'I gobbled this book up in one sitting. The emotions between characters were superb. The new hottest book couple!'

Jennifer Probst,
_New York Times_ bestselling author of _The Marriage Bargain_

'Leisa Rayven crashes onto the romance scene: laughing, flirting, and just daring us to put _Bad Romeo_ down. I couldn't!'

Christina Lauren,
_New York Times_ bestselling author of _Beautiful Bastard_

'An unputdownable debut! Filled with delicious tension that will make your palms sweat, toes curl, and heart race'

Alice Clayton, _New York Times_ bestselling author of _Wallbanger_

'The perfect combination of hot and hilarious, _Bad Romeo_ is utterly dazzling. I loved it!'

Katy Evans, _New York Times_ bestselling author of _Real_

'I can't even begin to describe how much I love this story without using cliché words like amazing and wonderful and itrocksmyworldsohard. I've honestly never read anything like this. I've reread it at least three times, and it never fails to make me laugh or cry (probably at the same time), even while in public. It's just so beautiful'

gladly beyond

'I have to say that this is one of the best stories I have ever read. The love story is epic'

Lingling Rose

'I loved this story so much, and it will remain one of my favourites of all time'                                                                KCBC

'Absolutely wonderful – witty, hilarious, and shows us how two people lose each other through a dangerous love and find each other in a healthier one. Love this story so much'                      Unfamiliar Faces

'Wow . . . just . . . wow. This story is captivating, and the emotions are amazing! It has been a while since I read something so raw and emotional—something that made me *feel* instead of simply going through the motions'                                    sleeplessinvirginia

'I loved how wrapped up I got in the story and the characters' emotions. I actually took way longer to read this than it normally takes me, simply because each chapter was so deeply emotional that it took me a while to process everything I was thinking and feeling as I read. I loved it'                                                    la-geologia

'A beautiful, wonderful tale weaving together two complicated and captivating characters'                                                  apennyshort

'This story totally rocks . . . It rates up there with the big-time classics'                                                            suzysalter

'I absolutely adored this story from the very first paragraph until the last'                                                              SparkleSwan

'The more I read the more addicted I became with the plot, the emotions, the characters, the mystery, the alternation between past and present. Everything is absolutely perfect!'                        mrt123

# BAD ROMEO

# BAD ROMEO

## LEISA RAYVEN

PAN BOOKS

First published 2014 by St Martin's Press

First published in the UK 2014 by Pan Books

This edition published 2015 by Pan Books
an imprint of Pan Macmillan, a division of Macmillan Publishers Limited
Pan Macmillan, 20 New Wharf Road, London N1 9RR
Basingstoke and Oxford
Associated companies throughout the world
www.panmacmillan.com

ISBN 978-1-4472-8295-2

1 3 5 7 9 8 6 4 2

A CIP catalogue record for this book is available from the British Library.

Printed and bound by CPI Group (UK) Ltd, Croydon, CR0 4YY

Visit **www.panmacmillan.com** to read more about all our books
and to buy them. You will also find features, author interviews and
news of any author events, and you can sign up for e-newsletters
so that you're always first to hear about our new releases.

*To everyone who told me I could do this when I thought I couldn't.*
*Apparently, you were right and I was wrong.*
*Don't get cocky about it.*

O nature, what hadst thou to do in hell
When thou didst bower the spirit of a fiend
In moral paradise of such sweet flesh?
Was ever book containing such vile matter
So fairly bound?

—Juliet, describing Romeo
*Romeo and Juliet* by William Shakespeare

# ONE

## TOGETHER AGAIN, TOO SOON

*Present Day*
*New York City*
*The Graumann Theater*
*First Day of Rehearsal*

I rush down the crowded sidewalk, and a nervous sweat has broken out in all my most unglamorous places.

I hear my mother's voice inside my head—*"A lady doesn't sweat, Cassie. She glows."*

In that case, Mom, I'm glowing like a pig.

Anyway, I never claimed to be a lady.

I tell myself I'm "glowing" because I'm running late. Not because of *him*.

Tristan, my roommate/life coach, is convinced I've never gotten over him, but that's crap.

I'm so over him.

I've been over him for a long time.

I scurry across the road, dodging the unstoppable New York traffic. Several cabdrivers curse me out in various languages. I merrily wave my middle finger, because I'm pretty sure flipping the bird means "fuck you" all over the world.

I glance at my watch as I enter the theater and head to the rehearsal room.

*Dammit.*

Five minutes late.

I can almost see the look of amusement on his bastard face, and I'm horrified that before I've even set foot in the room I have an over-whelming urge to slap him.

I pause outside the door.

*I can do this. I can see him and not fall apart.*

*I can.*

I sigh and press my forehead against the wall.

Who the hell am I kidding?

Yeah, sure, I can do a passionate play with my ex-lover, who broke my heart not once, but twice. No problem.

I bang my head against the wall.

If there were a Nation of Stupid People, I would be their queen.

I take a deep breath and exhale slowly.

When my agent had called with news of my big Broadway break, I should have known there'd be strings attached. She raved to me about the male actor who'd also been cast. Ethan Holt—the current "It Boy" of the theater world. So talented. Award winner. Adored by scream-ing fans. Handsome as hell.

Of course she didn't know about our history. Why would she? I never talk about him. In fact, I walk away when other people mention his name. It was easier to cope when he was on the other side of the world, but now he's back and tainting my dream job with his presence.

Typical.

Bastard.

Finding my game face isn't going to be easy, but I have to.

I pull out my compact and check my reflection.

Goddammit, I'm shinier than the Chrysler Building.

I slap on some powder and retouch my lip gloss as I wonder if I'll look different to him after all of these years. My brown hair, which used to be down to the middle of my back in college, now sits just below my collar, messy-layered and edgy. My face is a little thinner, but I guess I'm basically the same. Decent lips. Okay bone structure. Eyes that are neither brown nor green, but a strange combination of both. More olive than hazel.

I snap the compact shut and throw it back into my bag, pissed I'm even contemplating looking good for him. Have I learned nothing?

I close my eyes and think about all the ways he hurt me. His stupid reasons. His crap excuses.

Bitterness floods me, and I sigh in relief. That's the insulation I need. It brings my anger to the surface. I wrap it around me like iron and take solace in the aggressive simmer.

I can do this.

I pull open the door and stride in. Before I even see him, I can feel him watching me. I resist looking for him because that's what I want to do, and one thing I've learned with Ethan Holt is to push down my natural instincts. Following my gut is how things got screwed up between us. It told me I could have something from him, when in fact he offered me nothing.

I head over to the production desk where our director, Marco Fiori, is having a discussion with our producers, Ava and Saul Weinstein. Standing next to them is a familiar face—our stage manager, Ethan's sister, Elissa.

Ethan and Elissa are a package deal. He has it written into his contracts that she runs all of the shows he works on, which baffles me, considering they fight like cat and dog.

I'd say that Elissa is his security blanket, but of course, why would he need one? He doesn't need anyone or anything, right? He's untouchable. He's freaking Teflon.

Elissa gestures to a scale model of the set we'll be using, as she talks about the stage mechanics.

The producers listen and nod.

I have no issue with Elissa. She's a fantastic stage manager, and we've worked together before. In fact, a million years ago we used to be good friends. Back when I still thought her brother was born of a human mother and not spawned straight from Satan's asshole.

They look up as I approach.

"I know, I know," I say as I drop my bag onto a chair. "I'm sorry."

"It's fine, *cara*," Marco says. "We're still talking production details. Calm down, get a coffee. We'll get started soon."

"Cool." I dig in my bag for my rehearsal supplies.

"Hey, you," Elissa says, and smiles warmly.

"Hey, Lissa."

For a moment, my anger is tempered by a flood of nostalgia, and I realize just how much I've missed her. She's so different from her brother. Short to his tall. Rounded to his angular. Even their coloring is different. Blond and straight versus dark and chaotic. And yet, seeing her again reminds me why we haven't spoken for years. I'll always associate her with him. Too many bad memories.

As I pull out my water bottle, my bag slips off the seat and flops loudly onto the floor. Everyone stops to stare. I grind my teeth when I hear a low chuckle.

*Screw you, Ethan. Not even going to look at you.*

I pick up my bag and throw it back on the chair.

The chuckle happens again, and I swear to the Almighty God of Justifiable Homicide, I'm going to murder him with my bare hands.

Although he's on the other side of the room, he might as well be right next to me, because his voice vibrates through to my bones.

I need a cigarette.

I glance over at Marco, resplendent in his cravat as he flamboyantly describes the play. This is all his fault. He's the one who wanted

Holt and me to do this project. I convinced myself it would be a great career move, but in reality it's going to be the last show I ever do, because if the chuckling idiot in the corner doesn't shut up, I'm going to go on a murderous rampage any second and be put away for life.

Mercifully, the chuckle stops, but I can still feel his gaze searing my skin.

I ignore it and rummage through my bag. I have my cigarettes, but my lighter is MIA. I seriously need to clean this sucker out. Jesus, is there anything I don't have in here? Gum, tissues, makeup, painkillers, old movie tickets, small bottle of perfume, tampons, keys, a one-legged WWF action figure—what the hell?

"Excuse me, Miss Taylor?"

I look up to see a cute African American boy holding out what smells suspiciously like my favorite green bean macchiato.

"Wow, you look stressed," he says, with just the right amount of concern to prevent me from ripping off his ears with my teeth. "I'm Cody. The production intern. Coffee?"

"Hey, Cody," I say while eyeing the cardboard cup. "Whatcha got there, sport?"

"A double-shot green bean macchiato with mocha and extra cream."

I nod, impressed. "That's what I figured. It's my favorite."

"I know. I made sure to familiarize myself with the likes and dislikes of yourself and Mr. Holt, so I could anticipate your needs and facilitate an enjoyable rehearsal environment."

An enjoyable rehearsal environment? With me and Holt? Oh, you poor, deluded child.

I take the coffee from him and sniff it while I continue digging in the Tardis of Crap. "Is that a fact?"

*Where the fuck is my lighter?*

"Yes, ma'am." He pulls a lighter out of his pocket and hands it to me with a crazy-cute smile.

I sigh and drop my head back.

Sweet Jesus, the boy has been sent from God Himself.

I take the lighter and resist the urge to hug him. Tristan says I can be a little too touchy-feely. Actually, his term is touchy-fucky but I modify it to make myself feel better.

I smile at the kid instead. "Cody, I hope you don't take this the wrong way, because I know we've only just met, but . . . I think I love you."

He chuckles and lowers his head. "If you want to duck outside, I'll come get you when they're ready to start."

If he didn't look like he was sixteen, I'd probably kiss him. With tongue.

"You're a rock star, Cody."

I see a dark shape in my peripheral vision, slouching in a chair on the opposite side of the room, so I draw my shoulders back and strut like I don't give a crap.

The heat of his gaze follows me until I hit the stairwell, then I just go numb.

I tell myself I don't miss the burn.

The stairs are steep and dark and lead to an alley behind the theater. Before the door even closes behind me, I have a lit cigarette in my mouth. As I lean against the cool bricks, I inhale and look up at the thin finger of sky visible between the buildings. The nicotine does little to calm my nerves. Pretty sure nothing short of hospital-grade sedatives is going to help today.

I finish my cigarette and head back to the stage door, but before I can grab the handle, it opens, and the trigger for all my anger issues steps out. His dark jeans hug him in ways I really shouldn't be noticing.

His eyes are the same as I remember. Pale blue, mesmerizing. Dark, thick lashes. Intensity to burn.

Everything else, however . . .

Oh, Lord, I'd forgotten. I'd made myself forget.

Even now, he's the most handsome man I've ever seen. No, that's not right. Handsome doesn't do him justice. Soap actors are handsome, but in a completely predictable, bland way. Holt is . . . captivating. Like a rare, exotic panther: equal parts beauty and power. Enigmatic without even trying.

I hate how good he looks.

Strong, furrowed brows. Sharp jaw. Lips that are full enough to be pretty, but in the context of his other features seem powerfully masculine.

His dark hair is shorter than it was when I last saw him, and it makes him seem more mature. And taller, if that's possible.

He's always towered over me. Six foot three to my five foot five. And going by the width of his shoulders, he's been working out since college. Not a huge amount, but enough for me to see clear muscle definition beneath his dark T-shirt.

Blood rushes to my cheeks, and I want to slap myself for the reaction.

Trust him to show up looking more attractive than ever. Douche.

"Hi," he says, like I haven't spent the last three years dreaming of punching him in his gorgeous bastard face.

"Hello, Ethan."

He stares at me, and, as usual, I feel the vibration of him in the marrow of my bones.

"You look good, Cassie."

"You, too."

"Your hair is shorter."

"Yours, too."

He takes a step forward, and I hate the way he looks at me. Appraising and approving. Hungry. It draws me in against my will, like he's flypaper, and everything inside me is buzzing and trying to wrench itself free.

"It's been a long time," he says.

"Really? I hadn't noticed." I'm trying to sound bored out of my mind. I don't want him to know what he's doing to me. He doesn't deserve this reaction. More importantly, neither do I.

"How've you been?" he asks.

"I've been fine." Automatic response. It means nothing. I've been anything but fine.

His gaze stays on me, and I really want to be somewhere else, because right now he looks like he used to, and it hurts to remember.

"And you?" I ask with white-knuckle politeness. "How have you been?"

"I'm . . . okay."

There's something in his tone. Something buried. He's left just enough of it poking through to make me curious, but I don't want to dig to find out more, because I know that's what he wants.

"Wow, that's awesome, Ethan," I say with just the right amount of perky to piss him off. "Good to hear."

He looks at the ground and runs his hand through his hair. His posture tenses into the familiar form of the jackass I know so well.

"Well, there it is," he says. "Three years, and that's all you have to say to me. Of course."

My stomach rolls.

*No, asshole, that's not all I have to say, but what's the point? It's all been said before, and talking in circles isn't my idea of a good time.*

"Yep, that's it," I say cheerily, and push past him. I fling the door open and clomp down the stairs, ignoring the tingle on my skin where we touched.

There's a muffled *"Fuck"* before I hear him hurrying after me. I try to outrun him, but he grabs my arm before we reach the bottom.

"Cassie, wait."

He turns me to face him, and I expect him to press against me. To ruin me with his skin and smell like he has so many times before. But he doesn't.

He just stands there, and all the air in the narrow, dark stairwell is as thick as cotton. I feel claustrophobic, but I won't let him see.

No weakness.

He taught me that.

"Listen, Cassie," he says, and I hate that I've missed hearing him say my name so damn much. "Do you think we could just put all our bullshit behind us and start again? I really want to. I thought you might, too."

His expression is full of sincerity, but I've seen it before. Every time I trusted it, I ended up getting my heart ripped out.

"You want to start again?" I say. "Oh, sure. No problem. Why didn't I think of that?"

"It doesn't have to be like this."

The implication is that I'm being unreasonable. If I weren't so angry, I'd laugh.

"Then what should it be like, huh?" I ask, words like acid. "Please, tell me. After all, you're the one who always makes decisions about our relationship. How do you want to play it this time? Friends? Fuck buddies? Enemies? Oh, wait, I know. Why don't you play the piece of shit who broke my heart, and I'll be the woman who doesn't want anything to do with him outside the rehearsal room? How would that be?"

His jaw tightens. He's angry.

Good.

I can deal with angry.

He rubs his eyes and exhales. I expect him to yell, but he doesn't. Instead, he says in a quiet voice, "None of what I said in my e-mails meant anything to you, did it? I thought we might at least be able to talk about what happened. Did you even read them?"

"Of course I read them," I say. "I just didn't believe them. I mean, there's only so many times I can swallow bullshit before I despise the taste. What's the phrase? Fool me once, shame on you. Fool me twice—"

"I'm not fooling you this time. Or myself. In the past, I did what I needed to, for both of us."

"Are you kidding me? Do you actually expect me to thank you for what you did?"

"No," he says, voice brimming with frustration. "Of course not. I just want to . . ."

"You want *another* chance to ruin me? How stupid do you think I am?"

He shakes his head. "I want things to be different. If you want me to apologize, I'll do it until I lose my fucking voice. I just want things to be right between us. Talk to me. Help me fix this."

"You can't."

"Cassie—"

"No, Ethan! Not this time. Not ever again."

He leans forward. He's close. Too close. He smells just like he used to, and I can't think. I want to shove him away so I can clear my head. Or beat him with my fists until he understands I haven't been truly happy for years, and it's all his fault. I want to do so many things, but all I do is stand there, hating how powerless he can still make me feel.

His breathing is just as uneven as mine. His body's just as tense. Even after everything we've been through, our attraction still tortures us. Just like old times.

Thank God the door at the bottom of the stairs opens. I look over to see Cody staring up at us with a confused expression.

"Mr. Holt? Ms. Taylor? Is everything okay?"

Holt steps away from me and rakes his fingers through his hair.

I exhale a ragged, shallow breath. "Everything's fine, Cody. All good."

"Okay, then," he says brightly. "Just letting you know we're about to start."

He disappears, and it's just Ethan and me again. Oh, and the shit-load of baggage we carry.

"We're here to do a job," I say, my voice hard. "Let's just get it done."

His brows furrow and his jaw tightens, and for a second I think he's not going to let it go, but he says, "If that's what you really want."

I push down a vague sense of disappointment. "It is."

He nods, and without saying another word, heads downstairs and out the door.

I take a moment to compose myself. My face is hot, my heart is pounding, and I almost laugh when I think how he already has me tied in knots, and we haven't even started rehearsals.

The next four weeks are going to suck harder than a black hole.

I straighten myself up and head back into the rehearsal room.

By the time I grab my script and a water, there's only one chair left at the production table, and naturally, it's beside Holt. I drag it as far from him as I can and sink into the uncomfortable plastic.

"Everything okay?" Marco raises his eyebrows.

"Yep. Fine," I say with a smile, and it's like I'm back in the first year of drama school, saying what others want to hear so they'll be happy even if I'm not.

Playing my role.

"Then let's start at the beginning, shall we?" Marco says. There's a rustling of paper as everyone opens their scripts.

What a great idea. All good stories need to start somewhere.

Why should this one be any different?

# TWO

## IN THE BEGINNING

*Present Day*
*New York City*
*The Diary of Cassandra Taylor*

*Dear Diary,*

*Tristan has suggested I use you to help chronicle the events in my life that led me to being the maladjusted individual I am today. He wants me to look at some of the unhealthy relationships that have made me moody and emotionally unavailable, so I thought I'd start with the jackpot of all my regrets:*

*Ethan Holt.*

*The first time I saw him, I was simulating anal sex with someone I'd just met.*

*Wow. That sounds bad.*

*Let me explain.*

*I was auditioning for a place at The Grove Institute of Creative Arts, a private college that offered courses in dance, music, and visual arts, and also housed one of the most prestigious drama schools in the country.*

*Built on the bones of an old orchard, it was located in Westchester,*

New York, and in recent history, it had trained some of America's most talented stars of theater and screen.

I'd been dreaming about studying there forever, so in my senior year, when all my friends were applying to colleges to be doctors, lawyers, engineers, and journalists, I applied to be an actress.

The Grove was my first choice for many reasons, not the least of which was that it was on the other side of the country from my parents.

It wasn't that I didn't love my parents, because I did. But Judy and Leo had very specific ideas about how I should live my life. Because I was an only child and therefore programmed to do anything and everything to gain their approval, I basically lived up to all their unrealistic ideals.

By the time I reached my senior year, I'd never drunk alcohol, smoked cigarettes, eaten anything other than Judy's healthy-but-tasteless vegetarian crap, or slept with a boy. I was always home when I was supposed to be, even if it was so they could both completely ignore me, or snipe at each other, or not be there at all.

My mother was a fixer. She always felt like she should be bettering herself, or me. I was clumsy, so she enrolled me in ballet classes. I was chubby, so she watched every mouthful I ate. I was shy, so she made me go to drama classes.

I hated everything she forced me to do, except for drama. That one stuck. Turns out I was pretty good at it, too. Pretending I was someone else for a few hours? Yeah, that rocked my world.

Leo's main contribution to my upbringing consisted of laying down strict guidelines about where I could go, who I could see, and what I could do. Apart from that, he ignored me unless I was doing something really right or really wrong. I quickly learned there was less yelling and being grounded when I did stuff right. Getting good grades made him happy. So did winning awards for drama and public speaking.

So, I worked hard. Harder than a daughter should to get her father's attention. It's safe to say all of my people-pleasing hang-ups came from him.

*My parents weren't happy about my plan to go to drama school, of course. I believe Leo's exact words were, "Like hell." He and Mom were okay with me acting as a hobby, but with my grades, I could have had my choice of highly paid professions. They didn't understand why I'd throw that away for a vocation in which 90 percent of college graduates were forever unemployed.*

*I convinced them to let me audition by bargaining that I would also apply to the law program at Washington State. That bought me a roundtrip plane ticket to New York and the faint hope of leaving my approval-seeking husk behind.*

*I knew when I started the application process that my chances were slim, but I had to try. There were other schools I would have been happy to attend. But I wanted the best, and The Grove was it.*

**Six Years Earlier**
**Westchester, New York**
**The Grove Auditions**

My leg is shaking.

Not trembling.

Not shuddering.

Shaking.

Uncontrollably.

My stomach is tying itself in knots, and I want to vomit. Again.

I'm sitting on the ground with my back against a wall. Invisible.

I don't belong here. I'm not like them.

They're brash, and outrageous, and seem comfortable using the "F" word. They chain-smoke and touch each other's private parts, even though most of them have just met. They brag about the shows they've done or the films they've been in or the famous people they've seen, and I sit here getting smaller and smaller each second, knowing the only thing I'm going to achieve today is to prove how inadequate I am.

"So then the director says, 'Zoe, the audience needs to see your breasts. You say you're dedicated to your craft, and yet your misguided sense of modesty dictates your choices.'"

A perky blonde is holding court, telling theatrical war stories. The people gathered around look captivated.

I don't really want to hear it, but she's so loud I can't help it.

"Oh my God, Zoe, what did you do?!" a pretty redhead asks, her face contorting with exaggerated emotion.

"What could I do?" Zoe asks with a sigh. "I sucked his dick and told him I was keeping my shirt on. It was the only way to protect my integrity."

There's laughter and a smattering of applause. Even before we've stepped inside, the performances have begun.

I lean my head back and close my eyes, trying to calm my nerves.

I run through my monologues in my head. I know them. Every word. I've dissected each syllable, analyzed the characters, subtext, and layers of emotional subtlety, yet I still feel unprepared.

"So, where are you from?"

Zoe is speaking again. I try to block her out.

"Hey. You. Wall Girl."

I open my eyes. She's looking at me. So is everyone else.

"Uh . . . what?"

I clear my throat and try not to look terrified.

"Where are you from?" she asks again, like I'm mentally challenged. "I can tell you're not from New York."

I know her snide smile is directed at my department store jeans and plain gray sweater, as well as my boring brown hair and lack of makeup. I'm not like most of the girls here, in their vibrant colors, large jewelry, and painted faces. They look like exotic tropical birds, and I look like a grease stain.

"Uh . . . I'm from Aberdeen."

Her face crumples in distaste. "Where the fuck is that?"

"It's in Washington. It's kind of small."

"Never heard of it," she says with a dismissive wave of her lacquered nails. "Do you even have a theater there?"

"No."

"So you don't have any acting experience?"

"I did some amateur plays in Seattle."

Her eyes are bright. She smells an easy kill. "Amateur? Oh . . . I see." She stifles a laugh.

My self-preservation kicks in. "Of course, I haven't done all the amazing things you've done. I mean, a movie. Wow. That's must have been seriously awesome."

Zoe's eyes dull a little. The smell of blood is diluted by my suck-uppery.

"It *was* seriously awesome," she says as she smiles like a barracuda with lipstick. "I mean, I'm probably wasting my time taking this course, because I won't make it to the end before I get a big-budget deal, but it's something to keep me occupied 'til then."

I smile and agree with her. Stroke her ego.

It's easy. I'm good at it.

The conversations bubble around me, and I add a comment here and there. Every half-truth that spills from my mouth makes me more like them. More likely to fit in.

Before long, I'm guffawing and braying like the rest of the donkeys, and one of the gay boys pulls me to my feet and pretends we're at a rave.

He stands behind me as he thrusts against my butt. I play along, even though I'm horrified. I make vulgar noises and toss my head. Everyone thinks I'm hilarious, so I ignore my shame and keep going. Here, I can choose to be uninhibited and popular. Their approval is like a drug, and I want more.

I'm still pretending to be butt pumped when I look up and see *him*.

He's a few yards away, all tall and broad shouldered. His dark hair is wavy and unruly, and although his expression is impassive, his eyes show clear disdain. Sharp and unforgiving.

My fake laugh falters.

He looks like a vengeful angel with his intense gaze and ethereal features. Smooth skin and dark clothes.

He has one of those faces that stops you when you're flipping through a magazine. Not textbook handsome, but mesmerizing. Like a book cover that begs you to flip it open and get lost in the story.

My new false bravado feels heavy under his gaze. It slides off me all dirty and thick, and I stop laughing.

The gay boy pushes me away and turns to someone else. I've lost my vulgar butt-pumping charm.

The tall boy also turns away and sits with his back to the wall. He pulls a tattered book from his pocket. I catch the title: *The Outsiders*. One of my favorites.

I turn back to the noisy group, but they've moved on.

I'm torn between trying to regain my position and finding out more about Book Boy.

The choice is taken from me when the nearby door opens and a woman steps out. She's statuesque, with short black hair and bright red lips, and she assesses us with the focus of a laser beam. She reminds me of Betty Boop, if Betty Boop were pee-your-pants intimidating and had a patent-leather clipboard.

"All right, listen up."

The chicken coop falls silent.

"If I call your name, head inside."

She fires off names, her voice clear and sure.

When she yells, "Holt, Ethan," the tall boy pushes off the wall. He looks at me briefly as he passes, and it makes me want to follow. I feel false and uncomfortable without him.

Names keep coming. I estimate more than sixty people walk through the door, including "Stevens, Zoe," who squeals before strutting inside. I flinch when I hear, "Taylor, Cassandra!"

As I grab my knapsack, the intimidating woman says, "That's it for this group. Everyone else wait here. You'll be collected by other instructors."

She follows me through the door and pulls it closed behind her.

We're in a large, black room. A multipurpose theater space.

On the far wall is a long bank of collapsible bleachers. Most of the group is sitting on them, chatting quietly.

The final count is eighty-eight. Sixty girls and twenty-eight boys. None of them look as nervous as I feel.

I sit, feeling like a clueless hack in a sea of more experienced city kids. My leg starts trembling again.

The instructor stands in front of us.

"My name is Erika Eden, and I'm the head of the acting department. This morning we're going to do some character work and improvisation. At the end of each scene, I'll let you know who will stay. I know what I'm looking for, and if you don't have it, you're gone. I'm not trying to be a hard-ass, that's just the way it is. I don't need to tell you that the Grove only takes the top thirty drama candidates from the two thousand who will be auditioning over the next few days, so put your best foot forward. I'm not interested in seeing hackneyed theatrics and fake emotion. Give me the real deal or go home."

My fear of failure whispers that I should leave, but I can't. I need this.

We spend the next half hour doing focusing exercises. Everyone's desperately trying not to look desperate. Some people are more successful than others.

Zoe is loud and confident, as if her acceptance is in the bag. It probably is. *Holt, Ethan* is intense. Incredibly so. His interactions fire with restrained energy, like he's a nuclear power plant being used to light a single bulb.

I try to keep everything real and natural, and for the most part, I succeed.

After each scene, people are cut. Some take it well and some crash and burn. It's like a war zone.

The group numbers dwindle rapidly. Erika is fast and efficient, and every time she comes near me I think I'm gone. Somehow, I manage to survive.

When we break for lunch, we're all quiet. Even Zoe. We sit in a circle, our minds stumbling over our monologues while we try to ignore that most of us won't make it to callbacks tomorrow. A few times I feel my face burn and look up to see *Holt, Ethan* staring at me. He immediately looks away and scowls. I wonder why he seems so angry.

Back in the room, we're paired off. I get assigned to a boy named Jordan who has acne and a lisp.

Each duo is given a scenario, and the rest of us watch. It's like a blood sport. We're all hoping the others will screw up so we have a better chance.

Zoe and *Holt, Ethan* are paired together. They're supposed to be strangers at a train station. They talk and flirt while Zoe tosses her hair. I can't tell if she's more eager to impress Erika or Ethan.

Jordan and I play brother and sister. I have no siblings, so it's kind of nice. We banter and laugh, and I have to admit, we're pretty damn good. Erika compliments us, and the rest of the group grudgingly applauds.

At the end of the round, people are cut and tears are shed. I sigh in relief as I realize there are only about thirty of us left. The odds are getting better.

The partnerships are switched up. I get *Holt, Ethan*. He doesn't look happy about it. He sits next to me as his jaw clenches and releases. I don't think I've ever noticed a guy's jaw before, but his is impressive.

He turns and catches me staring, and his expression is a perfect blend of a frown and I'm-going-to-kill-you-and-remove-all-your-skin.

Wow. We are so going to suck as partners.

Erika paces in front of the group. "For this last session, everyone will be given the same task. Your scenario is 'Mirror Image.'"

Sounds easy.

"It won't be easy."

Dammit.

"This exercise is about trust, openness, and making a connection with the other person. No self-consciousness. No artifice. Just raw, pure energy. Neither of you leads or follows. You have to sense each other's movement. Got it?"

We all nod, but I have no flipping clue what she's talking about. Holt is rubbing his eyes and making a groaning sound. I figure he doesn't, either.

"Right, let's go."

The first pair takes their position. It's Zoe and Jordan. They take a few minutes to plan, then start to move. It's obvious Zoe is leading and Jordan is following. They're all hands and nothing more. At one point, Jordan giggles. Erika scribbles on her clipboard. I figure he just screwed the pooch. I smile. So does Holt.

Another one bites the dust.

The other groups perform in turn, and Erika circles them like a hawk, scrutinizing their every movement. She's deciding who will make the final cut for callbacks. Most people are cracking under the pressure. I'm thrilled beyond words.

At last it's our turn, and we stand in front of the group. Holt is jangling his leg. His hands are in his pockets, and his shoulders are hunched. It doesn't fill me with confidence. I'd really like to pee and/

or vomit. Because I can't do either, I shift my weight from one foot to the other and beg my bladder to stand down.

Erika studies us for a few moments.

I realize Holt and I have both stopped breathing.

"All right, you two," she says. "Last chance to impress me."

Holt glances at me, and I see my desperation mirrored in him. He wants this. Maybe as much as I do.

Erika leans into me and lowers her voice. "He moves, you move, Miss Taylor. Understand? Breathe his air. Find a connection." She glances at Holt. "You have to let her in, Ethan. Don't think about it, just do it. Three strikes and you're out, remember?"

He nods and swallows.

"You have three minutes to prepare."

She leaves, and Holt and I move to the back of the room. He stands close and he smells good. Not that I should be noticing something like that, but my brain is looking for a distraction from my nerves, and his good smell is it.

"Look," he says as he leans down. "I need this, okay? Don't screw it up for me."

I flush with anger. "Excuse me? You have just as much chance of screwing it up as I do. And what did Erika mean when she said 'Three strikes and you're out'?"

He leans in closer but doesn't look at me. "This is the third year I've auditioned. If I don't get in this time, I'm done. They won't let me re-audition. Then my father would say a big, fat 'I told you so' and expect me to go to medical school. I've worked hard for this. I need it, okay?"

I'm confused. I've been watching him all day. Are these people blind?

"Why haven't you gotten in before? You're really good." *In a disturbingly intense kind of way.*

His expression softens for a moment. "I find it hard to . . . mesh . . .

with other performers. Apparently Erika believes that's an important attribute for her actors to have."

"It didn't look like you had any problem with Zoe."

He scoffs. "There was no connection there. I felt nothing, as usual. Erika could tell."

I glance over at the dark-haired lady who is studying us. "She's auditioned you before?"

He nods. "Every year. She wants to offer me a place, but she won't give me a free pass. If I can't prove I can do this particular exercise, which I've completely sucked at each time I've auditioned, then it's over."

"One minute!" Erika yells.

My heart rate kicks into overdrive. "Listen, just do whatever it takes to 'connect' with me, okay? Because if I don't get this, I have to go back to my overprotective parents, and I seriously can't fluffing cope with that. I know this might come as a surprise, but you're not the only one with something to lose here."

He frowns. "Did you . . . did you just say 'fluffing'?"

I feel a fierce blush engulf my throat. He's laughing at me, just because I refuse to curse my head off like every other fluffer in this place. "Shut up."

His smirk widens. "Seriously? Fluffing?"

"Stop it! You're wasting time."

He stops laughing and sighs. He seems more relaxed, but I'm guessing that's because all his anxiety has transferred to me.

"Look, Taylor—"

"My name is Cassie."

"Whatever. Just relax, okay? We can do this. Look into my eyes and . . . Jesus, I don't know . . . make me feel something. Don't lose concentration. That's what's screwed everyone else so far. Just focus on me, and I'll focus on you. Okay?"

"Fine."

"And don't say 'fluffing' any more, 'cause that shit cracks me up. You know it's a porn term, right?"

*No, I didn't know it was a fluffing porn term. Do I look like a porn-watching pervert?*

I exhale and try to focus. My thoughts are chaotic. I need to be calm.

"Hey," he says as he touches my arm. It doesn't help my concentration at all. "We can do this. Look at me."

I look up into his eyes. His lashes are ridiculous.

As he gazes at me, something jolts straight into the pit of my stomach.

He must feel it, too, because his mouth drops open, and he inhales sharply. "Holy shit." He blinks but doesn't look away.

The energy crackling between us is too intense. I close my eyes and exhale.

"Taylor?"

"Cassie."

"Cassie," he whispers, his voice soft and so very desperate. "Stay with me. Please. I can't do this without you."

I swallow and nod. Then Erika yells at us, and we walk to the center of the room.

We turn to face each other, only a foot apart.

He's much taller than I am, so I stare at his chest, watching it rise and fall as he tries to calm himself.

"Ready?" he whispers.

I want to yell, *"No, God, please, I'm not fluffing ready!"* but instead I say, "Yeah. Sure," like this wasn't life or death, or at the very least, really important.

I take a deep breath before looking up. His expression is less desperate now, and it feels like I'm seeing him—really seeing him—for the first time. I feel his energy. It's like a wave of heat all around him. We stand there for a few seconds, just breathing, and as we gaze into each other's eyes, the air between us solidifies, connecting us like two parts of the same person.

He raises his hand, and I follow, as if we have thousands of tiny strings between our arms, tugging them into alignment. I match his speed exactly, moving when he moves, breathing when he breathes.

We move again, and our bodies are perfectly aligned. It feels so natural. More natural than I've felt in a long time. Maybe ever.

We step closer. He leans forward, and I lean back. I tilt sideways, and he follows. The invisible strings tighten between us. Our movements become faster, but every one is perfect and precise. Intricate choreography that we've never learned, but our muscles somehow remember.

It's thrilling.

We're in *the zone*. That magical state performers sometimes achieve when everything is flowing and open. Heart, mind, body. I've felt it before, but never with another person.

It's amazing.

Smiles spread on our faces. I notice Holt is kind of beautiful when he smiles.

Our arms are above our heads, and as we bring them down, our palms come together. His hands are big and warm. My skin tingles where we touch. Then I'm looking into his eyes, and we're both not breathing, and I don't know why.

In a second, Holt's expression fills with panic, and he tenses. He blinks and drops his gaze, and suddenly it's like all the buoyancy has gone out of the air. Our energy slams into the floor and drains away.

Holt steps away and exhales before looking over at Erika. "Are we done? Nobody else went for that long. We're done, right?"

Erika tilts her head and studies him. His posture is tense and challenging.

I lower my hands. They're cold now, and I clench them at my sides as my heart beats fast and unsteady.

"Are we done or not?" Holt says, and every good thing I felt about him fades in the shadow of his rudeness.

"Yes, Mr. Holt," Erika says calmly while glancing at me. "You and Miss Taylor completed the exercise. Well done. You two have some interesting chemistry, don't you?"

He glares.

She gives him a warm smile. "You may sit down. Everyone, give them a round of applause."

The whole group breaks into applause. I hear murmurs of surprise that we were so good.

No one is more surprised than I am.

Holt stalks back to the bleachers and sits. Zoe gushes beside him as she touches his bicep. She'd be more subtle if she ripped open her shirt and begged him to grope her. He ignores her and leans his elbows on his knees.

I make an effort to stop staring at him.

The rest of the afternoon passes in a blur. People get cut, and the pairs get swapped around as more scenarios are played out.

At the end of the day Erika dismisses us, and we file outside to wait for her to post the callback list.

We're all on edge. None of us know that we've done enough to move on to the next round. Even Zoe is unsure. She bites the inside of her cheek and paces.

I gnaw at my cuticles and chant, *"Oh please, oh please, oh please"* over and over again, as if begging the universe could possibly help me now.

At the end of the corridor, Holt sits with his back against the wall and his legs pulled up to his chest. He looks like he's in pain.

Despite his behavior today, I feel sorry for him. Everyone's nervous, but he seems really sick.

I walk over. He's leaning his head against the wall, eyes closed. When I touch his shoulder, he jolts like I've Tasered him.

"What the fuck?" He glares, but it's hard to find it intimidating when he's so green he could get a job with the Muppets.

"You okay?"

He drops his head down to his knees and sighs. "I'm fine. Go away."

I don't know why I even bothered. "You're a jerk, you know that?"

"I'm aware."

"Just making sure."

I go to leave, but he puts out an arm to stop me. "Taylor, look . . . I—"

"My name is *Cassie*."

"Cassie . . ."

The way he says my name is . . . Well, it does strange things to me. It might be best if he goes back to calling me Taylor.

He gestures for me to sit, and I do. "The thing is . . . we're not going to be friends, so I figure there's no use in wasting energy on each other, right?"

I blink a few times. "Uh . . . okay."

"That's it? Okay?" He seems disappointed, but I don't know why.

"Well, I've never really had the 'you and I aren't going to be friends' talk before, so I'm not sure of the protocol. Do I thank you for pointing out the obvious, or . . . ?"

He rubs his hands over his face and groans.

"What?" I ask. "I don't know what you expect me to say. I wasn't planning on being your friend."

"Good," he says, still rubbing his face.

I inhale and try to not lose my temper. "What is your problem? I pretty much saved your butt in there today, and you treat me like crap?"

"Yeah," he says, his shoulders tense and high. "Because you're so—"

"What?" I say. "Annoying? Irritating?"

"Bipolar."

That stops me in my tracks. "Oh. I . . . huh?"

He sighs and shakes his head. "I saw you earlier, playing the popularity game. Giving the cool kids what they wanted, which is ridiculous because most of them are obnoxious creeps who are about as genuine as a three-dollar bill. But with me, you're all prickly impatience and ball-breaking honesty. What, you don't like me enough to fake it?"

I hadn't realized it, but he's right. I've never, and I mean *never*, spoken to someone the way I've spoken to him. Letting people know I'm annoyed or impatient is not what I do. I get along with people. I've done it my whole life. If someone doesn't like me, I make them.

But with him, everything's different.

"Well, what about you?" I say. "What's your story?"

He shrugs. "I'm easy to figure out. I'm an asshole."

"I know that."

"No, you don't."

"Uh, yeah, I do. You've spent the afternoon treating me like I was going to infect you with Ebola. So I know what you are."

He nods. "Good. Then you'll know to stay away from me."

"I'm sure I won't have much choice about that, because after Erika posts the callback list, we'll never see each other again. Problem solved."

"Why do you think that?"

"Because you're probably going to get a callback, and I'm not, so . . . yeah."

He looks down and fiddles with his laces. "Don't be so sure. You did okay today. More than okay."

It takes a moment to realize he's just given me a compliment. "Well, gee, thanks. You were okay, too."

He looks up with a half smile. "Yeah?"

I roll my eyes. "Oh, please. You know you were amazing."

"Yeah, I was," he says and nods.

"So humble."

"And good looking. It must really suck to not be me."

I shake my head. "So, if you've been trying to get in here for three years, what have you been doing in between auditions?"

He looks down the hallway. "Mostly I worked construction for a company in Hoboken. They build sets for Broadway shows. Figured if I couldn't be onstage, I'd work behind the scenes."

"That's why your hands are rough?" He frowns. "During the mirror exercise," I say, "when we touched, your hands were calloused."

He looks at his hands. "I prefer to think of them as rugged. Lugging around tons of set pieces isn't delicate work. Hell of a workout though."

"So is that why you have all"—I point at his shoulders and arms—"that?"

He smiles and shakes his head. "Yeah. That's why I have all this. And enough money to pay for at least two years if I get in here."

"*When* you get in," I clarify.

He stares at me for a second, as if someone having faith in him is incomprehensible. "If you say so, Taylor."

I give up asking him to use my first name. It's probably better that we're on a last-name basis, considering we're not going to be friends or anything.

Except it kind of feels like we already are.

We sit there in silence for a while. Then the door opens and everyone jumps to their feet as Erika emerges with a piece of paper.

We all go silent, and expectation hums around us.

"For those of you on this list, congratulations. You'll be back tomorrow for the second round of auditions. Those who aren't, I'm afraid you've been unsuccessful. You may reapply next year. Thank you for your time."

She sticks the paper to the back of the door before disappearing back inside.

There's a huge rush of bodies as we all try to see the list. I push forward, my heart pounding, braced for disappointment.

When I finally get to the front, I hold my breath.

There are only three names.

*Ethan Holt.*

*Zoe Stevens.*

And . . . *Cassandra Taylor.*

The rest of our group is cut.

I'm in shock.

I made it.

*Fluff, yes!*

Holt reads over my shoulder and sighs in relief. "Thank fuck."

I turn as he drops his head and exhales. He looks like a death-row prisoner who's been granted a reprieve.

"Aw, it's sweet you're so happy for me," I say. "Did you really have any doubt?"

"About you? None at all. Congratulations."

"Congrats to you, too. I guess the medical world is safe from your scintillating bedside manner, for another day at least."

"I guess so." When he looks at me, the pit of my stomach tingles and flips.

I feel like I should say something else, but my brain is strange and clouded, so I just stand there.

He doesn't speak, either. He just stares. His face is fascinating in an annoyingly good-looking kind of way.

"Well," I say after an embarrassingly long pause, "I guess I'll see you tomorrow."

He nods. "Yeah. Sure. Later, Taylor."

He grabs his bag and walks away, but I know we'll see each other in the morning. I'm looking forward to it and dreading it at the same time.

I've never had this sort of reaction to a boy before.

I'm pretty sure it's not a good thing.

# THREE

## BACK TO BEFORE

*Present Day*
*New York City*
*The Diary of Cassandra Taylor*

*Dear Diary,*
*The final round of auditions for The Grove was grueling*
*The interviews were the worst. A panel of Grove lecturers sat at a long table and grilled everyone about life, family, likes and dislikes.*
*The panel expected me to just be myself. That was tough.*
*In the end, Erika turned to me and said, "Cassandra, you're a smart girl. You could have your pick of careers. Why do you want be an actress?"*
*I knew I should've said something about my passion for theater, or the importance of a vibrant, evolving culture in a world of disposable ideals and reality television. But as she stared at me, I wasn't able to think of anything clever enough to fool her, so I spoke without thinking.*
*"I want to act because I don't really know who I am. I find relief in being other people."*
*She held my gaze for a moment then nodded before writing something in her notes. Probably "crazy, emotionally dysfunctional teen with self-esteem issues. Don't make any sudden movements."*

*I walked out feeling like I'd left pieces of myself all over the floor.*

*Still, I must have done something right, because two months later, I received my acceptance letter.*

*The day I got it, I screamed so loudly, I scared the neighbor's dog.*

*I knew Mom and Dad weren't thrilled about the prospect of me moving to the other side of the country, but they also knew that acting was my passion, and being accepted at The Grove was a pretty big deal. It also helped that I was awarded a partial scholarship that covered half my tuition and on-campus accommodation. Considering that we weren't the Vanderbilts, that was a huge bonus.*

*In the back of my mind was the vague hope that Holt had gotten in.*

*I figured if he had, at least I'd know one person. One kind of annoying, strangely intriguing person.*

**Six Years Earlier**
**Westchester, New York**
**The Grove**
**First Week of Classes**

I walk through the apartment with a huge smile on my face.

There are two bedrooms separated by a poky bathroom, a combined living/dining area, and a small kitchen. The furniture is worn and dated, the carpet is hideous and stained with stuff I don't even want to think about, and I think the upstairs neighbor dances naked in the moonlight while he sacrifices small animals, because seriously, the dude is *weird*. But despite all this, it's perfect and beautiful and mine.

Well, I'm sharing it with a theater tech major named Ruby, but still . . .

I can do what I want. Eat what I want. Go to bed when I want. No parents cataloguing my every move.

I'm almost giddy with the possibilities.

"You owe me thirty bucks for groceries," Ruby says as she studies the receipt. "Oh, wait, make that thirty-four. The tampons are yours."

It's weird moving in with a stranger, but Ruby and I have been getting along great, considering she's my polar opposite. I'm mousy brown, she's fiery red. I'm average looking, she's spectacular. I'm a people pleaser, she's brutally honest.

She flops down in our ugly brown vinyl couch and lights up a cigarette. She holds the pack out to me, and I take one.

Oh, yeah, I'm a smoker now.

Well, I'm not, but when Ruby said she was, I just went with it. It was something for us to bond over. Plus, I knew most of the people at the auditions smoked, so it seemed like the thing to do. Also, my mother would have hated it.

All good reasons to take it up.

She lights me up, and I inhale shallowly, then cough. Ruby shakes her head.

I'm the worst apprentice smoker ever.

"So," she says as she blows out a stream of smoke, "it's your turn to cook, unfortunately."

"Hey. I thought what I made the other night was good, considering I've never cooked before."

"Woman," she says with a sigh, "you screwed up mac and cheese. Seriously, if you fail at cooking that crap, we're never going to survive the college experience."

"Then thank God you're here to teach me." I drag her off the couch, trudge into the kitchen, and get some steak and vegetables out of the fridge.

The thing is, Ruby isn't exactly a gourmet chef, either, so we end up with rock-hard steak, lumpy mashed potatoes, and green beans that are so limp I could knit them into a scarf.

"I'm writing to the Cooking Channel to complain," Ruby says as she pushes the food around on her plate. "Those bitches make cooking look easy. I'm suing them for false advertising."

That night we make a pact to purchase only frozen meals. It's the surest way to prevent starvation.

The next day is the first day of classes, and Ruby and I walk the short distance from our apartment to the main campus.

In the three days since we arrived, we've spent some time exploring our new school. The campus isn't huge, but it's well laid out, and the buildings are a nice mix between traditional and contemporary.

In the middle of everything is the Hub—a large, four-story building that houses the library, cafeteria, student lounge, and several large lecture theaters.

Placed around the Hub, like petals of a flower, are the various arts buildings, one for each discipline: dance, drama, music, and visual arts.

This morning Ruby and I are headed to the Hub to hear the dean's welcome speech.

We walk into the huge lecture theater where there are about two hundred freshmen milling around. Everyone is introducing themselves and checking one another out.

I hate this.

So many new faces. New expectations to meet.

It's overwhelming.

I can make out various cliques by the way they're dressed. The dancers are all Lycra and layers, the musicians have a vague, retro-geek air about them, and the visual artists look like they were stealing stuff from a thrift store when a paint bomb exploded.

The really loud, obnoxious kids are the drama students.

I feel my chest tighten as I wonder if I'll fit in here any better than I did in high school.

It's not like I didn't have friends in high school. I did. But I was always careful to be the Cassie I thought they expected. Happy, easygoing, nonthreatening. Smart but not intimidating. Pretty but not desired. The one who acted as the go-between when someone liked a boy, but never the one the boy liked.

I take a deep breath and let it out slowly. This is a new school, new people, new rules. Maybe someone here will see beyond my many fake faces.

"Come on," Ruby says. "Let's get seats so we don't have to talk to any of these fuckers."

In that moment, I love her.

We walk to the middle of the auditorium and take our seats. A few minutes later, I see a familiar face heading over to us.

"Hey, Cassie."

"Connor! Hi."

I'd met Connor at the callbacks. We'd been paired up for some scene work, and even though we didn't have the same crazy intensity I'd shared with Holt, we still had decent chemistry. He's also very cute and, as far as I can tell, straight.

He motions to the seat next to me. "May I?"

"Sure." I introduce Ruby, who already looks bored.

Connor folds himself into the chair beside me, and I give him a smile. Sandy-colored hair, brown eyes, open face I've yet to see frown. Definitely cute.

"I'm so glad you got in," he says. "At least I'll know one person in the class."

"Yeah, I haven't seen anyone else I know yet."

"I saw a couple of familiar faces." He looks around. "But I'm bad with names. I saw that blond girl who talks a lot . . ."

"Zoe?"

"Yeah. And the tall guy with the cool hair."

"Holt?"

"Yeah. He's right over there."

He points to the far side of the auditorium where I see Holt's lanky frame slouched in a seat. He has his feet up on the chair in front of him and his head in the same book he was reading at the auditions. He must really love *The Outsiders*.

I get a strange tingling in my stomach when I look at him. I'm happy he made it. Getting into this place meant a lot to him, and apart from his obvious personality disorders, he's really talented.

"He seems like a loner," Connor says. I don't miss that his arm is lying across the back of my chair. "But man, he can act. I saw him do Mercutio last year at the Tribeca Shakespeare Festival. He was amazing."

"I'm sure." I get a crystal-clear image of Holt as a modern-day Mercutio. All leather and denim and dark, glowering eyes.

As I'm staring at him, he looks up and catches my gaze. The corner of his mouth lifts and one of his hands comes away from his book as if he's actually going to smile and wave. Then he notices Connor, and within a second he's back to his book, like he hadn't seen me at all.

Connor raises his eyebrows. "Uh, did I just do something to piss him off? He looked like he wanted to kill me."

"Don't worry about it," I say with a sigh. "He's like that with everyone."

Before long, the dean steps up to the podium and welcomes us. He gives a speech about how proud we must be to have made it into the most prestigious arts college in the country, and even though he's probably given the same speech for years, his words make me puff up like peacock. For the first time in my life, I feel like I'm achieving something for me and not for my parents. It feels good.

When the dean finishes, the lecture theater empties quickly, and we all scurry off to our first day of classes.

Ruby waves good-bye to me and Connor, and heads to her stage management class. When she's gone, Connor drapes his arm around my shoulders and steers me toward our first acting class. Although it feels weird that he's so comfortable invading my personal space when we hardly know each other, it also feels nice. I'm not used to boys putting their nicely muscled arms around my shoulders, but I could *get* used to it.

We walk into a large, empty room with bare brick walls and a rough carpet. Following the example of those already there, we dump our bags at the perimeter of the room and sit on the floor.

I look around at the rest of our class. So many new people to meet and please. My pathetic need to make them like me flares to life, and a sick sweat breaks out on my forehead.

"You okay?" Connor asks, his hand on my back.

"Yeah. Just a little nervous."

"Here," he says as he moves behind me. "I'll help you relax."

When he massages my tense shoulder muscles, I almost groan.

Despite his talented hands, I've got Connor's number. He wants to be the caring, supportive boy. Fine by me. I want to be supported. It's win-win.

The rest of the class chats and laughs, but I only see a few faces I know. A short distance away is Zoe and the strawberry blonde I saw on the first day of auditions. I think her name is Phoebe. True to form, they're chatting loudly and saying "Ohmigod" a lot. In the corner are Troy and Mariska, a brother and sister who seem freaky and quiet.

There's a girl with spiky dark hair named Miranda, who I'm pretty sure hit on me at the callbacks, and a dark guy in a leather jacket called Lucas. He's sitting next to a curly headed jokester named Jack who had everyone in stitches at the callbacks. He's cracking Lucas up by beatboxing using Disney character voices.

As I scan the room, Holt walks in. When he sees Connor massaging my back, he rolls his eyes and takes a seat as far from me as possible.

Whatever.

I don't get Holt. Usually I know what people expect from me within minutes of meeting them.

You want me to laugh at your jokes? Okay.

Oh, please tell me about your hopes and dreams! That'd be great! A shoulder to cry on? No problem.

But with Holt . . . it's like he wants me to not exist. That's something I don't know how to do.

I should be hurt by his behavior, but I'm not. It just makes him a huge, moody, good-smelling puzzle that I'm determined to figure out.

Before long, Erika sweeps into the room and everyone falls silent.

"Okay. This is Advanced Acting, otherwise known as leave-your-bullshit-at-the-door-or-I'll-kick-your-ass class. In here, I don't care if you're tired or scared or hungover or high. I expect one hundred percent of your effort one hundred percent of the time. If you're incapable of that, then don't show up. I don't want to deal with you."

A few people look around nervously, including me.

"You're all here because we saw something in you that deserved to be developed, not babied and coddled. If you think because you can say a few lines with a modicum of emotion this class is going to be easy, think again. In here you'll find exactly where your weaknesses lie. I'm going to strip you down to your bones then build you back up, layer by layer. If that sounds painful, it's because it will be. But in the end, you will know every person in this room better than your own family. And above all, you will truly know yourself."

She looks at me as she says this, and I have a sudden, irrational urge to run from the room and never come back.

"Right. Everyone on your feet. It's time to get to know each other."

She orders us into two lines.

"The rules are simple. The line nearest the windows asks their partner a question, and the partner must answer honestly. Then you switch. You'll continue the pattern until the time runs out and you move on. The challenge here is to get to know as much about the other person as possible in the time given, and I'm not talking about name, age, and favorite color. At the end of this exercise, you should be able to tell me one interesting personal fact about everyone in this room. Your time starts now."

I turn to the person opposite me. It's Mariska. She has dead-straight, pitch-black hair that hangs around her face. Her eyes are just as dark. She's looking at me expectantly.

Oh, right. I'm supposed to ask a question. It's difficult to think of something. She's kind of off-putting.

"Uh . . . what do you do for fun?"

"I cut myself. You?"

I blink for a full five seconds as I process that. "Uh . . . I read. Why do you cut yourself?"

"I enjoy pain. Why do you read?"

"I . . . well . . . enjoy words."

For the next two and a half minutes we talk about books and movies, but I'm still hung up on the whole, "I hurt myself for fun," scenario. When the time is up, I gratefully move on to the next person.

The cycle continues, and I learn lots of interesting things about my new classmates. Miranda has known she was a lesbian since she was eight and thinks I have beautiful breasts. Lucas was arrested for armed robbery when he was sixteen because he was addicted to crack, but now he's off the hard drugs and only smokes pot. A tall, ebony-skinned girl named Aiyah emigrated to the United States with her family when she was twelve after her grandparents and two uncles were massacred in their village in Algeria. Zoe met Robert De Niro in a deli two years ago, and she's positive he hit on her. And Connor has two older brothers in the army who think he's a fag for wanting to act. They beat him up at every family get-together.

I feel like an idiot. A useless, vanilla-flavored waste of space.

Before today, I'd never met a lesbian. Or a drug addict. Or someone who'd lost half their family. I'd been too busy being safe and comfortable in my tiny hometown, thinking I had it tough because my parents expected a lot from me.

*God, I'm pathetic.*

By the time I stand in front Holt, my mind is pounding from my new-and-improved inferiority complex. I look up. He's frowning. Maybe his head hurts, too.

"Does your head hurt?" I ask with a sigh.

"No. Does yours?"

"Yes. Why do I seem to have zero verbal filter around you?"

"I have no idea, but feel free to fix that. Are you freaking out because compared to most of these people, you feel like a spoiled whiner?"

"Uh . . . yes. That's exactly how I feel, and thanks for putting it so eloquently. Is it that obvious?"

He gives me a small smile. "No. But that's how I feel. I just hoped someone else was, too."

For a moment, we're united in our freakish normalcy. Our remarkable unremarkableness.

"So, no deep, dark secrets you want to share with me then?" he asks.

"No. Apart from accidentally stealing a Pooh Bear pencil sharpener when I was five, I'm completely average in every way. Haven't you noticed?"

"No, I haven't." His eyes are doing that annoying intense thing again. "I did notice one remarkable thing about you."

I cock an eyebrow. "Really? And what might that be?"

He takes my hand, then pushes our palms together while he aligns our fingers.

The same heat we shared in the auditions flares, and for a moment I think he's going to say something about our amazing connection.

Instead he says, "You have freakishly large man hands."

*Excuse me?!* "I do *not* have man hands!"

"Yeah, you do. I noticed them when we did the mirror exercise. Look at them."

I examine our hands pressed against each other. His fingers are only slighter longer than mine, and that's saying something, 'cause if he picked his nose with those suckers, he could give himself a lobotomy.

"Maybe your hands are just girly," I say.

"Taylor, I'm six foot three and wear a size twelve shoe, and your hand is almost as big as mine. You can't tell me you don't find that bizarre."

I snatch my hand away and glare. "Well, thank you for pointing that out. Now I'm going to be super self-conscious about my mutant hands."

"Don't be. Some guys might find it sexy. Mostly gay guys of course, because those hands are kind of butch—"

"Shut up!"

"Fine. I won't mention them anymore. And I'll try not to stare. No promises, though. They're like giant attention-drawing satellites."

He thinks he's funny. He's *so* not.

"Why do you hate me so much?" I ask.

He looks at me for a moment, and blinks his crazy-pretty eyes. "I don't hate you, Taylor. Why would you think that?"

"Oh, I don't know. Maybe because when you're not getting off on annoying me, you're either ignoring me or scowling at me. And at the auditions you told me we weren't going to be friends. Why would you say that?"

He sighs and rubs his eyes. "Because we're not. Why, do you want to be friends?"

"Not particularly, which is really strange because usually I'm desperate to be everyone's friend."

"I've noticed."

"What's that supposed to mean?"

He waves his hand dismissively, which, I conclude, should give me free rein to punch him in the stomach. "Nothing. Forget it. Whose turn is it to ask a question?"

"No, I won't forget it. What do you mean by that?"

"I think it's my turn," he says, ignoring me. "So, are you dating that Connor guy?"

The question takes me by surprise. "What?"

"Did I stutter? Are you *dating* him?"

"Dating him as in . . . ?"

"Oh, Jesus, Taylor . . . as in going on dates. Seeing him naked. Fucking him."

"What?!" I'm so angry, I can barely breathe.

"The point of the exercise is to answer the question," he says calmly. "Honesty, please."

"It's none of your business!"

He leans in and lowers his voice to a whisper. "Do I need to get Erika over here and tell her you're not completing the exercise she assigned? She wants us to share, remember?"

The thought of Erika thinking badly of me makes me want to vomit. On him. "You are such a butthead."

"And you're being evasive. Answer the question."

"Why do you care if I'm"—I want to shock him by saying the "F" word, but I just can't push it past my lips—"dating him?"

"I don't. Just curious. You two looked pretty friendly earlier. In fact, it looked like he was going to feel you up in front of the whole class."

"God, you're disgusting."

"Just answer the question."

"No!"

" 'No,' you're not dating him, or 'no,' you won't answer the question."

"Both."

"Well, that's impossible. If it's 'no' to the first you're automatically saying 'yes' to the second."

"Stop. Talking." My face is white-hot.

"So is your answer to my original question 'no' or not?"

"No, my answer isn't 'no.'"

"No?"

"No!" Dammit, now I'm confused as to what exactly I'm saying "no" to.

By now, I can feel a blush crawling down onto my neck. I almost want to laugh about his assumption that I could be "dating" anyone, let alone someone as charming and good looking as Connor.

I'd kissed a few boys at various high school parties, but that was it as far as my experience went. Their sloppy mouths and probing tongues never gave me the urge to take it any further. If sex were baseball, I was still on the bench. The only action my bases had seen was courtesy of my own curious hands, and even then, I'd never achieved a homerun.

Of course, Holt doesn't know that.

I open my mouth to tell him I'm riding Connor like a rodeo bronco, but the look in his eyes stops me. Amid all his hard edges and stony stares, there's something fragile about him, and I can't do it.

I look at my feet and sigh. "No, I'm not dating him."

Holt's frown lessens. "Good. Just stay away from him. I don't like the way he looks at you."

Flashes of my father saying the exact same thing about every boy who bothered to look sideways at me jolt through my brain, and suddenly, my newfound freedom doesn't seem so free anymore.

"Maybe I like the way he looks at me," I say, and jut my chin. "And if I ever decide to date him, I sure as hell won't need your permission. You're not my big brother, you're not my father, and you've already made it very clear you're not my friend, so excuse me if I don't run my dating choices past you. Connor is a nice guy. I could do worse than date him."

Anger flashes in his expression, but he composes his face quickly. "Fine. Date the whole school for all I care."

"Maybe I will."

Before he can say anything else, Erika yells for us to move to the next person, and he's gone.

I'm left standing there wanting to rant at him some more, but Phoebe's in front of me, and the only thing she wants to talk about is Holt. How handsome he is. How tall he is. How intense he is. How much she wants to "date" him.

I hate her immediately.

After class, everyone stands around chatting, and even though Holt is across the room, I can feel him watching me.

I don't think I ever truly knew the meaning of the word "antagonize" before I met him, but I sure as heck know it now. I've never had someone rub me the wrong way so intensely before. If I'm being completely honest, I kind of like the spark.

I glance over at him to make sure he's looking before grabbing Connor's arm and doing my best flirty-Zoe impersonation as I ask him to walk me to the next class.

Holt doesn't speak to me for the rest of the week.

# FOUR

## MAKING THE FIRST MOVE

*Present Day*
*New York City*
*The Diary of Cassandra Taylor*

*Dear Diary,*

*The more time I spend with him, the more he invades my dreams. I don't want to remember, but he pushes through.*

*He's here, under my hands. His lips on my skin. It's perfect and warm, and I tell myself he won't run away this time.*

*I hold him to me, willing away the fear, willing him to lose himself in me. To stay. And even though he's already written a tragedy, I want to change his mind.*

*Then he's inside me, and it's perfection.*

*I give him the part of myself I can't imagine giving to anyone else. He tells me it's precious. That he doesn't deserve it.*

*Afterward, he holds me like he never wants to let go.*

*I believe he'll stay this way. That it won't change things.*

*Of course, it does.*

*He covers himself again, so disguised by layers that I don't even see him anymore, just the hurt he leaves behind.*

*I blame him, but it's my fault. Stupid, romantic, gullible me.*

*I saw what I wanted to see. Felt what I wanted to feel. He just played his part.*

*Sometimes he's behind my eyes, weeping and exposed, and he's the most beautiful thing I've ever seen.*

*But it was an act.*

*He's an actor.*

*And he's very, very good.*


**Six Years Earlier**
**Westchester, New York**
**The Grove**
**Second Week of Classes**

I walk out of my History of Theater class, my brain churning with information on Roman amphitheaters, when I run smack-bang into the chest of someone tall and still.

Of course, my notes go flying.

"Frack!"

The tall someone chuckles, and my hackles rise.

I look up into Holt's smirking face. My expression must scream of impending violence, because his smile drops faster than Zoe Stevens' panties on a Saturday night.

When I bend to pick up my notes, he's beside me. I want to slap his hands away, because since the getting-to-know-you exercise on our first day, he hasn't spoken a word to me. I'm not cool with that.

"Just leave them," I say as he gathers up my notes.

He holds out the notes, and I snatch them without looking up.

I bite back the instinct to say "thank you," because after the way he's treated me, he doesn't deserve it.

"Thank you," I mumble involuntarily.

Damn you, automated politeness!

"You're welcome," he says in his stupid smooth voice.

I push past him and stride down the stairs toward the Hub. Within a few seconds, he's walking beside me like it's the most natural thing in the world.

"Big week, huh?" he says. "I thought Erika was going to kick Lucas out when he showed up stoned, but I think she realized he's a better actor when he's half-baked."

I stop and turn to face him. "Holt, you do not get to ignore me for a week then start gabbing away like nothing happened."

"I haven't been ignoring you."

"Oh, yes you have."

"No, ignoring you would be to disregard your presence. I've noticed you. I've just chosen to not speak to you."

"Is that better or worse than ignoring me completely?"

"Slightly better."

I throw up my hands. "Well, thank God. I won't take offense then."

"Good for you."

"I was being sarcastic, butt-munch."

"Taylor, are you always this grumpy, or are you PMSing?"

"What?! I'm . . . What?! PMSing?! You are so . . . *God! Shut up!*"

I walk away, but he keeps pace, and my PMS is making me crazy-angry and weepy at the same time.

"Why are you following me?!"

"I'm not following you. I'm walking beside you."

*Holy Jesus, give me strength!*

"What do you want?" I ask, feeling like a tiny yappy dog next to him.

He sighs and looks down at his ridiculous, giant feet. "Nothing. Are you going to Jack's party tonight?"

"Why do you want to know?"

He rubs his eyes. "I have no fucking idea."

"Are you going?"

"Probably not."

"Then sure, I'll be there."

He looks at me for a few more seconds before frowning like he's trying to calculate how many watermelons will fit in a Winnebago. Then, without saying another word, he turns and walks away.

"Oh, okay, so we're done here?" I say to his back. "Well, thanks for making the effort. Your conversation skills are truly stimulating!"

Thank God it's the weekend. I won't have to see him for two whole days.

By the time I've stomped back to my apartment, any desire to go to the party has disintegrated. All I want to do is soak in the tub for a few hours, eat my own weight in Ben & Jerry's, and go to bed.

Ruby has other ideas.

"Get up."

"I don't wanna," I say, sounding like a two-year-old.

"You're going."

"Ruby . . ."

"Don't start with me, Cassie. It's our first college party, and you're going if I have to drag you there by your hair. Judging by your face when you walked in the door, you seriously need to get laid."

I roll my eyes. I wish I was the sort of girl who could solve her problems with white-hot animal sex. But considering my V-card is well and truly valid and flirting isn't exactly my forte, the best I can hope for is to not have a completely sucky time.

"I think the only person getting laid tonight will be you, Ruby."

She throws up her hands. "Cassie, you're gorgeous. You could have any guy you wanted if you just showed a bit of confidence."

"Yeah, right."

"Promise me you'll make a move tonight."

I laugh. "I don't think you understand. I have no moves. I'm moveless. I exist in a vacuum of moves."

She sets her mouth in such a way that I know I won't be winning an argument with her any time soon. "Do I need to remind you that you're an actor? Act like you know what the fuck you're doing. Now, get your ass into something sexy and let's go."

I don't really own anything sexy, so I settle for my tightest jeans and a low-cut sweater that makes my boobs look great. I even put on some makeup and do my hair. Ruby shrugs her approval.

Half an hour later we're pulling up to a huge house on a wide street.

"Whoa, who lives here?" Ruby asks as she slams the cab door.

"Jack Avery shares it with two other boys from my class. Lucas and Connor."

"Connor?" she says, raising an eyebrow. "That's the guy I met on the first day?"

"Yeah."

"He was cute. Any chemistry there?"

I smile when I think about how attentive Connor has been. "He hugs me a lot."

"Well, there you go," she says, as if all my problems are solved. "Make a move on him."

I shrug, because even though I like Connor, I don't know if I *like* Connor.

"Listen," she says, "I'm not asking you to walk down the aisle with him and squeeze out loud, chubby babies. Just have some fun. Make out. It's not going to kill you."

"Isn't the boy supposed to make the first move?"

"Dammit, Cass, stop being such a pussy. Look, I'll even sweeten the deal. If you get up the balls to make out with a boy tonight, I'll do your laundry for a month."

She has my attention. Our building has one ancient washing machine that takes more than an hour to go through its cycle, so laundry day can be a major time suck.

"Fine. I can't promise I'm not going to be awkward and embarrassing, but I'll try, okay?"

She smiles and pulls me toward the noisy house. "Good enough."

There are people talking and laughing on the front lawn. It looks like most of the freshman class has shown up.

I prepare to conjure a personality.

"Come on," Ruby says as she tugs me into the mess of people. "You need a drink."

"I don't drink."

"You do now." She grabs two bright green test tubes from a girl with a tray. "Two or three of these, and you'll be tackling boys and ripping off their shirts."

Despite doubting her prediction, forty-five minutes and three test tubes later, I'm leaning against a wall feeling frisky. I bounce my head to the beat as Ruby dances with a group of boys all desperate to impress her. She's flirting with a few of them, but one—a tall, well-built guy who's also in her tech course—is getting special attention. He leans down to whisper something to her. She glances at me and raises her eyebrows before taking his hand and going outside to the terrace.

She makes it look so easy.

*Okay, fine. I can do this. Find cute boy. Chat with cute boy. Be charming. Suck on his face.*

Panic shivers through me.

*Goddammit.*

I go down the hallway in search of the bathroom, the one party safe haven where it's acceptable to be alone.

Before I can find it, I spy Holt standing in the doorway to the kitchen.

What the hell is he doing here?

He leans down and talks to the short, pretty girl by his side.

He has a girlfriend?

Of course he does. Someone as attractive as he is probably has dozens of women throwing themselves at his stupid, large, clown feet.

I feel myself blush, fast and hot, and I don't like it.

The alcohol has made me slow, and before I can pretend I don't see him, he's walking toward me with his hand on the girl's back. She's smiling like she knows me.

"Hey, Cassie," she says. She does look familiar, but my brain is murky. "I'm Elissa. I'm in theater tech with Ruby."

"Oh, right. Hey, Elissa." She'd been talking to Ruby the other day in our semiotics class. Pretty face. Doe eyes.

I glance at Holt, and my face burns when I see that he's staring at my boobs. He quickly makes it back up to my face and clears his throat.

"Taylor," he says and nods.

"Holt." I try not to let my brain acknowledge how annoyingly handsome he looks in his dark jeans and blue button-down with the sleeves rolled up.

Forearms. Nice.

"I thought you weren't coming," I say.

"Well, I heard all the cool kids would be here, so I couldn't stay away."

Elissa glances between us, and I wonder if she realizes how much her boyfriend gets on my nerves.

"So, Cassie, you and Ethan are doing the acting course together?"

"Yeah, but we haven't done much acting yet."

"Well, it's only been a week," she says, smiling. "Auditions for the term one theater project are coming up soon. I've heard rumors they're doing *Romeo and Juliet*. You never know. You two could end up playing star-crossed lovers."

Holt and I burst into laughter like it's the most hilarious thing we've ever heard.

Elissa looks at us like we're both insane.

"Okay," she says as she claps her hands together. "I need to get hammered as soon as possible. See you guys later."

She brushes past me and walks down the hallway.

"I'm leaving in two hours," Holt calls after her. "If you want a ride home, find me before then, or else you can fucking walk."

Wow. If only I had such a charming boyfriend.

I shake my head in disgust.

"What?" he asks.

"You."

"What about me?"

"Do you always talk to her like that?"

"Yes."

"Why?"

"Why not?"

"Because it's *rude*."

He shoots me a lopsided grin and shakes his head. "That was me being polite. I say far worse things at home."

"At home?"

"Yeah."

"You live with her?"

"Well, I'd prefer not to, but I can't seem to get rid of her. I locked her out once, but she's pretty resourceful and managed to pick the lock with a blade of grass and a paperclip."

"God, Holt, you're just . . . so . . . ugh! Why does she put up with you? You're officially the world's suckiest boyfriend."

His eyes widen. Then he laughs. "Elissa isn't my girlfriend. Jesus, that's disgusting. She's my sister."

It's my turn to be surprised. "Your sister?"

"Yes."

Relief has never felt more odious.

"Don't worry, Taylor," he whispers. "I'm single. No need to be jealous."

I laugh. "I'm not jealous. I'm just glad you're not inflicting your toxic personality on some poor member of the opposite sex."

Something dark flashes in his eyes as he looks down, and I get the impression I've said something really wrong. I'm about to try to find out when Connor appears and drapes his arm around my shoulders.

"Hey, Cassie, I've been looking for you. Glad you could make it."

He hugs me, and I can feel Holt watching us.

"Wouldn't miss it," I say and hug him back.

"Hey, Ethan," he says and claps Holt on the shoulder. "Thanks for coming, man."

Holt smiles, but it's tight and forced. "Wouldn't miss it."

"So," Connor says. "A lot of our class is in the basement playing drinking games. Wanna join?"

I smile. "Sure."

Holt shrugs. Connor leads the way.

When we get downstairs, about twenty people from our class are sitting in a circle with a collection of bottles, beer cans, and shot glasses littered across the floor.

"I found two more," Connor says as he guides us into the circle. The group gives what can only be described as a drunken roar.

Zoe immediately pulls Holt down next to her and hands him a drink. Connor sits next to me. Jack sets us all up with a shot glass of brown liquid. Holt downs the shot and refuses a refill, muttering something about having to drive. It's ironic that he's one of the few people in our class who's twenty-one and yet he's the only one not drinking.

I drink my shot, then cough like I've swallowed acid.

Everyone laughs, and the games begin.

I try to concentrate, but I don't really know the rules. I end up drinking a lot.

Too much.

After a while, everything's funny. Everyone's pretty. I want to hug and kiss them all because they're just so nice and pretty and funny.

Then there's music. Loud and pounding.

Someone pulls me to my feet. Connor.

He puts his arms around me, so I put mine around him, and I'm trying to dance, but all I can do is shuffle. Connor doesn't care. He's warm and grazes his nose down my throat.

"You smell so good, Cassie."

I smile, because his nose tickles. Because he's sweet. Because I like the way he holds me. I'm hanging off him and smiling, but my body feels heavy.

Then his lips are where his nose was, and I'm tingling. But something's wrong.

The room is tilting. I pull back. I tell myself I'm not looking for Holt, but I am.

Everywhere people are dancing and laughing. Making out.

I see Holt across the room, sitting on a couch sipping a Coke. Zoe is talking to him and touching him in ways that say, "I'll let you do whatever you want to me." But he's not listening to her. He's looking at me, and now I'm tingling a whole lot more.

I don't want him to make me feel things, so I turn back to Connor. He's stroking my back. It feels nice.

His face is close, and he has that look in his eye. The one that says he wants me.

I've always yearned for a boy to look at me like that. Now one is, but all I can think about is the scowling face across the room.

"Cassie, I want to kiss you."

He seems to search my face, looking for an answer. I want to be kissed, but I think it's the alcohol.

Ruby's voice is in my head telling me to stop being a pussy and just do it.

Connor's gazing at my mouth as his face gets closer and closer, and I'm too hot and too drunk.

Then Connor's kissing me, and there's part of me that wants to kiss him back, but I can't.

I pull away. "Connor . . ."

He smiles and drops his head.

"I'm sorry," I say. I think I must be defective for not kissing him, because he's really handsome and sweet.

He shakes his head. "Don't worry about it."

"I want to, I do . . ." I say, slurring but sincere.

"Yeah, but I get the feeling you want to kiss someone else more."

He touches my cheek, and I don't have a chance to tell him he's wrong before he's disappearing up the stairs.

The music changes, and it makes the floor shift so much I have to sit down.

I stagger toward the couches. They seem so far away.

Someone grabs my arm and guides me. Without looking, I know it's Holt.

Jack appears on the other side and laughs. "Taylor, you are sooooo fucked up!"

Hyena giggles all around.

Warm hands are trying to push me onto the couch, but Jack gives me the bottle again, and it would be rude not to drink. I slap at the helpy hands and take the bottle.

I sip it and pull a face. It's gross but awesome.

Everyone laughs, and so do I. Too loud. Too shrill. Drunk me laughs like an idiot.

"Okay, that's it, she's had enough."

Holt's voice. Gruff. Sounds like my father.

"Dude, no one's forcing it down her throat. She's a big girl."

"Pass the bottle to someone else, Avery. *Now.*"

I stumble and everyone giggles.

Obviously, drunk-Cassie is hilarious.

They're all blurry now. I'm blinking way too long. I sway, and warm hands are on me again.

"Christ, Taylor, would you sit before you fall down?"

Cranky voice. Doesn't approve of Drunk Cassie.

Drunk Cassie doesn't give a flying fuck.

Giggles.

Just said the "F" word. In my brain.

Naughty Drunk Cassie.

I flop down on the sofa. It's soft, and I'm tired. Seriously tired.

I lean against his body. Hard and warm. Smells good. I turn my face so I can smell better. Cotton shirt. Shoulder. Grab and sniff. Nice.

"Fuck me." Man-voice. Sexy.

I grab more of him. Tug at his collar so I can get closer. Under the collar is skin. Warm. Tingly under my fingers.

"Jesus, Taylor . . ." His voice isn't angry anymore. Different. Begging. "Stop."

"No. S'nice. Smellsgood."

Want more warm so I climb onto his lap. Legs either side of hips. Nose in neck. Hands in hair. So good.

"For fuck's sake." He pushes me away, and I pout.

I look at his face. So handsome when he frowns.

"Taylor, stop. You're drunk."

I flop forward.

"Please," I say, fitting myself against his body. "Juswanna sleep for a minute."

Nuzzle into neck again. Breathe in warm boy-skin.

He's tense underneath me, but I'm comfortable. He smells amazing.

"Hey, check it out!" *Shhh, Jack. Too loud.* "Taylor's finally found a way to rattle the unflappable Holt. I think he's blushing!"

More laughter.

I whisper, "Shh," and my lips touch his neck. He groans, and I want to do it again.

"Avery, you asshole." He's talking softly, but it's still too loud. I try to cover his mouth with my hand, but he pulls it away. "She drank too much and she's going to be sick."

"She's fine, man. Look at that smile. She can't get enough of you. I wouldn't be complaining if I was in your shoes."

I want everyone to stop talking. Just wanna sleep.

I moan and bury my head further into Holt's neck. He squirms underneath me.

"Get her some water before I kick your fucking ass." His chest vibrates against my boobs when he talks. Feels nice. Manly.

"Okay, okay. Christ, take a fucking pill."

I snuggle down. "Stoptalkin. Shh. Need to sleep."

"Taylor." His voice is softer, less cranky. "You need to get off me. Please."

"Donwanna. Feels good." I put my hand inside his shirt. Nice muscles. So nice.

"Fuck, Taylor. For the love of God, stop, before I do something really fucking stupid."

His hands are on my hips, trying to move me. I move but not off him. I press down.

I feel him against me. Hard. God. So hard.

He groans again, his face in my neck. "Jesus . . ."

My whole body burns. Aches. Wants.

I move against him.

He swears, and it's all sexy. His lips are near my ear.

"Cassie, not like this." He grabs my hips and stills me. "Not when you're drunk and won't remember it tomorrow. Stop."

I'm burning, but he won't let me move.

I slump. Defeated.

"Cassie, look at me."

Eyes open.

Oh, not a good move.

Everything is swaying.

Feel seasick.

"Cassie?"

The world is tilting. He's watching me. Concerned.

"Cassie?"

"Mnotfeelingsogood."

Stand. Almost fall over. Hands on me. Strong. Burning.

"Shit, woman. Slow down."

"Mfine."

Pull away. Stagger down the hall.

The bathroom. Close door. Toilet too far away. Crawl to it.

Stomach tightens, mouth opens.

Brown liquid and corn chips explode out. It burns coming up like it did going down. Stomach heaves till there's nothing left, and I'm tired. So tired.

I close my eyes. Swirls of black and gray are there, and I'm on a boat in a storm, swaying and tilting.

When I open my eyes, I'm being lifted out of a car and he's carrying me. He has my keys, and as soon as the front door opens, I make a groaning sound. Then I'm in front of the toilet, vomiting while he holds my hair and rubs my back. I'm crying and gross while he's shushing me and wiping my face with a cool washcloth.

Then he puts me in bed. The swirls of black wrap around me, and I'm gone.


I wake up, and everything hurts. The sun is too bright. A stabbing pain shoots straight through my eyeballs into my brain. My stomach is crampy, and my abs feel like I've done a thousand crunches.

I groan and pull my pillow over my head, but there are hands pulling it away. I crack open an eye to see Holt next to me, holding out water and Tylenol.

"Take these." He talks quietly, but even that's too loud for my pounding head.

I try to sit up, but it hurts too much. I roll onto my side and take the pills with the full glass of water. It does nothing to flush away the horrible taste in my mouth. I slump back onto my pillow.

I must fall asleep again, because when I wake up I can smell bacon cooking and hear someone moving around in the kitchen.

I stumble to the bathroom and pee like I've never peed before. The lure of a warm shower is too much to resist, so I peel off my clothes and stand under the spray until I feel more or less human. I wash my hair and scrub my body, then wrap myself in a towel before brushing my teeth and tongue. Twice.

By the time I'm done, I feel a little better. My head's still pounding and my stomach is unsettled, but I can function.

I open the bathroom door to find Holt standing there. He takes in my wet hair and my towel-covered body before he makes it back up to my face.

He clears his throat. "Uh . . . hey."

"Hey," I say. It's so bizarre to see him in my apartment, I wonder if I'm still incredibly drunk.

"I . . . uh . . . made you something to eat," he says and shoves his hands in his pockets.

I frown. "We have no food."

"I went and bought some. You should eat. It'll make you feel better."

"Okay."

He stands there, towering in the doorway, staring and biting the inside of his cheek.

"Uh, Holt?"

"Hmm?"

"You have to move so I can go to my room and put on some clothes."

"Oh . . . right."

He turns and walks back to the kitchen.

I throw on some sweats and run a brush through my hair. Then I'm sitting at our tiny dining table with Holt. He's cooked eggs, bacon, and hash browns. There's a cup of coffee in front of me, along with a glass of orange juice. It's a truly bizarre situation.

"Uh . . . wow," I say. "This is . . . wow. You . . . you made hash browns? From scratch?"

"Yeah," he says and pops some egg into his mouth. "It's not hard."

"Maybe not for you. I can't even boil water without a recipe."

He's watching me, and even though my stomach is refusing to get excited about food, I eat.

"Hmm," I mumble around a mouthful of hash browns and bacon. "This is really good."

"My mom's a private chef. She's taught me stuff." He shrugs and keeps eating. Every now and then he glances up at me, his eyes dark and unreadable.

When we're done, he clears the plates as I sip my coffee. I don't mean to, but I stare at his ass as he washes the dishes.

I shouldn't stare at his ass. No good can come of it. Still, he's being nice to me, so I decide to be nice to his ass and allow myself to notice how hot it looks in his jeans.

He turns around to lean against the sink and without planning it, my focus is now firmly on his crotch.

He catches me staring. I grab my coffee and take a huge gulp, but it goes down the wrong way. I choke and cough.

"You okay?"

"Yep."

Smooth.

No wonder I've never had a boyfriend.

"So . . ." he says, and gestures to my phone on the kitchen bench. "Your roommate called to see how you were and to tell you she'll be home later."

"Oh, yeah?"

"She said to ask if she needs to do your laundry for the rest of the month."

I smile.

Well, I did sexually harass Holt. Even though we didn't kiss or anything, I wonder if Ruby would count that as making out.

I blush when I think about it.

"Look, Holt, about last night—"

"Yeah, about that," he says while rubbing his eyes. "What the hell were you thinking, drinking that much? You could have gotten alcohol poisoning."

"I was"—*trying to be something I'm not*—"trying to have a good time."

"Did you have a good time projectile vomiting? Was that fun?"

I shake my head. "For a while I felt good. People were laughing."

"That's because you were shitfaced and rubbing yourself on every man in the room."

"Not every man," I say defensively. "Only Connor. And . . . you."

"Yeah, well, that's enough," he mutters. "What's up with you and Connor, anyway? One minute you're kissing him, and the next you're all over me."

"I didn't kiss Connor. He kissed me."

"Semantics."

"And it was barely a kiss, anyway."

"So, I guess you're a horny drunk."

"I wasn't horny," I say indignantly.

Oh God, I was so horny.

"Well, it certainly felt like it from where I was sitting."

"I was . . . well . . . you were there and I was . . . uh . . ."

"Horny?"

"*Drunk*, and that's why it happened. No other reason. Normally, I wouldn't do that. To you of all people."

"Because you hate me."

"Exactly."

"But you still want me."

"What?! No!"

"Yes."

"You're delusional."

"Hey, you were the one sniffing me and kissing my neck and grinding yourself on my . . . well . . . on me. If I wasn't such a gentleman, we probably would have fucked right there in front of all of our classmates."

His words are ridiculous, but my body doesn't know that because the tingling ache I felt last night is back with a vengeance.

"Holt, two people who hate each other do not . . ."

"Fuck?"

"Have sex."

"Sure, they do. Happens all the time."

"Not to me, it doesn't."

"Pity."

We fall into silence.

I smile and shake my head.

He frowns. "What?"

"I can't figure you out, that's all. One minute you give off this bad-boy vibe, like the world's going to end if you're nice to me, and the next minute you're this really good guy who takes me home, buys food, and cooks me breakfast. Why would you do that?"

He picks at his fingernails. "I've been asking myself the same question all night."

"And what did you come up with?"

"I have no fucking clue."

"A moment of weakness?"

"Obviously."

"Maybe you're more good guy than bad boy after all."

He gives a short laugh. "Taylor, I'm a lot of things, but I can assure you that the one thing I'm not is a good guy. Just ask my ex-girlfriends."

His face drops. Like he just told me something he didn't mean to.

Before I can say anything else, he stands, brushes himself off, and takes a step toward the door.

"Well, I'm outta here. You've probably got things to do."

"I don't have anything planned," I say. He stops to look at me. "You can . . . ah . . . hang out if you want."

I never expected to crave Holt's company, but part of me does. A lot.

"I . . . uh . . ." He looks at his feet. "Nah. I have to go."

I don't like that I'm disappointed.

"Oh. Okay. Well, thanks for the, you know, hair-holding and breakfast and stuff."

"Yeah, no problem."

I walk him to the door. He steps outside and turns to face me. "So, I guess I'll see you Monday."

"Yeah. Guess so."

As he turns to go, I say, "So, are you going to talk to me next week, or was this a momentary lapse in your resolve to not be friends?"

He turns back, almost smiling. "Taylor, us being friends would be . . . complicated."

"More complicated than whatever the hell we are now?"

"Yes."

"Why? Is the world going to end if we hang out?"

He fixes me with an intense expression. "Yes. The seas will boil, the skies will darken, and every volcano in the world will erupt, thus bringing an end to civilization as we know it. So for the sake of humanity . . . in fact, for the sake of everything you hold dear . . . stay away from me." He's so serious, it makes me think he isn't joking.

"Ethan Holt, you're the strangest person I've ever met," I say.

He nods. "I'm going to take that as a compliment."

"You would."

He stares for a moment longer before shaking his head and walking to his car.

I watch until his taillights disappear around the corner.

After I close the door, I retreat to my room and crawl into bed. As I snuggle into my pillow, I wonder which Holt I'll see next week: the douche with a giant chip on his shoulder who boils my blood, or the sweet man who made me hash browns from scratch.

Part of me hopes for both.

# FIVE

## BIRTHDAY WISHES

*Westchester, New York*
*The Diary of Cassandra Taylor*
*Fourth Week of Classes*

*Dear Diary,*

*Today is my birthday.*

*Yep. Nineteen years of trying to be everything to everyone and ending up as no one to myself.*

*How the hell did this happen?*

*I don't know if I'm depressed because I feel I should have achieved more with my life by now, or because I'm a nineteen-year-old virgin who desperately wants sex.*

*I'm pretty sure it's that second thing.*

*I've never had a boyfriend. Never had a truly toe-curling kiss. Never had a boy touch my boobs or my butt, or pretty much any part of my naked body, and Lord, I'm desperate for it.*

*Most nights I touch myself, pretending the hands aren't mine as I search for the crashing pleasure I keep reading about in Harlequin romance novels and* Cosmo. *But every night I give up, because even though I can feel something building—something shining and explosive and just out of* reach—*I can never grasp it. It's like I'm hovering on the edge of a sneeze, and I'm inhaling and inhaling and inhaling, but the orgasmic exhale never comes. Literally.*

*Of course, it doesn't help that I've recently discovered Internet porn and have become obsessed with it.*

*At first I was embarrassed as I watched extreme close-ups of male and female genitalia thrusting against each other, but the embarrassment was quickly replaced by fascination. Horny, aroused fascination.*

*Mostly with penises.*

*Oh, the pretty penises. Not flaccid ones of course, because they're just floppy, wrinkly, and gross. But the erect ones? Wow. Beautiful. Magnificent. Incredibly sexy.*

*I'm enthralled by them.*

*I bet they feel amazing. Is that why men are so obsessed with their own?*

*The closest I've ever come to one was the night I drunkenly ground myself against Holt, and although that felt nice, I want to feel one in my hand.*

*Maybe Holt will let me touch his. I bet he has a very nice penis. I bet it's glorious, like his stupid perfect face, and gorgeous eyes, and muscled body. I bet if he entered his penis in a competition, it would win "Best in Show" and he could walk around with a giant blue ribbon stuck to his crotch.*

*If I asked nicely, I wonder if he'd use his pretty penis to remove my pesky virginity.*

*I'm willing to bet I'm the only virgin in my class. I was holding out hope that Michelle Tye was still in the "V" sorority, but she came to class the other day bragging about how she finally met up with a guy she'd been cyber-sexing, and they humped each other senseless last weekend. She whispered to me that she came four times. Four!*

*Good God, I'd be happy just to come once, and she gets four? That's plain greedy.*

*I haven't spoken to her for a few days. My jealous vagina forbids it.*

*I swear that I'm so desperate sometimes I just think I'm going to grab*

*the next guy who comes up to me, tear his clothes off, and molest him on*
*the spot. That I'm going to—*

"Hey, Taylor. Writing a novel?"

I slam my diary and legs shut with equal panic. When I look up,
Holt's looking down at me with one of his signature irritating smirks.

"What do you want?" I say as I shove my diary deep into my bag.
With much effort, I stop myself from petting his crotch.

I fan myself because, oh sweet Jesus, my face is burning hot.

"What the fuck is wrong with you, woman? Are you sick?"

He places the back of his fingers on my forehead. All I can think
is that I want those fingers touching me in intimate places.

*Yes, I'm sick. Extremely perverted and sexually sick.*

"I'm fine," I say and stand to get away from him. I wind up over-
balancing and tilt toward the ground. Then his arms are around me,
and my horny, deprived body is against his, and I'm trying desperately
not to hump his thigh.

"Shit, you can't even stand up today," he grumbles. "What the hell?"

I have a moment to savor how his arms feel under my hands before he's pushing me away and doing that thing where he exhales while
running his fingers through his hair.

I have to get away from him, because if I don't, I swear to the tiny,
sweet-smelling baby Jesus, I'm going knock him to the ground and
straddle him.

I turn and walk away.

"Where the hell are you going?" he calls after me.

"Elsewhere."

"Taylor, the Benzo Ra performance starts soon. In the theater.
Which is in the opposite direction to the one in which you're currently traveling."

I stop in my tracks. In my sex-obsessed haze I'd almost forgotten
about the world-famous performance troupe visiting our school for
an exclusive performance.

I spin on my heel and stalk past him. "I knew that."

He falls into step beside me. I speed up to lose him, but there's no outrunning his stupidly long legs.

"You auditioning for Juliet next week?" he asks.

I scoff and shake my head. "No."

"Why not?"

"Because there's no way I would get the lead. I'm probably going to end up playing 'third partygoer from the left' and spend the whole production doing crosswords in the dressing room."

He stops and stares at me. "Why the hell wouldn't you audition?"

"Because I might suck."

"Why would you suck?"

"Because," I say, "I look around our class, and everyone, and I mean *everyone*, has more of a clue about what the hell they're doing. Nearly all of you have had some kind of professional experience and training, while I've had none. I feel like you guys are all driving sports cars while I'm still trundling away on my pink kiddie bike with the training wheels."

He frowns. "That's ridiculous."

"Is it? Holt, they didn't even have a drama course at my high school. I had a couple of private acting classes with a guy whose greatest claim to fame was being an extra on *The Bold and the Beautiful*, and the other day when I walked in on a conversation between Zoe and Phoebe about Stanislavski, honest to God, I said, 'Oh, wow, I love him. I think I saw him play in the finals of the U.S. Open.'"

He looks at me for a few seconds, his aggravatingly blue eyes unblinking. "Well, hey, that's an easy mistake to make. The father of modern characterization does sound like a tennis player."

He keeps his composure for a grand total of three seconds before his face cracks as he doubles over in laughter.

"I hate you," I say as I walk away.

"Aw, Taylor, come on," he calls as he comes after me.

"I tell you I'm feeling insecure and inferior, and this is how you react? See, *this* is why we're not friends."

"I couldn't help it."

"I know. Apparently my ignorance is hilarious."

He grabs my arm to stop me, and his laughter fades. "Cassie, you're not ignorant. Do you honestly think a casting director is going to care if you know who Stanislavski is when you go to an audition?"

"I don't know. I've never auditioned for a casting director, because I have *zero* experience."

"But you've done plays . . ."

"I was in the chorus of two musicals for which the only audition requirement was showing up. I'd hardly credit that to my stellar technique."

"Well, you got into this place, for God's sake," he says, gesturing around him. "Out of thousands of people, they accepted *you*, and that wasn't because of how many castings you've been to or how many lame-ass plays or movies you've been in. They accepted you because you're really fucking talented, okay? Stop being so goddamn insecure and own it."

I look up at him. "You think . . . I'm talented?"

He sighs. "Jesus, Taylor, yes. Very talented. You've got just as much chance as anyone of getting the lead role. Maybe more, because you have a sort of . . . intense vulnerability when you act. It's . . . well, it's kind of remarkable."

For a moment, the way he's looking at me is almost affectionate. Then he clears his throat, and says, "You'd be freaking nuts not to audition for Juliet. You'd be perfect."

The phrase "you'd be perfect" resounds in my brain like a sweet, sexy echo.

"Well, maybe I will try out," I say, practically toeing the pavement. "Even on my suckiest day I'm still better than Zoe."

He chuckles. "That's true."

"So what about you?" I say, walking slowly as he falls into step beside me. "Are you auditioning for Romeo?"

He shakes his head. "No way. I'd have to have my balls removed to play that pussy."

"Hey, that's no way to talk about one of the greatest romantic heroes of all time."

"He's not a hero, Taylor, he's a limp, fickle dick who confuses lust with love and kills himself over a chick he's just met."

"Harsh!" I say and laugh. "You don't believe he loved Juliet?"

"Fuck, no. He was dumped by Hot Girl Number One—Rosaline. He pines over her like a kid who's lost his puppy, or his pussy, as the case may be. Then, through a chain of unlikely events, he meets Hot Girl Number Two—Juliet. He immediately forgets all about Hot Girl Number One and is so pathetically desperate to fuck Hot Girl Number Two that he proposes marriage to her within *hours* of meeting her. I mean, come on. Her vagina could offer shiatsu massage and whistle the national anthem—it's still not worth marrying her to get a piece of it."

I shake my head over the massive mound of cynical walking beside me in human form.

"So you don't think there's the slightest possibility he just fell in love at first sight?"

"Love at first sight is a myth invented by romance novel authors and Hollywood. It's bullshit."

"Jeez, how did you get to be so jaded?"

"I'm not jaded. Just realistic."

"Sure you are."

He stops and turns to me, his face all serious. "Think about it like this. Just imagine you see a hot guy. You have an immediate, powerful reaction to him. Do you love him?"

Not sure I'm entirely comfortable with this line of questioning.

"Well . . . I . . . uh—"

"Okay, I'll turn it around. I see a girl. For some reason, looking at her is like . . . God, I don't know. Like finding something precious I never knew I lost. I feel something for her. Something primal. Are you trying to tell me that what I feel is love? Not lust?"

"I don't know. Is this hypothetical girl hot?"

"Fuck, yes. Hot in a way I never thought hot could be. Just looking at her turns me on. It's annoying as hell."

*Okay. This conversation has taken a seriously arousing turn. Just what I need today.*

"I . . . well . . ."

"Come on, Taylor. Am I in love?"

I'm looking at his crotch. "Well . . . uh, I don't know. It's hard"—God, I said *hard* while looking at his crotch—"to say. I mean . . . uh . . . wow."

"Of course I'm not in love! It's a bizarre chemical reaction that'll pass. I'm not going to ask her to marry me just so I can fuck her."

My mind goes to very porny places.

"Taylor!" He clicks his fingers in front of my face. "Focus."

"So . . . uh . . . you think a strong reaction to someone of the opposite sex is always purely physical?"

"Yes. If *Romeo and Juliet* had happened in real life, minus the ridiculous deaths, Juliet probably would have destroyed Romeo in the end by fucking Mercutio."

He's dead serious. It's funny and tragic at the same time.

"Think about it, Taylor," he says as he leans forward. "If Romeo thought he loved Rosaline and she broke his heart, why wouldn't he be *terrified* of Juliet, considering his connection to her is a hundred times stronger?"

I raise my eyebrows. "Maybe he's brave enough to think it's worth the risk."

"Yeah, and maybe he's just horny and stupid."

"The romantic argument would be that if they'd denied their . . .

love . . . connection . . . whatever you want to call it, they'd be hollow. Isn't that the point of living? To find the one person in all the world who's your perfect match?"

"Actually, Taylor, the point of living is not dying. Romeo and Juliet failed at that part."

I shake my head in disbelief. "What you're telling me is that if you were Romeo, you'd have walked away from Juliet."

"Yes," he says, unblinking.

"Hmmmm."

"What's that supposed to mean?"

"Nothing. It's a contemplative sound."

"Contemplating what?"

"How much you're deluding yourself." I narrow my eyes while tapping my chin with my finger. "Hmmmm."

He exhales and glares. "Don't fucking 'hmmmm' me, Taylor, okay? I don't need your condescending little sounds."

"Hmmmm."

"Goddammit." He looks at his wrist and says, "Wow, look at the time. We have to go. The show's starting soon."

Right. Benzo Ra.

He walks off, and I follow, saying, "Uh . . . Holt? You know you're not actually wearing a watch, right?"

"Yeah, I know."

"Just checking."

When Holt and I emerge from the theater an hour later, we're barely out the door before we're snorting out all the repressed scorn that built up during the performance.

"Oh . . . man," Holt says as he starts to calm down "That was the funniest thing I've seen since Keanu Reeves did *Much Ado About Nothing*."

I wipe the laugh tears from my eyes as we walk to our next class.

"Seriously." I sigh. "That's a *professional* theater company. That could be our future."

He laughs and groans at the same time. "It would be the ultimate torture. Those guys couldn't actually classify themselves as actors, could they? Surely their résumés say 'Professional Pretentious Prick.'"

We continue chuckling as we make our way into acting class. Erika is already there, sitting on her desk.

As the class settles around her, she says, "So, that was one of the most highly respected avant-garde theater troupes in the world, ladies and gentlemen. What did you think?"

The class babbles excitedly. Phrases like, "Oh my GOD, it was AMAZING!" and "SO unique! Really powerful!" and "The most stunning piece of theater I've ever seen!" fly around the room, overlapping.

My mouth drops open.

They loved it. They *all* loved it.

They saw the same collection of embarrassingly obtuse scenes as I did, and they all came to a completely different conclusion.

God, I'm such an uncultured idiot.

"Their use of stylized movement was so precise," Zoe says excitedly. "It was incredible!"

Next to me, Holt scoffs, and Erika turns to him.

"Mr. Holt? Did you have something to say?"

"Nothing good," he says and raises his chin defiantly. "I thought it was a pile of shit."

Erika tilts her head. "Really? And why did you think that?"

"Because," he says, exasperated. "There's supposed to be a difference between random noise and movement, and theater. Even experimental theater is supposed to represent ideas and emotions. It's not supposed to be a bunch of idiots walking around the stage like they have sticks up their asses."

"You don't think the performance achieved communication on an emotional level?"

He laughs. "Not unless they were trying to communicate that they were all enormous jerk-offs."

Zoe rolls her eyes, and there are murmurs of disagreement from other members of the class.

Holt looks at them with disdain. "I can't believe you guys didn't think it was crap. Did you all see a completely different show? Or were you blinded by their 'reputation' because you're a bunch of fucking sheep?"

I hear several murmurs of *"Fuck you, Holt,"* until Erika shushes everyone as she turns to me.

My stomach convulses.

*No, no, no, no, please don't ask me.*

"Miss Taylor? I haven't heard your opinion yet. What did you think?"

*Oh, God.*

Holt is looking at me.

I don't want to look ignorant. I want to be accepted and say the right thing.

"Well . . ."

"Come on, Taylor," Holt says. "Tell them what you think."

"It was . . ."

They're all staring. Him. Them. Erika.

"I thought it was . . ."

So many expectations. My head hurts.

"Yes, Miss Taylor?"

Holt's gaze is piercing. "It's not a hard question. Just give them your opinion."

No matter what I say, I'm screwed.

"I thought it was amazing," I finally mutter. "Really incredible. I loved it."

The silence is broken as everyone mumbles their approval.

Everyone but him.

I can almost see Holt's anger shimmering like a current in the air.

"Well, that's very interesting," Erika says. "It seems you're all of the same opinion about it except Mr. Holt, and I have to say"—she gives him a surprised smile—"I agree with him."

There are gasps of surprise.

I feel like crap.

Wrong again. Of course.

"Just because someone has a reputation for excellence doesn't mean you should view everything they do as tacitly good. Even the finest actors in the world have had terrible performances. Just look at Robert De Niro in *Analyze This*."

Everyone laughs.

Erika crosses her arms over her chest. "I've seen Benzo Ra perform many times over the years, and I have to say, this performance was disappointing in the extreme. It was comprised of unimaginative theatrics that, in my opinion, alienated the audience rather than drawing them into the experience."

She keeps talking, but I've zoned out. I feel sick.

After being at each other's throats for weeks, Holt and I were starting to get along. Then I go and throw him under the bus because I want people to like me.

*Idiot.*

"So, ladies and gentlemen," Erika says, "your assignment tonight is to write a thousand words analyzing the Benzo Ra performance and why you did or didn't like it, citing references to other experimental theater practitioners, including people like Brecht, Brock, and Artaud. I look forward to reading your thoughts."

She dismisses us, and before I can stumble through an apology, Holt is striding out of the room. I scramble to my feet to follow him, but he's so damn fast I have to run to catch up.

"Holt."

He ignores me.

"Holt, wait up."

He keeps walking. I get in front of him and put my hand on his chest to stop him.

His face is stormy. "What?"

"You know what."

"Oh, that little thing back there where you completely screwed me over? Yeah, I do know what. Take your fucking hand off me."

He steps around me and keeps walking while I stumble after him.

"I'm sorry! I didn't know what to say. I thought I must be defective because I didn't get it. They all thought it was great. I didn't want to seem like I was too ignorant to have the right opinion."

He stops and turns to me. "So you think *I'm* too ignorant to have the right opinion?"

His expression is so intense, he's almost scary.

"No! God, you said exactly how you felt, and I should have. I just—"

"For fuck's sake, Taylor," he says as he throws up his hands. "An opinion isn't right or wrong. It's your interpretation of a subject or situation. You can't *be* fucking wrong!"

"So, if I look at the sky and have the opinion that the clouds are pink, I'm right?"

"Yes! Because it's an *opinion*, not a *fact*, and maybe to you, the clouds are pink because you're nuts. An opinion doesn't need to be true for anyone else in the world but *you*. Stop trying to fucking please everyone, and just say what you think."

I feel like he's slapped me.

"And you know what makes me even crazier?" he asks, poking his finger at me. "Whenever you're with me, you're the most opinionated person on the fucking planet, and you *constantly* browbeat me with your opinion, whether I want to hear it or not. But the moment you get around those dicks in our class, you have zero fucking backbone.

You're so damn paranoid about being accepted, you turn into a sheep, just bleating along with the herd. It makes me want to slap you, because you forget about everything that makes you cool and fun and . . . Cassie, and you become some sort of people-pleasing autobot who tries to be whatever the fuck people expect instead of just yourself."

He's so worked up, he's panting. I have nothing to say because he's said it all.

No one has ever known me well enough to call me on my issues before, and I guess that he's so upset because he actually . . . cares.

"You're right," I whisper.

"Yeah, I am," he says. "So fucking quit it."

I shuffle my feet as the quad starts clearing of people. "So, what are you doing now?"

He slings his knapsack over his shoulder and sighs. "Going home to write a thousand words on experimental theater, I guess."

"Well, you could come to my place to write your paper. I could pick your brain, so I don't come off sounding like an idiot."

He thinks about it for a few seconds. Judging by his expression, he's weighing whether or not to sell one of his kidneys.

"Jeez, Holt, I'm not asking you to get married. I just thought you could help me out."

"Okay," he says reluctantly. "But you owe me snacks."

"I can do that." Apart from the preprepared meals filling my freezer, the only food I own is snacks. My mother would be so ashamed.

We detour to the library and I grab a few books that might be useful. Then we make our way back to my apartment.

I walk into my bedroom and dump my bag on the bed before I turn to see him hovering in the doorway.

"What the hell?" I say and laugh. "Are you like one of those vampires on TV? You need to be invited in before you can enter?"

He shakes his head and walks into the room. "No, it's just weird to be in here when you're not either vomiting or passed out."

"I have 'vomiting and passing out' on the schedule for nine o'clock. Stick around. Should be fun."

I'm about to unpack my books when my phone rings. I fish it out of my pocket to see my mom's number.

"Be back in a second."

I head out to the living room, because I know why she's calling.

"Hey, Mom."

"Sweetheart! Happy birthday!"

I put my hand over the speaker and look over my shoulder.

"Thanks, Mom."

"Oh, sweetie, I wish we could be with you. Are you having fun? What are you doing tonight?"

"Uh, not much. Studying."

Holt pokes his head out of my bedroom and says, "Taylor, where are the library books? I'll start on the research."

My mother's talking, but I cover the phone and whisper, "In my bag, on the bed."

He nods and disappears.

Mom stops. "Who was that?"

"Just a boy from my class. We're studying together."

There's a beat of silence before she says, "You're alone with a boy in your apartment?"

Oh, Lord. Here we go.

"Mom, it's not what you think. We're working."

Just then Holt yells, "Jesus, Taylor, your bed is fucking uncomfortable! How the hell do you sleep on this thing? Or is that the point? You don't want guys trying to snuggle when you're done with them?"

I cringe, and my mother gasps.

"Mom— "

"Cassie! I raised you better than to jump into bed with the first boy you meet."

"We're just friends." *Sort of.* "It's not like that. Really."

"Why don't I believe you?"

"Hurry up, Taylor! I think your bed has put my back out. I can't get up!"

I'm going to *kill* him!

My mother launches into a rant about how many rapes occur on college campuses, and how irresponsible I'm being, and crows that this is what happens when she's not around to supervise me. Usually I'd just let her get it out of her system to keep the peace, but I have a tiny little Holt on my shoulder, urging me to stand up for myself.

"Mom, just stop. Whether or not I have a man here is none of your business. I'm an adult now, and I don't need your approval for my every decision. Now, I love you, but I have a very good-looking man in my bed and I have to go."

She's silent for a few seconds, and I'm terrified I've given her a heart attack.

"Mom?"

There's more silence. I picture my mother lying glassy-eyed in her living room, the phone still clutched in her hand.

"Mom?!"

"How good looking?" she finally asks.

I sigh. "You have no idea."

She laughs. It's fake, but at least she's trying.

"Be careful of the good-looking ones, sweetie," she says. "They'll break your heart."

"Mom, Dad's good looking."

She pauses. "Yes, well, your father sends his love. He'll call you later tonight when he gets home from work."

"Thanks, Mom."

I get a pang of homesickness. Despite bitching about them, I really miss my parents.

I say good-bye and feel a kernel of pride for speaking my mind.

I've never stood up to my mother before, and I got through it without crying or killing her. Maybe Holt is onto something after all.

I smile as I walk back into the bedroom to find him sitting on the edge of my bed, bent over a book, raking his fingers through his hair.

"Wow, that looks like a thrilling read," I say.

He jumps up in surprise. "Taylor . . . I didn't mean to. It was in your bag. One of the other books had pushed it open, and I saw my name and I . . ."

A wave of sickening horror washes over me as I realize what's in his hand.

I swallow embarrassment and nausea. My face blazes.

"How much did you read?" I whisper, my voice hoarse with shame.

"Enough."

"Everything I wrote today?"

"Yes." He pauses. "It's your birthday?"

I'm going to be sick. He's read it all. Me ranting about my virginity. How horny I am. How much I want him and his award-winning penis.

All of it.

"Cassie . . ."

"Holt, if you say 'happy birthday' to me right now, I'm going to destroy you."

I cover my face and refuse to cry, but he can't be here anymore. I can't be near him. Ever again. Maybe longer.

"Goddammit, Taylor . . ." he says. "What you wrote about me? I can't know that. I seriously fucking can't—"

"Get out."

I hear him exhale, but I can't look at him.

"Cassie—"

"Get. The Hell. Out. Now."

I hear a dull thud and I look over to see that he's dropped the diary on the bed. He comes over and grabs his bag from the floor behind me.

When his body brushes mine, he makes a noise and pulls back. I open my eyes to find him right in front of me, studying my face. I feel like if he doesn't stop, my skin is actually going to burst into flames.

"How is it possible?" he asks quietly.

"What?"

I press my back into the door of my closet as he moves forward and continues to stare. "How is it possible you've never . . . ? That no man has ever . . . ?"

I want him to finish the sentence, but he just keeps staring with an incredulous expression. "It's a fucking crime that you haven't been kissed properly."

I stare at his chest. It's rising and falling fast. So is mine.

I close my eyes. "You do it, then." It's out of my mouth before I can stop it, but I don't want to take it back. "You show me how I should be kissed."

I open my eyes to see him staring at me with such intensity, it takes my breath away.

For a moment, he doesn't move, and I want to climb into the wall to escape my mortification. But then he leans forward, so slowly it barely looks like he's moving. I think I stop breathing because my chest hurts. I didn't know how much I wanted to be kissed by him until this moment, but now, every cell of my body craves it. Everything tingles with vicious anticipation.

Holt's expression is serious. Eyes dark and searching. His hands go to my hips, and I lean back against the door as his fingers squeeze and release in a rough rhythm.

I finally inhale, and he's so close now, I breathe in his warm, sweet air.

*This is going to happen. Oh, God, please let this happen.*

I close my eyes and part my lips, almost crying from the expectation of having his mouth on me.

But then, everything stops. His air is no longer washing over my face, and his warm hands disappear from my body.

"You really think after reading all of that, there's any way I can fucking kiss you?" he says in a rough voice. "Jesus, Taylor, I can't even cope with being in the same room as you."

When I open my eyes he's slinging his bag over his shoulder and striding out the door.

Mortification and embarrassment fill all the space in my lungs, and I slide down the wall and cover my face, wishing myself invisible.

I'm still waiting for the earth to open up and swallow me when I hear the front door slam closed.

# SIX

## COURAGEOUS CASTING

*Present Day*
*New York City*
*Day Four of Rehearsal*

The coffee shop is noisy, but they have free Wi-Fi. A perfect place to haul out my iPad and lose myself during my lunch hour. I've been writing in my diary most days. Mainly because Tristan keeps insisting it will keep me sane within the craziness of my current situation. As usual, he's right.

Of course, these days I use an online journal with an encrypted password and more security than a presidential motorcade, but it's not quite the same as writing on real paper.

Every day, Elissa and Ethan ask me to join them for lunch, but there's no way I'm going there.

I come to work, do my job, and try to stay as far away from Ethan as possible in the time we're offstage. He keeps trying to ambush me into talking, but I've learned to duck and weave better than a world champion boxer.

Talking will achieve nothing, other than taking us for a stroll down Excruciatingly Painful Memory Lane. Neither of us needs that.

I'm in the middle of typing my latest diary entry when a giant Caesar salad is plunked next to me. I'm about to protest that I didn't order it when I look up to see Elissa.

"You're getting too skinny," she says as she sits beside me with her own lunch. "A woman can't survive on caffeine and nicotine alone, you know."

"Wrong," I say and give her a smile. "I'm a shining example."

"Well, your stage manager thinks you're beginning to look like a bobblehead, so eat up. My treat."

Looking at the salad, I realize just how hungry I am. "Yes, ma'am."

As I pack away my tablet, I notice Holt on the far side of the café at a table by himself.

Goddammit. Of all the diner joints in all the towns in all the world, he has to come to mine. This is supposed to be a Holt-free zone.

As if anticipating my next question, Elissa says, "I'm having lunch with you because I'm sick of his company. Whenever I ask about how things are going between you guys, he clams up."

I shrug and keep eating. I gave up trying to figure out Holt's motivations a long time ago.

"You barely say a word to each other in rehearsals. You won't even look at him, but he spends all his time staring at you. Wanna tell me what's up?"

I sneak a glance over at Holt, who's reading and absently picking at a bowl of fries.

"Nothing's up," I say, and take a sip of my drink. "Just working hard."

She tilts her head, studies me for several seconds, then says, "Are you fucking my brother?"

I laugh and cough at the same time. A dribble of Coke runs down my chin, and I grab a wad of napkins to clean myself.

Holt seems oblivious to our conversation. Thank God.

"Of course I'm not," I whisper. "Do you think I have zero sense of self-preservation?"

She glances at Holt before whispering back, "I think that when it comes to my brother, you can't think straight, and if he wanted to get you into bed, you'd have your legs in the air in about three seconds."

"Not true."

"Really?" she says. "Because I could power half of New York with the heat you two generate in rehearsals. You both look guilty. If you're not fucking, then what?"

This really isn't a conversation I wanted to have today. Or ever.

I sigh and shake my head. "Look, I'd be lying if I said I wasn't still attracted to him. But God, Elissa, that's it. I have no intention of getting back into something with him. Ever."

"But you must still have feelings for him. I thought you'd run a million miles away when you heard he was going to be your leading man. Why didn't you?"

I shrug. "I have no idea."

That wasn't entirely true. I had to see him. I needed for him to tell me he'd made a mistake and was sorry, but I'm starting to doubt that's ever going to happen. Now I think I'm just trying to get through it to prove I can move on without him.

"Well, you have guts, that's for sure," Elissa says. "I mean, I love my brother, but if someone had done to me what he did to you . . ." She wipes her mouth with her napkin. "Let's just say, I understand why you stopped taking my calls. When Ethan told me you'd been cast, I thought this was our chance to mend bridges."

"Lissa, you never burned any bridges. Your brother did."

"I know. But I'm glad we're talking again. I've missed you."

I take her hand and squeeze. "I've missed you, too." I hadn't realized how much until now.

"So, Marco's working on the kiss after lunch, huh?" she says as she swirls a fry in some ketchup. "Nervous?"

"No. It's not the first time I've been cast opposite your brother when I couldn't stand the sight of him."

"True. But last time there was less water under the bridge."

"And I was a lot younger and less able to separate reality from fantasy." I take a mouthful of salad, even though I'm not really hungry anymore.

Elissa finishes the last of her grilled cheese before saying, "So you won't have a problem kissing him? It's not going to bring up old feelings?"

I shrug. "There are no old feelings to bring up. They died a long time ago."

She gazes at me for a few seconds, then shakes her head. "Sure they did."

We continue to make small talk, neither one mentioning Ethan again. Our friendship too often revolved around him when it should have just been about us.

As we chat, I notice a trio of girls has gathered around Ethan's table. His groupies. There are always a few of them waiting for him outside the theater. They seem to have a sixth sense about where he's going to be. It's irritating.

They squeal and ask for his picture and autograph. Gaze at him like he's a gift from God. Push out their boobs like they have a chance with him.

If only they knew the truth. Despite having the face of an angel, he's an evil, Cassie-abandoning bastard.

I spear the last of my salad with a little too much gusto as a barrage of giggles fills the café.

*Damn his stupid angel face.*

When Elissa and I are done eating, she says, "See you back there.

Don't forget Chapstick. Ethan hasn't shaved. Don't want you getting chafed." She gives me a quick hug before taking the check up to the cashier.

When she's gone, I let out a long exhale.

I'd almost forgotten about the kiss. Well, not forgotten so much as blocked it out. As Tristan will attest, my talent for denial is impressive.

I'm packing up my stuff when I feel someone at my back. I'm not surprised my body reacts before I see who it is.

"So, you'll talk to my sister but not me?" he says as I turn to face him.

"That's because I still like your sister."

He's wearing his trademark frown. "We have to talk sometime, Cassie."

"We really don't." I grab my gear and push past him to the exit.

Of course, he follows. "You think we can get through this play the way we are now? That it won't affect our performances?"

I step out into the street, and the traffic noise makes me raise my voice. "I won't let it affect my performance. This is my dream job. And despite the universe screwing with me by casting you, I'm going to make it work." I turn to him. "If you can't, then do us both a favor and quit."

He leans down, purposefully invading my personal space to mess with me. "Cassie, don't fool yourself into thinking you could do this role justice opposite someone else, because we both know that's bullshit."

"I'd be willing to try," I say and give him my sweetest smile.

He's about to protest when more groupies show up.

They all but push me out of the way to get to him.

They're welcome to him. I'm done being his fangirl.

As I walk away, he calls my name.

I don't stop.

\* \* \*

*Six Years Earlier*
*Westchester, New York*
*The Grove*
*Sixth Week of Classes*

He's staring at me.

I keep my focus on Erika and try to concentrate. It's tough. His gaze gives me an electric tingle that starts at the back of my neck and spreads all over my body.

I'd tell him to knock it off, but that would involve acknowledging his existence, and there's no muffing way I'll be doing *that* in the foreseeable future.

Since he read my diary nearly two weeks ago, I've avoided him at all costs. Whenever I look at him, a huge wave of humiliation washes over me, followed quickly by vicious anger, and ending with a strong urge to rub myself all over him. I thought he was going to kiss me. It looked like he was. Then he left, and now I have no idea what's going through his brain.

Just thinking about our almost-kiss has my girl parts all excited. I don't have the heart to tell them we're going to die without ever experiencing an orgasm. It would depress them too much, and I really can't afford to have a sad vagina.

"Miss Taylor?"

"I'm sorry, what?"

Erika's looking at me. So is everyone else. Except him. Oh, the irony.

"I asked why you think we become actors," Erika says. "What drives us to pursue this profession?"

*Okay, stay cool. Answer her question honestly. Don't just give her the answer you think she wants to hear.*

"Miss Taylor," Erika says, "I promise this isn't a trick question. Why do you think we act?"

"Well . . ." I take a deep breath and try to ignore all of the eyes on me. "I think it's a way to communicate ideas and concepts. I guess we're like mediums. Channeling different personas and characters in order to bring other people's work to life."

Erika nods. "You don't think you're a collaborator in that work? That your character choices add something to the original vision?"

"Well, yes. But only if my choices don't suck."

People laugh.

Holt scoffs.

"Mr. Holt? Your thoughts?"

He leans back in his chair. "We're actors because we want attention. We're standing around saying someone else's words and trying not to screw up."

Erika smiles. "So, you don't think there's anything artistic in what you do?"

He shrugs. "Not particularly."

"What about a musician, interpreting someone else's music? Do you consider them artistic?"

"Well, yeah . . ."

"And a visual artist? A painter who interprets images through their brushes? Artistic?"

"Of course."

"But not actors."

"Not really. We're parrots, aren't we? We learn lines and repeat them."

"So then," she says, "if you don't think acting is a creative endeavor, why do it, Mr. Holt? Why act? If you're merely a puppet and have no personal investment in what you're performing, why dedicate yourself to it for three years of your life? Surely you can find something you're more *passionate* about."

"I didn't say I wasn't passionate. I just think we're fooling ourselves if we think it's difficult."

"Perhaps it's not difficult to you. But to most people, getting on stage in front of hundreds or thousands of people would be impossible."

He laughs.

"Mr. Holt," Erika says patiently, "did you know that in a recent survey, almost ninety percent of participants said they would rather run into a burning building than get up and speak in front of a large group of people?"

"What? That's ridiculous."

"Not when you look at people's top ten fears, with 'fear of public speaking' at number two. Other items on the list relevant to acting are 'fear of failure,' 'fear of rejection,' 'fear of commitment,' and 'fear of intimacy.'"

"Coincidentally," Jack says, "they are all the exact reasons Holt doesn't have a girlfriend."

Holt shoots him a glare. "Running into a burning building takes a hell of a lot more courage than getting rejected or being intimate."

Erika looks at him like a spider studying a fly. "More courage, you say?"

He nods, not realizing he's about to get eaten.

"I think it's more accurate to say that it's a different type of courage, and that the choices you make decide the depth of that courage."

Holt doesn't look convinced. Erika studies him again. "Hmmmm."

He rolls his eyes. He hates that contemplative sound.

Erika walks to the front of the room and writes words on the whiteboard.

"Mr. Holt?" she says and gestures for him to stand next to her. He unfolds himself from his seat and does as she asks.

"Could you kindly read the two words on the board?"

"'I'm sorry.'"

"Okay," says Erika. "I'm the playwright. Those are my words. What's my intention?"

Holt shrugs. "You tell me."

"No, Mr. Holt, that's not my job. As a playwright, it's my job to give you words. As an actor, it's your job to interpret them. So . . ."

She gestures at him to repeat his line reading.

He puts his hand to his ear and pretends he didn't hear her. " 'I'm sorry?' "

She nods. "See? You made a choice. A very safe, boring choice, but a choice nonetheless."

"But it's not always up to the actor to make the choice," he argues.

"True," Erika says. "Directors often push actors to make bolder, riskier choices, so let's explore that." She walks to the other side of him and crosses her arms. "This time I want you to say it like you're speaking to someone important to you. A family member or lover."

A dark shadow passes over Holt's face. "What am I supposed to be apologizing for?"

"You tell me," Erika says with a smile.

He exhales and rubs his hand over his face. "Just tell me what to do, and I'll do it."

"No, that's not how it works. Your job is to create something—an idea, an emotion—within the parameters I give you. The parameters are those two words being said to someone who means something to you. You have your instructions. What are you going to do with them?"

He looks around the room, restless and uncomfortable.

"Mr. Holt?"

"I'm thinking," he snaps.

"About what?"

"Who I'm apologizing to."

"Who's it going to be?"

He glances at me briefly before saying, "A friend."

"And what are you apologizing for?"

He stops fidgeting. "Why do you have to know that? Does it matter?"

She shakes her head and gestures for him to begin. "Not at all. Whenever you're ready."

He closes his eyes and draws in a huge lungful of air before releasing it in a long, steady exhale. There's a sense of expectation in the room.

When he opens his eyes, he picks a point at the back of the room and focuses on it. His face changes. It's softer. Contrite.

"I'm sorry," he says, but it's still not sincere.

"Not good enough," Erika says. "Try again."

He stays focused on the same point as his face twitches.

"I'm sorry," he says again, but he's resisting the emotion.

"Dig deeper, Mr. Holt," Erika urges. "You're capable of more. Give it to me."

He blinks and shakes his head, and his eyes are getting glassier by the second. "I'm sorry!"

His voice is getting louder, but he's still protecting himself. Spark without flame.

"That's not enough, Ethan!" Erika says, her voice rising with his. "Stop fighting the emotion. Let us see it. All of it. No matter how messy it is."

He swallows and clenches his jaw. His hands curl into fists as he moves from one foot to the other.

He stays silent.

"Mr. Holt?"

He blinks a few more times then drops his gaze to the floor.

"No," he whispers. "I . . . can't."

"Too personal?"

He nods.

"Too vulnerable?"

He nods again.

"Too . . . frightening?"

He glares at her. He doesn't need to answer.

"Sit down, Mr. Holt."

He strides over to his chair and sits heavily.

"So, would you like to change your opinion that acting is easy and doesn't require courage?" Erika asks softly.

He swallows hard. "Obviously."

Erika looks around at the rest of us. "Acting deals with delicate emotions. Finding them within ourselves and letting them out for others to see. But in order to do that, the actor has to be willing to show parts of himself he's ashamed of. He has to have the courage to give light to every terrifying insecurity and shameful regret. Nothing can be hidden. Contrary to popular belief, it's not about eliciting a response from the audience. It's about manifesting something from within *yourself* and letting the audience witness it."

She gestures to Holt, who's looking at the floor and chewing his fingernail.

"What happened to Mr. Holt today will happen to all of you at some point. There'll be times when you think you can't portray a character or emotion because it's too frightening or personal. But it's your *job* to find the courage to let others see your vulnerability. That's what makes a good actor. In Kafka's wonderful words, you have the power of 'melting the ice within, of awakening dormant cells, of making us more fully alive, more fully human, at once more individual and more connected to each other.' That's why we do what we do."

Her words resonate with me. I look at Holt. He's staring at the floor, shoulders slumped. He knows she's right, and it scares the hell out of him.

"Now," Erika says as she walks to her desk and picks up a piece of paper, "you all auditioned for our first-year theater production, a little-known play called *Romeo and Juliet* . . ." Everyone laughs. "And I'm happy to say that casting has been completed."

We all sit up straighter as excitement ripples around the room.

I thought my audition went well, and despite my lack of experience, I want this role. So much.

Erika starts by reading out the minor characters. There are murmurs and curses and some squeals of delight, but as we get to the leading roles, the whole room falls silent.

"The role of Tybalt goes to . . . Lucas."

Lucas woots loudly and pumps his fist in the air. I can see him playing Tybalt, high as a kite and slightly unhinged.

"Benvolio will be played by . . . Mr. Avery."

Jack nods and smugly says, "That's right. Badass Benvolio in da house."

There are laughs and cheers.

"The nurse will be played by Miss Sediki."

There's a round of applause, and Aiyah looks like she's going to cry.

She announces Miranda, Troy, Mariska, and Tyler will play the parental Capulets and Montagues. Then it's time to reveal the lead roles.

My mouth goes dry and my stomach acid churns. I close my eyes as I chant silent entreaties.

Erika clears her throat.

"Our Juliet"—*God, please, please, please, please*—"is Miss Taylor."

*Yes!*

My stomach soars as my heart pounds. I don't think I've ever been so happy.

Everyone applauds and my chest feels like it's going to explode with pride.

I'm Juliet.

Me.

The no one from nowhere with no experience.

*Hell, yes!*

I glance at Holt. He's not looking at me, but he's smiling. Probably thinking "I told you so" and giving himself credit for making me audition.

"Finally," Erika says, looking around the room, "casting the two male roles caused a heated discussion among the audition panel, but I think we've made the right decision. It's not an obvious casting choice, but then, sometimes they're the most interesting."

Holt sits up in his chair. I know he wants Mercutio. He's done the role before, and from what I hear, he nailed it.

Connor would be perfect for Romeo, and I think he and I would work well together. He looks over at me and holds up his crossed fingers.

"In this year's production, Mercutio will be played by Mr. Baine. The role of Romeo goes to Mr. Holt."

The class applauds, but I don't join them.

I feel like a lead weight has dropped into my stomach.

By the looks on their faces, Holt and Connor feel the same way.

All three of us stare at one another, not sure what the hell just happened.

Erika claps to signal the end of the lesson.

"That's it, everyone. If you didn't receive a role, then you'll be in the chorus. Don't worry, you'll still have plenty to do. Please pick up a script and a rehearsal schedule before you leave."

People congratulate me on their way out, but I barely hear them.

Connor comes over and gives me a hug.

"Congrats," he says warmly. "You'll be an amazing Juliet, I have no doubt."

"I wanted you to be Romeo," I say, aware that Holt hasn't moved from his chair.

"That would have been nice," he says, "but I'm not gonna lie, Mercutio is a kick-ass role. I mean, 'a plague on both your houses'? Doesn't get much better than that."

When he leaves, I walk in a daze to Erika's desk to pick up a script.

It has my name on it next to the character name—Juliet. I see the only other script left there. Romeo—Ethan Holt.

No.

No.

*No.*

"Miss Taylor? Are you all right?"

I try not to show how sick I feel. "Uh . . . yeah. Fine."

She smiles. "I would have thought you'd be happier about getting your first leading role. It's one of the classics. Very few actresses will ever get to play Juliet."

"Oh, I know," I say. "God, I'm thrilled. Really. I just . . ."

Erika looks at me expectantly.

"She doesn't want me as her Romeo," Holt says as he comes and stands beside me. "And quite frankly, that makes two of us. You *knew* I wanted Mercutio. And you knew how much I fucking hated Romeo. What is this bullshit?"

"In the immortal words of the Rolling Stones, Mr. Holt, you can't always get what you want. You wanted Mercutio because you've done the role before, and you'd be comfortable doing it again. Being an actor isn't about being comfortable. It's about challenging yourself. I know you hate Romeo, and that's one of the reasons you were cast. You're not the typical romantic hero. You're brash and cynical and sometimes, downright rude. You have an edge I think Romeo needs. Likewise, Mr. Baine has a sensitivity that will make him a sympathetic Mercutio. Believe me, I didn't make this decision lightly. I knew you'd be resistant, and considering I have to direct you, I just made my job a whole lot harder. I happen to think if I can draw the performance out of you I believe you're capable of, it'll be worth it."

Holt glares at her and crosses his arms over his chest.

"What if I refuse to do it?" he asks. "Because even if it was possible for me to comprehend playing such a pussified dipshit, which I can't, I highly doubt Taylor here would be thrilled about me doing it."

Erika looks at me questioningly.

"It's true," I say. "He's an asshole."

Erika places her hands on the desk and hangs her head.

"And what do you suggest? That you play Mercutio and Mr. Baine plays Romeo?"

"Yes!" Holt says. "He'd be great at the lame-ass lovey-dovey stuff. I could just die loudly and call it a night. Everyone wins."

"No, they don't, Mr. Holt, because you'll have achieved nothing in your development as an actor, and I'll miss out on exploiting the remarkable chemistry I witnessed between you and Miss Taylor at the auditions."

Holt stops dead. "Is that why you cast me in this role? Because of that stupid fucking mirror exercise? Jesus, Erika!"

"That's not the only reason, but it's a part of it. Do you think that sort of chemistry comes along every day? Because I'm here to tell you, it doesn't."

"But that's . . . It wasn't something that I . . . I can't just—"

"Ethan," Erika says, "I understand dealing with that kind of connection is scary, but it's exactly what you need to do to grow. You're so talented in so many ways, but anything that requires you to be open and vulnerable with another person is your Achilles' heel, and believe me when I say you won't get very far in this industry, or this course, or *life,* if it continues to be a problem."

She looks from Ethan to me. "Now, you two have been cast as the leads in one of the greatest romantic tragedies in the history of the world, so stop your bitching and be grateful. You'll play the roles as they're assigned, or you'll both get an F for the semester. I don't care how you do it, but you need to find a way to work together. Show up on Monday with your lines learned and your game faces on, because I'm going to make you look like you're in love if it's the last thing I ever do. Bullshit will not be tolerated on any level. Are we clear?"

Holt and I both mumble, "Yes, Erika," and look at the floor.

Erika sighs and gathers up her things before saying, "Don't forget your scripts," and leaves.

Holt and I just stand there, not looking at each other and not speaking.

I should be happy about being cast, but I'm not.

Holt grabs his script and rehearsal schedule and shoves them into his bag.

"This is so fucked," he mumbles under his breath. "This whole goddamn year is going to shit, and it's all your fault."

"My fault?! How the hell is it my fault that you were cast as Romeo? You can't always play the brooding, untouchable rebel, you know. At some point you're going to have to play the romantic lead."

"That's crap. Not every actor has to be the leading man. Samuel L. Jackson, Steve Buscemi, John Turturro, John Goodman. They all have *amazing* careers and don't do the romantic bullshit."

"Don't take this the wrong way, Holt, because I really don't want to give you a compliment right now, but *you don't look like any of those guys*. You're tall and handsome and have freakishly cool hair. People are going to cast you as the leading man, whether you want them to or not."

"So you want me to be your Romeo? Is that what you're saying? Because last time I checked, you couldn't stand to even look at me."

"No," I say, "you wouldn't be my first choice to be Romeo, mainly because you're an almighty jackass who goes around reading people's diaries!"

"Fuck this." He grabs his bag and strides toward the door, but I grab his arm.

"Holt, what the hell is wrong with you? It's been two weeks, and you haven't even *tried* to make things better between us. Apologize already, you diary-invading douche!"

He spins around to face me and his eyes are full of fire. I take a few steps back, but he follows. It's not until my back hits the wall that we both stop.

"It was a fucking mistake to read your diary, I admit. I wish I could unread it, because it would make my life *so much easier* not to know all that shit about how you feel about me. But what the fuck were you thinking writing it all down in the first place? Of *course* the person you're writing about is somehow going to read it, mortifying you both and screwing up *everything*!"

"Oh, no," I say as a flash-fire of blood rushes to my face. "You did *not* just blame me for *you* reading my diary!"

"Yeah, I'm pretty sure I did."

"You're unbelievable!" I throw my hands up in exasperation. "That's it. I'm done trying with you. I don't even want your apology anymore. Just stay the hell away from me."

I push past him, but he follows me.

"How do you propose I stay away from you, when we have to perform countless love scenes in this stupid play, huh? Believe me, I'd love to not have to go through that fucking torture, but I don't have a choice in the matter."

I walk faster. "I'd rather stick needles in my eyeballs than have to pretend to be in love with you, but I'm going to do it because this production accounts for *forty percent* of our acting grade for the semester, and you will *not* screw with my GPA!"

"I wouldn't dream of it, princess. After all, you'd probably just bitch about it in your diary."

"Yeah! I probably would!"

"You know," he says while striding easily beside me and my scrambling legs, "millions of people survive their whole damn lives without writing about their sexual fantasies and innermost thoughts in a book that anyone can find and read. You should try it!"

"As soon as you saw what it was, you should have stopped reading!"

"Oh, right, like it was possible to stop reading when I saw you were talking about my *cock*!"

I stop dead and punch him in the arm.

"Ow! Fuck!"

"This is not *my* fault! Screw you!"

He grabs my arms and pulls me toward him. "Well, according to your diary, that's exactly what you need. Is that where all this aggression is coming from? You're angry I didn't kiss you the other day and you need to ride my dick for a while?"

"God, you're an asshole!"

"I notice that *wasn't* a 'no'!"

I instinctively go to hit him, but he grabs my wrist and holds it tight.

"Wrong part of my body to put your hands on, sweetheart. Don't you want to give some relief to the part of me that's been hard as fuck ever since I read your stupid diary? Don't you want to feel the *hell* you're putting me through? You want to touch a cock so much? Go right ahead. Put your fucking hands on me and put me out of my misery."

I wrench my wrist free.

"You're disgusting," I say before walking away.

"So that's a no to the hand job then?!" he calls after me.

I get away from him as fast as I can, and when I turn the corner, I see him still standing where I left him, his head bowed and his hands in his hair.

I walk home on trembling legs, and it's only when I get inside my bedroom and slam the door that I realize my eyes are wet.

# SEVEN

## POINT OF NO RETURN

*Present Day*
*New York City*
*Graumann Theater Rehearsal Room*
*Day Four of Rehearsals*

I'm biting my fingernails. I've pretty much destroyed all of them and have moved on to the rough skin of my cuticles. It doesn't help with my nerves, but it stops me from pacing.

Marco is talking to Ethan. Taking him through *the* scene.

My stomach lurches with a combination of nausea and irrational anticipation. It makes me want to barf up my lunch.

Marco talks quietly, but I can hear every word.

"Sarah is here to confront you about why you're pushing her away. Her mother has revealed she's not the small-town girl you thought she was, and in the process, it's made you feel like you'll never be good enough for her. Deep down you've always believed this was too good to be true, and now all your doubts have been confirmed."

Ethan nods as he frowns in concentration. His arms are crossed over his chest. Defensive stance.

He glances at me, then back to Marco, his face stone.

I've run out of cuticles. I need a cigarette, but I have no time.

"I want to feel that you think she's better off without you, but it's killing you. Understand?"

He nods and his leg judders.

He's nervous.

Good.

"Cassie?"

My turn.

Marco comes over and puts his arm around me. "You're confused by Sam's behavior. You love him, and you don't care how different your backgrounds are. He seems to have given up, but you want him to fight. Yes?"

I nod. It makes me dizzy. I want to sit down.

"This is where we feel your desperation. You haven't seen him for days. All you want is for him to stay, okay?"

"Yeah. Sure."

I sound more sure than I feel. He trusts me to do my job. I don't want to let him down.

"Take a few minutes to prepare, then we'll take it from Sarah's entrance."

Prepare? How the hell do I prepare for this? To feel these incredibly personal, relevant things? To kiss him?

I pace. I want to find my character, because she's the insulation between fantasy and reality. But all I find is me. *My* hurt. *My* confusion.

I close my eyes and breathe. Long, measured breaths in through my nose, out through my mouth. I try to imagine a white sheet on a clothesline, blowing in the breeze. It's my focus.

Today I can't get it. The image is blurry and inconstant, like a TV channel I can't tune.

My eyes are still closed when I hear footsteps. Then heat is in front of me, and I know he's staring.

"What?" I ask, eyes still closed. I try to hold on to my focus. It shimmers like a mirage.

"Do you want to talk about anything?"

"Actually, yes. I have this weird burning sensation whenever I pee. What does it mean?"

I keep my breathing steady.

He sighs. "I meant about the scene."

"I know what you meant."

"Of course you did."

"Let's just get it over with and see what happens." If I run screaming from the room, then I'll deal with it.

"Are you sure about that?"

I've never been less sure of anything in my life.

I open my eyes. "Fine. What do you want to say?"

He shoves his hands in his pockets. "Where do I fucking start?"

I wait. I know he's thinking, because he looks like he's in pain. Some things never change.

"Cassie, don't you think it's insane that we haven't spoken about any of the crap that's gone down between us, and in just a few minutes I'm going to be kissing you?"

"No, you're not," I say.

"Yes, I am. It's in the script."

"What I mean, dumbass, is that Sam is going to be kissing Sarah. You and I will be elsewhere, right?"

He takes a step forward, and I resist retreating. I don't do that anymore.

His body heat burns through my clothes. As much as I don't want to look into his eyes, he doesn't give me much choice.

"We both know it doesn't work like that," he says so softly only I can hear. "As much as we want it to be the character's emotions, it's still going to be my arms around you, and my mouth on yours. Now, I feel pretty weird about that considering all our baggage could fill a goddamn department store, but since you seem cool not discussing anything, let's crack this fucking thing open and see what falls out."

His ability to make me viciously angry within thirty seconds is remarkable. He wants to talk now because it suits him?

The only thing worse than his ability to make relationship decisions is his sense of timing.

"You had three years to talk," I say. "But the only time you'd contact me was when you were drunk and unintelligible."

"That's not true. The e-mails—"

"Were full of mind games and pathetic attempts to get me to chase you . . . again. They were vague and self-pitying, and not once did you apologize, you arrogant bastard."

"Is everything all right?" Marco calls to us. We plaster fake smiles on our faces and nod.

"We're fine," Holt says, voice tight. "Just workshopping some ideas."

"Excellent. Let's get started, then."

Holt turns back to me, but I'm done with this conversation.

"Let's just get it done," I say, not in the mood to be in the same room with him, let alone play a love scene. "Grab your script, and let's go."

He laughs, but the sound is hollow. "I don't need a script for this scene."

"No, I don't suppose you do."

We take our starting positions on opposite sides of the space.

Marco claps his hands to silence the room. "Okay, when you're ready, Cassie."

I enter the space, more angry than I should be at this point in the play, but fuck it. I'll take the anger and make it work.

We play the scene, strong words and bitter emotions parrying between us. I circle him. He keeps his distance. Hurt and evasive.

He's nailing it.

"Do you honestly think we stand a chance?" he asks. I can feel his intensity from across the room. "We don't. You know it. I know it. Your country club bitch of a mother knows it, and she's the only one with enough guts to say it out loud. Stop fighting the inevitable. The inevitable always wins."

My voice is small but simmering. Anger floods me. He's wrong. As usual.

I crawl into Sarah's skin and make her reactions mine. "When did you become such a coward?"

"About the same time I found out I knew nothing about you."

"You do know me! You know the only things that are important."

"Bullshit! I knew the person you were pretending to be, and lady, you're one hell of an actress. You had me completely fooled."

The room is humming with tension. He's looking for an out. I'm not going to give it to him.

I step closer. "Sam, I know you love me. I know it like I know the sky's blue and the world's round. If you leave now, you'll wake up in five years and wonder what the hell you've done, because people search their whole lives to find what we've got, and you're throwing it away. Don't you see that?"

My anger is filling the air, making it thick and hard to breathe.

He can't even look at me. A wounded animal about to go to ground.

"I can't be your project, Sarah. I'm not something you can fix." He turns to leave.

"Wait!" The torment in my voice stops him. "You were never a project to me. And you're not leaving until you tell me you don't love me."

His shoulders slump, and he mutters a curse word.

"Say it!"

He turns. His expression is full of conflict. Brimming with pain.

"If you want to ruin us," I say, my voice tremulous, "then at least do the job right."

He's struggling, but I won't back down. "Say it."

He takes a breath. "I don't love you."

I can practically hear his heart cracking through the pain in his voice.

I order him to say it again. He does, but quieter. I'm breaking him, so he can't walk away. He has to stay and be broken with me.

I tell him to say it one more time, and he can barely breathe with the effort. "I . . . don't . . . love you."

His attention is focused on the floor. Shattered.

"Do you believe it yet?" I ask.

When he looks at me with eyes full of agony and saltwater, I feel like I'm drowning.

"No," he says, and before I have time to think, or prepare, or run, he's striding toward me, and his hands are on my face. His touch makes me gasp. As the air rushes into my lungs, he covers my mouth with his.

Everything explodes. My body and mind seize. Senses overload, and three years disappear in a blinding millisecond.

His lips are just as I remember. Warm and soft. Delicious beyond words. He inhales sharply, and his hands tighten, one on my cheek, the other at the back of my neck. He makes a small sound in his throat, and heats flood me. My body is against his, and my hands are in his hair, and every single reason I should stay away melts as our mouths open to each other.

It's rough and desperate and full of passion I don't want to feel. But this . . . *this* is where all the best memories of him live.

*This* is what we should have been. Always. Mouths and hands on each other, breathing each other's air. Reveling in our soul-deep connection, not running from it.

His hands trail over a trembling body that hasn't felt this fire for far too long.

*This* is why I haven't had a long-term relationship for the past three years. It's why I sleep with men once and never call them again. Because they don't feel like this.

I desperately want someone else to ruin me the way he does, but they don't even come close. This is the first time I've truly felt aroused since he left, and I hate myself for it.

I pull my mouth free and manage to gasp, "Ethan," before he mumbles, "God . . . Cassie," and kisses me again.

My body can't get enough of him, even if my brain knows it's wrong. Every part of me craves him.

The noises he's making are plaintive and desperate. Hands pull me closer. Arms wrap around.

I can't believe that in the world of wrong we've created together, this can still feel so right.

"Okay, that's enough," Marco says before clearing his throat. "Let's stop there before we need to get you two a room. Good job. Excellent chemistry."

The spell is broken, and as I pull back, Holt's eyes snap open. "Cassie . . ."

I push him away. He can't kiss me like that and say my name with that tone, and completely own me without my fucking permission. He steps forward, but I can't cope anymore. Before he can touch me again, I slap him.

He steps back, his expression so confused that for few seconds, I feel bad for doing it.

I shouldn't. This is his fault. He knows what sort of power he has over me. He counted on it, and he exploited it. Now my body is pounding and aching. Needing him in ways I can't deal with.

I hate that he can still make me feel like this. That with one kiss, he can demolish every single defense mechanism I've ever had against him.

I hate him for doing it, but I hate myself more for wanting him to do it again.

\*    \*    \*

*Six Years Earlier*
*Westchester, New York*
*The Diary of Cassandra Taylor*

> *Dear Diary,*
> *After all the crap he's put me through in the past two weeks, Holt ad-*
> *mitted he was attracted to me.*
> *Well, he said reading my diary made him hard, which I guess is the*
> *same thing.*
> *Why do I even care? He's a rude, egotistical, apology-phobic ass, and*
> *nothing good would ever come of us hooking up. Except maybe some mind-*
> *blowing sex.*
> *Oh, the sex. I can just imagine.*
> *I can't deny it anymore. I want him, even though he drives me in-*
> *sane.*
> *And now that I've admitted that to myself (and to you, dear diary),*
> *I'm absolutely terrified he's going to read this, because according to him,*
> *it's inevitable. As soon as I write down something highly mortifying, the*
> *universe is going to find a way to let him see it.*
> *Well, in that case: Hey, Holt! Yeah, you diary-reading jerk! I want to*
> *grope you. Wanna have angry sex and blow my horny, virginal mind?*

I drop my pen and rip the page out of my diary before scrunching it
up and throwing it at the trash can. It bounces off the edge and joins
the other seven balled-up pieces of paper littering the floor.

"Fudging corksucker!" I launch my diary across the room, and it
hits the door with a loud thud. I flop back onto my bed and throw
my arm over my eyes.

It's no use. I can't write in my diary anymore. He's ruined the ritual of it, because I can't get past the terror that he'll read it again.
The one thing that helped me make sense of my ridiculous feelings
for him is now unavailable, and that sucks beyond all words.

"Cassie?" There's a knock at the door, and Ruby's head appears. "You okay?"

"No," I say before rubbing my face and sighing.

"Holt?"

"Yes."

"What happened?"

"He's playing Romeo. I'm Juliet. We got into a fight."

"About the diary?"

"Among other things."

"Still no apology?"

"Of course not. Plus, he practically demanded I give him a hand job."

"That's not cool. He should have at least said 'please.'" She walks over and sits on the edge of the bed. "You know he likes you, right?"

"I don't care."

"Yes, you do. You like him back."

"I don't want to."

"Sometimes liking someone has nothing to do with what you want and everything to do with what you need."

"Ruby, he's a dick."

"You're passionate about him."

"We'd be terrible together."

"Or wonderful."

I exhale and sit up. "So what are you saying?"

"I'm saying you should make a move."

I rub my eyes. "God, Ruby, no. We just don't mesh. It's like we're oil and vinegar. No matter how much we shake each other up, we're never going to blend."

"Cassie," she says, giving me her best heed-the-pearls-of-wisdom-I'm-about-to-impart expression, "you forget that even though oil and vinegar don't blend, they still make delicious salad dressing."

I narrow my eyes. "Okay, that makes zero sense."

She sighs. "I know. I'm sorry. I had nothing. Still, salad dressing is delicious. My point is this: You should fuck Holt. It'd be yummy."

I look at her in shock. "What?! I should . . . what? I mean . . . I can't even comprehend—"

"Don't you *dare* tell me you've never thought about jumping that boy's bones, because I know you have."

I slump and pout. "Okay, fine, I've thought about it. Doesn't mean I'd actually do it."

"Need I remind you that you dry-humped him shamelessly when you were drunk? And from all reports, he wasn't complaining."

"That doesn't count."

"You rubbed your girl flower on his love muscle, Cass. It counts."

I pull my hair over my eyes and groan. "Ruby . . ."

She parts my hair and glares at me. "Cassie, you're obviously hung up on this guy. You're going to have to deal with whatever's bubbling between you before you both have a complete meltdown. You can't go on with all this unresolved sexual tension. It's not healthy. I vote for fucking him until you both can't stand, but hey, that's just me."

I grunt in frustration and flop back onto my bed.

She stands and walks over to the door before turning back to me. "You know, a wise man once said, 'Love cannot be found where it doesn't exist, nor can it be hidden where it truly does.' Think about it."

"That's deep, Rubes. Is that out of your *Philosophy Quotes 101* book?"

"Nope," she says with a smile. "David Schwimmer. *Kissing a Fool*. Terrible movie."

I laugh.

"'Night, Cass."

That night, I dream of Holt, and thanks to Ruby, the rating is definitely X.

On Monday, as I walk to our first day of rehearsal, I'm still unsure how I'm going to deal with him.

When I turn the corner to the drama block, he's there, leaning against the railing outside the theater, sunglasses on, a cardboard cup in each hand. As I get closer, he sees me and stands up straight. I stop in front of him.

"Hey," I say.

"Hey." He looks down at me and chews on the inside of his cheek.

We stand there for a few seconds before he thrusts one of the cardboard cups at me and says, "Oh, shit. This is, uh . . . this is for you."

I take it and hold it up to my nose.

"What is it?"

"It's an I'm-a-dick-achino."

I try to stop the smile that lifts the corners of my mouth. "Huh. Smells like plain old hot chocolate to me."

"Yeah, well, it turns out they were out of dick-achinos. I offered to make some more, but they said I was overqualified."

"They were right."

We sip our drinks in silence, and I figure a hot chocolate is about as close to an apology as I'm going to get from him. For the moment, I'm okay with that.

"So," I say. "You know your lines?"

He nods. "Unfortunately. Shakespeare really could have used a good editor. Dude was wordy."

"Found any love for Romeo yet?"

He looks down at his cup and fiddles with the edge. "No. The more I worked on the lines, the clearer it was how fucking stupid this casting is. I can't play this role, Taylor. I really can't."

"Erika thinks you can."

"Yeah, well, Erika's deluding herself. She thinks I'm someone I'm not."

"Or maybe she has faith in the someone you could be."

He shakes his head. "She can have all the faith in the world. All I'm capable of giving her is a bad Romeo."

"Maybe that's what she wants. A perfect Romeo is boring. It's more interesting to watch him struggle with his emotions. You know, triumph over his insecurities."

He studies his cup for a few seconds before saying, "And if he doesn't triumph? What happens then?"

I'm wracking my brain for an encouraging answer when Erika arrives. We file past her and throw our empty cups into the trash as we enter the dim theater. After we dump our bags in the auditorium, we join Erika onstage.

"How are you guys feeling today?" she asks.

Holt and I mumble something vaguely positive, then the small talk is done.

"I don't want to scare you," Erika says, looking at each of us, "but the success of this whole production hinges on you two and the believability of your relationship."

Holt exhales. "Jesus, Erika. No pressure or anything."

Erika gives him a sympathetic smile. "The good news is, I know you're both more than capable of making these characters come to life." Holt rolls his eyes. "But you're going to have to trust me and each other, and give yourself over completely to the experience. Do you understand?"

We both nod. Holt looks like a spooked horse, shifting his weight and ready to bolt.

"This is the party scene where you first lay eyes on each other, and as corny as it sounds, you have to convince us that it's love at first sight."

"Holt doesn't believe in love at first sight," I say.

"He doesn't have to believe it," Erika says, smiling. "He just has to make the audience believe it. Right, Mr. Holt?"

He looks at the floor. "Whatever you say."

She laughs and positions us on opposite sides of the stage.

"Okay, so you have to imagine the space is filled with partygoers. Romeo, you're bored out of your mind. Your friends have promised to make you forget all about Rosaline by introducing you to other beautiful women, but you couldn't be less interested. As far as you're concerned, Rosaline has ruined you for any other woman, and you're just counting the minutes until you can leave.

"Juliet, you're desperately trying to avoid your mother and Paris. When you see Romeo for the first time, it's like something awakens inside you. Everything and everyone fades to black and all you can see is him. You're scared by your extreme attraction."

I nod as nervousness bubbles inside me. I look at Holt. He's pale as a sheet.

"Do either of you have any questions?"

Holt swallows and shakes his head. I do the same.

"All right, then. Let's go from when you see each other across the room. I want to see the passion. The sense of destiny. Let's have a go and see what happens."

She goes and sits in the front row of the auditorium with her script and notebook. Holt and I are alone onstage. He looks as nervous as I feel.

"Okay, when you're ready," Erika calls.

I take a deep breath, then push it out slowly. I look over at Holt. His eyes are closed, and he's frowning in concentration, like he's psyching himself up to jump out of a plane or walk over hot coals. He takes several deep breaths and shakes his hands. I can see his lips moving but can't hear what he's saying.

At last, he opens his eyes and looks over in my direction, starting at my feet. He seems satisfied with them before he moves to my knees. I wore a skirt today. Denim. Kinda short. His gaze moves higher, up my thighs before continuing over my stomach, my breasts, then onto my neck and finally, my face.

He looks at my mouth for a few seconds then . . . oh, God . . . he looks into my eyes. I gasp as I feel our energies connect. It's like I'm falling into him and absorbing him at the same time.

I can see him trying not to be scared, but he is. For a moment, I think he's going to run. His body goes rigid while a flash of panic lights his eyes. Then he exhales, and I see Romeo emerge, intense and desperate. He's channeling his emotions into the character. Using the fear. Transforming it.

I look at him through Juliet's eyes, and he's the most beautiful man I've ever seen.

Friday afternoon we were screaming at each other. But now . . .

Now, he's everything.

We move toward each other. My skin is alive with fluttering excitement. My body, filled with expectation. His eyes burn into mine, deep and intense. When he stops in front of me, I can barely breathe.

He's looking at me like I'm beautiful. Like I'm some miracle of nature that was made just for him.

I need to touch him, to feel that he's real and here and wants me, but I know Juliet wouldn't. So I stand there and drink him in. His strong jaw and high cheekbones. His beautiful eyes and riotous hair.

All his parts have their own unique beauty, but when they're added together, he's magnificent beyond my ability to describe.

The fear is still in his eyes, lurking, but he pushes through it. His hand comes up to my face. He touches me gently, but my reaction is intense. His eyelids flutter as he strokes my cheek. There's heat under my skin, and it builds with every soft pass of his fingers. His fear peeks out a little more, flickering behind his resolve.

His attention is fixed on my mouth, and he clears his throat before he murmurs, "If I profane with my unworthiest hand this holy shrine, the gentle fine is this: My lips, two blushing pilgrims, ready stand to smooth that rough touch . . . with a tender kiss."

The words are formal and archaic, yet the way my body reacts to them is timeless.

His fingers are still on my cheek as he leans down, slowly. All I can see are his lips, parted and soft. I know that Juliet would pull away, but I don't want to.

I remember my purpose and remove his hand from my face. I hold it and softly stroke his fingers.

"Good pilgrim, you do wrong your hand too much, which mannerly devotion shows in this; for saints have hands that pilgrims' hands do touch. And palm to palm . . . is holy palmers' kiss."

I press our hands together, and my voice is airy. My rhythm's off. I can't think straight. He's so close I can smell him—soap, and cologne. The sweet scent of chocolate on his breath.

I can feel him in every part of me, and my hands tremble.

He brings his other hand up to cover mine, then caresses it. The soft hush of skin moving against skin is the most intimate thing I've ever experienced. The intense current that passes between our hands shimmers in my blood.

It must affect him as well, because his voice becomes low and quiet. "Have not saints lips, and holy palmers, too?"

I can feel the vibration of his voice against my face.

"Ay, pilgrim," I answer, as he caresses and weaves his fingers between mine, stroking the soft skin there and making me shudder. "Lips that they must use in prayer."

"O, then, dear saint," he says, focusing on my mouth again, "let lips do what hands do; they pray, grant thou, lest faith turn to despair."

The intensity of his energy is filling me up. I barely have enough air to speak.

"Saints do not move," I whisper, "though grant for prayers' sake."

"Then move not," he murmurs as he moves closer, "while my prayer's effect I take. Thus from my lips, by yours, my sin is purged."

I hold my breath as his lips get lower, suspended above mine, so far away from where I want them to be. I'm just about to close my eyes and savor the moment when he stops. He blinks and shakes his head. His grip tightens on my hands.

*Ethan, no.*

He squeezes his eyes shut and makes a frustrated, strangled noise.

"Mr. Holt?" Erika calls from the auditorium. "That's your cue to kiss her. Is there a problem?"

He drops my hands and steps back. The fear he was trying so hard to suppress has broken free. It fills his expression and bunches his muscles.

"I told you I couldn't," he says, his voice is tight with panic. "I told you both."

"Mr. Holt?"

He shakes his head and shoves his hands in his pockets. Shoulders hunched. "Why does no one ever fucking listen to me?"

He strides off into the wings, and although Erika calls after him, he doesn't stop.

I start to follow, but Erika motions for me to wait.

"Cassie," she says as she comes onstage to join me, "be careful with him. He clearly associates emotional intimacy with painful consequences, and it's possibly a trigger for much deeper issues. I have no doubt he can do this role, but he needs to be convinced. Realistically, you're the only one who can help him."

"I don't know about that. Our usual form of communication is screaming at each other."

She smiles. "Haven't you noticed you're the only person in the whole class he makes an effort with? He barely talks to anyone else."

I feel bad that I hadn't realized how alone Holt is. At lunchtime he disappears when I sit with Connor and Miranda. After class when everyone else is leaving and chatting, he's the first out the door.

Alone.

I thought that he was just avoiding me, but maybe he was avoiding everyone.

"I'll talk to him," I say.

She smiles. "Sometimes people put up walls, not only to keep people out, but also to see who cares enough to tear them down. Understand?"

I nod and exit the stage. As I weave through the backstage darkness, I hear a scraping noise and head toward it.

"Holt?"

I find him in one of the dressing rooms, slumped in a chair with his head in his hands. The lights around the mirror glow behind him like a halo.

I step inside the doorway. He looks so miserable, I want to tell him it's going to be okay, but I'm not sure what to say.

"Just let me quit," he says without looking up. "You need someone else. Not me."

"I don't want someone else," I say, moving toward him. "I just think if you trust yourself, and me, we could create something really amazing."

"Taylor . . ." He pushes out of the chair and goes over to the windows. "I know my limit, and this is it."

"Just *try*," I say as I come up to stand behind him. "That's all I'm asking. I know this stuff is hard for you, but don't quit without at least trying."

"Is there any use in trying, when I know how it's going to turn out? I'll choke and bring you down with me. You're better off cutting your losses while there's still time to rehearse someone else into the role."

"It's already too late for that," I say, watching how his shoulder muscles strain against his T-shirt and wanting to soothe them. "I know the other day I said I didn't want you to be my Romeo, but I was wrong. It's supposed to be you. I can't imagine anyone else doing it."

He puts his hands on the windowsill, and his shoulders slump as he drops his head. "Why do you have to say shit like that?"

"Like what?"

"Stuff that makes me like you. It's fucking annoying."

I can't stop myself any longer, so I place my hand between his shoulder blades and rub gently.

His muscles tense under my fingers, and when he inhales, it's loud and ragged.

"Just get Connor to do it," he says as he turns to face me. "He'd probably cream his shorts as soon as you kissed him, but he'd get the job done."

"I don't want to kiss Connor," I say. "I want to kiss you."

He freezes, and I think he's stopped breathing.

He studies me for a moment before taking the smallest step forward. I keep my focus on him despite every instinct screaming at me to run. He could very well reject me again, but I've come this far. I can't back down now.

"You really want me to kiss you?"

"Yes. Please, Ethan."

"You don't know what you're asking." His brows furrow.

"I do," I say, and step forward. "If this is what you need to do to see if you can play this role, then let's do it. It's just a kiss."

He steps back, panic building in his expression as I move forward.

"What if it's not *just* a kiss?" he asks, as his back hits the wall. "What do we do then?"

I put my hands on his chest and feel how fast his heart is pounding. A noise vibrates in his throat, and I look up to see him staring at me. The need emanating from him makes my brain fuzzy and my legs weak.

"Stop being so dramatic," I whisper, as I run my fingers up his neck and along his jaw. "If we kissed, we'd probably figure out that our bodies are as grossly incompatible as our personalities."

God, I'm such a liar. I'm already turned on more than I've ever been in my entire life. Every part of me is screaming for him to touch me. He feels amazing under my hands.

"Taylor," he says as he weaves his arm around my waist and pulls me closer. "The one thing we are definitely not is physically incompatible."

He pulls me against him, and I gasp. I can feel him, long and hard on my stomach. Knowing I did that to him brings me feral satisfaction.

I press closer. He closes his eyes and groans. "This is a bad idea. Seriously."

I weave a hand into his hair. "Kiss me."

I touch my fingertips to his lips, and they open. His breath is warm against my hand. I run my finger across his top lip, then stroke the bottom one.

So silky. Soft.

He looks bewildered. "I've been nothing but an asshole to you since the first day we met."

"I know."

He rests his forehead against mine as his hands move across my back. "I've pushed you away, time and again. Yet you still want me to kiss you?"

"Yes. A lot."

He grazes his hands over my ribs, and his voice is soft and breathless when he says, "Don't you see how fucked up this is? How bad I'd be for you?"

"I know," I say, unable to stop looking at his mouth, "but do you *want* it? Do you want . . . me?"

*Just say it. Please.*

He swallows again, and whispers, "Fuck, yes."

I stand on my toes and tug his head down. When his mouth is close enough, I gently press my lips against his.

*Oh. God.*

We both inhale loudly, our bodies tensing as our connection explodes. My insides coil and tie themselves in knots, and he makes a grunting sound that's a perfect blend of both pleasure and pain.

I release his lips and pull back. His mouth is open and soft, and

I kiss him again, a little harder. I feel him exhale against my face, and I don't know what the hell I'm doing, but I suck gently on his lips. Heat oozes under my skin. Fires in my belly. He makes another tortured noise, then he's sucking on my lips, too. Every inch of me blazes. Heat from his mouth pulls into my lungs, and I curse myself for not having been kissing this man from the first day I met him, because what he's doing to me is beyond incredible.

"I can't believe no one's ever done this to you before," he says between increasingly desperate kisses. Then he pushes his tongue into my mouth, and all hell breaks loose. I'm lost in the sensual slide of him. Dizzying pheromones make me ravenous. There's nothing in the room but him. No feeling in my body but what he's giving me. No sensation in the world except his skin beneath my hands.

In that moment, I'm *that* girl. The one who's confident, and beautiful, and desirable. I'm all of those things because of him. Because of what he's bringing out in me.

I pull back to look at him, panting and overwhelmed. His eyes are wild, chest heaving. He looks how I feel. Raw and insatiable.

"Oh, God," I say, because now I'm always going to want him like this. There's no going back. "This is bad. Bad, bad, bad, bad."

"I warned you," he says, breathing heavily and cupping my face. "Why the hell didn't you listen?"

Then he's kissing me again, and everything I thought I knew about kissing is obliterated by his lips. His tongue. His small groaning noises. His hands and arms are everywhere and nowhere. I rake my fingers across his scalp while moaning into his mouth, trying to get enough of him and failing miserably.

"Oh, God." I gasp as he moves to my neck, his mouth open and sucking. Driving me insane.

He walks me backward until my ass hits the bench in front of the mirrors. He hoists me onto it and pushes his hips between my legs. My skirt rides up as his swollen crotch presses against me.

We kiss, and grind, and tangle together, desperate for more. There's too much fabric and not enough air. His hard is pressing against my soft, and I never knew anything in the world could feel so damn good.

"Jesus." He groans, one hand grasping my hair as he uses the other one to find my breast. "This is just . . . Goddammit, Taylor. I'm so fucking stupid, because I knew you'd ruin me, and I let it happen anyway. I'm so screwed."

"We both are." I grab his head and make him kiss me more, because I'm addicted to the taste of his lips and tongue, but my hands need more, so they push under his T-shirt and find his stomach, flat and warm, trembling under my touch.

He grunts into my mouth and kisses me deeper. Then his hands are under my shirt and on top of my bra, caressing and fondling. Making the ache inside me so hungry, it's painful.

He presses against me harder, but it's not enough. I'm winding tighter and tighter, and nothing he's doing is enough. I need more. All of him.

"Please." I don't even know what I'm asking for. For him to have sex with me? Here? Is that what I want?

"We shouldn't." He pants as he leaves my lips and kisses down past my ear, his breath hot and shallow on my skin. "This is fucking insane. Tell me to stop."

"I can't."

He sucks hard where my shoulder and neck meet. I know he's leaving a mark, but the pain doesn't matter as much as him claiming me in that way.

He lifts me, then turns to press me against the wall, and when he grinds between my legs, I cry out with pleasure.

God, he's so hard. I want him inside me, quieting the ache. Feeding the hunger.

"Jesus." He rocks his hips faster as he cups my ass. "Cassie, if you don't tell me to stop right now, I swear to God, I'm going to fuck you against this wall. You feel so good. I knew it. I knew you would."

I writhe against him. I couldn't tell him to stop right now if I had a gun pointed at my head. He rocks against me, and all I can do is hold on and pray for him to keep moving. Everything inside me is drawing up, contracting, tightening with unbelievable pleasure. It's like nothing I've ever felt before, and I never want it to end. I feel like I'm climbing to the top of a mountain. If he just keeps moving, I'm going to launch into space.

"Cassie, I can't . . . I shouldn't." He pants in rhythm with his hips. He has to keep going. He has to.

I bury my head in his neck and suck on the sweet skin there, marking him the way he marked me, the tang of his cologne tingling on my tongue as we both groan and curse. I hold my breath, waiting to fly.

"Ethan . . ."

"Jesus. Cassie . . ."

*"Mr. Holt? Miss Taylor?"*

We freeze as we hear Erika's voice. He stops moving. Stops breathing. The tension inside me unwinds and dissolves.

*No, no, no, no, no!*

I hear footsteps, then her voice. "There you are. I was wondering if I'd lost my lead actors, but it seems you're actually doing some character work. How dedicated of you."

She's right behind us.

Inside the room.

I detach myself from Holt's neck, and he looks at me, panic filling his eyes. We're both panting. Our lips are swollen and red.

Erika clears her throat as I unwrap my legs from Holt's waist, so he can lower me to the floor.

I push down my T-shirt and skirt, and I see Holt run his hand through his hair before shoving his hands in his pockets and exhaling.

I glance over at Erika. She's assessing us calmly.

"So, it looks like you two have had an interesting . . . discussion. I take it you've worked through your issues about kissing Miss Taylor, Mr. Holt?"

Holt clears his throat. "Well, I was just getting to the . . . crux of the issue when you found us."

Erika smirks. "So I heard."

A nervous giggle escapes me, and I cover my mouth because I think I'm about to lose it in a big way. My body is still pounding and throbbing, my heart is beating out of my chest, and just feeling Holt behind me is doing nothing to help matters.

"So, can I assume that you won't be quitting the show, Mr. Holt?" Erika asks.

Holt shifts his weight. "Doesn't look like it."

Erika nods and smiles. "Excellent. In that case, we have a lot of work to do. I'll see you onstage in five minutes."

She turns and leaves the room. It's just Holt and me again, wrapped in layers of sexual tension so thick they could insulate a house.

I glance at him. He looks like a prisoner plotting an elaborate escape.

"Listen, Taylor . . ." He rubs his eyes. "That kiss was . . ."

*Amazing? Stupendous? Earth shattering?*

Because I know he's not going to use any of my adjectives, I say, "It was stupid, I know. I also know you want to try and pretend it never happened, so sure, let's do that. Solid plan."

I can't believe one kiss has turned my world upside down. I used to think I wanted him, but now what I'm feeling isn't even in the same universe as want. It's *compulsion*. Powerful and hungry. I wish I could go back to the vague yearning I used to feel.

He knew this would happen. I should have listened.

He shuffles nervously. "I'll do the show and whatever that involves, but offstage, we're just—"

"Friends. Yep. I get it." We should avoid the train wreck we'd no doubt make of each other.

Keep our distance and try to not become obsessed.

Except, I'm afraid I already am.

# EIGHT

## EMAILS AND ZEN

*Present Day*
*New York City*
*End of Day Four of Rehearsal*

When I enter my apartment, I'm met by rainforest noises. Goddamn running water and birds calls with some annoying melodic/electronic crap that makes me want to tear my hair out.

"Fuck."

"I heard that," says a very relaxed voice from the living room. "Please don't pollute our sanctuary with aggressive language. You're harshing my calm."

My emotional exhaustion weighs on me like a blanket of lead. I drop my bag in the hall before zombie-walking into the living room and collapsing onto the couch.

"Please turn off this crap." I sigh as I tilt my head back and look at the ceiling. "It's not relaxing. It makes me want to torture puppies. And you."

My roommate, Tristan, is sitting on the large rug in front of me, legs crossed, hands on his knees. His eyes are closed, and his breathing is even and measured. He's wearing tiny shorts. Nothing else. I take a moment to reflect on how years of yoga have sculpted all six-foot-four of him into the pinnacle of masculine perfection. His long black hair is pulled back into a ponytail, and his face is smooth and free of tension. Having a Japanese mother and a Malaysian father has given him the sort of exotic good looks that should be immortalized by an artist. He'd make a great statue.

Hot Buddha.

Unlike me, he's the epitome of goddamn Zen.

"Bad day?" he asks.

*I spent most of the day making out with my very attractive ex-lover who I'm not even remotely over. Bad doesn't cover it.* "You have no idea."

Tristan opens his eyes and assesses me with a glance. "Oh, God, Cass. Your chakras are all over the place. What the hell happened?"

"Holt and I kissed." My voice is tired and croaky. My brain is muddy. I'm so turned around, I can barely speak.

Tristan sighs and shakes his head. "Cassie, after everything we talked about. After you *swore* to me you wouldn't jump back into something with him. After you wrote the *Oath of Self Preservation*."

"It wasn't spontaneous, Tris. It was part of the scene."

He turns off the stereo. Thank God.

"Oh. And?"

"And . . ."

He waits for me, but I can't speak. If I open my mouth, a storm of bitterness will swirl out of me and strip the skin from my bones.

"Cassie?"

I shake my head. He knows.

He sits beside me and wraps me in his giant arms.

"Sweet girl." He sighs as I hug him like he's the only thing anchoring me to reality.

"Tris, I'm so screwed."

"You knew this would be hard."

"Not this hard."

"What about him? How's he dealing with things?"

"He's being a prick."

"Really?"

I sigh again. "No, not really. Mostly he's being kind of semi-decent and concerned, but that's almost worse. I don't know how to deal with him like that."

"Maybe he's changed."

"I doubt it."

"Has he apologized?"

"Of course not."

"What if he did?"

I thought about it. Would I accept it? Could he ever apologize enough for me to forgive him?

"Cassie?"

"Let's say he did apologize, which is about as likely as small, furry animals flying out of your butt. It wouldn't change anything. He's still him, and I'm still me. We're like these giant magnets that keep flipping over and over again, pulling each other in, then pushing away, and I just— I . . ."

I deflate and go still.

I can't say it. I can't admit that the first time I've felt whole in years was when he was kissing me today. It makes me crazy to realize he's the only one who can make me feel that way.

I rub my face. "I don't know what to do."

"You need to talk to him."

"And say what? 'Gee, Ethan, even though you completely destroyed me when you left, I still want you, because I'm the world's biggest glutton for punishment'? I can't give him that kind of ammunition."

"You two aren't at war."

"Yes, we are."

"Does he know that?"

"He should. He started it."

Tristan gives me a look. I know he's about to say something profound, enlightened, and thoroughly freaking annoying. Whatever he says will be right. He's always right. I hate that about him.

I also love that about him.

Ever since the night he waited for me at the stage door to tell me how amazing I was in the off-Broadway version of *Portrait*, we've had a connection. I felt like he was meant to be in my life, and I hadn't had that since Ruby moved overseas in our senior year.

He needed a place to stay, so when my roommate turned out to be a compulsive shoe-napper and fled in the middle of the night with my entire footwear collection, I didn't think twice about asking him to move in.

We've been best friends ever since, and over the past three years, he's seen me in every stage of my "I Hate Holt" evolution. He's helped me overcome many of my destructive tendencies, but today is a definite setback.

"Cassie, what do you want?"

It seems like a deceptively easy question, but I know better. Tristan doesn't ask easy questions.

"I don't want him to make me feel these things anymore."

"I didn't ask what you *didn't* want, I asked what you *want*. If you could have anything, regardless of present, past, and future, what would it be?"

I think hard. The answer is simple. And impossible.

"I want to be happy again."

"And what's going to make you happy?"

Ethan.

*No.*

Yes. Ethan holding me and kissing me.

*Don't. You can't. He won't.*

Ethan. Running his hands over my body as he undresses me.

*God, no.*

Ethan groaning my name as he moves inside me and declares his undying love.

*Oh, Jesus.*

I stand and stride into the kitchen. My hands tremble as I grab the nearest bottle of wine, tear off the cap, and pour a huge glass. Tristan leans against the doorframe. I feel his disapproval as I drink too much, too fast.

"Cassie—"

"Don't wanna hear it."

"I'm going to take you out."

"No."

"Yes. You need to chill and stop obsessing over the gorgeous Mr. Holt."

"Please don't refer to him as 'gorgeous.' Or 'Mr. Holt.' In fact, don't mention him at all. That'd be great."

"Let me take you to the Zoo. It's straight night. You can ogle to your heart's content."

I drain the rest of the glass. "Tristan, what I need tonight is to drink myself into a semiconscious stupor at home, alone. If I go out, you know that I'll end up fucking a stranger who'll make me forget all about the asshole-who-shall-not-be-named for a few short hours. Then you'll give me a lecture in the morning about meaningless one-night stands and how I use them to desensitize myself to the pain of my past rejections by His Royal Assholeness, and how eventually I'm going to have to treat the cause of the gaping hole in my heart and not just the symptoms."

He exhales and blinks. "Well, you've just packed more self-awareness into that mini rant than you've shown in the entire time I've known you. I was beginning to think you didn't listen when I talked."

"I do listen. And maybe I'm learning." I refill my glass.

"Thank the ever-loving Sun God," he says, and walks over to hug me. "Now, when are you going to talk to him?"

I sigh and shake my head. "I don't know. When I can manage it without falling apart?"

"That would be never."

"Tristan . . ."

"Cass, stop procrastinating. The sooner you do it, the sooner you can start planning how to purge all the bad energy between you two."

"I don't even know if that's what he wants."

He rolls his eyes. "Even I know that's what he wants, and I've never met the man. I've read his e-mails, remember? When are you going to stop hiding and let him talk? If you can find a way to forgive him, then maybe . . . just maybe . . . you can figure out how to be happy again. With or without him in your life."

He's right. As usual.

"You know I hate you, right?"

"No, you don't."

I take a giant swig of wine. "Just let me get through the next few days, then . . . I'll talk to him."

He hugs me again. "Good. I love you."

"Love you, too. Have a good time at the club."

"You know I will. See you tomorrow."

I kiss him on the cheek before taking the wine into my bedroom and closing the door.

After I put on some music, I open my laptop and spend a few minutes checking e-mails. There's one from Ruby that makes me laugh, as well as several from very helpful companies telling me how to improve my penis size. I delete the junk and switch to my desktop.

*There it is.*

The little icon that forever taunts me. It's labeled *Asshole's E-mails.* I sip my wine and stare at it, with my finger hovering over the mouse button.

I've read them all before. Dozens of times. Always with eyes clouded by bitterness and pain.

I wonder what I'd see if I tried to get past all that. Would they portray a different Holt than the one I'd spent so many hours cursing?

"Fucking fucking fuck."

I open the file.

The familiar words fill the screen, and I take a deep breath.

The first one is dated three months after he left me.

. . .

From: EthanHolt <ERHolt@gmail.com>
To: CassandraTaylor <CTaylor18@gmail.com>
Subject: <none>
Date: Fri, July 16, at 9:16p.m.

Cassie,
I've been sitting here looking at my screen for two hours trying to get up the courage to e-mail you, and now that I'm typing, I have no fucking idea what I'm going to say.

Should I apologize to you? Of course.

Should I beg for your forgiveness? Absolutely.

Will you give it to me? I doubt it.

But even though I hurt you, I still think I did the right thing by leaving. I needed to go while one of us still had a chance to be whole.

Now I'm smiling, because I can imagine you rolling your eyes and calling me an asshole. You'd be right. I warned you on the first day we met, remember? I was so damned frightened of you, I said we shouldn't be friends, but you made us friends anyway.

You wound up being the best friend I've ever had.

I miss our friendship.

I miss you.

*I guess that's all I wanted to say.*
*Ethan.*

. . .

The next one is a month later.

*From: EthanHolt <ERHolt@gmail.com>*
*To: CassandraTaylor <CTaylor18@gmail.com>*
*Subject: <none>*
*Date: Fri, Aug 13, at 7:46p.m.*

*Cassie,*
*I've decided to keep writing to you, even if you never reply, because I'm going to pretend you read these and think of me. You know how good I am at pretending.*
*The show's going well. The cast is good, and I'm glad I'm back playing Mercutio instead of Romeo. Playing the romantic lead was never my strong suit, as you know.*
*I often get chest pains when I think of you. It's not fun. I'm too young to have a heart condition, but I'm afraid to get it checked out in case they tell me what I already know: that it's defective and can't be fixed.*
*I sometimes wonder what you're doing and hope you're moving on. That's what you deserve, but there's a part of me that hopes you're miserable I'm gone.*
*I miss you.*
*Ethan.*

. . .

And the next one. The one I've read more than any other. The one I read when I miss him so much I can almost feel his hands on my body.

*From: EthanHolt <ERHolt@gmail.com>*
*To: CassandraTaylor <CTaylor18@gmail.com>*
*Subject: <none>*
*Date: Wed, Sept 1, at 2:09a.m.*

*Cassie,*

*It's two a.m., and I'm drunk. Soooooo fuking drunk. I want you so bad. I wannt you naked and panting. I wanna see your face as you come, and . . . God . . . I want you.*

*Of course, I never did figure out how to fuck you, did I? Coulnd't just detach and treat it liek sex, 'cause it never was. Ever. It was so much more.*

*I brought a girl home with me tongiht. A pretty girl. Beautiful, even.*

*Not as beautiufl as you, but then no one is.*

*She wanted me to fuck her, but I coudn't. Couln't barely kiss her because her lips didn't taste like yours, and she didn't smell right because she wan't you.*

*Now I'm hard as a fucking rock sitting here writing to you and, I know I'll never be inside you again, and it's all I can thing about. So when I finish writing trhis, I'll probably fuck my hand while I fantasize about you, and then hate myself just a little bit more.*

*I'm pathetic.*

*I don't want to obsess over you anymore. It hurts too much.*

*I miss you too much.*

*Ethan.*

. . .

And then, there's this.

*From: EthanHolt <ERHolt@gmail.com>*
*To: CassandraTaylor <CTaylor18@gmail.com>*

*Subject: No excuse*
*Date: Wed, Sept 1, at 10:16a.m.*

*Cassie,*
*I'm so ashamed of the e-mail I sent you last night. I have no excuse.*
*I drank too much, and, well, you know the rest.*
*Please delete it and forget it happened.*
*That's what I'm going to try to do.*
*Ethan.*

. . .

After that I didn't hear from him for months. Then this arrived.

*From: EthanHolt <ERHolt@gmail.com>*
*To: CassandraTaylor <CTaylor18@gmail.com>*
*Subject: <none>*
*Date: Thu, Jan 13, at 12:52p.m.*

*Cassie,*
*Happy New Year.*
*It's been a while.*
*How are you?*
*Of course I don't expect you to answer that. You never answer me.*
*That's understandable.*
*I've been getting help. Talking to someone about why I continu-*
*ously fuck things up. I'm trying to get better. I know I should've done*
*this a long time ago, but better late than never, right?*
*My therapist says I need to let go of my fear, so I can let people in.*
*I don't fucking know anymore.*
*I think maybe I'm not meant to be happy. If I couldn't be happy*
*with you, I have no hope.*
*I want to make things better between us. Maybe get back to being*

*friends. But I have no idea how to do that. And even if I did, I doubt
you'd want to. Would you?*

*I'd like to be your friend again, Cassie.*

*I miss you.*

*Ethan.*

. . .

There are more, but I can't read them. The wine is gone, and my
eyes are stinging.

I compose an e-mail.

. . .

*From: CassandraTaylor <CTaylor18@gmail.com>*
*To: EthanHolt <ERHolt@gmail.com>*
*Subject: End of the week*
*Date: Fri, Sept 4, at 9:46p.m.*

*Ethan,*
*For the sake of the show, I guess we should make time to talk. How
about tomorrow night, after rehearsal?*
*Cassie.*

. . .

I click send before I chicken out.

My dreams hate me. They always take me back to a time when all
I was trying to do was forget. Or remember. I never could work out
which.

The man kisses my neck as he increases his pace. Long, deep strokes.
I make all the right noises, but I'm not even close.

"Cassie, look at me."

I can't. That's not how this works. Looking at him shatters the illusion, and as flimsy as it is, the illusion is all I have.

"Cassie, please."

I push him onto his back and take control. Ride him with desperation. Try to make it more than it is.

He groans and grabs my hips, and I know it's almost over. He trails his hands over me, reverent and loving. I don't deserve it. How does he not know this by now?

"Cassie, please look at me."

His voice is all wrong. I move faster, making it so he can't speak. When he grunts and goes still, I don't get satisfaction. Just relief.

I pretend to come and collapse onto his chest, and even though he wraps his arms around me, the distance between us widens.

I listen to his heart. So strong. Fast and steady. Unafraid of loving. The sound is foreign to me.

I climb off and collect my clothes. He follows my every step with his eyes.

"You can't stay?"

"No."

He exhales. He's tired of that answer. So am I.

"Just tell me one thing," he says and sits up.

"What?"

"Are you ever going to think about just me when we make love?"

I pause, then pull on my T-shirt. I hate that I'm so obvious.

"Cassie, he left you."

"I know."

"Let him go."

"I'm trying."

"He's on the other side of the world, and I'm here. I love you. I have for a long time. But that's never going to make a difference, is it? No matter how much I want it to."

He gets up and pulls on his boxers. Sharp, frustrated movements. I don't blame him. He deserves more.

I sit on the bed, defeated. This started out of spite, but now I want it to work. I'd give anything to not be this dysfunctional.

But I am. Trying to pretend otherwise isn't working. And the relief I feel at hurting someone instead of being hurt makes me hate myself.

He stands in front of me, and when I hug him, he squeezes me tight.

"I can't believe Ethan Holt's screwing things up for me, even when he's not here."

The mere mention of his name makes my chest tighten.

I pull back and run my fingers over frown lines, trying to get them to loosen.

"I'm sorry," I say. "I know it's a total cliché, but it's absolutely not you. It's me."

He laughs. "Oh, I know that." His expression softens. "Still, I hope you get closure one day, Cass. I really do."

I nod and look at his chest. "Me, too."

Then he kisses me, gentle and slow, and I nearly cry because I want it to feel so different.

Leaning his forehead against mine, he says, "And I hope that bastard realizes that letting you go was the stupidest thing he's ever done."

He walks me to the door and kisses me once more before saying, "See you tonight at the theater?"

I nod and say good-bye, and just like that, we're back to being onstage lovers only.

It's better this way.

As I leave, I vow not to inflict myself on innocents anymore. Get in, fuck, get out. No strings attached.

Love is weakness.

That's not the only thing Holt taught me, but it's the thing I remember most.

* * *

I almost fall off my chair as I jolt into consciousness.

My heart pounds furiously, fueled by latent guilt.

*Jesus, what time is it?*

I look at the clock. Ten forty-five. I've been asleep at my desk for an hour.

My mouth is dry, and when the room tilts, I'm reminded I drank a whole bottle of wine. I groan and push away from my desk, my whole body protesting as I get up and go into the bathroom.

I take a quick shower and brush my teeth as a pit of dread yawns in my stomach.

I e-mailed him.

I e-mailed him and said that we should talk.

I'm so not ready for that to happen. If he tries to excuse his behavior, I'll end up punching him in the head. I know it.

I towel dry my hair and don't even bother brushing it before I pull on my favorite pajamas and crawl into bed. I open a book and try to read, but my eyes are blurry. I rub them and sigh.

I'm tense, horny, and drunk. Damn, I need to get laid.

I can't remember the last guy who gave me pleasure. Honestly, I have no idea what his name was. Matt? Nick? Blake? I know it had one syllable.

Whatever his name, he was an adequate lover, but he didn't make me come. Few of them do. They feed my ego and make me forget for a while, but they never make me feel like Holt did. Then again, they never rip my heart out of my chest and shred it into a thousand pieces, either, so there's that.

My phone rings. I know it's Tristan wanting to tell me about the latest piece of delicious man-meat he's discovered at the club.

I pick up the phone and jab the answer button. "Listen, dancing queen, I'm drunk, horny, and in no mood to hear about pretty men who aren't going to fuck me. So for the love of my poor neglected vagina, order yourself another Cosmo and please fuck off."

There's a pause and an uncertain cough. "I'm more that happy to fuck off, but if it makes a difference, I wasn't going to talk about dicks. I'm far more interested to hear more about your poor neglected vagina. How's she been? We haven't had a face-to-face in a while."

Heat floods my cheeks. I shouldn't have any shame left around him, yet I always seem to find just a little bit more.

"What do you want, Holt?"

"Well, considering you're horny and drunk, I'd really like to be within groping distance. Failing that, I just want to talk. I got your e-mail."

I rub my eyes. I have no patience for his charm tonight. "Yeah. Okay."

"Saturday night would be great. Thanks."

"Don't thank me yet. There's a strong chance we won't make it through the evening without me throwing something at you, but I guess things can't get much worse between us, right?"

He laughs. "I don't know. There were times when we were less civil than we are now. Still, I appreciate the chance to clear the air."

He goes silent, and so do I. We used to be able to talk on the phone for hours. Now, we've barely made it through a minute before the awkward sets in.

"So, was that all you called to say? Because you could have just told me tomorrow."

There's silence for a moment. Then he says, "I called to tell you something that couldn't wait until tomorrow."

A chill runs up my spine. "And what's that?"

"I just needed to tell you . . . I'm sorry, Cass."

I stop breathing and squeeze my eyes shut as a bizarre storm of emotions swirls within me.

Those words. Those simple, powerful words.

"Cassie? Did you hear me?"

"I don't think so. It sounded like an apology, but in your voice."

He sighs. "I know you didn't hear me apologize nearly enough during our relationship, and I'm sorry for that, too. But before we spent one more day together, I had to say that. It was killing me not to."

In my shock, I almost miss how slurred his speech is.

"Ethan, you've been drinking, haven't you?"

"A little," he says.

"A little?"

"Well, a lot, but that has nothing to do with me apologizing. I should have done it the moment I saw you on the first day of rehearsal, but . . . you didn't want to listen. And, well, you were scary."

"You haven't seen my hair since I got out of the shower. I'm still scary."

"Bullshit. I bet you look beautiful."

He's really drunk. He only ever compliments me when he's lost feeling in his extremities.

"What are you drinking?"

"Whiskey."

"Why?"

"Because . . . because of you. Well, you and me. And kissing. Definitely because of the kissing."

I don't tell him that I drank a whole bottle of wine for the same reason.

He sighs. "Jesus, Cassie. Kissing you?" He groans. "I've been fantasizing about it for three years, but none of my fantasies compared to what happened today."

His voice lowers so much, I don't know if he's even talking to me anymore. "I've missed kissing you. So much."

Goddammit. I can't hear this.

"Holt, please . . ."

"I know I shouldn't say any of this, but I'm drunk, and I miss you, and . . . did I mention being drunk?"

I laugh, because like this, he's my friend again. But I know that it's not real and it won't last.

"Go to bed, Ethan."

"Okay, pretty Cassie. 'Night. And don't forget how sorry I am. Please."

I smile despite myself. "You know you're going to have a giant hangover in the morning, right?"

He chuckles. "Has anything I've said tonight made you hate me any less?"

"Maybe."

"A little or a lot?"

"A little."

"Then it'll be worth it."

# NINE

## FAKING IT

The next day, Holt's apology is still echoing in my brain as I walk to rehearsal. I thought him apologizing would give me some sense of closure, but it hasn't. Instead it's given rise to a strange, simmering anxiety.

I blow out a breath and pull back my shoulders.

What's the worst that could happen? He says he didn't mean it?

*No*, my conscience whispers, sounding annoyingly like Tristan. *It would be worse if he said he* did *mean it, because then you'd actually have to decide to either let him in or let him go. Realistically, both options scare the hell out of you.*

I grind my teeth.

Conscience Tristan is as annoyingly right as Real-life Tristan. Who knew?

As I reach the theater, I contemplate today's rehearsal. We're supposed to block the sex scene, then do the morning after. I shudder as images of Holt running his hands over my body hijack my mind.

*Lord.*

Just thinking about him sexing me up, pretend or not, is enough to make my vagina start slow-clapping in anticipation.

I take a deep breath and pull open the door. When I walk into the room, Cody, caffeine angel extraordinaire, hands me my coffee. As I dump my bag and sip the coffee, Holt appears in front of me, looking way too good for someone with a monster hangover.

"Hey," he says quietly.

"Hi."

We just stand there for a few seconds in awkward silence.

"So . . ." he says, looking down at his hands.

"Yeah, so . . . you look like shit this morning," I say out of spite.

"Thanks. Seems I can't drink nearly a full bottle of Jack like I used to."

"That's a shame. Didn't you list that on your résumé as a special skill?"

"Yeah. Never had to use it for a role, though, but I've done it a lot for research."

"Oh, yes. Very important, drunky research."

"Yep." He smiles, the kind-of-cute, one-sided smile that's annoyingly endearing.

"Listen," he says. "How much of an ass did I make of myself last night? Feel free to lie and say none at all, because I have a feeling it was bad."

I nearly drop my coffee. "You don't *remember*?"

He swallows and pauses before saying, "No, I remember, I just . . . I don't know how much you laughed about it after we hung up. I wouldn't blame you if you did."

"I didn't laugh at all," I say, trying honesty on for size. "I was too shocked by you apologizing to do anything but convince myself I wasn't dreaming."

He nods. "Yeah, I realize I have issues with that. It's one of the things I've been working on."

"Too bad you didn't work on it when we were together."

I feel bad for the hurt that crosses his face, but what can I do? It's not like I can stop being a bitch to him overnight.

Marco sweeps into the room, and there's a flurry of activity as set pieces are moved into position. There's a bed in the middle of the rehearsal room, and it's raised on an angle so the audience can see us when we're lying down.

My mouth goes dry just looking at it.

I sneak a glance at Holt. He's taking large, even breaths, either warming up or settling his nerves. I follow his lead. My heart is beating way too fast.

Five minutes later, Marco has placed us into the most awkward position two ex-lovers could ever find themselves—Ethan is between my legs, his hands framing my face, his mouth just above mine.

He kisses me, soft and sweet, as his hips rock back and forth, and then he lets out a quiet moan as he closes his eyes.

"Look at me, Sam," I whisper.

He opens his eyes.

So beautiful. Full and complicated. Always.

"Kiss her again," Marco calls out. "Kiss her mouth, then go down to the neck."

Ethan looks at me, hesitating for a moment before obeying, his lips soft but closed.

I lie there, too frozen to kiss him back but aware I should.

He pulls back and looks at me, confused.

Dammit, I need to start thinking like Sarah.

He's Sam. He and Sarah have a happily-ever-after. I've read the script.

He kisses me again, and I respond awkwardly.

"You need to make some noise, Cassie," Marco says, sounding frustrated. "Nothing you're doing is reading from out here. Make it bigger."

I unfreeze and try to do my job.

I start by wrapping my arms around him and groaning loudly while lifting my hips and arching my back. It's fake and porny, but at this stage I have no idea what the hell I'm doing.

I grab his ass and push him against me. He whispers, "Fucking hell, Cassie," before exhaling hard against my shoulder.

"I believe the line is, 'Oh, Sarah, I love you,'" I say, before moaning and kissing his neck.

Instinctively, I reach over his shoulders and grab his T-shirt. I tug it over his head and toss it on the floor.

"So we're taking my clothes off now?" he whispers. "I thought we were just marking this through."

"What can I say? Apparently nothing I'm doing is reaching the audience. I'm guessing getting you naked will reach them."

It feels good to be aggressive. It helps me disconnect.

More fake noises pour from my mouth, but as his muscles ripple under my fingers, all thoughts of Sam fly straight out the damn window.

*Semi-naked Ethan.*

He feels incredible. More incredible that he used to, if that's possible.

I'm so distracted by his bare chest, I suddenly have no idea what the hell I'm supposed to say. Sarah's gone bye-bye.

I run my hands down his stomach before reaching around to his back and fingering the waistband of his jeans. He mumbles something that sounds vaguely like "Jesus motherfucking Christ."

He drops his head onto my shoulder and the sheets on either side of my head bunch as he curls his hands into fists. All of his muscles tense, and I don't think he's breathing.

"Is there a reason why you've stopped?" Marco asks, bewildered. He turns to Elissa. "Why have they stopped?"

Ethan still isn't breathing.

"Ethan?" I whisper.

He doesn't move, but there's a gust of warm breath as he exhales against my neck. "What?"

"Are you okay?"

He pauses and sighs. "Yep. Fine."

"Is it your line?"

He tenses. "Is *what* my line?"

"Is it your turn to *say* a line?"

He pushes up onto his arms and looks down at me, his jaw tense.

"Cassie, I have no fucking clue what my name is right now, let alone what lines I'm supposed to be saying. Let's just get through this and we'll figure out the dialogue later, okay?"

He sounds angry, but I know he's just frustrated. I'm frustrated, too.

"Okay. Sure." When I wrap my legs around him and pull him close, I feel the source of his frustration, hard against me. He lets out a strangled cry then slides down my body so I'm pressed against his stomach instead of his groin. "Jesus, Cassie, I'm really trying to think of dead puppies here, but . . ."

"It's harder than you thought?"

He glares. "Are you trying to be funny?"

"No, because if I start laughing now, I don't think I'll be able to stop."

He drops his head. "Goddammit."

"Less chat, more acting please, children," Marco bellows. "Ethan, you've stopped moving. Do I need to explain how to make love to a woman? Because although I've never had the pleasure, I'm fairly certain it involves thrusting."

Ethan sighs and starts fake thrusting again. Even though I know he's trying to keep his erection away from me, I feel it graze the inside of my thigh.

"Shit. Sorry," he says, adjusting his angle again. "Damn thing has a mind of its own around you."

"Don't worry about it," I mumble, because really, what else am I going to say? *"How dare you get aroused when you're simulating sex with me? The nerve of you!"* Never mind that it's wetter than a Slip'N Slide in my panties right now. He doesn't need to know that.

It's not as if either of us can help it.

Our physical attraction was never something we could control.

All too often, we gave in to what our bodies wanted without sorting out all of our other crap, and most of the time, we ended up regretting it.

Now everything's wrong, because we're trying to filter our debilitating attraction through our characters.

We're faking not feeling it.

After a few more minutes of lackluster lovemaking, Marco sighs in frustration.

"All right, let's stop there," he says and waves his hand as he walks over to us. "This isn't working. You two look as uncomfortable as vegetarians in a sausage factory. What's going on?"

Ethan rolls off me, and we both sit up. Neither of us answers.

"Is it too intimate?" Marco asks, looking from one to the other. "Are you embarrassed? Because frankly, I've seen you both perform much more controversial scenes than this. Yet here you are, fumbling about like a couple of virgins. Where's the passion? The fire? The gut-wrenching need for each other? You had it yesterday. What happened to make it fizzle?"

What happened is that Ethan unexpectedly apologized to me, and now we're in some sort of weird relationship limbo, because we're not friends, and we're definitely not lovers. As strange as it is to say, we're not even enemies, so . . . yeah.

Marco sighs and shakes his head. "Okay, then. Let's skip over the sex scene and go straight to the morning after."

The relief on our faces must be extreme, because Marco laughs. "You both look like I just donated bone marrow to save your lives."

Not gonna lie. It feels a bit like that.

Marco talks us through the scene and tells us to go with our instincts. Like most directors, he likes to see what his actors come up with on their own before he starts shaping it. That's all well and good, as long as his leading lady can keep her shit together and not collapse in an emotional heap.

When we take up positions on opposite sides of the bed, Holt says, "This will be easier, right?"

"Sure," I say, with fake confidence. "I wasn't the one who used to freak out after we made love, remember?"

He exhales. "Yeah, well, that was then. I'm fresh out of freak-outs."

We lie down beside each other. He puts his arm around me and draws me in to his bare chest. I can feel his heart pounding under my hand, hard and irregular.

*Out of freak-outs, my ass.*

Despite my assurances, I'm freaking out, too.

Now that I'm here, I realize this position—my hand over his heart, his lips on my hair, our bodies pressed together—is more intimate than any sex scene I've ever done.

Sex is about hormones and body parts.

This is about closeness. Love. Trust.

All the things that scare the living hell out of me.

The first time Ethan and I made love, we held each other like this afterward. I was so happy. So in love with him.

Then everything went to hell.

In this position, with my head against his chest, I can hear Ethan's heart pounding, fast and erratic. Just like it did back then.

A familiar ache starts in my chest and weaves up into my throat. I clench my jaw to stifle a groan, but I don't think it works, because Holt tightens his arm around me and whispers, "Hey . . . what's wrong?"

His hand comes up to my cheek.

I close my eyes and try to push down the panic.

This is ridiculous.

"Cassie? Hey . . ." His voice is all liquid comfort and unspoken affection.

A whole mess of past emotion surfaces and floods my body with too much adrenaline.

I sit up as my head starts to spin.

Within seconds, Holt's arm is around me. "You look like you're going to barf. It's been a while since I've made you physically ill. Good to know I haven't lost my touch."

He waits for my comeback, but I stay silent. I'm in a full-blown panic attack, and it feels like my stomach is trying to crawl up my windpipe and strangle me.

"Cassie?" he says, frowning. "Seriously, are you okay?"

"No." I'm wheezing, and his expression is too concerned. "Stop looking at me like that. You can't."

"I'm sorry," he says, like it's perfectly normal for those words to leave his mouth. Like he says it every day, and I'm used to hearing it.

"Miss Taylor?" Marco says as he comes over to us. "Is everything alright?"

I exhale and try to shove my anxiety back into its box. "I'm sorry, Marco. It's been a long week. Do you think we could leave this scene until Monday?"

Yeah, because by Monday, I'll be able to do all those highly intimate things to Ethan without unraveling, won't I?

Idiot.

"Okay, fine," Marco says. "You're both tired. Let's call it a day."

He heads back to the production desk, and Elissa stares at us for a second before telling the rest of the company we're wrapping for the week.

I feel movement and turn to see Ethan picking up his T-shirt. He pulls it on and swings his legs off the bed before resting his elbows on his knees.

"I remember the first time we had to do a scene like this," he says as he turns to face me. "You were less forgiving of my . . . excitement."

"You were less apologetic about it. In fact, if I remember correctly, you exploited your power over me."

"My power over you?" he says, giving me innocent eyes. "You have no idea what you did to me that day, do you? Jesus, I was in real physical pain."

"You deserved to be."

He nods as he picks up the edge of the sheet nearest him and fiddles with it.

"Listen," he says, and tugs at the seam. "I get that you may never forgive me, but I want to at least try to make things easier for you. Tell me what to say, and I'll say it. Tell me to fuck off, and I'll try to. Just tell me, okay? What do you want me to do?"

I take a deep breath and blow it out slowly. "Well, for a start, let's pretend I didn't just freak out in front of everyone because you hugged me. That's just mortifying."

He smiles. "I'm not going to lie—for once it's nice to not be the one freaking out."

I shake my head. "Yeah, not going to lie—our role reversal sucks giant yak balls."

He stands and offers me his hand. "Still up to going out tonight?"

I'd almost forgotten about our talk-date. "Do we have to?"

"Yeah, we really do."

"Can I at least have lots of alcohol?"

"Sure," he says as he pulls me to my feet. "I'm buying."

"Good. Then I'll order the expensive stuff."

*Six Years Earlier*
*Westchester, New York*
*The Grove*

I arrive at rehearsal and do a few warm-up exercises, intent on chilling out and having a good day.

I'm doing some yoga stretches when Holt walks in. He dumps his bag in a seat in the second row and flops down next to it, before putting his feet up on the chair in front of him and closing his eyes. I can see his lips moving, probably running his lines.

The tension between us has reached awkward levels since the kiss. We show up to rehearsals, say our lines, act like we're in love, kiss passionately. Then, when rehearsal finishes and we have the opportunity to talk? Nothing. We're too weirded out to have a conversation. It's driving me crazy.

It doesn't help that when he kisses me, I get so damned turned on I can barely breathe. I've spent the last three days in a state of totally debilitating arousal, and today we have to block Romeo and Juliet's sex scene.

Frick.

I refuse to be one of those girls who makes a fool out of herself for a man. If Holt's determined to ignore whatever is happening between us, I will, too. I don't need him.

Well, I kind of need him to give me an orgasm, but apart from that, he's just a guy.

A guy with whom I'm going to have to simulate sex for the next seven hours.

Fluff my life.

Erika appears onstage and gestures for us to join her. For the purpose of rehearsal, our "bed" is simply a black rostrum covered in a sheet.

So romantic.

"Okay," Erika says. "The marriage night scene is historically controversial because of its graphic content, so we're going to aim for something realistic but tasteful, okay?"

Holt and I nod, but I'm not sure what she means. I'm not well acquainted with real sex, let alone the fake kind.

"Now, because we're a drama school, we need to be seen as taking certain risks. So for that reason, I'd like to create the illusion of nudity."

I'm pretty sure the look of terror on Holt's face is mirrored on mine.

"Don't panic." Erika laughs. "You won't *be* naked. You'll just look like you are." She reaches into a bag at her feet and pulls out what looks like underwear.

"Miss Taylor, you'll wear this beneath your costume." She holds up a flesh-colored leotard. "And Mr. Holt, you'll wear these." I smirk as she reveals flesh-toned boxer-briefs. "Now, I understand that you may be a little hesitant about this, but believe me, they're quite modest. You'd reveal more of your bodies going to the beach."

"I usually wear board shorts," Holt mumbles.

"I wear jeans and a hoodie."

Erika and Holt turn to me.

"I come from Washington state. Our beaches are freezing."

Erika pulls out a white T-shirt with a pair of white drawstring pants for Holt and an ivory robe for me. "These are your costumes for this scene. I need you to rehearse in them, since removing them is part of the blocking."

Oh, hell. I have to practice undressing Holt? In my current state, this isn't going to end well.

Holt and I take our costumes and undergarments from Erika, then slink away to separate dressing rooms. When we reemerge, I swear we're wearing identical blushes.

He looks good in his costume. Tall and lean. The stark white makes his eyes look even bluer than usual. He goes to shove his hands in his pockets, but the pants don't have any. He sighs in frustration. I stop in front of him, and he eyes the deep vee at the front of my robe before dropping his head and muttering "*Shit*" under his breath.

"Okay, let's do this," Erika says as she claps. "We'll begin by talking through the sequence of events. Miss Taylor, you'll start by sitting on the bed. You're awaiting your new husband, full of anticipation and longing. Mr. Holt, with the help of the nurse, you've managed to sneak into Juliet's room. You'll have a few short hours to consummate your love before you're banished from the city. You both want to savor every inch of skin, memorize every part of each other's body. Any questions?"

I shake my head and squirm as the elastic of my leotard rides up my left butt cheek. Holt shakes his head and cracks his knuckles.

"Start slowly. Take your time exploring each other. Romeo, this is your first time having sex with someone you truly love. It's a profoundly different experience for you. And Juliet, your apprehension about giving yourself to a man for the first time is completely overridden by your desire for your new husband. As the passion builds, your movements can become more frantic. But when you come together, it's a revelation for both of you. I'm not looking for porn here. Just simple, honest, pretend lovemaking. Are we clear?"

"Clear," we say in unison.

My palms are sweaty, and Holt's biting the inside of his cheek. The theater feels very small.

"Right. Take a moment to chat about what you're going to do, then take your positions."

Erika goes down into the auditorium, while Holt and I turn to each other and shuffle nervously.

"So . . ." I say, looking up at him.

He nods and lets out a breath. "Yeah. So . . ."

"We're going to have fake sex."

"Yep."

"You and me."

"Apparently."

"I have to take your clothes off, and . . . well . . . touch you and stuff."

He tries for his nonexistent pockets again before putting his hands on his hips. "Fuck this fucking play."

"Don't worry about it," I say. "I'm sure after a few minutes, we'll be bored out of our minds."

He gives me the world's most skeptical look.

"Are you two ready?" Erika calls.

We stare at each other for a second before Holt stalks off side stage.

*Okay, so we're really doing this. A sex scene between a virgin and the man who hates that he wants her. Should be fun.*

I sit on the edge of the bed and bounce my legs.

"When you're ready," Erika says as she opens her notebook.

I take a few breaths, then Holt walks onstage, bare feet and beautiful face, eyes full of fear, need, and want.

I stand and face him as he approaches, a low flutter starting in my belly. It moves lower as he runs his gaze up and down my body.

*Okay, Cassie, focus. Find your character. Juliet. It's all about Juliet.*

Dear God, Holt looks good in that costume.

Romeo, Romeo, wherefore art thou, Romeo.

He stops in front of me, and it looks like he's just run a mile rather than walked a few steps across the stage. His breathing is fast, and his chest rises and falls as he locks eyes with me.

Lord.

His eyes.

He's completely committed to this scene. No fear or hiding. Just honest, raw passion.

He focuses on me, and I melt. That look is going to be the death of me.

His expression screams that he'd walk over hot coals to have me, and my whole body reacts. A deep ache starts low and grows more intense with each passing second.

He cups my face and gently rubs his thumb over my cheekbone. Every piece of skin under his hand tingles fiercely. My heart races, pounding loud and fast, making me dizzy.

I step toward him. Now our bodies are touching. I mirror his hand and touch his face. He has light stubble on his cheek and chin. I graze my fingers over the sandpapery texture. His lips part, and I run my thumb over them, fascinated by their softness.

Such beautiful lips.

Need to taste them.

I stand on my toes, and place my hand at the back of his neck as I pull him down. He's in the middle of an exhale, but when I press my lips against his, he inhales sharply. He grips the back of my head with one hand and winds the other around my waist.

All of me melts against him. The way we react to each other is elemental. Candle wax and flame. Wherever he touches me, scorching heat flares beneath my skin.

His lips move slowly as he tastes me, filled with restrained passion and breathless anticipation.

"That's good," Erika calls out.

I open my eyes and pull back in surprise.

"Don't," he whispers. "Ignore her."

He kisses me again as he pulls my body flush against his, and Erika no longer exists.

When I inhale, it's like pieces of him make their home inside me. His taste. His smell. Just as debilitating as the rest of him.

I run my hands down his chest, and as I reach his stomach, he pulls back and looks down at me.

I grip the bottom of his T-shirt. It needs to go. I have to see him. He helps me by yanking it over his head and dropping it on the floor.

And there he is.

Shirtless Holt.

I take a deep breath and really look at him. His broad shoulders, smooth and firm. His wide chest peppered lightly with hair. His flat stomach and narrow waist. Muscular but not bulky.

Lean.

Hard.

Sexy.

He watches me assess him, and his breath speeds up.

"Put your hands on me," he orders quietly.

I run my fingertips over the backs of his hands and graze my palms up his forearms, over his triceps, and onto his shoulders. He takes in a shuddering breath and closes his eyes as I trail over his clavicle, his chest, down his ribcage and onto his abs.

I breathe through all the emotions I'm feeling, trying to make sense of why he affects me so powerfully.

I've always found him attractive, but this is more than that. An intense feeling of familiarity washes over me. A whisper of "yes" even as my mind screams "no."

He opens his eyes, and his gaze travels down my chest, then lower, until he reaches the tie around my waist. He frowns when he tugs at the silky fabric to pull it loose. The robe falls open, and I'm incredibly aware that the only thing stopping Holt from seeing me naked is a skimpy leotard that is doing nothing to camouflage my nipples.

He draws in a loud breath and looks into my eyes before he steps forward. He bends down to press warm kisses down to my collarbone, onto my chest, then lower, between my breasts. The thin fabric of the leotard does nothing to insulate me from the effect of his lips on my body. He kisses his way back up, retracing the path he just took until his mouth is against my ear.

"Bored yet?" he whispers.

I run my hands down his chest and graze my fingernails along his abdominals, stopping at the waistband of his pants. I dip my finger under the elastic, and he grips me tighter as I kiss his chest.

"Practically comatose," I whisper into his skin.

Holt makes a groaning sound, and that's when the gloves come off.

He grabs my face and kisses me fiercely. All pretense of being gentle and patient flies out the window as our rapid breathing and low moans fill the quiet space.

"Oh, good," Erika says. "Nice sense of urgency. Keep going."

"As if I'm going to fucking stop," he says against my mouth.

He lifts me, and I wrap my legs around his waist. He grunts and continues to kiss me while he carries me to our makeshift bed. He lays me down and climbs on top of me. I gasp when he settles between my legs.

He's there. Right where all my tension has been building over the past few days. He's hard and hot against me, and nothing he's doing is enough. I want to consume him. Draw him inside until I can't take anymore.

I grab his butt to pull him more firmly against me. He moans and circles his hips, making my fingers curl into his skin as tension builds inside me. I gasp when I feel a warm hand on my right breast.

"Okay, you're walking a fine line now," Erika calls out. "Watch where you put your hands."

"Would it be okay to touch my new husband?" I call to her. "I mean, I've never experienced that part of a man before." Onstage or off.

"Well," she says. "I guess that's true, but it can't be too gratuitous. Touch his thigh and I'll see what it looks like from here."

I reach between us, and in the process, the back of my wrist brushes again Ethan's erection.

He tenses up. "That's not my thigh."

"Sorry. My bad."

He tenses his jaw. "I didn't say it was bad, just not my thigh."

"Okay, that looks good from out here," Erika says. "It's indicative of you touching him without being too obvious. Nice realistic reaction, Mr. Holt."

"Thanks," he says in a strangled voice as I turn my hand around so I can grip him gently.

God, he feels amazing. If he feels this good through clothes, how good would he feel naked in my hand?

I run my palm along the length of him.

"Fuck," he says quietly. "You'd better stop."

"Why?"

"Jesus," he groans. "Please . . ."

He grunts and tries to pull away.

I kiss down his chest as I squeeze him more firmly. He hisses a loud exhale.

"Okay, Miss Taylor, that's enough," Erika calls. "It's looking repetitive now."

"Thank Christ," Holt says as I remove my hand.

I grab the back of his neck and pull him down. We tangle again in a long, deep kiss that makes the hunger inside of me intensify.

I want him inside so much, it's painful.

"At some point you have to take off his pants, Miss Taylor," Erika says. "Otherwise consummating your marriage is going to be very difficult."

Holt looks at me, panic written all over his face.

"She can't see you," I say as I push the pants down over his hips, revealing his flesh-toned trunks. He lifts his pelvis so I can get the pants down to his knees before he kicks them off.

"This is the most fucking embarrassing thing I've ever done," he mutters as he settles back against me.

"Ditto."

"Okay," Erika says. "Now, we need to see the moment of actual consummation. I know this is probably challenging, and I'm sorry. It doesn't have to be over the top, but it has to be there."

Holt lowers his pelvis onto mine, and his face softens.

"Are you ready to lose your virginity?" he asks, and even though I know he's joking, there's something in his tone that makes my stomach tingle.

"Absolutely."

"If this was real, it would hurt."

"I know."

He pulls his hips back and puts his hands between us as if aligning himself with me. His fingers brush against me, and I inhale in surprise.

"Here we go," he says.

He thrusts against me, and I gasp as a look of wonder passes over his face.

Is that what he'd look like if he were inside me? *Sweet Jesus.*

I play my part, wincing in pain as he pushes himself hard against me.

"You okay?" he asks softly, and I don't know who wants to know, him or Romeo.

I give both of them a small smile. "I'm fine."

He smiles back. "Good."

He moves, slowly and carefully. I don't have to act to show both pleasure and pain as he slides against me, because my body is alternating between screaming out for more and moaning that it's all too much. He watches my face, and I'm sure he can feel my desperation.

"Still haven't had an orgasm?" he asks as he kisses down my neck to the faint mark he left at the beginning of the week. He licks it before closing his mouth over it and sucking hard.

"Don't," I say as I wind my fingers in his hair and tug.

He pulls back and looks down at me, his hips circling . . . pressing . . . grinding.

"Don't mark you? Or don't make you come?" He's breathing just as heavily as I am.

I don't answer.

I can't.

I can feel it. The elusive feeling. It's spiraling inside me, spinning and coiling in tighter and tighter circles. I hate that he can make me feel it, and I can't. It's too much power for him to have, and he knows it.

"If you don't want it, just say the word and I'll stop," he says, his voice becoming low and rough.

I don't say anything. I can't speak. I'm clinging to him as he thrusts, and I hold my breath while squeezing my eyes shut and concentrating on the hard, heavy pulses that are threatening to overtake me.

"Tell me you want it," he says, demanding and begging at the same time.

He's moving faster, thrusting in long, firm strokes.

"I want it."

*Oh . . .*

"Say please."

"Please. God."

*Oh . . . oh . . .*

"No, 'Please, Ethan.'"

*Oh, God, yes. Don't stop now. Don't stop.*

"Please, Ethan."

*Please, please, please, Ethan.*

It's close. So very, very close.

"Please." I moan. "Please, Ethan."

He presses down, circling and thrusting and whispering my name. I can't even think, because I'm so full up with chasing down what's just out of reach.

"Let go, Cassie. Let yourself feel it."

He kisses me, and as he thrusts one more time, it happens.

*Oh, dear God!*

I gasp and arch my back as my orgasm hits me, because none of the descriptions of waves or pulses or unwinding jolts of pleasure can prepare me for the absolute knee-buckling sensation that rages through me. My breath catches, and my muscles seize. I'm sure my eyes are as wide as saucers as I experience what has eluded me my entire life.

"God, Cassie," he whispers reverently. "Look at you."

I cling to him as he drops his head into my neck and grunts softly. Then he's moaning as all the muscles in his back tense and he pushes against me one last time.

"Fuck." He makes a long, plaintive noise that's the perfect accompaniment to my own sounds.

Pleasure is thick in my veins as he breathes against me, shallow gasps and long moans.

Oh.

Ohhhh.

That was . . .

Wow.

Reality filters back in as the last shudders fade inside me. Holt and I are panting, sweaty, and spent.

"Okay," Erika says with a slight edge to her voice. "Well, that was certainly a . . . committed performance. But I think we either need to work on the orgasms or fade to black before they happen. They were a little clichéd."

The bed rattles as we both suppress our laughter.

Two hours later, Holt and I emerge from the theater, and I'm laughing like an idiot as he does Romeo's lines in the style of Marlon Brando from *The Godfather*. For once, there's no bickering. Orgasmic rehearsals obviously suit us.

Near the end of the hallway, a group of third-year students are clustered together, practicing in commedia dell'arte masks and cracking each other up. We're almost past them when one of them says, "Well, well, well. Ethan Holt."

The whole group goes silent as Holt and I stop. When a pretty brunette removes her mask and emerges from the group, I don't miss how tense Holt's posture becomes.

She fixes him with an aggressive stare. "You look good, Ethan."

His jaw clenches. "You, too."

"I heard you finally got in. Did Erica make you get a psych evaluation to get over the line? Or did she just get tired of auditioning you year after year?"

He shakes his head and gives her a wry smile. "You'd have to ask her."

"Maybe I will. I heard she'd cast you as Romeo. What a joke. It's like she doesn't know you at all."

He shoves his hands in his pockets. "It wasn't my preference, believe me."

"I bet. First Romeo who's ever been played by a heartless bastard."

Someone murmurs, "Ooh, burn!" and although I expect Holt to fire up and fight back, he just drops his head and sighs.

"Nice to see you again, Olivia," he says before turning to me. "Gotta go, Taylor. See you tomorrow."

He strides away, and the girl directs her attention to me. "So you're his new Juliet, huh? Has he ruined you yet?"

"I . . . ah . . ."

She leans in. "Run while you still can. Trust me on this. You do not want to be around when that boy self-destructs. He'll just take you with him, and the damage he'll do will fuck you up forever. Just ask my therapist. And my sponsor."

The conviction of her tone makes goose bumps break out on my arms.

She and her friends walk away, and I'm left wondering what the hell Ethan did to her to make her so bitter.

# TEN

## CONNECTION

*Present Day*
*New York City*
*Graumann Theater Rehearsal Room*

I pack up my bag as I watch Holt out of the corner of my eye.

He's nervous and keeps glancing over like he thinks I'm going to walk out and leave him behind.

That would be nice, but my brain is telling me we need go somewhere, so he can explain and I can rage. Then maybe we can break each other down and see if our pieces fit together anymore. But my heart is cowering like a dog that's been beaten too many times.

What's been happening between us the last few days scares the hell out of me. The connection I've tried to forget for three years is back, just as strong as it ever was, with barely any effort.

Even now, as I watch him shrug on his jacket and shove his script into his bag, the giant magnetic pull that always drew me to him is there, demanding I move closer.

I hate the familiar compulsion.

"Cassandra?"

I turn to see Marco, script in hand, with his hat perched on his head at what can only be described as a "jaunty angle."

"Is everything okay?" he asks as he throws a glance at Holt, who is now conspicuously hovering on the other side of the room. "You and Ethan seemed out of sorts during the sex scene today. Should I be concerned?"

He's been counting on our natural chemistry to smooth over the divots and potholes of our past. But unless Holt and I unload some of our baggage, the chemistry isn't going to be enough. This whole journey will come to a screeching halt, and our impossible desire for each other will just be a dot in the rearview mirror.

"We're figuring things out," I say with as much sincerity as I can muster. "It's complicated."

He nods and looks at Holt again. "I can see that. But make no mistake, regardless of your issues, my first priority is the play."

"I understand."

"When Mr. Holt begged me for this role, I knew I was taking a risk on your torrid past. However, I trusted that you could put your differences aside for the sake of the show. If that's not the case, tell me now, and I'll have him recast."

My stomach drops. "Wait, what? Holt begged for this show?"

Marco sighs. "Yes. After I'd decided I wanted you, I'd had discussions with another actor. A very talented unknown. But out of the blue, Mr. Holt called me and campaigned for the role. Of course, I knew his horde of rabid fans would practically ensure a box office hit, and physically, he was perfect, but I'd heard rumors about what he did to you and was skeptical it could work. He called me three times a day, every day, for two weeks. He reminded me about my reaction to seeing you both in *Romeo and Juliet* at The Grove. He was quite annoying. But his passion is what finally made me relent. The way he spoke about you . . . I couldn't ignore that."

"I'm sorry, Marco. I had no idea."

"Don't be sorry. Be better. If you can't work with him, tell me. It's still early. I could have him replaced by the end of next week, if that's what you want."

He looks at me expectantly. It's a tempting offer. If Holt wasn't in the show, I wouldn't have to confront all the ghosts from our past. We could go back to our separate lives and never see each other again.

The thought of it makes a lump form in my throat.

"His fans would riot if we replaced him," I say.

Marco shrugs. "Perhaps. But better that than have critics pan us for awkward, mopey lead actors."

"Can I think about it?" I say, and he takes my hand.

"Of course. Personally, I hope you work it out. You're both obviously miserable without each other, and it's depressing to watch. Him, in particular."

He nods toward Holt, who's now pacing slowly, watching his feet in between glancing at us.

"I thought the story was that he broke *your* heart," Marco whispers. "From where I'm standing, it seems the other way around."

I quash the nervous giggle that bubbles in my throat. "I assure you, I was the breakee, not the breaker. I just don't know if . . ."

He raises his eyebrows. "If what?"

I sigh. "If there's too much damage. If we can ever be fixed."

He smiles and leans in to kiss my cheek. "Dear Cassandra, sometimes it's not about trying to fix something that's broken. Sometimes it's about starting again and building something new. Something better." He looks over at Holt, who's stopped pacing and is staring at us. "It seems like the old foundation is still there. Use it."

He leaves and pats Holt on the shoulder as he passes. "I hope to see you on Monday, Mr. Holt."

Ethan frowns before looking back at me. "Ready to go?"

I nod, and we head out.

We walk in silence as we climb the stairs that lead to the foyer. He holds the door for me, and we step out into the street.

"Marco wants to replace me, doesn't he?" he says as warm fingers settle in the small of my back, guiding me closer to him as we cross the street.

"He doesn't want to, but unless we get it together, he will."

As we reach the opposite sidewalk, he stops me. "Is that what you want?"

I rub my eyes so I don't have to look at him. "I don't know. Marco told me you campaigned to be in the show. I thought this whole thing was fate throwing us back together, but it's not. Maybe this play is a bad idea."

For a moment, his composure falters before steely determination slides into place. "I don't want to screw this opportunity for you, Cassie. If you want me to quit, I'll quit. But if you're only doing it to avoid dealing with me, that's not going to work, because I came back to New York for *you*. The show was just a bonus."

"Ethan . . ."

"I know I've been an idiot in the past, but this? Being with you again? It's all I've wanted for so long I can't even comprehend it not working."

"But it's not working. That's the problem."

"It will. I'm going to prove I've changed. Then you're going to fall back in love with me, and we'll get the happy ending we should have had the first time around."

All of the air leaves my lungs. "That's your plan? God, Ethan! What the hell?"

"Don't do that," he says, his expression dead serious. "Don't second-guess us before we've even tried."

"I'm not second-guessing. I'm saying what you're hoping for is *impossible*. Why would you have such unrealistic expectations about us? After all this time?"

He sighs, and when he speaks again, his voice is softer but still firm. "You keep your expectations low if that's what you need to do to protect yourself, but don't tell me to lower mine. It's not going to happen. If they're too high, the only person who's going to get hurt is me."

"Ethan, no . . ."

He takes my hand and brushes his thumb across my skin. Such a sweet, simple gesture, but I feel it everywhere.

"Look, Cassie, I get it," he says. "I understand how you're feeling, because I used to feel it, too. It's easier to expect nothing, because then nothing can be taken away from you. But it doesn't work like that. I tried to convince myself I wanted nothing from you and ended up losing everything."

He looks into my eyes, and I think Marco is right. As much as he broke my heart, I broke his as well.

"I don't want *nothing* anymore. If you kick me from the play, I'll understand, but I'm not going to let you shut me out of your life without a fight. Are we clear?"

I can see why Marco caved. His passion is very persuasive.

He wants to fight for us? That makes a nice change.


*Six Years Earlier*
*Westchester, New York*
*Diary of Cassandra Taylor*

> *Dear Diary,*
>
> *It's the morning after "O" day—a day that will forever linger in my memory with thigh-clenching fondness.*
>
> *I can't even put into words the feelings Holt brought out in me.*
>
> *It can't be natural for one man to be so infuriatingly sexy. Maybe he's made a pact with the devil. See, that I could understand.*
>
> *He's sold his soul to Lucifer in return for sexual powers over frustrated virgins.*

*It would explain a lot.*

*It seems Olivia feels the same. She was pretty pissed with him.*

*I have to wonder about their story. Or perhaps it's best I take the old head-in-the-sand approach to dealing with intense, brooding bad boys. What I don't know can't hurt me, right?*

*Right?*

As I approach the theater, Holt's there, waiting. I cringe when I realize how excited I am to see him.

*Jeez, Cassie. Be cool. Don't let him work his devil powers on you.*

*Oh, God. Too late. Look at him.*

Dark jeans. Black V-neck tee tucked haphazardly into his waistband. Vintage belt buckle I want to unclasp with my teeth.

He looks up as I approach. He has two cardboard cups in his hands. I assume one's for me, although surely he's not offering me a Dickachino today. Not after his expert dry-humpage.

Perhaps Starbucks makes an Orgasmalatte.

As he watches me, he stands a little taller. His chest rises and falls in a deep sigh.

Oh, yeah. He totally wants to orgasm me. He wants to orgasm the hell outta me.

Maybe he'll use his fingers this time.

Please, God, let him use his hot-assed fingers.

I smile at him. He swallows but doesn't smile back.

Alarm bells go off in my head.

"Hey," I say, trying to be casual.

"Hi." He's no better at casual than I am.

He's nervous. Sweating a little. He hands me a cup, and I take it. I suspect it's a Dickachino after all.

He puts his own cup down on the bench beside him and straightens up. His brows furrow as he says, "Listen, Taylor, about yesterday . . ."

*Dammit, Holt. Don't say it.*

"I really shouldn't have done . . . you know . . . *that*. To you."

He's looking anywhere else but at me.

"It was fucking stupid and wrong . . . and . . . I used you."

"No," I say vehemently. "You didn't. I wanted you to—"

"Taylor," he says, "I humped you like a fucking dog. In front of our acting teacher. What the hell is wrong with me?"

"Holt—"

"Olivia is right. I need a psych eval. Whenever I get around you, I lose my head. It's fucking crazy, not to mention completely wrong."

"But, we can just—"

"No, we really can't."

"Stop cutting me off! I'm trying to—"

"I know what you're trying to do, but this isn't up for negotiation! What we're doing stops now, before either one of us gets hurt!"

I want to hit him with a witty comeback, but nothing comes to mind. I consider just hitting him instead.

His expression softens as he steps toward me. "Look, the path we're heading down isn't going to end well for either of us. Trust me on this. I can already feel you want things from me that I can't give you, and if you fall for me? Well, that'd be one of the stupidest fucking things you'd ever do. There's a whole bunch of girls who'll attest to that."

A flash of anger runs up my spine. "God, egotistical much? Maybe I don't want anything from you."

"Then tell me I'm wrong," he says and holds out his hands. "Tell me the look on your face when you saw me a moment ago wasn't excitement with a touch of 'please fuck me now.' Tell me you don't think about me. Dream about me."

I don't say anything, because I can't deny it. But I don't understand why having those feelings is such a bad thing. With the way he's talking, it seems like us becoming closer is tantamount to a crime.

"You want me, too," I say.

"I'm not denying that," he says as he steps closer. "And that's part of the problem. You're enough of a distraction already. If we start giving in to temptation, then . . . Jesus, Taylor, that's all there's going to be for us. Forget about us concentrating on our acting. Your virginity? Gone. My sanity? Gone. Our time here would become a blur of fucking and hormones, and I don't want to get into that with any girl, especially you."

"What the hell does that mean?"

He leans forward, so close I can smell his cologne. "It means fucking won't be enough for you. You'll want emotions and hand-holding and romantic bullshit. And you deserve all that stuff, but that's not me. Not anymore."

"Why not?"

He looks down and doesn't answer.

"God, Holt, some girl really did a number on you, didn't she? Was it that girl from yesterday?"

There's silence, but he gives me a look that warns me to not push it.

"What did she do to you?"

"Nothing. What happened between us was my fault, and I'm not going to make the same mistake twice. I'm sure she told you to stay the fuck away from me. Take her advice."

I feel like he's breaking up with me, even though we've never actually been together.

All of a sudden, I'm really tired. I feel like I'm always fighting to be with him, while he's fighting to push me away.

"Fine," I say. "You're right. I shouldn't have feelings for you. You're obviously not worth it."

I hate that he looks hurt when he says, "Obviously."

Feeling too drained to argue, I walk toward the theater door. Just before I pull it open, I turn back to him.

"Holt, there aren't many people in the world who connect like we do, for whatever reason, and saying that we shouldn't feel it isn't going to make it go away. One day you might figure that out, but by then it'll be too late."

I turn my back on him and close the door behind me.

"Okay, Miss Taylor, let's take it from 'What's here.'"

We're rehearsing the death scene. Holt is lying in front of me, motionless. Romeo has poisoned himself.

Idiot.

As Juliet, I'm distraught, seeing the love of my life dead on the ground. Killed by his own hand because he couldn't go on without me. He didn't know I was just sleeping. You'd think he would have checked for a pulse, right?

I try to pull his body up and hug him, but he's too heavy, so I'm resigned to lying across his chest. Too shocked to cry, too emotional to not. I run my hands over him as if the force of my need will bring him back to life. Save him from himself.

But there's no saving to be done. His rash decision has killed us both, because without him in my world, I'm dead inside, even though I still have the illusion of life.

With the acceptance of death in my heart, I just need to find the means.

I run my hands down his arms and discover him clutching a small vial.

"What's here?" I say, my voice hoarse with emotion. "A cup, closed in my true love's hand?"

Holding it under my nose, I sniff, then groan in anguish. "Poison, I see, hath been his timeless end."

I look inside, needing just a remnant, but it's empty. Furious, I hurl it away.

I grab Romeo's head and scold his still, beautiful face as the tears spill over.

"O churl! Drunk all, and left no friendly drop to help me after?"

His lips are parted, and I lean over and close my streaming eyes as our foreheads touch.

"I will kiss thy lips. Haply some poison yet doth hang on them . . . to make me die . . . with a restorative."

I gently press my lips against his. Still so soft. How can he be dead and still feel so alive?

I suck at them gently, desperate to find any trace of the poison. Holt tenses beneath me.

"Thy lips are warm." I sigh against his mouth.

He tenses even more.

I swipe my tongue along his bottom lip, and he grunts as his body twitches.

"Stop there!" Erika calls out.

Holt sits up and glares at me.

"Well, Juliet," Erika says. "It seems your lips have miraculous healing properties. If only Shakespeare had written Romeo's dramatic recovery in the way Mr. Holt has just improvised, there'd be a whole lot less tragedy at the end of this play and people could go home whistling a happy tune."

"She licked my lips," Holt protests.

"That's totally what Juliet would do," I say. "She's trying to ingest his poison. You're lucky I didn't stick my tongue in your mouth and swirl it around like a toilet brush."

"Oh, because that's what Juliet would do, right? Not you."

"Yes."

"Bullshit."

"Oh, my God would you two just *fuck already*!" Jack Avery calls from the auditorium.

There's a huge laugh from the rest of the cast, and Holt and I exchange embarrassed glances.

If only it were that simple, Jack.

Erika urges the cast to quiet down. "Mr. Holt, what Miss Taylor did seemed perfectly acceptable to me. Perhaps you just need to modify your reaction. You're dead. It shouldn't matter if she licks your entire mouth and starts on your tonsils. You don't move. Understand?"

Holt shakes his head and laughs bitterly before turning to glare at me.

My smile couldn't be smugger if I bought it from Smuggy Mc-Smugster at the Smug Store in Smugville.

He rolls his eyes.

"Now, Miss Taylor," she says, looking at me, "when you grab the knife to stab yourself, I want you to straddle him."

"Oh, for fuck's sake," Holt mutters.

Erika glances at him. "Mr. Holt, when Miss Taylor collapses on you, I don't want you both looking like you've been gunned down in a gang war. You need to die as you've lived—like lovers."

I'm taking in everything she's saying, but my brain is fixated on two words. *Straddle him.*

Legs akimbo. Parts pressed against other parts.

Oh, boy.

Holt is rubbing his face and groaning.

Erika smiles at us. I think she enjoys our mutual discomfort.

"Let's go back to the kiss, and let's see if we can get through to the end, okay? Can I have the rest of the cast involved in the end of this scene in their places side stage please?"

There's a bit of shuffling as people take up their positions. Holt is scowling at me.

I give him my most innocent smile.

He looks at me with an intensity that would be scary if I wasn't enjoying his frustration so much.

"Lie down, lover," I whisper sexily. "I have some straddling to do."

He curses under his breath and lies down.

Methinks the gent doth protest too much.

"Okay, here we go. Thank you, Miss Taylor."

I start the scene again. When I get to the kiss, I purposefully make it as erotic as possible. I can feel Holt breathing heavily as a small sound escapes him.

*Uh uh uh. Play dead please, hot corpse.*

He exhales and stays still.

*Good boy.*

There are voices offstage, and I look toward them. Juliet is running out of time.

"Yea, noise?" I say, panic coloring my voice as I look around in desperation. "Then I'll be brief."

I spot the knife, and after throwing one knee over his middle, I straddle Holt's groin as I grab the prop dagger he has strapped to his hip

"O happy dagger," I say as I pull it from the scabbard and bring it up to my chest, "this is thy sheath."

I push the collapsible blade into the center of my chest and cry out, face contorting in pain. To the audience, it looks like I've just fatally wounded myself.

"There . . . rust." I groan and fling the knife onto the floor as I clutch my chest. I fist Holt's shirt and tenderly kiss my Romeo once more before whispering, "And . . . let me . . . die."

I collapse onto Holt. My face presses into his neck, one hand on his chest, the other in his hair. If someone took a snapshot of us, we'd look like a young couple sleeping in an intimate embrace.

Other characters rush onto the stage and continue the scene, lamenting our deaths and breaking down the series of events that led to them. I can feel Holt tense beneath me, trying to control his breathing. His groin is pressed hard against me, and I feel it getting gradually harder. I try to ignore it. My vagina has other ideas. I try to explain to her she's dead and therefore has no further need for Romeo's impressive erection, but she's finding it difficult to suspend her disbelief.

I slow my breathing and listen to the scene playing out around me. The archaic language and its rhythm has a sedating effect. Soon I'm concentrating on Holt's heartbeat beneath my ear. It's hypnotic, so strong and steady. As my muscles soften and my heart rate slows, my body sinks into him, and I have a brief moment of thinking I must be very heavy, before his smell and warmth lulls me into a half daze.

Before I know what's happening, a hand is shaking my shoulder. I open my eyes to see Jack standing over us with several other cast members behind him.

"Wow. Glad to see you guys so excited by our performances," he says with a smirk. "Maybe next time you could try not to snore."

I sit up quickly and look down at Holt. He's bleary-eyed and confused. His eyes come into focus when he registers me on top of him. I take the hint and climb off, but my muscles are loose and weak.

Jeez, who knew straddling cuts off so much circulation?

Jack grabs me around the waist and helps me upright. There's laughter as my legs give out again, making me stumble against him.

"Whoa! Steady there, Cassie. You've been dead for a while now. You'd better take it easy."

I steady myself as Holt gets to his feet. He glances at Avery's arms around me before looking away.

"Mr. Holt, Miss Taylor," Erika says as she climbs the steps to the stage, "can I assume your final positions were comfortable?"

I step away from Jack and smooth down my hair, trying to distract myself from my rising blush.

"It was okay."

People laugh under their breath. I'm beyond embarrassed. I've kissed Holt in front of these people. Hell, I've had fake sex with him. But what I just did? *Snuggled* him? Melted into him and fallen asleep? That's more intimate than anything else I've done.

We sit on the stage as Erika gives us notes, but generally she seems pleased with our progress. Jack's sitting next to Holt, whispering and snickering. Holt grabs the front of Jack's shirt and hisses something in his face. Jack goes pale and shuts up immediately. When Holt releases him, Jack moves away while muttering under his breath. Holt runs his hand through his hair before glancing over at me.

He looks furious.

When Erika calls an end to rehearsal, conversations fill the air as everyone packs up the stage and props. Miranda and Aiyah invite me to go to dinner with them, but I'm not in the mood. I thank them for the offer and hug them good-bye. The rest of the theater slowly empties as I pick up the dagger and take it over to Holt. He still looks angry as he takes it from me.

"You okay?" I ask as he unclasps the scabbard from his belt.

"Fine."

"What was with you and Avery?" I ask.

"He's an asshole." He shoves the dagger into the scabbard.

"Why?"

"He kept asking if I was fucking you."

"What did you tell him?"

"I didn't answer."

"And?"

"And he assumed I wasn't."

"Which is true."

"Yeah, but then he thought it was okay to tell me how much *he'd* like to fuck you."

"And what did you say to that?" I ask and take a step forward.

His gaze runs the length of my body before he says, "I told him if he went anywhere near you, I'd cut off his balls and feed them to my Rottweiler."

"You have a Rottweiler?"

"No, but he doesn't know that."

I touch his belt buckle. It's a rectangle with what looks like some sort of crucifix. Strange that he'd be wearing God's symbol when he's in league with the devil.

"So, let me get this straight," I say while running my fingers over the cool metal. "You don't want to be with me, but you also don't want other guys to be with me?"

"He's not other guys. He's Avery. If you slept with him, your IQ would automatically drop forty points."

"Have you stopped to analyze why you're so jealous?"

"I'm not jealous. I just don't want that fucking mouth-breather touching you. That's just common sense."

"What about Connor? Am I allowed to sleep with him?"

His expression turns stormy. "Do you *want* to sleep with him?"

I curl my fingers into his T-shirt and resist tearing it off. "If I did, would that be okay with you?"

He looks feral. "Fuck, no. Too vanilla."

"What about Lucas?"

"Too stoned."

"Troy?"

"I think he's gay."

"And if he's not?"

"Too ambiguous."

"And you say you're not jealous."

"I'm not."

"Then give me a name," I say. "*You* tell me who I'm allowed to sleep with."

He throws up his hands. "Why the fuck are you so obsessed with sex?"

"Because I haven't had any! And if it were up to you, I never would!"

He swallows and drops his head. "What the hell do you want from me, Taylor? Huh? Do you want me to fuck you? Or are you just looking for some random cock to pop your cherry? I'll buy you a damn vibrator if that's all you want."

"That's not all I want, and you know it."

"Then we're back to the reason we need to stay away from each other. You want what I'm incapable of giving. Why do you have so much trouble understanding that?"

"What I don't understand is how you can feel *this*," I say as I step into him and put my hands on his chest, "and just pretend it doesn't exist."

He doesn't even blink as I run my hands over his pecs. "Haven't you noticed? I'm really good at pretending."

I shake my head and sigh. "So that's it. You decide we can't be together, and that's just the way it is."

"Pretty much."

"And you think you can abide by your own rules?"

"Do you mean, can I stay away from you?"

He leans down, his lips just above mine, so close I can taste his breath, all warm and sweet.

"Yes," I whisper, wanting nothing more than to rise up on my toes and kiss him.

His exhale is slow and measured. "Taylor, I think you underestimate my level of self-control. Apart from my slip during the sex scene, I've shown the restraint of the fucking Dalai Lama around you. Our first kiss? That was initiated by you. Today in the death scene? All you. Right now? You."

"So your theory is," I say, "that if it wasn't for *me* jumping *you*, then you would have never had laid a finger on me."

"Exactly."

"Bull."

"Please note that your hands are currently all over me, and mine are by my sides."

I look down as I absently stroke his abs. I immediately step back.

*God, he's right.*

It's me.

Everything has been initiated by me.

"Okay, fine," I say, and step back farther. "I won't touch you outside of the show, unless you ask me to."

"Do you think you're capable of controlling yourself?" he asks, and I swear he's putting some sort of sex mojo into his voice that makes me want to lick him. "Should we make it interesting?"

"What, like a bet?"

"Why not?"

I think for a second. "Okay, then. The first one to touch the other in an intimate way loses and has to give the winner an orgasm."

He laughs and runs his hands through his hair, but I don't miss how he rakes his gaze over my body. "That kind of defeats the point of the bet."

"Not in my mind. We'd both end up winners."

He grabs his bag and slings it over his shoulder. "Go home, Taylor. Have a drink. Try to stop thinking about me."

"The bet is about touching. I can think about you in a hundred different sexual positions if I like, and there's nothing you can do to stop me."

He drops his head and sighs, and I know I've won the round.

"See you next week."

"Yes, you will."

Then he's gone.

# ELEVEN

## STAGE FRIGHT

*Present Day*
*New York City*

Holt and I are heading to a wine bar not far from the theater for our "talk."

Walking beside him is both strange and familiar, with just a hint of impending doom—much like most of our time together.

The cautious part of me is whispering that being with him is like wearing the world's most comfortable pair of shoes that sometimes catapult you headfirst into a wall. It's like having an allergy to shellfish and refusing to give up lobster. Like knowing you're about to fall, face-first, into a patch of poison ivy but refusing to halt your steps.

His arm brushes against mine as we walk.

God, how I itch for him.

When we reach the wine bar, he opens the door for me and requests a table in the back. The hostess eye-fucks him within an inch of his life before seating us.

He's oblivious. As usual.

I wish I could say the same. I have no business being jealous. I'm sure in the years we were apart, he's lost count of his conquests. Women have always thrown themselves at him, but his popularity exploded when he was touring Europe. His character spent most of the show shirtless, and when sexy promo shots of him hit the Internet, he had women following him from city to city to see him perform.

I didn't blame them.

I remember how I'd felt when I saw the pictures online. I'd tried to look away, but it was impossible.

Just thinking about it makes my face burn.

I pick up the tapas menu and fan myself. Holt looks at me and frowns.

"You okay?"

"Yep."

"You look flushed."

"Menopause. Hot flashes."

"Aren't you a little young for that?"

"You'd think so, huh? Being a girl sucks."

"Except for that whole thing about having multiple orgasms," he says and raises an eyebrow. "Someone once told me that's pretty incredible."

"Well, yeah." *If you want to break it down into the most provocative terms possible.* "There's that."

*Multiple Ethan,* that should be his nickname. The night he first discovered he could make me do that, I swear, I saw the face of heaven.

I fan myself again.

Dammit, he's not allowed to talk about this stuff. Certainly not when I'm trying to ignore his sex appeal.

All topics related to sex are out.

How does he not know the rules I just made up?

"Why are you scowling at me?" he asks with a frown.

"Why aren't we drinking yet? We came here to drink."

"And talk."

"And drink."

"Does menopause make you an alcoholic, too?"

"Yes. And psychotic. Watch your step."

"Trying to. Not easy with a scowling, menopausal psycho."

I scowl at him for real.

He laughs.

Add laughing to the list of things he's not allowed to do when I'm trying to ignore how attractive he is.

He notices I'm not laughing and looks at me with concern.

Concern? On the list.

"Cassie?"

Also, saying my name.

"I'm fine. I need alcohol."

"Okay. Sure."

He stares at me for a few more seconds, and sure enough, staring goes on the list. I mentally give up and accept that the list is going to be constantly updated. I try to put it from my mind.

At last a waitress arrives. She introduces herself as Sheree, and proceeds to ogle Ethan as he picks up the wine list. I want to punch her in her lip-glossed mouth.

As Sheree rattles off her wine recommendations, Ethan glances up at me. He's not listening to her. He's trying to figure out what I want to drink.

It used to be a game we played, and he never lost. He knew what I wanted even when I didn't. When to order sweet, or dry, or spicy.

When the waitress finishes, he looks back at the list.

"The question is, Sheree . . . does my friend want red or white?"

The waitress frowns. "Uh . . . shouldn't you ask her that?"

"There's no fun in asking. I need to deduce. Like a sommelier Sherlock. If I get it wrong, my perfect record will be tarnished."

"And if you get it right?" Sheree asks with a raise of her eyebrow.

I shake my head. When he used to get it right, I'd reward him with my mouth. No chance of that happening tonight.

"If I get it right," Ethan says, "maybe she'll see that, despite all my screw-ups, I still know her better than anyone else ever will."

He stares at me, and when heat stretches across the table, I have to look away.

Sheree shifts her weight as I pick at the edge of the tablecloth.

If you looked up the word "awkward" in a dictionary, there'd be a picture of this moment.

Before it can go on any longer, Ethan clears his throat and orders the Duckhorn Vineyards Merlot with absolute confidence.

It's the perfect choice. I don't know why I'm so surprised.

When the waitress leaves, he leans back in his chair and laces his fingers together on the table in front of him.

"Nailed it, didn't I?"

I shrug. "Maybe."

He seems pleased. "I wasn't sure if I could still do it. It's been a while."

"Yeah."

He stares for a few seconds, before saying, "Too long, Cassie."

A thick silence settles between us.

We both know this is the last chance for us. Our final opportunity to salvage some good from the train wreck that's been our relationship.

The pressure is stifling. I clear my throat. My mouth is drier than the Sahara.

How long can it possibly take to grab a bottle of wine and two glasses? Is Sheree tramping the damn grapes herself?

Nerves squirm in my belly. I could really use a cigarette, but there's no smoking in here.

Holt cracks his knuckles, and I can see him brewing sentences in his brain.

I gaze at his fingers. His thumbs are slowly rubbing against each other, his hands tense and restless. I want to reach out and still them, and reassure him that . . . what? I'm not going to be a bitch? That I'll listen calmly and carefully, consider all his justifications in a level-headed way?

I can't tell him that. It wouldn't be true.

There's a very good chance this evening could end badly. That, by talking about all of this, all my good intentions of being friends will disappear.

He knows this as well as I do.

After what seems like several lifetimes, Sheree brings our wine. Holt and I look at her with desperate gratitude as she pours. When she leaves, we both drink deeply, then set our glasses down.

He sighs in frustration and rubs a hand across his face. "It wasn't supposed to be this difficult."

"Haven't you met us?" I say. "We don't do easy."

"That's true."

My stomach cramps, and I swig more wine to try to get it to relax.

Holt frowns. "You okay?"

I take another mouthful and nod. "Yep. Great. Nice wine."

I'm not lying about the wine. It's delicious. I am lying about being okay. I've drunk too much, too soon, and as much as I thought I was ready to deal with Ethan, my stomach is telling me I'm really not.

It cramps again, and I wince.

"Cassie?"

I start to sweat because I know what's coming. Saliva floods my mouth as I run for the bathroom.

I make it just in time.


I'm rinsing my mouth when there's a knock at the door.

"Cassie? You okay?"

Pause. "Not really."

"Can I come in?"

"If you have to."

As bathrooms go, this ones pretty classy. Very clean. High-end fittings. Fresh flowers.

He comes in and closes the door as I finish up washing my hands.

"I used to be the one with the barf nerves," he says.

I dry my hands with paper towels, then throw them in the trash. "Now, it's me."

"Feeling better?"

"A bit."

He goes to touch my shoulder, but I instinctively move away. Being comforted by him is not something I can handle right now.

He drops his head and sighs. "When I rehearsed this night in my mind—and let me tell you, I rehearsed it a *lot*—I was a whole lot smoother. There was very little vomiting involved. Now, not only have I made you sick, but I can't remember any of the things I needed to say to you."

I turn to check my reflection. I look like hell. No, not even that good. I look like hell after it's gone through an atomic winter and the zombie apocalypse.

I'm contemplating trying to fix the damage with makeup when Ethan takes a step forward and brushes my hair over my shoulder. It makes goose bumps shiver up my spine.

"Jesus, Cassie," he whispers. "Even when you're sick to your stomach, you're still the most beautiful woman I've ever laid eyes on."

I freeze as he stares at us both in the mirror.

"Ethan, you can't say stuff like that."

"Why not? Look at us. We're perfect together." He grazes his fingers over mine. I close my eyes and inhale. "We always were. No matter how fucked up things got behind the scenes, we always looked like we were made for each other. And we are."

"Ethan . . ."

I turn to face him. He leans forward, but I put my hand on his chest to stop him.

He exhales and clenches his jaw. "Touching me right now is probably not a good idea. Not unless you want to shatter my cool, calm demeanor."

I remove my hand and lean back against the vanity. It does nothing to ease the pull I feel to him. It's filling every corner of this tiny room.

"How is it after all this time, you still affect me like this?" he asks, inching forward.

"Like what?" I know exactly what he means, but I want to hear him say it.

"Nervous and calm at the same time. Crazy and serene. Feral and civilized. Having you near me makes me want to forget about all the crap we've been through and just . . ."

"What?"

His expression turns hungry. "Just bury myself inside you and block out everything. Make our past go away."

If only it were that easy.

"I've missed you so fucking much, Cassie. You have no idea. You really, really don't."

I hesitate. The cautious side of me whispers that I'm about to put on those damn shoes and smash my head into a wall. It warns that I really can't eat lobster. It screams that I'm about to fall into a giant patch of poison ivy.

I consider my impending fall for about three seconds before putting my arms around his neck and pulling him into a hug. He wends his arms around me, and as he pushes his head into my throat, he lets out a shuddering sigh.

True to form, I start to itch.

\* \* \*

*Six Years Earlier*
*Westchester, New York*
*The Diary of Cassandra Taylor*

*Dear Diary,*

*It's opening night, and it's been a week since Holt and I made our bet about keeping our hands off each other. Since then, things have been . . . weird between us.*

*Well, weirder.*

*Our dynamic has been off, even while acting. Because we're both determined to win this ridiculous bet, our kisses have been restrained, our embraces false. A sanitized version of our filthy animal lust.*

*Erika has felt it, too. She thinks she's over-rehearsed us and made us stale. But it's not her fault. It's ours. And apart from jumping Holt's bones, I really don't know how to fix it.*

*Add to that the sick squirming of opening night nerves, and it's fair to say that I'm kind of terrified. (And when I say "kind of" I mean "absolutely." And when I say "absolutely" I mean it will be a miracle if I make it onstage without experiencing an epic freak-out that involves screaming and/or crying and/or clinging desperately to the wing curtains as the stage manager tries to drag me onto the stage.)*

*Please, God, let me get through tonight without making a complete fool of myself. Let me be good.*

*I'm begging you.*

As I walk to the theater, I puff on a cigarette. I'm getting better at smoking. Not sure if this is a good thing, but it takes the edge off my nerves.

The show opens at seven thirty. It's now three o'clock in the afternoon. I'm hoping that being in the theater will help me focus and loosen the tightness in my chest.

That's the plan, anyway.

Things to do over the next few hours: yoga and tai chi, walk around the set, get in Juliet's head, place my opening night cards and presents in the dressing rooms, get dressed, try not to barf, enter stage without being coerced by a cattle prod, be amazing.

Simple.

Things not to do: obsess about Holt, barf, run screaming from the theater.

Not so simple.

When I get inside, I go straight up to my dressing room.

Most of the dressing rooms are behind the stage, but there are half a dozen on the mezzanine level. Erika has assigned them to the lead actors. I'm in a room with Aiyah and Mariska, and Ethan is sharing with Connor and Jack.

I unpack my bag and lay out my makeup and hair accessories. Then I pull on some leggings and my lucky Tinkerbell T-shirt before making my way down to the stage.

It's dark, and the dim glow from the work lights casts long, ominous shadows around the set.

*Great. What I need is even more fear pumping through my body, 'cause really, I'm not wound tight enough.*

I take a deep breath and walk around the set. Run my hands over the Styrofoam stone and canvas wood as I look out into the rows and rows of empty seats. I try to ignore the goose bumps that rise on my arms when I feel the glow of several hundred pairs of phantom eyes.

I want to be great tonight.

I want Holt to be great.

The whole play kind of hinges on us getting our crap together. I have zero idea how to do that.

I stand in the middle of the stage and breathe while going through several of my yoga poses. Stretch my muscles. Focus my mind.

After a while, the yoga morphs into tai chi. I close my eyes to concentrate on my breathing. In. Out. Move slowly. Synchronize air and movement. Exhale the fear. Breathe in confidence.

I concentrate on images that bring me pleasure. Inevitably, my thoughts turn to Holt. The strong line of his jaw peppered with stubble, masculine and sexy. His lips, unbearably silky and soft. His eyes. Fiery. Nervous. Scared and terrifying at the same time.

My whole body heats up as I think of him.

Staying away from him this week has been torture. I try not to look at him too long, even during scenes, or else the ache gets to be too much. I focus on the wall behind him, or a piece of set, or the top of his hair. Anywhere but in those deadly eyes that make me want to do bad, bad things to him for hours on end.

As I push out a final exhale, I feel calm. Focused and ready.

When I open my eyes, I almost pee my pants because Holt's face is mere inches away.

"Jebus freaking shit!" I scream as I flail like a sky-diving octopus.

Holt jumps several feet backward and holds his hand over his heart. "Fuck, Taylor! You scared the crap out of me! Jesus Christ!"

"I scared *you*?!" I walk over and shove him hard in the chest. "You nearly made me urinate!"

That makes him crack up.

"It's not funny!" I say as I slap at his arm.

"Yeah, it is," he says, and backs away as I continue to hit him.

"What sort of freak are you to just sneak up on someone like that?!"

"I didn't want to disturb you," he says while trying to grab my slappy hands. "Fuck, stop hitting me."

He pulls my hands against his chest, but I'm having enough trouble coping with my pounding heart to acknowledge the warm hardness of his pecs under my fingers.

I yank myself free before striding over to the bedroom set and flopping onto the bed.

"What the hell are you doing here? I thought I was alone."

He stands in front of me, his laughter dying as he shoves his hands in his pockets.

"I thought the same thing. I like to be in the theater for a few hours before opening night. Helps my nerves."

I run my hand through my hair. "Yeah? How do you feel now, Señor Scare Tactics? Calm?"

"As hilarious as it was, it wasn't my intention to scare you. I just wanted to . . . watch."

As my shock dissipates, I take a moment to register what he's wearing.

White wife beater, long navy running shorts, and silver and black Nikes.

What the hell?

He's not allowed to wear that.

I mean . . . That's just . . . He's . . .

Dear God, *look at him!*

Broad shoulders. Beautiful arms. Wide chest. Narrow waist. Muscular calves.

Unfair! Obscenely sexy. Not allowed!

"Why are you looking at me like that?" he asks, and shifts his weight.

"Like what?" I manage to ask through my haze of lust.

"Like you want to spank me."

My tongue tries to choke me at this point. I cough and sputter. "Why are you wearing that?"

He glances down at himself and shrugs. "I jogged here. Thought it might help clear my head."

My brain seizes on an image of him jogging—arms pumping, face flushed, long legs striding, hair blowing in the breeze.

"You . . . jogged?"

"Yeah."

"In that?"

He looks at himself again and frowns. "Yes. What's your issue? It's just a tank and a pair of shorts."

"Just a . . . You think that is . . . just a . . . No! Bad Holt!" My brain has stalled.

He looks at me like I'm a crazy person, yet I can't stop staring.

What genius decided to call that particular piece of clothing a "wife beater"? It's not a wife beater. It's a *vagina arouser*. A *drool inducer*. A *panty destroyer*.

Fricking hell.

"Taylor?"

He takes a few steps toward me, and all the lust I've been suppressing floods my body. I jump off the bed and step back.

I will not lose this damn bet just because he decided to dress like a hot-bodied edible man treat. I will freaking *not*.

I need to get very far away until the urge to push him down onto the stage and grope him disappears.

"I have to go . . . do stuff," I say as I stumble offstage.

"Taylor?" he calls after me, but I don't stop. I can't look at those shoulders again. The biceps. The forearms.

*Fricking frick!*

I run up to my dressing room and slam the door before spending the next two hours doing breathing exercises. The whole time I tell myself that begging Holt for sex on our opening night is a *really* bad idea.


At five thirty I start getting ready. I want to get it done quickly so I can put all my opening night cards and gifts in people's dressing rooms before they arrive.

Good luck cards are traditional to give cast and crew on opening night. I'm also giving them little heart-shaped chocolates to represent the love at the heart of our show.

Yeah, it's lame, but I'm poor, and the chocolates were cheap.

I finish my makeup, brush out my hair, secure my lucky silk robe, and grab the bag that contains all my goodies. I move through the dressing rooms quickly, all the while pondering that I haven't finished writing on Holt's card yet. All I have so far is 'Dear Ethan.' After that, I'm at a loss for what to say.

"Good luck on opening night," seems lame and impersonal, and "Please have sex with me" just seems wrong. I need to aim somewhere in between, but that's easier said than done.

I've delivered most of the cards when I pass his dressing room. I poke my head inside. The room's empty.

Working quickly, I sneak in and put Connor's and Jack's cards in their spots, telling myself I'll finish Holt's and give it to him later.

As I turn to leave, he appears in the doorway, his face in shadow from the dark hall.

"What, no card for me?" he asks, and something about his voice is wrong.

"Uh . . . there will be. I just haven't finished writing your message yet."

I go toward the door, but he steps inside, cutting me off. He's still wearing the *panty destroyer.* His shoulders look amazing. I want to bite them.

"You've written messages to everyone else, Taylor, why not me? Am I not good enough for a card from you?"

His face is dark and a little sweaty.

"Holt? Are you okay?"

"Nice robe," he says as he stares at my breasts. He touches the tie around my waist. "Wearing anything underneath?"

"Just my delightfully fashionable nudie-tard," I say, as I pull his hand away. "No peeking. You've seen it before."

"Too many times."

"It's not that bad, is it?"

He grabs the tie again. "Not if you expect me to continue ignoring you and your fucking ridiculous body." He runs the silky fabric through his fingers. "I've been trying so hard. To be good and respectful. It'd be so easy not to be."

The energy that's been missing between us for a week is back, thick and heavy. Desperately magnetic.

My breath catches. "You're the one who set limits. I want you to do exactly what you want to do to me."

He exhales as he wraps the silky tie around his hand and steps forward.

"You're not allowed to say stuff like that."

His voice is strained. His hands tremble. The small amount of sweat on his forehead is still there, but it's now shimmering on his neck and shoulders, too.

"Seriously, are you okay?" I ask as he swallows and winces.

The words are barely out of my mouth before he clutches his stomach. He staggers back and flops onto the sofa.

"Fuck."

"Holt?"

After a few deep breaths, he leans his head back and closes his eyes. "It's just nerves, okay? Really fucking bad nerves."

"About the show?"

"Among other things, yeah."

He exhales a long, controlled breath. "My anxiety goes straight to my stomach. I get cramps and nausea. Such a pussy."

"You're not a pussy," I say. "I understand how you feel."

He rubs his face. "Unless you have a father who's only coming to your performance so he can tell you that you're wasting your life with this acting bullshit, then no . . . you don't."

"Your dad isn't happy with your career choice?"

"That would be a massive understatement."

"Ah."

He drops his head into his hands and tugs at his hair. "It doesn't matter. I'm going to suck tonight, anyway. He'll have a ball saying 'I told you so.'"

"You're not going to suck," I say.

"We've been fucking terrible all week. You know it as well as I do."

"Not terrible, just . . . kind of off." He shoots me a look. "Okay, we've been atrocious. But it's because we're trying so damn hard to deny our attraction that our performances are suffering. We can't shut ourselves down and expect our characters to look like they can't live without each other. It's impossible."

"So what are you suggesting?" he asks. "That I throw you down on this revolting couch so we can believably play lovers?"

"Well, that'd be nice—"

"Taylor . . ."

"Okay, fine. We don't give into our urges offstage. But onstage? We need to let our connection happen. No more fighting it. Because when we open up and let each other in, that's when the magic happens."

He looks skeptical. "Just onstage? You think it's going to be easy to turn it on and off?"

"No, I don't," I say as I kneel in front of him so our faces are aligned. "But we have a cast full of people depending on us to get our crap together and make this show work. If we go down in flames, we drag all of them with us. So let's just get it done, and you can go back to denying your feelings for me next week, okay?"

For a moment I think he's going to touch my face. Instead, he runs his fingers down the front of my robe. My breath catches.

"Okay. You win. If I can stop feeling like I want to hurl every five seconds, I'll turn myself on for you."

The tone of his voice makes the hair on my arms stand on end.

"I have some focusing methods that might help," I say as he continues to stroke my robe.

"I have to shower and get ready first."

"No problem," I say as I stand. "I'll come back at the half-hour call. When we're through, we'll be so damned focused we'll nail these characters to the wall."

He sighs and shakes his head.

"What?" I ask.

"Nothing."

"Tell me."

"I now have a mental image of me nailing you to the wall. You'd better leave."

I start to laugh, but the animal hunger in his eyes tells me he's absolutely serious.

He stands, and my heart races.

*God. He's going to do it. He's going to nail me against the wall.*

I hold my breath as he moves forward.

To my dismay, he steps around me and grabs the towel off the back of his chair before heading toward the bathroom.

"Get out of here, Taylor," he says over his shoulder, "before I forget why I let you keep that damn robe on."


By six fifteen, the theater is buzzing. There are good-luck cards and presents strewn all over my dressing room. My parents sent a huge bouquet of flowers with a card telling me how proud they are and how they wish they could be here.

I wish they were here, too. My first big role, and no one I love is here to see it.

I head down to the stage to do a final check of my props. Everyone I come across wishes me luck, and we hug, but I'm not convincing. I feel nauseated, and my nerves are growing steadily worse as showtime approaches.

By the time I make it back up to Holt's dressing room, I feel like the chicken sandwich I had for dinner is staging a *Mutiny on the Bounty*–style revolt.

I take a deep breath and knock on the door. Jack yells at me to come in.

"Hey," I say, lingering in the doorway.

"Hey, sweet Juliet," Jack says as he finishes swiping some powder over his face. "Loverboy's in the bathroom."

"Still?"

I hear some muffled retching noises.

Jack cringes. "Yeah." He gets up and hugs me. "Have fun kissing him tonight."

He gives me a sympathetic squeeze before closing the door behind him.

I go to the bathroom door and knock.

"Go away."

"It's me," I say into the wood. "Can I come in?"

"No," he says, his voice cracking. "I'm fucking disgusting."

"Yeah, well, I'm used to that."

I push open the door and step into the bathroom. The air is filled with the acrid smell of bile. It almost makes me gag. Then I see Holt slumped against the wall, his face pale and slick with sweat.

"Oh, hell, are you all right?" I crouch in front of him. "You look like crap."

As a sad testament to my self-esteem, I still find him incredibly attractive.

"I thought you were supposed to be making me feel better," he says as he pulls his legs up to his chest. "If you're just going to insult me, I can be miserable and disgusting all by myself."

"I'm going to help," I say. "But you'd better do as you're told. No questions asked."

"Sure, whatever. Just make it stop."

He's already in his costume. White button-down shirt with the sleeves rolled up. The top few buttons are open, revealing a distracting amount of chest. On the bottom half he wears black jeans and boots.

I grab his left foot and start untying his laces.

He tenses. "What the hell?"

"No questions, remember?"

"Okay, but that rule starts after you tell me what you're doing."

"I need to get your shoe off."

"Why?"

"That's another question."

"Taylor . . ."

"Because I need to massage your foot."

He snaps his leg back and shakes his head."Nuh-uh. That's a deal breaker. My feet are gross."

"I'm sure I can handle it."

"Yeah, well, I can't."

"Holt." I sigh in exasperation. "Do you want to go out there and kick ass tonight, or do you want to suck like a Hoover and give your dad ammunition to say you're wasting your life?"

His face drops.

I feel bad for not playing fair, but what the heck? He needs to suck it up.

He grunts in frustration and thrusts his foot at me. I quickly finish unlacing his boot and pull it off, along with his sock.

For a few seconds, I just stare.

His foot is beautiful. Perfect. He could be a goddamn foot model.

I glance up at him and he shrugs. "They're ugly. Too long. Bony toes."

"You're insane."

I pull his model foot into my lap, and he flinches.

"Trust me, okay? My mother is an expert on every form of alternative therapy around, and while I think most of them are bogus, reflexology is something that's always worked for me. I'd learned all the pressure points by the time I was twelve, so chill. I won't hurt you. Much."

He flinches as I dig my thumbs into the spot where the ball of his foot ends and the arch begins.

"Painful?" I ask. If an organ is inflamed, the pressure point can be tender. Just ask my uterus pressure point around the time of my period.

"No," he says. "I'm . . . uh . . ."

"What?"

He sighs and levels me with a glare. "Don't you dare give me shit about this, but I'm really fucking ticklish, okay?"

I suppress my laughter. "Ticklish?"

"Yes."

"You?"

"Yes."

"Big bad you with the fuck-off attitude?"

He glares at me. "Fuck off."

"See?"

He exhales and grabs his stomach. "Just get on with it."

I smile and massage him again. One part of my brain registers that him being ticklish is adorable, while the other part focuses on getting him in a fit state to walk onstage in half an hour.

After a few minutes, his breathing slows.

"Is it making a difference?" I ask as I massage all over his arch, hitting points for his intestines, colon, and pancreas.

"Yeah." He sighs. "The cramps are letting up a little."

I keep circling my thumbs, and his foot gets heavier as he relaxes.

It's a big foot. My brain dredges up a piece of trivia I once heard about foot size being related to penis size.

I try to concentrate on what I'm doing. Thinking about his penis right now could end in disaster.

I continue for a few more minutes until his pinched expression releases. Then I pull his sock and boot back on and watch as he laces it up.

"Thanks," he says, and gives me a grateful smile. "I feel better."

"Feel well enough to get out of this stinky bathroom?"

"Yeah." He stands and heads over to the sink where there's a tooth-brush, some toothpaste, and a bottle of mouthwash. "Uh . . . just give me a minute, okay? Don't want you kissing someone who tastes like regurgitated turkey sub."

I quickly wash my hands before he shoos me away. Back in the dressing room, I slump into the couch while I listen to the most thorough mouth cleansing since the toothbrush was invented. He finishes with a world-record-length throat gargle. I shake my head as I realize that even gargling sounds sexy coming from him.

I'm clearly disturbed.

At last he emerges, smelling minty fresh. I motion for him to sit cross-legged on the floor.

Helping him has calmed me a little, but I'm still not feeling confident I can pull off a good performance tonight.

As if sensing my anxiety, Holt gestures to my feet. "Uh . . . do you want me to . . . you know . . . do you, or something?"

He looks so uncomfortable with the idea, I almost say yes just to torture him.

"I'll pass," I say. "We don't have a lot of time. Let's just get focused so we can go out there and rock this show."

He nods and looks grateful.

I tell him to close his eyes and focus on an image he finds calming. I try to picture a plain white sheet blowing in the breeze. It's something Meryl Streep uses to calm herself. It usually works well for me, but not tonight.

I'm too aware of Holt sitting close to me. His scent and energy make my body thrum and pound, ruining any chance of finding my happy place.

I don't think he's faring much better, because his breathing is choppy and uneven. He grunts in frustration before saying, "This isn't working."

I open my eyes.

He's staring at me. "You're too close and too far away."

Just then, the intercom above the door crackles to life and the stage manager says, *"Ladies and gentlemen of the* Romeo and Juliet *Company, this is your fifteen-minute call. Fifteen minutes until places. Thank you."*

I'm certain my face is the definition of panic.

I'm not ready. Not even close. I'm unfocused. Characterless.

Where the hell is Juliet? I can't find her.

I scramble to my feet and pace. "We should have started earlier. We've been here all afternoon, for God's sake!"

"Taylor, calm down. We can do this." His voice is remarkably peaceful.

"No, we can't," I say as I shake out my hands and roll my head. "There's not enough time."

"Just breathe."

I walk over to the door and press my forehead against it as I drag in uneven breaths.

I can picture the audience, filing into their seats, flicking through their programs. Full of excitement and anticipation for a performance that isn't going to suck. They're going to be disappointed.

"I have to go," I say as I grip the door handle.

"Where?"

"Away. I need to do . . . yoga . . . or something."

I turn the handle.

He covers my hand. "Taylor, stop."

I pull the door open, but he slams it shut.

"Holt! Open the door!"

"No. Calm down. You're freaking out."

"Of course I'm freaking out!" I say as I turn to face him. "The show's starting in less than fifteen minutes, and I have no idea what the hell I'm doing!"

"Taylor—"

His hands are on my shoulders. I ignore them.

"It's my first big role. Erika said directors and producers from Broadway are going to be in the audience."

"Stop—" He frames my face with his hands. I ignore him.

"There are reviewers out there, for frick's sake! They're going to say I killed the show. Me. Killed it dead."

"Cassie—" He strokes my cheeks. I ignore it.

"They're going to print stuff about how terrible I am, then the whole world is going to see how much of a fraud I—"

Then he's kissing me.

I can't ignore that.

He pushes his weight against me and groans as he sucks gently at my lips. I draw in a noisy lungful of air as my whole body blazes to life.

I hear myself moan, then I'm kissing him back, frantic and desperate, trying to find solace in his delicious mouth.

He freezes before pulling back and staring at me in shock.

"Oh . . . dammit."

We're both breathing heavily, staring at each other.

"You kissed me."

"I didn't mean to. You were freaking out. I wanted to make you stop."

"By putting your tongue in my mouth?"

"I didn't use tongue."

"I'm still freaking out a bit. Maybe some tongue is warranted."

He sighs and looks down. His hands are still on my face, his body still pressed against me. "Jesus. I just lost our bet."

"Yes, you did."

"Fuck."

"If you insist."

He pushes away and runs his hand through his hair.

*"Ladies and gentlemen, this is your ten-minute call. Ten minutes, thank you."*

Panic grips us again.

We have to do something. Now.

"I have a crazy idea," he says.

"Does it involve your tongue?"

"No."

"Damn."

He grabs my arm. "Come here," he says and pulls me over to the couch.

He sits and tugs me toward him. I understand what he's trying to do and place my knees on either side of his hips. I sink into him and mimic our position in the death scene. As our bodies connect, we both expel groaning sighs.

I bury my face in his neck and just breathe, and all of a sudden, every ounce of panic melts away.

He makes a noise and tightens his arms around me.

"Best focusing exercise ever," I murmur into his skin.

I push my fingers into his hair and massage his scalp. He moans and slumps down as his hips push into me.

"Fuck, yes."

The churning in my stomach eases, replaced by tingling expectation.

He squeezes me tighter, and I marvel over how well we fit. He knows how to hold me, and I know how to soothe him. It's instinctual. Our bodies talk to each other without us having to say a word.

It makes no sense for us to not be together. I wish I knew what keeps holding him back.

"Are you ever going to tell me about your ex?" I ask.

"Which one?"

"Any of them."

"Wasn't planning on it."

"So you're just not going to date ever again?"

"That's the plan."

"It's a dumb plan."

His arms tighten around me. "Better that than to inflict myself on someone again."

"Nay, gentle Romeo," I say, borrowing Mercutio's lines, "we must have you dance."

He strokes my back. "Not I. Believe me, you have dancing shoes with nimble soles. I have a soul of lead so stakes me to the ground I cannot move."

The intercom crackles again. *"Ladies and gentlemen, this is your five-minute call. Five minutes, thank you."*

We stay wrapped around each other for as long as we can, exchanging energy. By the time the next call comes, I feel like I'm a part of him.

I'm eerily calm.

*"Ladies and gentlemen of the* Romeo and Juliet *Company, this is your call to the stage. Please take your places for Act One. Thank you."*

We silently unfold ourselves and stand. He takes my hand before opening the dressing room door and leading me downstairs.

Backstage, everyone is in their positions. Tension and expectation are thick in the air. A few people look at us as we pass, and they raise their eyebrows when they see Holt holding my hand.

I don't care. I feel like an electrical transformer, buzzing with energy. I glance at Holt, and his face is calm but intense. He has the air of a superhero, all restrained strength and disguised power. Where his fingers are wrapped around mine, there's a thrumming of energy, and I know we're ready. Our characters are just lingering beneath the surface, waiting to inhabit us as soon as we walk onstage.

Then the lights change, and everything goes quiet as we hear the opening lines of the prologue.

*"Two households, both alike in dignity, in fair Verona, where we lay*

*our scene. From ancient grudge break to new mutiny, where civil blood makes civil hands unclean. From forth the fatal loins of these two foes, a pair of star-cross'd lovers take their life."*

As I exhale with excitement, Holt pulls me into a dark corner behind a curtain and turns to me, every inch my Romeo.

"Ready?" he asks quietly.

"I'm amazing," I say with absolute confidence.

I hear the sounds of the Montague and Capulet boys fighting, and I know it's almost time for his entrance.

He stares at me, eyes glittering from the stage lights. "Me too. Let's show them a Romeo and Juliet they'll never forget."

All I can do is nod, because he's the most beautiful thing I've ever seen.

He leaves me to take his place on the brightly lit stage, and just like that, the make-believe is real.

# TWELVE

## NEW ROLES

*Present Day*
*New York City*

By the time Holt and I return to our table after our bathroom encounter, there's a jazz combo playing in the corner. The plaintive sound of the sax wafts over to us as the smoky-voiced singer launches into the first verse of "Nature Boy."

*"There was a boy . . . a very strange, enchanted boy . . ."*

I tune her out.

Don't really need to add any more emotional layers to my night.

Holt's looking at me, and by the prickle of nervousness that runs up my spine, I know he's about to say something that's going to make me uncomfortable.

"Dance with me," he says quietly.

It's not a question.

"Uh . . . why?"

He smiles and glances over at the few couples on the dance floor before looking back at me

"Because I have things I need to say to you, but I don't want us separated by this damn table." He takes a sip of wine and looks at his fingers. "I want to be close to you."

Just the thought of it makes me angry. Not because I don't want to dance with him, but because I want it so badly it hurts.

I take a swig of wine. A big one. It's pointless. There's not enough wine in the world for this.

I watch in slow-motion horror as he stands and walks around to my side of the table.

"I don't think we should," I say.

He holds out his hand. "Please, Cassie."

I look at his hand. His perfect, warm, Ethan hand. Then I look at his face. There's such fragile hope in his eyes, I find it impossible to say no.

I press my palm against his, and our fingers curl around one another. They fit back together more perfectly than they have any right to.

He leads me to the dance floor and pulls me into his arms. I sigh without meaning to.

"Do you remember the first time we danced together?" he asks, his mouth near my ear.

"No," I say, because I want to hear his version of events.

"It was the night we shot that commercial for the supper club on West 46th Street, remember? You, me, Lucas, and Zoe were cast. We were all supposed to be young, hip, and in love."

"Yeah, but I was partnered with Lucas, and you were with Slut Barbie. She was all over you like a rash."

"You were jealous as hell."

"Says the man who spent the night acting like he wanted to tear Lucas's arms off."

"He touched your ass."

"He was your friend."

His gaze drops to our clasped hands. "I used to think that anyone who touched you like that wasn't my friend."

"You tried to punch him out."

He pauses for a few seconds before saying, "I'm not proud of how I acted that night. It made me realize you deserved so much better than an insecure, jealous asshole."

I remember his jealousy well. At first I thought his possessiveness was sexy. By the end, it was just one more nail in our coffin.

"That night," he says. "I wanted so much to be different. More than anything, *I* wanted to be different. But I wasn't."

He twirls me around and pulls me back, arm strong around my waist.

"So you destroyed us."

He tightens his arm around my waist. "I thought I was cutting the cancer that was me out of your life."

"I never saw you like that."

"I know, and that was the problem. You couldn't see the damage I was doing even while it was happening."

We dance for a while, lost in our own thoughts.

After a few minutes, he pulls back and looks down at me. "You know, when I begged Marco for this show, I hadn't even read the script. I didn't care what the role was, as long as it was you and me onstage together. Then I saw you for the first time in too many years, and . . . our whole past came rushing back. How it felt to be near you. How you could drive me insane with a single look. I was hoping that when you saw me, you'd remember we had good times, too. That you'd missed me as much as I'd missed you. But you were so angry—"

"I had reason to be."

"I know," he says, still swaying with me even though the music has stopped. "I expected it."

"And deserved it."

"But when we rehearsed the kiss, I—"

He stops and brushes my hair away from my neck, grazing my skin. "I guess there was part of me that hoped kissing you would wash away all the bullshit I'd put you through. That I could tell you without words how I felt, and you'd just magically forgive me."

"It's not that easy." I fist my hands in his shirt, because I want to push him away and hold him closer at the same time.

"I realize that. But you know what kills me?" Frustration is sharp in his voice. "What slays me every day I come to rehearsals? Is that I can be there, in bed with you, kissing you and pretending to make love and . . . I still miss you. Because it isn't real. And I want it to be. So fucking badly."

I try to swallow and can't. I want to look away, but it's impossible.

A kaleidoscope of regret fills his eyes. "Cassie, I felt like a ghost while I was away from you. Now, I want to feel real again."

He searches my face, but I can't look at him anymore. All the fault lines inside me are flaring to life.

My throat is too full of emotion to speak. He nods in understanding before pulling me back into his arms.

We start to sway again. We're not actually dancing, just rocking side to side. Not moving forward or backward. Just moving.

Like most of our time together, we're treading water.

Trying not to drown.


*Six Years Earlier*
*Westchester, New York*
*The Grove*
*Opening Night*—**Romeo and Juliet**

There are times in every actor's life when the enormous mess of possibility and make-believe is distilled into a crystal-clear point of clarity.

When the line between imagination and invention blurs, and talent and conviction converge for a brief, shining moment.

Tonight is one of those nights.

The moment I stepped onstage, my transformation was complete. Juliet inhabited me completely.

Now, I'm living her reality, and as the play wears on, my voice says her words, my body feels her emotions, and my brain struggles to understand that the man I'm looking at is real, perfect, and mine.

He's under my balcony, drawn here by his need to be with me. I'm embarrassed he's just overheard me lamenting about how much I love him, but I wouldn't have him unhear it for all the world.

He climbs the trellis, his face dark and determined.

"How camest thou hither?" I whisper down at him. He's being so reckless. "Tell me, and wherefore? The orchard walls are high and hard to climb, and the place death, considering who thou art. If any of my kinsmen find thee here—"

He jumps onto the balcony with a thump and smiles while I look around nervously.

"With love's light wings did I o'er-perch these walls," he says as he walks forward. "For stony limits cannot hold love out, and what love can do that dares love attempt. Therefore thy kinsmen are no let to me."

He touches my face, then leans forward to brush his lips against mine. Featherlight but heavy with desire.

"If they do see thee," I say, breathless against his mouth, "they will murder thee."

"Alack," he says as he runs his thumb across my cheek, "there lies more peril in thine eye than twenty of their swords. Look thou but sweet, and I am proof against their enmity."

There's a drunken roar from inside my house and I push him back against the wall, into the shadows.

"I would not for the world they saw thee here," I whisper. My hands are on his chest, caressing him. He's watching them in awe.

"I have night's cloak to hide me from their sight," he says as he places his hand over mine and presses it more firmly over his heart. "And but thou love me, let them find me here. My life were better ended by their hate, than death prorogued, wanting of thy love."

He's looking at me, torn and passionate, and I don't know how I thought I was truly alive before I met him.

This is what love feels like. To no longer belong to yourself. To be pulled from what you know into what you feel.

No wonder people live and die for this feeling.

Time passes in a blur, and over the course of the next couple of hours, my world is altered. Completely upended. Everything I've known is now rewritten by my need for him.

We ignore everything and everyone to be together, and just when I think we've outwitted our disapproving parents and friends, I wake up to find him gone.

Dead.

Just as quickly as he gave my life new meaning, my life without him instantly amounts to nothing.

So I choose to die. To swallow down my hurt like poison, take his dagger, and join him.

It's only as I sink down onto his still-warm body that I feel the peace being a part of him brings. I close my eyes and inhale. His scent is the last thing that registers as I become still and silent.

I float in semi-consciousness, but a huge percussive cacophony makes me stir. For a moment I'm confused.

I open my eyes and see Holt's neck, his pulse beating strong and fast. The roar of the crowd bombards me, and it's then I know for sure we've been amazing.

I feel amazing.

Bulletproof.

High as a kite and dizzy from it all.

The curtain falls. Holt folds his arms around me and sits up while urging me to my feet.

"Come on," he whispers as he drags me offstage. "Bows."

He holds my hand in the wings. My heart pounds fast and loud as our castmates file onstage to take their applause. The audience whoops and whistles. When the main characters appear, they get louder and more appreciative.

Holt and I walk out together. My feet move confidently, even though the enormous cheer that greets us is completely surreal. I present Holt, and he bows, beaming. I'm so proud of him, I feel like crying.

Then it's my turn to bow. My body is tingling all over, electrified by the adrenaline of my performance and being with him. The audience screams their approval, and I'm so full of happiness, I feel like my skin is going to burst right off my body.

Holt takes my hand, and as we bow together, the audience explodes out of their seats. Their cheering and whistling is almost deafening.

I look at Holt in disbelief. He smiles, radiant and stunning.

The applause seems to go on forever, but eventually the stage manager lowers the curtain, and the entire cast gives a huge cheer of self-congratulation. Everything's a blur of embraces, kisses, and excited chatter, and I don't want this feeling to ever end.

I turn around and see Holt, happy and laughing. He's hugging guys, kissing girls, and slapping people on the back. So normal and unguarded.

A warmth blooms in my chest as I watch him, then he turns to face me. Without a moment's hesitation, he strides over and wraps his arms around me.

"You were fucking astonishing out there tonight," he whispers against my ear. "Astonishing."

I wind my arms around his neck. "So were you. Just incredible."

We pull back to look at each other, and it's like everything around us fades to black. It's just his face, his eyes, the feel of our bodies pressed together, the magnetic pull of his lips, so close.

"Hey, guys! You were average tonight. Must suck to be so talentless. Coming to the party?"

We both receive claps to our backs and turn to see Jack's smiling face. Holt scowls at him, and Jack's smile only grows wider.

"We'll be there," I say.

"You driving?" Jack asks Holt. "Or do you want to ride with me and Connor?"

Holt looks at me. "Uh . . . Taylor, do you need a ride? I don't have my car."

"Because you jogged in today."

"Yeah."

"I remember." The image of him in his jogging outfit is burned into a very horny part of my brain. "No problem. I told Ruby I'd go with her and your sister."

"Great!" Jack says and claps us on the shoulders again. "We're going to have a blast. Woohoo!"

Jack heads off to harass other partygoers.

"Miss Taylor! Mr. Holt!"

I turn to see Erika walking toward us, accompanied by a man I've never seen before. He's wearing a dark red velour jacket and a purple cravat. He could have stepped right off the set of *Pygmalion*.

"Cassie, Ethan," Erika says as she stops in front of us. "I'd like you to meet Marco Fiori. Marco's a very dear friend of mine and one of Broadway's finest directors. His recent production of *Death of a Salesman* just won the Outer Critic's Circle Award for Best Revival."

The man holds his hand out to me, and I shake it with trembling fingers.

A real Broadway director. This is surreal.

"Pleased to meet you, Miss Taylor," he says warmly as he covers my hand in both of his. "That performance tonight was . . . well, let me say that if I need a Juliet in the near future, I know who I'll be calling. You were remarkable, my dear. Truly."

A blast of heat hits my cheeks, and I don't think my smile could be wider without surgical assistance.

"Thank you so much, Mr. Fiori," I say, trying to talk around the huge lump in my throat. "I'm . . . wow . . . I'm honored."

"And Mr. Holt," he says as he releases my hand and turns to Ethan. "You've managed to do the impossible. To portray a Romeo I didn't want to beat with my umbrella. Bravo. You're a very talented young man."

Apparently Holt isn't above blushing, either, because the tops of his ears go bright red as he shakes the older man's hand.

"Uh . . . thanks," he says with a self-conscious smile. "I'm glad you don't want to beat me. Now if you could only convince Taylor not to, that'd be great."

Marco turns to me and raises his eyebrows. "You beat your leading man, Miss Taylor?"

I shrug. "Only when he deserves it."

Marco laughs and claps. "Oh, you two have some interesting chemistry, don't you? Directing them must have been delightful, Erika."

Erika shakes her head and smiles. "That's one word for it. The experience was certainly never boring. Still, the results speak for themselves."

Erika smiles at us proudly. I feel like my chest is going to explode from happiness.

Marco points to Holt and me. "Yes, I have to say, you two onstage together is a rare and special phenomenon. Quite remarkable. I haven't witnessed chemistry this powerful since I saw Liza Minnelli cradling a triple Scotch at the opening night of *The Boy from Oz*. I predict big futures for the both of you. Especially if you continue working together. I'd certainly love to direct you one day."

Holt and I glance at each other. I can't believe what I'm hearing. Judging from his expression, neither can he.

"Well, you two had better go get changed," Erika says as she takes Marco's arm. "I believe you have a party to attend, and you've certainly earned a night of celebration."

Holt and I say our good-byes before we head toward our dressing rooms. He walks beside me on the stairs and grazes his hand down the small of my back. We're silent, but I can tell his head is reeling just as much as mine.

"That was a Broadway director," he says in awe.

"Yep."

"He complimented our performances."

"Yes, he did."

"He actually implied he'd hire us. You and me. For a Broadway show."

"So I didn't just imagine that part, then?"

"No."

"Wow."

"Yeah. Wow."

When we reach his dressing room, he takes my hand and pulls me inside. The room's empty, and he shuts the door behind us. He turns to face me, his expression intense as he moves forward, urging me back against the door.

"I'm sorry," he says as he leans down, "but what just happened has officially blown my mind. I need to do this."

He presses against me and kisses me. It's long, slow, and deep, and although I've kissed him a lot onstage tonight, this is different. We may be still wearing our costumes, but this has nothing to do with our characters.

When he pulls back, his breathing is fast, his face flushed, and his eyes are bright with lust.

"Come and meet my parents."

I can't believe what I'm hearing.

"Uh . . . okay."

"I feel like you're my good luck charm tonight. Maybe being with you will make talking to my old man bearable."

I smile. "I don't mean to freak you out, but you just said something nice to me. On purpose."

"Yeah, I did," he says and screws up his face. "It felt weird."

"It sounded weird."

"But nice?"

I stand on my toes and kiss him softly. Although he tenses, he lets me. He even kisses me back.

I pull back and sigh. "Very nice. Thank you."

He wraps his arms around me and grazes his nose along my neck.

I shiver as his lips brush against my throat when he whispers, "You're welcome."

Ten minutes and one more knee-buckling kiss later, we reach the stage, dressed for the party. Elissa is there, waiting.

When she sees us, she stops in her tracks and looks between us.

"Oh my God. Did you two just have *sex*?"

"Jesus, Elissa, no," Holt says, frowning at his sister.

"Well, it looks like you have," Elissa says as she wipes some lipstick off Holt's neck and smoothes down my hair. "Now let's move it. You guys are the last ones out. Mom and Dad will think we've forgotten about them."

"Wouldn't want that," Holt mumbles as we head toward the door.

We push through into the foyer, and it's packed with friends, family, and fellow students. I have another pang that my parents couldn't be here.

There's a slight rumble of recognition and a smattering of applause as Holt and I emerge, and people say nice things as we pass. Holt seems to take it in stride, but he's more experienced with this kind of thing. Still, I acknowledge as many people as I can and try to smile.

We push through the crowd until Elissa yells, "Mom! Dad!" before dashing toward an attractive middle-aged couple. The man is almost as tall as Holt but with sandy brown hair, and the lady is short like Elissa, and nearly as blond. I can definitely see shades of Elissa in her mom, but I struggle to see Ethan in either of his parents.

Elissa hugs her mother first, then her father wraps his arms around her. Ethan leans in to give his mother a kiss. He looks at his father and shuffles nervously. There are several awkward seconds before his father reaches his hand out, and Ethan shakes it.

Elissa ushers me forward. "Mom, Dad, this is Cassie Taylor, our *amazing* Juliet. Cassie, our parents, Charles and Maggie Holt."

"Mr. and Mrs. Holt," I say as I nervously shake their hands. "It's very nice to meet you."

*Pleaselikeme, pleaselikeme, pleaselikeme.*

"Cassie, you were a *wonderful* Juliet," Maggie says, smiling. "So much better than the girl who played her in the Shakespeare Festival last year. What was her name, Ethan?"

"Uh . . . Olivia," he says, looking uncomfortable.

*Oh. Now her crack about me being his new Juliet makes more sense.*

"Yes, Olivia," says Maggie. "Nice girl, but she couldn't hold a candle to your performance tonight. But I'm not surprised. You were playing opposite my amazing son."

She pulls Holt down so she can kiss him on the cheek. He blushes. Hard.

"Well, Ethan made the whole process very easy," I say, and shoot him a knowing look.

Holt leans over and whispers, "Such a liar," and I have to laugh.

"I loved Ethan as Mercutio," Maggie says. "But this? Oh . . . this was something special. You two have so much chemistry."

I catch Maggie giving her son a pointed look.

Holt sighs and shakes his head, and I have a feeling he's used to his mother giving him a hard time. It makes me smile.

"Cassie," his father whispers as he leans over. "I believe what my wife is implying is that she thinks Ethan should ask you out on a date."

"Jesus!" Holt says as he runs his hand through his hair. "Can everyone in this family please stop talking now?"

Everyone is silent for a moment, then Charles whispers a little softer. "I also think he should date you. You seem nice, and it's been a while since he's let us meet one of his many—"

"Dad!" Holt says firmly, frustration and embarrassment creeping into his voice. "Stop. Please."

Charles laughs and holds up his hands in resignation. I wonder why Holt has such an issue with the man. So far, he seems kind of cool.

Elissa turns to her father. "So, Dad, did you enjoy the show?"

Charles rubs the back of his neck and glances at his son. "Well, Shakespeare isn't really my thing, but . . . it was well done, I suppose. Everyone seemed to know what they were doing. And Cassie, I agree with my wife. You were very good."

He gives Ethan a tight smile before turning to pull Elissa into a hug. "And of course," he whispers, then kisses her cheek, "the lighting was genius."

I feel Holt tense beside me, and when I look around, his jaw is tight. Obviously I'm not the only one who thinks it's strange his dad didn't say anything nice about his performance.

Is the man deaf, dumb, and blind? Did he not see what everyone else saw?

"And Ethan was also amazing, right?" Elissa says, as her brother exhales and shoves his hands in his pockets. "Wasn't this the best thing you've ever seen him in?"

Mr. Holt sighs. "Elissa, your brother is always very competent in his acting. He doesn't need my approval to validate him."

Ethan lets out a short laugh. "Just as well."

Competent? What the hell? He was freaking spectacular.

"But Dad," Elissa says, holding his hand, "can't you at least appreciate that the performances Ethan and Cassie gave tonight were remarkable? I mean, you just don't see stuff like that every day."

Mr. Holt looks at her patiently. "Sweetheart, I appreciate that acting takes a certain amount of dedication, but I'd hardly call it remarkable. Curing cancer? That's remarkable."

"Here we go," Holt mutters.

"Healing broken bones? That's remarkable. Saving someone's life on a daily basis? *That's* remarkable. Actors may think that what they're doing is important, but really, what difference would it make if we didn't have them? Suddenly there are no gossip magazines and the rehab centers are empty? No great loss as far as I can tell."

Holt scowls, and his mother puts a hand on her husband's arm.

"Charles, please."

"It's okay, Mom," Holt says. "As if I care what he thinks anyway."

"Ethan," she says in an admonishing tone.

"You think actors aren't important?" he says. "What about artists, Dad? Musicians? Might as well lump us all together in a useless pile, huh? Do you really want to live in a world with no color? No music? No entertainment? You realize the human race would implode if that happened, right? Every culture on earth has art. Every . . . single . . . one. Without it, humans would be a bunch of primitive psychos whose only compulsions would be eating, fucking, and killing. But art's not important, right?"

Mr. Holt looks at his son sternly, and I get the feeling his father is holding back because I'm here.

"As usual, son," Charles says, "you misunderstand me. I'm merely comparing the importance of acting to other essential roles within our society. I hardly think you can place actors in the same category as *doctors*, for example."

"Okay, you two," Maggie warns. "That's enough."

Mr. Holt ignores her. "Ethan, with your intellect, you have the opportunity to do something truly great with your life. Instead you choose to do something that has very little chance of being anything more than a frivolous hobby. I just don't understand how you can have no ambition—"

"I *do* have ambition," Holt says. "I've worked my ass off for three years to get into this place. I came back time and again, even when they kept telling me no, because I want to be the best that I can be, doing something I love to do. *That's* ambition, Dad. It's just different from yours. What a fucking crime, huh? Oh, and thanks for shitting on my chosen profession. And Cassie's, too. Way to be an unsupportive prick."

Before his mother can admonish him again, he turns to her. "Sorry, Mom. I can't deal with him tonight. I'll talk to you later."

He pushes roughly through the crowd as we all watch him in awkward silence. My face is hot with anger and embarrassment. How dare Mr. Holt speak to his son like that?

Charles drops his head as his wife whispers, "When are you going to stop? This is what he's chosen to do. Accept it."

He looks over at me and winces. "I'm sorry you had to see that, Cassie. I just . . ." He shakes his head. "For the past few years, Ethan and I haven't exactly seen eye-to-eye. It's hard to witness your brilliant son choose a career that's so . . ."

"Frivolous?" I offer sarcastically.

He gives me a guilty look. "I was going to say different from what I'd expected. I think every parent wants their child to change the world. I'm no different. I didn't mean to put down your chosen profession."

"But if your child finds something they're truly passionate about," I say, "who are you to tell them that they're wrong?"

He studies me for a second. "So, your parents are happy you chose acting as your career?"

That stops me dead in my tracks. "Well, not exactly happy. But I can guarantee that if they were here tonight, they would have told me I did well and were proud of me. I know that much for sure."

I watch Mr. Holt's expression carefully, knowing I probably just offended him, but he doesn't seem angry. If anything, he seems sad.

"I guess I saw a different path for Ethan. Ever since he was eight years old, all he ever talked about was being a doctor. Then in his junior year of high school, someone convinced him to join the drama club, and suddenly medicine took a backseat to plays and student films. I honestly thought he'd grow out of it."

"The thing is, Mr. Holt," I say, "people never outgrow their passion."

On one hand, I can totally understand why Holt has so much animosity toward his father. But on the other, I know that it's hard for parents to let go of their expectations and trust their children to find their own way, no matter how much they love them.

"You'd better go after him," Elissa says, gesturing toward the doors. "He won't talk to any of us when he gets like this, but you might stand a chance."

Ethan's parents look at me expectantly. "Well, it was nice meeting you both," I say and quickly head off to find Holt.

I push through the doors and run as fast as my shoes will allow, click-clacking on the pavement stones. I breathe a sigh of relief when I see his familiar frame striding toward the Hub.

"Ethan! Wait up!"

He turns and looks as me, and for a moment he lets me see how tired he is. How completely beaten down by whatever it is that makes him act the way he does.

"That bastard," he says as he shoves his hands in his pockets. "He couldn't say it, could he? Couldn't just fucking pat me on the back for once and say, 'Well done, son, I'm proud of you.' Asshole."

I touch his shoulder. "I'm sorry."

"That theater was full of people who thought I was good. Who fucking loved me. Complete *strangers* who have more faith in me than my so-called father."

"It's not that he doesn't have faith in you, it's just that he—"

The words die in my throat when I see the look on his face. "Are you actually *defending* him?"

"No, I just think that . . . God, he's a parent. The uncertainty of a career in acting is scary for someone who doesn't understand that's it's something we're compelled to do, even if the pay is lousy."

He stares at me for a moment before dropping his head and shoving his hands in his pockets.

"He didn't offer me one kind word about my performance, Cassie," he says, lowering his voice to a bitter whisper. "Not. Fucking. One. He complimented Elissa, and even you. But me? I get the lecture on how I'm wasting my life."

The hurt in his voice makes my throat tight. I take his hand, and for once, he doesn't pull away.

"Do you know the last time he said he loved me?" he says to the pavement. "September seventh, two years ago. I remember it clearly, because it doesn't happen that often. He was drunk. Nice to know that he needs liquid courage to tell his son how he feels."

"Ethan . . ."

I move forward and try to hug him, but he takes a breath and steps back.

"I gotta go."

"What? Where?"

"I need to get out of here for a while." He starts to walk away.

"Ethan, wait."

He stops but doesn't turn around.

I walk around him and put my hands on his chest. He looks at me then, but his eyes are cold.

"Don't do that," I say. "Just . . . don't."

"What?"

"Shut down."

He stares at me, and for a moment I think he's going to slip into his usual mode of deflect and deny, but the fatigue I saw earlier lingers behind his eyes.

He sighs. "Taylor, you don't understand. The way I am . . ." He shakes his head. "I don't mean to shut down. It just happens."

"Yeah, well, don't let it," I say as I rub his chest and feel the muscles relax a little. "Did you even consider that you might actually benefit from having someone who's there for you? Who's willing to listen?"

"You *really* don't want that job."

I sigh in frustration. "Dammit, Ethan, can't you just trust that I *like you*? That I want to be there for you. Support you or whatever. But you have to let me."

He doesn't say anything. He just looks at me like I've requested he jump out of a plane without a parachute.

"Please don't freak out," I say.

"I'm not," he says, but his body is rigid and tense.

"Such a liar."

"Look," he says. "Needing things . . . being needed . . . only ever leads to disappointment."

"It doesn't have to."

"But it usually does."

I stroke his frown lines. His expression softens, but only a little.

"I just need some time to cool off," he says. "I'll see you at the party."

He steps around me and walks away.

Just when I thought we were making progress.

# THIRTEEN

## NOT CARING

*Present Day*
*New York City*

Dear God. He's in my apartment. Like, *in* my apartment. Not only that, he's wandering around, looking at my stuff.

Having him in my formerly Holt-free Sanctuary is making my skin prickle with heat.

This is the place where Tristan and I have talked about him. Where I write angsty-emo vitriol in my diary night after night. Where I've brought countless men who always ended up having *his* face. *His* hands. *His* body.

And now he's here. Pulling off his jacket and laying it on the couch. Turning to look at me with a small, nervous smile. Showing me that no matter how many men I bring back here, he's the only one who truly looks like he belongs.

Dammit.

How did this happen? Why did I let it?

Today's rehearsal was a crapfest. Ethan was nailing his characterization, while I was still flubbing simple lines. When Marco invited us out for drinks afterward, I didn't miss how he finished only half of his spritzer before leaving us alone. Subtle.

He may as well have hired a skywriter to say, "Sort out your shit with Holt and stop ruining my play."

Even though I turned down his invitation to have Holt replaced, I'm still having trouble being completely open. So I vowed to try harder as I stayed with Ethan and drank.

When Holt offered to walk me home, I figured it might help us bond.

My mistake was letting him walk me up to my apartment. He'd practically put his neck out trying to see inside when I opened the door, and when he flat-out asked to come inside, I was unable to say no.

So now, here we are—him wandering around my living room, and me watching like he's an exhibit in a zoo.

He examines my book collection and smiles as his fingers settle on my dilapidated copy of *The Outsiders*.

"I haven't read this in a while," he says, and pulls it out, then leafs through it. "I've missed it."

"I thought you read it every year."

He gives me a smile before placing it back in its slot. "Yeah . . . well . . . I gave my copy to some chick. Haven't gotten around to getting a new one yet."

The day he gave me that book, he was so proud. A birthday present I'd never forget, given to me by a perfect boyfriend.

Pity the boy who gave it to me didn't really exist.

I hear the front door lock click open, and Tristan's booming voice calls down the hallway.

"Cass? You here? I'm taking you out tonight, and 'no' isn't a word I'm accepting. Get out that hot black dress with the low back. I want to show you off."

The hallway closet slams as he puts away his yoga mat, and the look on Holt's face screams, "You didn't tell me you lived with someone. Especially not a man."

Tristan walks into the room and freezes when he sees Holt. Just like dogs in the street, the two men size each other up.

"Hello," Tristan says coldly before giving me a dark look. I shrug as he turns to assess Holt with narrowed eyes. "From the pictures Cassie showed me right before she burned them, I'm guessing you're Ethan Holt."

Holt bristles, but with more grace than I've ever seen from him, he composes his face and holds out his hand. "That's right. And you are?"

I roll my eyes as Tristan steps forward to face off with Ethan. He's only an inch taller, but the black tank he always wears to yoga class shows off his stupidly ripped physique.

He ignores Holt's hand and says, "I'm Tristan Takei. I live here. With her."

"I see," Holt says and drops his hand. "Nice to meet you, Tristan. Cassie didn't tell me she lived with someone."

"Maybe she thought it wasn't any of your business."

Testosterone is thick in the air, but before I can explain I don't have a live-in lover, Tristan grabs my arm and hisses, "Cassie? I need to speak to you in the kitchen," and drags me out of the room.

When we get into the kitchen he turns to me, fury on his face. "What the hell do you think you're doing?"

"Tris, calm down."

"I'm calm."

"No, you're not. Your chakras are flying around like fireworks."

"You don't believe in chakras."

"Yeah, well, if I did, that's what they'd be doing. Chill."

He glares at me for a few seconds before closing his eyes and taking a deep breath. Then he lets it out slowly and sighs. "Okay. I'm calm . . . ish. Now, answer the question."

"I'm not doing anything. We were hanging out."

"Hanging out doesn't involve bringing him back here. You know very well that when you bring a man home, it's for one reason, and if you think you're going to jump back into bed with him—"

"I don't! I'm not. I was a little tipsy. He walked me home."

"You've been *drinking*, and you let him in here?! For the love of Krishna! It's a wonder I didn't find you giving him a damn lap dance! You know that if you're within twenty feet of an attractive man when you're drunk, they're likely to be stripped naked and humped in record time! Let alone your handsome ex who you've never really gotten over!"

"Dammit, Tris, would you please keep your voice down?!"

He exhales again. Nothing ruins his equilibrium faster than the idea of me regressing to my old ways.

I touch his arm. "Do you honestly believe that a couple of weeks of him being decent is going to convince me he's no longer an emotionally defective asshole? Even I'm not that naive."

"I'm not saying you are, but that man is your Achilles' heel. If he asked you to sleep with him right now, would you even be capable of saying no?"

My whole body blushes. "Tristan, God . . . that's not what he wants."

"Bull. I see how he looks at you. If you gave the word, that boy would sex you up ten ways from Sunday."

I run my fingers through my hair. "Tris . . ."

He sighs and puts his hands on my shoulders. "Look, sweet girl, I know this whole thing is difficult to navigate, but you have to remember everything we've talked about. Boundaries. Respect. Honesty. Emotional availability."

"Are you referring to him or me?"

"Both. Don't be blinded by your hormones. I can't watch you go through all that heartache again."

He pulls me into a hug, and I sigh. "Thanks, Tris."

"You're very welcome." He pulls back. "But I just have to do one more thing before I can leave you two alone. You might want to look away, because this will be embarrassing."

Before I can stop him, he steps around me and strides back into the living room. Holt is sitting on the edge of the couch, but he stands when Tristan enters.

"Okay, you," Tristan says, pointing at Holt's face. "I'm going to say this once, so listen up. I spend a good portion of my waking hours trying to find calm in this world and be at one with my serenity, but I love this woman more than pretty much anyone else on the planet, so if you hurt her, in *any* way, I swear by mighty and powerful Buddha that I will not hesitate in ending you. Do you understand me?"

Holt glances at me before nodding, and I'm surprised to see that his face shows not fear but steely determination.

"Yeah, I understand you, Tristan. But just so you know, hurting her is the furthest thing from my mind. I know I've been an idiot in the past, and I have a lot to make up for, but I intend to see this through to the end. Whatever that may be. So you'd best get used to seeing me around, because I'm not going anywhere this time. Do *you* understand?"

Tristan stares at him for a moment before relaxing his stance, a look of surprise on his face. "Well . . . good, then. You have a pretty face. If you treat her right, I won't have to ruin it."

I suppress a smile, because in all the time I've known him, I've only seen Tristan get this alpha-male once before, and that was when a guy he was dating called Gandhi a "grandstanding hypocritical über-pussy." It took Tris a long time to find his serenity again after he punched the guy in the face.

He gives Holt one last evil eye before clapping his hands together and saying, "Okay, I need to shower. You two behave yourselves while I'm gone."

Tris departs, leaving Holt and me facing each other awkwardly.

"So . . . yeah. That's Tristan," I say. "He lives here and apparently threatens my ex-boyfriends. Would you like some wine?"

"Fuck, yes," Holt says, and follows as I head into the kitchen.

I grab a bottle of red and pour two overly generous glasses. I hand one to him and take a large mouthful of mine before leaning against the counter.

"So, Tristan's kind of protective of you, I take it," Holt says.

"Oh, you picked up on that?"

"Yeah, a little. It's not often I'm threatened by a scary-tall super-fit Japanese dude. Can't say I enjoyed it."

"He's only half Japanese. And he's not usually like that, but I guess seeing the Antichrist in his house pushed him over the edge."

He laughs and rubs the back of his neck. "Well, I'm just going by Satan these days, but if you want to be all formal about it . . ."

"Can I call you Lucy?"

"Huh?"

"Short for Lucifer."

"Oh, sure, but only when we're alone. I can't have you calling me that in front of my evil minions. They might laugh and . . . well . . . that would just hurt my feelings."

We head back into the living room and sit on the couch.

"So, you and Tristan. Are you guys"—he looks ill when he says the word—"together?"

I almost laugh. "No."

"Have you ever been?" He looks at me way too intensely as he waits for my response.

"No. I don't have the . . . uh . . . necessary *equipment* to satisfy Tristan."

He looks at me blankly for a few seconds as my words seep into his wine-clouded brain. Then a virtual lightbulb goes on behind his eyes.

"Oh! Well, thank Christ for that. My blood pressure just lowered by about twenty points."

I laugh and take a sip of wine, and when I look back, he's staring at me. "I saw pictures of you guys together, you know."

"When?"

"When I was in Europe. For the first few months after I left, my nighttime ritual was to get shit-faced drunk and google you. There were pictures of you and Tristan together when you were working off-Broadway. When I saw them . . . I . . . fuck, Cassie, it gutted me. I thought he was your boyfriend. That you'd moved on, while I couldn't stop pining for you."

I get a mental image of him, bottle in hand in front of his computer, seeing me with Tristan and cursing me for not being miserable. But I *was* miserable, even though the pictures showed me smiling.

"Yeah, well, you always did underestimate my feelings for you," I say, and turn away from him to fiddle with the stem of my glass. "That was one of our major problems."

"I know it sounds like a cop-out, but . . . I just couldn't comprehend how you could love me as much as I loved you. It just didn't seem possible."

For a moment, I can't believe what I've just heard. He always had trouble saying the "L" word. It was the one thing that made what we had too real for him.

When I glance over, he looks like an arachnophobe who just trumped a roomful of spiders.

"Impressed?" he asks. "Look at me go with the 'L' word. Didn't even stutter."

"It's like a miracle, only less likely."

Now it's his turn to gaze at his wine. "It's only taken three years for me to realize that not saying it didn't help me deny my feelings. Whether or not I loved you wasn't dependent upon a word. It was just a fact. Plain and simple. You'd be surprised how often I say it these days."

I go back to my wine, because his face is so full of emotion that I just can't look at it.

"Music?" I say, and head over to my iPod.

I spend a few moments looking mindlessly through my playlists before he says, "Need help? Because if you pull out any country music, I'll be forced to mock you."

"You're never going to let me live that down, are you?"

"What, that you once spent real folding money on a Dixie Chicks album? Nope. Never living that down."

"Hey, there were some good songs on that album."

"Cassie, there was fucking *yodeling* on that album. I'm pretty sure that album killed the stereo in my old car."

I laugh. "You used to blare AC/DC out of that car every day. Those speakers were completely shredded. You can't possibly blame two minutes of yodeling."

He walks over and takes the iPod from me. "That two minutes scarred my eardrums for life. I can only speculate about what it did to my poor stereo. Now, step aside, woman. Allow me to find the perfect music for us."

I shake my head and sit down. I'm once again struck by how surreal it is to have him in my apartment. Six months ago, it would have been inconceivable. Now he's trying so hard to show me that he's matured and grown. If only I had. Even now, I can feel resentment bubbling inside of me, waiting for him to make one wrong move so it can explode.

"Oh, wow," he says with a nervous glance over his shoulder. "Don't hate me for putting this on, but . . . God . . . this album . . ."

The opening strains of Radiohead's *Pablo Honey* filter though the speakers, and I immediately tense.

I take another mouthful of wine.

"I can change it if you want," he says. "I just . . . I haven't heard it in a while."

*Yeah, me neither.*

"It's fine," I say, before drinking again. The alcohol makes it easy to lie. This album was the soundtrack of so many memories, and although they're pleasant ones, they're also the parts of him I miss the most.

He joins me on the couch, far enough away to make it look like he's respecting my personal space but close enough to make my wine-addled brain crave him closer. I lean my head back and let the music distract me.

We're on the third song by the time Tristan appears in front of us, freshly showered and ready to go out.

He takes in the scene before him and frowns. "If I didn't know any better, I'd swear you two were meditating. Although I'm not sure why you'd be meditating to sex music."

Holt squirms a little.

"Cass, are you sure you don't want to come out with me?" Tris asks. "It's bubble night at Neon. You could even bring tall, dark, and brooding here. Looks like he could use some bubbles."

"No, thanks," I say with a sigh. "I'm kind of enjoying my meditation. You should be proud."

Tristan's mouth presses into a thin line as he turns to Holt. "So that's how this is going to work? You just waltz back into her life and get her to do something I usually have to bribe her with chocolate to do?"

Holt blinks at him lazily. "What can a say, man? I don't need to use chocolate, 'cause I'm just naturally sweet."

Tristan looks at me in confusion, like he's struggling with either really liking Holt or really hating him.

*Welcome to my world.*

"Okay, I'm leaving," Tristan says as he frowns at Holt once more. "But Cassie? Just remember what we spoke about. I don't want to arrive home and have to cleanse your aura of douche vibes."

Ethan tenses. "I've worked very hard to rid myself of 'douche vibes,' but if by chance some still exist, I promise not to infect Cassie with them."

"You do that," Tristan mumbles as he heads down the hallway to grab his jacket. "See ya, Cass."

"Bye."

The door opens and closes, and Holt and I sink further into the couch.

"Call me crazy," Holt says as he turns to me, "but I think Tristan really likes me."

"Well, that's one theory."

"What the other one?" he asks.

"That he wants to tear off your head, poke out your eyeballs, and use your skull as a bowling ball."

"Oh, he bowls?" he deadpans.

"Occasionally. On disco night."

He smiles—one of those beautiful, lights-up-his-whole-face smiles. When he notices me staring, his smile fades into a more wistful expression.

"Man, I've missed this. I never realized how much it hurt to not be with you until I saw you again, and the pain went away."

My smile falters. The wine is making his tongue loose and his eyes intense, and I'm not drunk enough to hear him say stuff like that.

"Did you miss me?" he asks, almost whispering.

"Ethan . . ."

"Not the bastard me," he says. "The me who was good to you. Made you laugh. Who . . . loved you."

"Unfortunately, he was locked inside the bastard you," I say, glancing up at him. "I could never have one without the other."

"You can," he says. "I promise, you can."

"It's going to take me a while to believe it."

"I get that. I never thought making things right with you would be easy, but I know it will be worth it."

"What if it's not?" I say, unable to bear him thinking we're just going to walk off into the sunset. "What if, after all of this time, you're just fooling yourself into thinking we can rekindle something that's been over for a long time?"

His eyes cloud over, and the familiar pull I feel for him thickens the air between us.

"Cassie," he whispers as he leans forward, so close I can smell the sweet scent of wine on his breath. "We've never been over. You know it as well as I do. Even when I was halfway around the world and you hated my guts, we weren't over. You can feel it between us now. And the closer we are, the stronger it gets. And that's what scares you."

He looks at my lips, and it takes every ounce of my dwindling self-preservation to turn away.

"If you can tell me you don't feel it," he says quietly, "then I'll back off. But I'm pretty sure you can't do that, can you?"

I only hesitate for a moment before saying, "I don't feel it." The line falls flat.

He touches my fingers, grazing warm fingertips over the back of my hand until he reaches my wrist. He wraps his hand around the thin bones and squeezes gently.

"You can say what you like, but your pulse doesn't lie. It's pounding. I'm doing that to you."

"How do you know it's attraction and not fear?"

"I'm certain it's a bit of both. But the attraction is definitely there."

I pull my hand away and drain the rest of my glass. I've drunk too much. So has he. Lack of inhibition isn't going to help anything at this point.

I yawn, and stand. "Well, it's getting late."

He nods and smiles. He can read me like a book. "Yeah, I'd better get going."

When we reach the door, he turns to me, one hand on the handle.

"Cassie," he says hesitantly as he leans on the doorframe. "Before I go, I just need to know one thing."

"What?"

He leans forward, his voice low. "You and Tristan weren't exactly whispering in the kitchen. I heard him say you wouldn't be able to resist me if I asked you to sleep with me. Is that true?"

I take in his tall frame filling my doorway, the long line of his throat leading up to his remarkable, emotional face. I remember how his body feels under my hands, the noises he makes when I touch him. The incredible look he got on his face every time his body was joined with mine.

"Ethan . . ."

"Wait," he says and shakes his head. "Don't answer that. Because if you told me that you wanted me . . . well . . ." He looks down at me, and I can tell how much he wants to touch me; how his fingers flex and clench at his sides, how his breathing gets a little rough. "There wouldn't be enough self-restraint in the world."

Thankfully, before either of us does anything stupid, he takes a step back. "Good night, Cassie. For both our sakes, shut the door. Now."

I close the door in his face.

Even through the wood, I can hear his sigh of relief.

*Six Years Earlier*
*Westchester, New York*
**Romeo and Juliet *Opening Night Party***

The music is too loud. It vibrates through my skull and makes my eyeballs hurt.

The living room is packed with people swaying and laughing. Some of them are actually attempting to talk to each other over the noise that's trying to pass itself off as music.

On the couch next to me, Lucas is smoking a joint. He offers it to me, and when I refuse he passes it along to Jack, who's so glassy-eyed he could be labeled Glassy McStaresalot in Madame Tussauds.

I'm a little freaked out that someone is smoking illicit drugs so close to me. I keep expecting my father to burst through the door and go ballistic, but of course, he's on the other side of the country, and even with his finely tuned dad nose, he couldn't smell it from over there.

I'm pretty sure he couldn't, anyway.

"Cassie!"

I look over at Ruby, and she mimes the "drink up" gesture. I sigh and down the shot of tequila I've been holding. She jabs a wedge of lemon at me and gives me a thumbs-up. I shove the lemon in my mouth, and she smiles broadly.

After putting the lemon and shot glass on the coffee table, I slump back onto the couch and sigh. For the millionth time in the last two hours, I look around, hoping that Holt's decided to make an appearance.

Of course, he hasn't.

"I'm going to get some air," I yell as I stand and move past Ruby. She nods and pours herself another shot.

When I reach the front of the house, Elissa is sitting on the stairs, sipping something from a large cup.

I flop down next to her. "Enjoying yourself?"

"Sure," she says. "I love getting ruptured eardrums every time Jack has a party. Just because he's half deaf, he's determined to drag us all down with him. His neighbors must hate his guts."

"His dad owns all of the neighboring houses. That's the only reason he gets away with it."

She offers me her drink as she gazes out into the street.

"Waiting for Ethan?" I ask.

"Yeah."

"Think he'll show?"

She shakes her head. "Every run-in with Dad turns Ethan into a ball of rage. I've tried to tell him to just let it go, but he won't listen."

"Has their relationship always been so . . . complicated?"

"Yes." She laughs. "It's like Dad just doesn't know how to deal with him. He's fine with me because I'm a girl, but with Ethan? I don't think he knows how to communicate with him on an emotional level. My theory is it's because our grandfather didn't believe men should be openly affectionate with each other because it made them soft, or whatever. So now, whenever Ethan challenges Dad, they fight instead of talking things through."

"That must be tough."

"It is. And it got worse a few years ago. I blame Vanessa, the bitch-whore."

My ears prick up. "Oh, so it wasn't Olivia?"

"No," she says, and sighs. "Vanessa was patient zero for all his issues. She's the reason it went south with Olivia."

"What happened between them? Ethan and Vanessa, I mean."

She looks down and runs her finger around the edge of her cup. "You should talk to him about it."

"Elissa, please. I've tried asking him, but he clams up."

"Yeah, but he'd kill me for telling you."

"I get that, but if it makes you feel any better, he read my diary, so he knows a whole stack of personal stuff about me I'd rather he didn't."

Her mouth drops open. "He read your *diary*?"

"Yeah. A few weeks ago. I *might* have written something about how much I wanted to touch his . . . uh . . . penis."

"Oh my God."

"And I kind of implied his dick could win awards."

"Oh . . . whoa."

"I know."

"Plus . . . ew. That's my brother."

"I know. But in my defense, your brother's extremely hot."

She looks at me doubtfully. "If you say so."

"I do."

Elissa sighs. "Well, as gross as it is to me, I'm kind of glad you feel that way, because you're the only girl I could see him getting serious with since the whole thing with Vanessa played out. I can understand why he's hesitant, but still . . ."

"Please tell me that statement is going to segue into the full story." I give her my best puppy-dog eyes.

She gives me an eye roll before saying, "Vanessa was Ethan's high school sweetheart. They started dating in sophomore year."

I nod and try to hide the vicious jealousy that flares inside me. It's stupid to be jealous of a girl I've never met, right?

"At school, Ethan and Vanessa were like the golden couple. But behind the scenes, they argued a lot. Vanessa liked pushing his buttons. If she thought he wasn't giving her enough attention, she'd flirt with other guys. She thrived on making him jealous. I totally think she was a sociopath. She even used to flirt with Ethan's best friend from grade school, Matt. She used jealousy to keep Ethan in line."

"Why didn't he just dump her?"

"I don't know. It was like she had him under her thumb. She could manipulate him into anything. Used his insecurities against him."

"So what happened?"

"Well, one night during senior year, after Ethan had finally told Dad he wasn't going to medical school and would be applying to The Grove instead, they had a really bad fight. I couldn't hear exactly what they were saying, but the next thing I know, Mom's crying and Dad's yelling at Ethan to get out. After that, he went to Vanessa's place, but she wasn't there, so he headed over to Matt's. When he got there, he walked in to find Matt and Vanessa. In bed."

"Oh, God."

"Ethan was devastated. I would have expected something like that from Vanessa, but not from Matt. He and Ethan were like brothers. The next day at school, Matt tried to smooth things over and apologize, but . . . Ethan was just so angry. He snapped and beat the hell out of Matt. Ended up breaking his nose and getting suspended for two weeks. Vanessa thought the two of them fighting over her was awesome. I'm sure she was playing them both for fools."

"What a bitch," I say, feeling violent hatred toward her. I expel a long breath. I can't even wrap my head around how traumatic it must have been to be betrayed by your closest friends. No wonder Holt had intimacy issues.

"That's when he really shut down," Elissa says. "Getting rejected by The Grove didn't help. He stopped communicating with me and Mom and became even more distanced from Dad. Threw himself into his theater work. Drank too much. Got into fights. Slept with every woman who came across his path, then never called them again. It was hideous to watch."

My face must give away how much I hate thinking about him with other women, because she quickly adds, "There wasn't ever anything serious."

"Not even Olivia?" I ask.

Elissa scrunches up her face. "Yeah, they had a thing. But honestly, Ethan treated her so badly it was doomed from the start. And she was a nice girl, too. Nothing like Vanessa. I never thought my brother could be cruel, until I saw him with Olivia. She would have done anything for him, and he destroyed her. He hasn't dated since."

I think about all the cruel things he's said or done since I've known him, and I feel sorry for his previous Juliet.

"So that's the story," Elissa says as she stands and pulls me to my feet. "Now, can we please stop talking about my deadbeat brother and start having a good time? I doubt he'll show tonight. He's probably in a bar somewhere, scowling at the wall and causing paint to blister."

We head back inside, and half an hour and two tequila shots later, Elissa and Ruby have convinced me to dance. I twirl and sway with them, but I can't help thinking about Holt and what he's been through.

When I hear a huge round of applause at the front of the room, I turn around to see Holt there, a nearly empty whiskey bottle in his outstretched arms as he yells, "Wassup, fellow thespians?! Romeo's in da house! Let's party!"

The whole room roars its approval, and beside me I hear Elissa say, "Oh, God. What the hell is he doing?"

I watch in disbelief as Holt hugs and high-fives everyone around him while making his way through the throng like a rock star with his fans.

When he reaches us he smiles sloppily and says, "Hello, ladies," in a voice I'm guessing is supposed to be sexy.

"Ruby," he says as he pulls her in for a hug. "You hate me, don't you? A lot of people hate me. Even my own father. Don't worry. I don't hold it against you."

Then he turns to his sister and wraps his arms around her. "Oh, Elissa. Sweet, ball-breaking Elissa. Why do you put up with me? I don't understand. But I love you. I really, really do."

"Uh . . . Ethan?" she says, wincing as he squeezes her. "Did you happen take a whole bunch of Ecstasy tonight?"

He kisses her cheek before turning to me. His smile immediately falters, but he takes another swig of liquor and then steps forward as he reaches out to cup my face.

"And Cassie. Beautiful, beautiful Cassie. Are you okay?"

"Yes. Are you?"

"I'm great! I don't even care about what happened tonight with my father. And you wanna know why? Because I've decided not to care about anything. It's such a simple concept, I don't know why I didn't come up with it years ago. Look at how happy I am!"

He throws his head back and laughs. It's the saddest sight I've ever seen.

"Holt . . ." I begin, but he puts his fingers on my lips.

"No, don't 'Holt' me." He puts down his bottle. "It's a party, and I want to dance. See ya."

He pushes into the crowd, and they whoop around him as he starts to move, energetic and ungainly.

"Wow," Elissa says. "I've never seen my brother dance before. There's . . . God . . . there's too much wrong for me to comprehend."

"He's a truly terrible dancer," Ruby says. "It looks like he's having a vertical seizure."

He's the life of the party. He talks to everyone—is *polite* to everyone. Heck, he even laughs at Jack's jokes and doesn't sneer when Zoe flirts with him.

He probably feels like raging and punching people in the face, but instead he's being the Holt he thinks everyone wants him to be.

I grind my teeth in frustration.

I know Holt can be an ass, because he's been one to me on more than one occasion, but at least he was being real. This new Holt? He's as fake as Zoe's boobs.

Now I know how he felt watching me be a people pleaser. It's aggravating as hell.

When I can't take anymore, I push through the crowd to get to him. He's talking to Zoe, smiling and laughing. She's making sexy eyes at him, and I have an urge to smash her face into the bowl of Doritos on the table beside her.

Holt looks up as I approach, and once again his smile falters for a second before it slams firmly back into place.

"Taylor!" he says warmly. "What's up? Zoe here was just telling me that if she'd been my Juliet instead of you, she wouldn't have been faking the sex scene. Isn't that hilarious?"

"Totally hilarious," I say with zero enthusiasm. "Zoe?" I pick up the bowl of Doritos. "Want some chips?"

*Pow. Right in the kisser.*

She rolls her eyes. "Yeah, right, Cassie. As if I'm going to eat carbs."

I exhale and plaster a nonviolent expression on my face. "Holt, can I talk to you for a second?"

"Actually," Zoe says as she links her arm through his possessively, "he's talking to me right now. Maybe you could come back later."

*Woman, you'd best get your hands off him before I give you a hydrolyzed-cheese-starch facial.*

I slam the chip bowl down on the table and force myself to smile. "I won't keep him long. I'm sure he'll be back listening to your amusing pornographic hypotheticals before you know it."

I grab Holt's arm and tug, and thankfully, he follows me to the kitchen.

I spin around to face him. "What are you doing?"

He shrugs. "Having a good time?"

"Really? Is that what you call it? Talking to Slut Girl. Pretending you like her."

"'Slut Girl' is a very unkind nickname," he says, his words slurred. "And maybe I actually enjoy her company."

"Oh, what a crock."

"You jealous, Taylor?"

"Yes. Very. Now would you please drop this stupid act and kiss me?"

That stops him dead in his tracks. He blinks three times. I don't even flinch. Guess I'm getting pretty good at saying what I really think.

Jack walks in and heads to the keg in the corner, ignoring the staring match going on as he fills several cups with beer. "Hey, Holt, buddy. You're not slowing down, are you? Come on, have one of these."

Holt turns around just as Jack holds out one of the cups, and the entire beer splashes down the front of Ethan's shirt.

"Shit!" Jack gasps. "Sorry, man. Total accident."

Jack grabs a dishtowel and tries to dry Holt's shirt as he mumbles more apologies.

"It's fine," Holt says and forces a smile. "I really don't care. Got a spare T-shirt I could borrow?"

Jack nods. "Yeah, upstairs in my closet. Wear anything you like."

Holt slaps him on the shoulder a little too hard as he passes and mutters, "Thanks, buddy."

He pushes through the crowd and strides up the stairs, and it's all I can do not to follow him.

"You know," Jack says. "I've never seen anyone be a happy-angry drunk before, but Holt somehow pulls it off."

I nod. "It's a rare and special gift."

He picks a beer up off the counter and sips it thoughtfully. "I should jump online and see if there are any reviews of tonight's performance out yet. I heard the reviewer from *Online Stage Diary* was there. I wonder if he had anything nice to say."

I get a sudden knot in my stomach. "He was there?"

"Yeah. Him and about four others. One from the *Broadway Reporter*." He looks at me and quirks an eyebrow. "You never know, Taylor. In the morning, you could be a star."

"Yeah, right. Or they could hate me." I laugh, but seriously, if they hate me . . .

Just the thought of it makes me prickle with nervous sweat.

"I'm sure they'll say awesome things about you," Jack says, putting an encouraging hand on my shoulder. "And if they don't? Well, there's still half a keg of beer left. You could drink until you forget about it."

He grabs his beers and wanders off.

I stand there for a few seconds, contemplating my possible impending public humiliation, and I realize there's only one thing that can help me stop freaking out, and he's upstairs, maybe shirtless.

I push through the living room before climbing the stairs and heading down the hall to Jack's room. The door is open, and as I peek around the corner, I see Holt seated on the bed, bare chested, his sodden shirt on the floor, his head cradled in his hands. He grips his hair and sighs, raw frustration emanating from him like an aura.

"Hey," I say, and take a tentative step inside the room.

He looks up sharply before pushing off the bed and striding over to the closet.

"Hey." He swings the doors open wide and flicks through Jack's impressive range of T-shirts. "Some party, huh?"

I can't look away from the muscles in his naked back as they move and flex. Well, that's not true. I *could* look away, but I don't want to.

"You okay?" I ask, coming closer.

"I'm great." He holds out a shirt that says, *To Err Is Human. To Arr Is Pirate.* "Does Avery actually wear this out in public?"

"Holt . . ."

"Or what about this one?" He brings out a shirt that says, *Here's to nipples. Without them, titties would be pointless.*

"Listen . . ."

"I mean, seriously. Did he buy these or were they paying people to take them away?"

"We need to talk."

"No, we really don't." He replaces the hanger and flicks roughly through the rest of the rack. "Does this guy own nothing but goddamn joke shirts? Nothing sporty? Or, God forbid, plain?"

He keeps flipping through the hangers, his posture becoming more and more tense.

"Ethan," I say and place my hand in the middle of his back.

"No." He spins around and steps away from me. "Just fucking . . . don't, okay?"

"Why not?"

"Because you touching me never ends well. Because when you touch me, I . . . fuck, I think stupid thoughts and want stupid things, and . . . so . . . just . . . don't . . ."

I take a step forward, and he presses his back into the closet door. When I place my hand in the middle of his chest, he inhales sharply and clenches his jaw.

"I don't know what you're so scared of. I'm not Vanessa."

His expression hardens. "What the fuck do you know about Vanessa?"

I take a deep breath. "Elissa told me about her. And the other girls. And Olivia." He sighs heavily, and I step a little closer. "Don't be mad. I forced her."

His fists clench by his sides. "She still had no goddamn business telling you."

"I wanted to know." I bring my other hand onto his chest where I can feel the frantic thrumming beneath the surface. "And now I understand a little more about why you're so hesitant to date again. What Vanessa did to you was horrible. But I'm not her. I'm nothing like her."

He looks down at me with less anger, but it's replaced with tired resignation. Like he's already had this conversation in his head, many times.

"You don't get it," he says. "It doesn't *matter* that you're nothing like her. Some part of me thinks you are, and it's just . . . waiting . . . for everything to go to shit again. It's not logical, but I can't help it. And as much as I'm afraid of you hurting me, I'm more afraid of hurting you. What happened with Olivia? I can't do that to someone again, especially not you."

He thinks he's trying to protect me, but as someone who's been so afraid of being wrong all my life, I finally know, without a shadow of a doubt, that I'm right for him.

"Ethan, no relationship comes without out its risks, and even though you think you can keep pushing people away forever, I'm here to tell you that you're absolutely going to fail."

I graze my hands up his forearms, his biceps. Skim across his warm, soft skin.

"The thing is," he says, looking at me as he tentatively cups my cheek, "as much as you frighten the living fuck out of me, and as much as I know one of us, if not both, is going to absolutely regret it . . . I want to fail with you."

We stare at each other for long moments, and as I look into his eyes, I see the exact second he makes his decision. I stop breathing as his fingers tighten in my hair. Then he leans down, his mouth lingering just above mine, sweet warm air fanning over my face as time stops.

"Looking at me like that isn't fair," he whispers. "Not even a little bit fucking fair."

Then the space between our lips is gone, and he's kissing me, hard and needy. A sharp inhale from both of us sounds incredibly loud in my ears. We kiss each other desperately, lips connecting and pressing, fitting together like it's their purpose, then parting to make way for low moans.

The effect he has on my body is instantaneous and powerful, and I take full advantage of him being shirtless. My hands roam everywhere. Across his broad shoulders and arms. Around to his back and up to his shoulder blades. Back down his sides and onto his stomach.

He groans into my mouth and explores me just as hungrily. "Jesus . . . Cassie."

He kisses me unreservedly, passionately, and at last I feel that, after taking so many steps backward, we're finally moving forward. Toward what, I have no idea, but just knowing he's open to the experience is better than any other feeling I've ever had.

"I've wanted to do this all night." He pants in between kisses. "Staying away from you was fucking exhausting."

Somehow we start walking back toward the bed, still kissing, deep and frantic. Before I know it, I'm on my back with him between my thighs. I clutch at him as he grinds against me, slow and insistent.

"Oh, God. Yes."

He buries his head in my neck, then he's sucking. He moves along my throat and onto my chest where he cups my breasts as he continues to move against me, stealing my ability to breathe.

I angle my hips up to meet him and boldly grab his butt to push him against me more firmly.

"Fuck." He groans into my shoulder as he freezes. The room is silent, apart from our ragged breathing.

"What's wrong?" I ask, gripping his shoulders as my heart thunders way too fast.

"Nothing," he says, still not moving. "Just give me a minute. Don't move."

I'm secretly thrilled that I affect him so powerfully. It's good to know our attraction is definitely two-sided.

"Talk to me," he says as he drops his head onto my shoulder. "Anything to distract me from your total fucking hotness."

"Uh . . . well, I'm sorry about your dad tonight." I gently stroke his back. "He was totally out of line. And I certainly wouldn't let two years go by without telling you I loved you. That's ridiculous. If you were mine, I'd say I loved you every day."

I inhale quickly. "I mean, I'm speaking as if I was your dad, you know? If you were my *son* I'd say that. I'm not saying *I* love you. I'm not saying that. I just . . ."

"I didn't think that you were . . ." He smiles. "Maybe you should shut up and kiss me again."

I push him onto his back. "Well, if you insist."

He pulls me down to him, and we're kissing again, and it's like I'm in a warm, aching dream I never want to end.

The kiss becomes more frantic, mouths and hands moving hungrily until we hear a distressed voice say, "Oh, God, you guys, come onnnn! Not in my bed!"

We look up to see Jack in the doorway, swaying like he should have stopped drinking about an hour ago.

"Did you not get the memo that no one's allowed have sex in my bed tonight? That *Star Wars* quilt cover is vintage!"

"What do you want, Jack?" Holt sighs, while I suppress a laugh.

"You gotta come downstairs," he says as he leans against the door and spills his beer. "The first critique of our show is in, and it's . . . well . . . it says some really bad stuff about you two."

Holt and I look at each other, panic and fear crossing our faces.

"Just messing with you!" Jack laughs. "It's completely awesome. Get your asses downstairs so I can read it to everyone. Come on!"

He staggers out the door. Holt reluctantly climbs off me and grabs a T-shirt from the closet. He pulls it over his head and smoothes it down with a smirk. It has a huge red cross on it and reads, *Orgasm Donor.*

"Well, at least I got one that's accurate."

I shake my head and laugh as I straighten myself up.

He walks over and puts a hand on each side of my face before leaning down and kissing me.

"I'm not going to kiss you in front of them," he says. "Or hold your hand. I just don't want them talking about us. Assuming stuff."

"Okay," I say, disappointed I have to hide how I feel about him. "But isn't Jack going to tell them that we were making out?"

He shakes his head. "The state he's in, he probably forgot about us five seconds after he left the room."

He kisses me again, and then we head downstairs, trying to ignore the whispers that filter through the crowd as we emerge together.

"Finally!" Jack says. He shushes everyone as he puts down his beer and holds up the pages he's printed out. "Okay, listen up guys. This review is by Martin Kilver from *Online Stage Diary.* He's notoriously hard to please, so keep that in mind when you hear what he has to say."

The whole room goes quiet, and I can feel Holt tense beside me as Jack starts to read:

"With any production of a classic Shakespearean play, the actors run the risk of imitating and re-creating much of what's gone before. In the most recent production of *Romeo and Juliet* by The Grove's Dramatic Arts Academy, this couldn't be further from the truth. The production is sparse and modern, which in itself isn't groundbreaking. What is revolutionary is that after seeing countless productions over the years, I finally believe in the truth and power of two young people in love. To say it provided this reviewer with one of the most thrilling nights of theater I've ever encountered would be an understatement."

There are murmurs of surprise and some light applause, and Jack smiles before continuing: "Director Erika Eden has shaped her young charges into a slick, powerful company of exciting players, and while they all show maturity in their performances, they lose nothing of the rambunctiousness of youth that is so central to the story."

More hoots of agreement. I feel the light pressure of Holt's hand on the small of my back.

"Okay, keep it down," Jack says. "We're getting to the best part." He clears his throat. "Although the entire cast is truly exceptional, special mention must be made of Aiyah Sediki as the nurse, who brings a wonderful sense of dignity to the role, and Connor Baine as Mercutio, a role that is often played as two-dimensional in its brashness, but to which he brings a surprising and welcome sensitivity."

There are huge yells of approval as Aiyah and Connor beam. I applaud them both, so proud.

Jack looks at us knowingly before continuing: "But the major triumph of this production is the casting of the two lead actors—Ethan Holt as Romeo, and Cassandra Taylor as Juliet." The crowd whistles and hollers, and my face burns bright red. "In playing Romeo, Mr. Holt brings to the role a prickly vulnerability that plays directly against the acres of flowery prose the character has to utter. His intense, panther-like energy is a refreshing change from the foppish, wet-eared Romeos I've seen in the past, and I predict that if this performance is anything to go by, Mr. Holt will have very bright future on the professional stage."

I swallow a lump in my throat as pride for Holt wells up inside me. I turn to look at him, bright-eyed and emotional. I want to hug him and whisper how proud I am, but that will have to wait until later.

I look back at Jack who's now staring at me. "Cassandra Taylor as Juliet is equally as compelling and truly epitomizes a heroine of the twenty-first century. Beautiful and bold, her Juliet is no shrinking flower. She's a headstrong, passionate woman whose strength of purpose will make the audience fall in love with her every bit as much as her doomed Romeo. Miss Taylor displays a stunning emotional range in her finely tuned performance and has what can only be described as 'star quality.'"

I try to swallow, but I'm too choked up. I clench my jaw to stop myself from crying, and when I feel Holt's fingers gently brush mine, I'm grateful he's there.

"But," Jack says, coming into the home-stretch, "as exceptional as these two young performers are in their own right, it's their astounding combined chemistry that really makes this production soar. For in our modern, cynical world, filled with a staggering divorce rate and disposable ideals, it's not easy to convince an audience to believe in the power of true love. Well, I'm here to tell you these two pulled it off beautifully, and I defy anyone who witnesses their onstage love affair to leave untouched by their extraordinary passion. It certainly made this somewhat-jaded reviewer wish there was more true love in the world."

The entire crowd "awwws" in unison, and when I look at Holt, I swear he's blushing just as furiously as I am. The room explodes with chatter as everyone discusses the review and what it all means, but I'm too stunned to even make conversation.

Jack pulls out his phone and orders Ethan and me to pose for a photo. Without even thinking about it, we put our arms around each and beam for the camera.

After the flash pops, Jack shows us the picture.

It's beautiful.

Our smiles are so dazzling, it makes me believe that no two people in the history of the world have ever looked happier than we do in that moment.

We're stars.

# FOURTEEN

## PUSH AND PULL

*Present Day*
*New York City*

Marco's apartment is a bit like him—large and flamboyant. It's filled with plush velvet and opulent antiques, making it feel like it's inhabited by an eccentric Prussian czar instead of a theater director.

We're celebrating the end of our third week of rehearsal, and Marco has invited the entire company to a cocktail party. It's the first time in over a week that I've seen Holt outside of rehearsal. He often asks if I'd like to get a drink after work, but I've always declined. While I'm more and more drawn to him, the idea of spending time alone with him makes me sweat. I only agreed to come tonight because I knew we'd be surrounded by people.

I watch him on the other side of the room, talking to Marco's partner, Eric. He's attentive and enthusiastic as Eric points out his favorite antiques and tells of how he found them.

Holt asks questions, smiles, laughs, and I get a twinge in my stomach as I realize how different he is from the impatient, sullen man he used to be. I wonder if he ever looks at me and notices how different I am. How jaded I've become. How fragile.

I wonder if he ever thinks that after all the effort he's gone through to be with me again, I'm no longer worth it.

"A toast!" Marco says, and we all mill around the living room as Cody refills our champagne glasses. "To this remarkable company and our wonderful play. May the finished product be as incredible as I predict. I haven't had a Tony nomination in two years, and I'm starting to suffer withdrawals! So please, dear colleagues and friends, raise your glasses—to us!"

I smile and raise my glass before glancing across at Holt. He looks at me warmly as he makes his toast. "To us."

See? This is why I have to stay away from him, because with two words he can make me feel like a schoolgirl with her first crush.

I seek out the bathroom, but on the way I come across Marco's study. Just inside the door is a huge glass-fronted cabinet filled with brightly colored glasses.

I walk into the room and gaze at the goblets and tumblers, wine and champagne flutes, all glinting in every color of the rainbow, some with gilt work in gold and silver.

"Ah, Miss Taylor, I see you've discovered my pride and joy."

I turn to see Eric enter the room, with Holt following close behind. "I was about to show Mr. Holt my most passionate indulgence. Marco keeps threatening that we're going to need a bigger apartment if I don't stop buying antique glass, but I can't help myself. The Internet makes it entirely too easy to feed my addiction."

Holt stands behind me, and the heat from his body leaches into my back.

"You have an amazing collection," Holt says as he examines the display case. "Have you been collecting long?"

Eric nods. "About twenty years. I prefer Italian glass, anything from Murano in particular. But I also have some Russian and English pieces, some dating back to the early eighteenth century."

"Really?" I ask. "How did they survive that long?"

He smiles. "Well, to be honest, quite a lot of it is chipped or damaged in some way, but that's part of the appeal. It speaks of its history. Knowing that it's had a life—maybe many lives—before I discover it is the wonder of antiques. Let me show you what I mean."

He opens the door and retrieves a tall, thin wine glass. It's not brightly colored like most of the others. It's plain, clear glass, and the only decoration is some light etching on the bowl.

"This is one of my favorites," Eric says, holding it reverently. "It's said to have belonged to Lady Cranbourne of Wessex. Her tumultuous relationship with her husband was infamous. One year, he gave her a set of six glasses as an anniversary present. Later that night, it's alleged he made a comment that offended her. I believe it was in relation to her relationship with one of the stable-hands. It's said this is the only glass that survived. The rest were smashed to pieces when she threw them at him."

He holds the glass up to the light and points at a thin line that runs the length of the bowl. "Do you see that crack? It occurred when Lord Cranbourne caught it after his wife flung it at his head. That was in 1741. For nearly three hundred years, this glass has survived, despite the damage. Remarkable, no?"

He places the glass carefully back in the case and turns to Holt and me. "I guess that's part of my fascination. It seems so fragile, yet it somehow manages to endure, even with cracks and scratches. Personally, I find perfect glass boring. I love all of these pieces, and the scars of their survival make them even more beautiful in my eyes."

"But doesn't damage like that make the glass worthless?" I ask, calling on my limited antique knowledge.

Eric looks at me thoughtfully. "Worth is such a subjective issue." He walks over to a large cabinet and pulls out a walnut box. While holding it out to me, he asks me to open the lid. When I do, I see the interior is lined in plush blue velvet. There are six indentations for goblets, but instead of containing intact glasses, there's simply a pile of broken pieces.

I look at Eric in confusion.

"When I bought the Cranbourne glass," he says, "this was included in the lot. It's what remains of the other five glasses. The auctioneer suggested I throw it away. After all, it's just a collection of broken glass. But to me it was much, much more. Lady or Lord Cranbourne must have retrieved the broken glass after their fight. What the glasses represented—their marriage, their history, their love—was too important to throw away, even broken beyond all repair."

He smiles at Holt and me before closing the box and placing it back in the cabinet. "The auctioneer considered it to be worthless, because it had no monetary value, but I think it's priceless. It represents passion, and without passion, life is meaningless, yes? At least, that's what I've always believed."

After pausing to give us a smile, he heads toward the door. "I'd best help Marco with the dessert. He gets tense if people don't have something in their mouths every five minutes. Look at the glass as long as you like. Handle it, if you wish. It's really not as fragile as it seems."

He disappears down the hallway, then it's just Holt and me, standing too close as Eric's words hang in the air.

"So," I say. "Who do you think saved the broken glass? Lord or Lady Cranbourne?"

"Lord," Holt says without hesitation.

I look at him questioningly.

"He bought her the glasses," he says, "and he said something to hurt her. He'd feel guilty."

"Yes, but she was the one who smashed them," I say. "And maybe what he said to her was true."

Holt shakes his head. "Doesn't matter. For her to fly off the handle like that, he had to have been an insensitive asshole."

"Or maybe she was just a drama queen."

He pauses for a moment and looks at me, his eyes intense. "Maybe they both saved it. Maybe they carefully collected all the pieces, then had incredible make-up sex in front of the fireplace."

I raise an eyebrow. "There's a fireplace?"

"Of course. Possibly with the head of a dead animal hanging above it."

"Wow. Romantic."

"I know. Nothing says 'I love you' like broken glass and decapitated wildlife."

I laugh, and so does he. Then his smile fades into the familiar shape of longing I see so often these days.

"You've been avoiding me," he says quietly. "Did I do something to piss you off? Because if so, I'd like a chance to apologize."

I look back at the cabinet, trying to ignore how amazing his eyes look reflecting the glass.

"It's nothing."

"With the way you've been looking at me, I'm pretty sure it's something."

He stands behind me, his chest pressing into my back. "If I were a betting man, I'd say you're pissed because of how much you want me." He weaves an arm around my waist and turns me to face him. "Don't you realize I know all the tricks? The dark looks, the anger, no touching. I did the same to you because I was scared of letting you in. But you didn't let me keep you out. You pushed me, time and again. Maybe that's what I should do now. Make you face your feelings for me."

My heart pounds as he runs his fingers through my hair. My breathing becomes shallow and I instinctively fixate on his mouth. How soft it looks. How delicious it would taste.

"You want me to kiss you," he says. "You'd never admit it, and if I tried to actually do it, you'd stop me, but . . . you want it. Don't you?"

I look down. "No."

"Bullshit."

He cups my face. "Look into my eyes and say it, then maybe I'll believe you."

My stomach tightens, and my whole body flushes, but I force myself to meet his gaze. "I don't want you to kiss me."

My voice is unsteady and weak. Just like my resolve.

"Jesus, Cassie," he says as he strokes my cheek. "You're a critically acclaimed actress and that's the best you can do? That's fucking appalling. Try again."

"I don't . . . I don't want you to kiss me."

"Yes, you do," he says, quiet and confident. "I'm not going to do it. I just want to hear you say it."

He might as well ask me to walk a tightrope a hundred feet above the ground without a net. I stare at his chest.

He sighs, and I'm not sure if it's out of frustration or relief.

"Cassie, look at me." When I hesitate, he puts a finger under my chin and tilts it up until I'm looking at him. "I just need you to know that the second you're ready to try again with us, I'm going to kiss the hell out of you. I'm going to kiss you until you see stars, and hear angels, and can't stand up for a week. I hope you realize that."

My heart is thundering when I say, "Holt, if I'm ever ready, you'll be the first to know. I promise."

He gives me a half smile. "So kissing is off the menu, but you should know I'm also offering free hugs today—strictly platonic—for the first beautiful woman who requests them."

I laugh, probably a little too loudly, and step forward as he wraps his arms around me. His face settles in my neck, and I squeeze him tightly as our bodies connect.

"God, you smell amazing," he whispers into my skin. "Nothing on this planet smells as good as you."

"That doesn't sound too platonic to me."

"Shh. Don't talk. Just let me smell you."

I pull back and cock an eyebrow.

"Okay, fine," he says and rolls his eyes. "No more sniffing. Jesus, ruin all my fun."

He hugs me again, and I sigh.

"Ready for that kiss yet?" he asks as his arms tighten.

"Not yet."

He runs his nose along my throat and inhales. "Just checking."

*Six Years Earlier*
*Westchester, New York*
*The Grove*
*The Diary of Cassandra Taylor*

*Dear Diary,*

*It's been nearly two weeks since Holt and I officially decided to become nonofficial, and in that time I've experienced more sexual frustration than I'm sure any human was meant to endure.*

*We've shared the occasional kiss-and-grope session when he's walked me back to my apartment after class, but that's it. If I didn't occasionally catch him looking at me like he wanted to make a three-course meal out of my boobs, I'd never know he actually liked me.*

*My problem is I'm sure everyone can tell I really like him. I laugh too loudly at his jokes and sit too close to him in class. His demonic sexual voodoo has kicked into overdrive, and I can't get enough of him.*

*It doesn't help that I've had some highly erotic dreams about him recently. Dreams in which I get to see what he's been hiding in his pants. Subsequently, my allotted porn-viewing time has been extreme. I've watched countless film clips about how to pleasure a man, and although I'm pretty nervous about putting my pseudo-knowledge into practice, I really want to.*

*He's coming over tonight so we can study for our History of Theater*

*quiz tomorrow. I want to seduce him, but I'm not really sure what se-*
*duction entails. I guess I have two hours to figure something out.*

"Name the six most famous ancient Greek playwrights," he says, all
sexy voice and glorious eyes.

"Um . . . okay. Ancient Greek playwrights. Uh . . . just give me
second."

I tap my pencil on my notebook as I try to remember the answer.
He's watching me as he sits cross-legged, leaning back against the
couch. His crotch is foremost in my line of sight.

There's no way in the world I can concentrate while he's basically
flaunting his penis in front of me. What the hell is he thinking?

I huff and squeeze my eyes shut. "Um . . . Ancient Greek guys . . .
ah—"

"Come on, Taylor, you know this."

"I know, but"—*you're distracting me with your possibly beautiful man*
*member*—"my brain's tired. We've been studying for two hours."

I open my eyes. He's staring at me, and a familiar heat emanates
from him.

"When we've finished with the ancients, we'll take a break. Okay?"

There's a slight sheen of moisture on his lip. I can't look away.

"When we break, will you let me kiss you?"

He pauses and tries not to smile. "Maybe."

"Grope you?"

"Possibly."

"See your penis?"

His eyes bug out of his head, and he chokes on his own saliva.
"What the hell, Cassie?!"

Okay. Seduction fail. Time for plan B.

"Please?" Did I mention plan B was flat-out begging?

He laughs and runs his hand through his hair. "I'll say one thing for you, Taylor. I never know what's going to come out of your mouth."

I desperately want to say something about what I'd like to go *into* it, but I figure I've already freaked him out enough.

"Okay, how about a challenge, then?" I sit up onto my knees. He looks at me quizzically. "For every answer I get right about the ancients, I get to take off a piece of your clothing."

He laughs again, but this time it's tinged with mild hysteria. "And if you get questions wrong?"

"Then you get to take my clothes off."

He looks at me before dropping his gaze to the floor. "I thought we agreed to take things slowly."

"We did, and we are," I say and take his hand. "Holt, the only thing going slower than the two of us right now is a glacier in New Zealand, and quite frankly, it's gaining." I look down at his fingers and stroke them. "I just . . . I want to touch you. Would it really be so bad if I did?"

He squeezes my fingers. "You do realize it's usually the guy who pressures the girl into getting naked, right? I mean, you're kind of usurping my manly duties here."

My heart pounds faster as I see how large his pupils have become. "Then pressure me."

He stares at me with an expression of disbelief.

"Nothing about this scares you, does it?" he asks quietly.

I almost laugh. "Of course it does. It terrifies me. *You* terrify me. But not enough to make me think you won't be worth it."

His gaze is intense. "You think I'm worth it?"

I nod. "I have no doubt."

He swallows. "That's the sexiest goddamn thing anyone's ever said to me."

In a second, he pushes me onto the floor. He kisses me hard, and as he presses his weight into me, I part my legs for him. As we connect, he buries his hands in my hair and makes my favorite groaning sound in his chest.

"If we flunk this test tomorrow," he says between panting and kissing my neck, "it's going to be your fault. You know that, right?"

I kiss him deeply then push him over so he's on his back. I straddle his thighs and grip the collar of his shirt. "Oh, please. We can so do this and keep studying. Uh . . . the six most famous ancient Greek playwrights." I flick open his shirt button. "Thespis."

"Aeschylus." The second button goes.

I pull fabric aside so I can kiss his chest. He grabs my hips and squeezes as he pushes his crotch up into me.

"Keep going," he murmurs, and I don't know if he's talking about my mouth or the Greeks.

"Number three would be . . . Sophocles." I open another button and continue to kiss him; his skin is crazy-warm and soft under my lips. "Four is . . . um . . . Euripides." I open the last button and pull open his shirt before kissing a trail down his stomach. He lets go of my hips and digs his fingers into the carpet. "And five is . . ." The muscles in his stomach tense as I kiss them. "Uh . . . five is . . ." I lick his abs.

"God . . . Cassie."

"Nope. Not 'God' or 'Cassie.' I'm thinking it starts with an 'A.' "

I kiss back up to his nipple. I have no idea if men's nipples are as sensitive as women's, but I kiss it anyway. He arches his back and swears so loudly the neighbors probably heard it.

*Okay. Note to self: He likes having his nipples kissed.*

"Five is . . . Aristophanes." I move to the other side. I'm amazed by how he tastes. Salty and perfect.

"Number six is . . . uh . . . God . . ." He grinds into me, and I can't think. I can't stop tasting him as I run my hands over him, loving how fast his heart is pounding because of what I'm doing.

"Six is . . . it's . . . Aw, hell, I have no idea."

He sits up and kisses me, his tongue sweet and warm as I push his shirt off his shoulders.

"Menander," he says, his voice tight. "Guess you have to lose a piece of clothing. Let me help you."

He leans back and yanks off my T-shirt as he mutters, "God bless Menander for being so fucking forgettable." He cups my breasts through my bra and squeezes gently.

*Oh, Lord. Holt's hands. On my boobs. I may pass out.*

He pushes my breasts together and kisses a path across the top of them. The light stubble on his jaw scratches in a completely pleasurable way.

"I've been fantasizing about doing this for weeks. They're fucking perfect. Soft. Warm. Beautiful."

I push his face further into me and moan as he continues to fondle and kiss. My skin is burning up. Everywhere he touches me tingles. I can barely breathe, but I don't want him to stop.

I tilt my pelvis so I can press against him more firmly, and when I do, I gasp. The hard of him makes me ache to feel more.

I push him back onto the floor and straddle his thighs, before kissing a line down his stomach. Within a few seconds, my face is hovering just above the waistband of his jeans. I stroke the light smattering of hair below his belly button as he watches with heavy eyelids.

"I want to see you," I whisper.

He exhales. "Taylor, you're the most forward virgin I've ever met. Most are frightened of the things lurking inside men's pants."

"Have you known a lot of virgins?" I ask.

"Heaps. None of them ever asked to see my dick. In fact, they always asked me to keep it well away from them. Mind you, we were all fourteen at the time."

I smile. "Silly girls."

I kiss the skin just above his waistband, and when I look up at him, he's leaning on his elbows, watching me.

"You've read my diary," I say, keeping eye contact as I lick his hip. "You know my fascination with what's inside here."

"Fuck, yes." He squeezes his eyes shut and groans. "Please don't remind me about what's written in your diary. After I read that damn thing, I had an erection for over a week. It was torture."

"So, you remember what I wrote?" I ask as I run my hands over his hips.

"Taylor," he says, his voice low and deep, "I'm absolutely fucking ashamed to say that I remember every word. Your diary is like literary Viagra."

He tightens his jaw as I stroke his thighs, my fingers getting a little higher each time. A little closer to the bulge I'm dying to explore.

"You said my penis would probably win awards," he says, his voice cracking. "I have no idea why I found that so sexy. Oh, fuck . . ."

He gasps as I gently graze the line of him, feeling the pressure of the tight muscle beneath the fabric.

"Jesus." His jaw clenches and releases. "You have no idea what you do to me. You really don't."

When I unbuckle his belt and begin to unbutton his fly, he doesn't stop me, and I'm hit with a sudden revelation that although this is all new to me, he's no doubt had heaps of girls do this in the past.

I'm scared I won't measure up.

"Keep going," he says when I pause, a desperate edge to his voice. "Have pity, woman. Do you not fully understand how much I need you to put your hands on me right now?"

His words give me confidence, and as I continue, he watches me, his chest rising and falling quickly. Small sounds accompany each exhale. When the fly is completely unbuttoned I pull it open and look down.

"Oh . . . wow."

Holt's not wearing underpants.

*Breathe, Cassie.*

I glance up at his face. He half shrugs, half smiles. "Laundry day."

I direct my attention back to his crotch.

As I pull his jeans down, his erection settles on his stomach, allowing me to really see it for the first time.

My predictions about what it would look like were spot-on. This is an award-winning dick.

My porn research has taught me that dicks come in all shapes and sizes, and I truly appreciate a pretty peen no matter the dimensions. But Holt's erection is just like the rest of him. Inexplicably gorgeous. Large and arousing.

I touch it gently, grazing my fingers over the taut skin. The texture is incredible; far silkier than I'd imagined. I graze my fingertips over the length of it, and watch in awe as a myriad of emotions play across his face.

"Is this okay?" I ask, touching him more firmly.

He doesn't answer, just nods. His approval spurs me on, so I work up the courage to wrap my fingers around it and squeeze.

"Oh, wow," I say. "That feels amazing."

He groans. "You can say that again."

I gently move my fist up and down, blown away by the sensation of skin moving over muscle. I alternate between watching my hand and watching his reaction, and soon I become more confident with my pressure and rhythm.

"Oh . . . Cassie . . ."

*Look at him. Look at how beautiful he is.*

His face is stunning. Mouth open, brows furrowed. Every pass of my fingers makes him gasp, or moan, or curse.

I need to kiss him, so I keep moving my hand as I crawl back up his body and claim his lips. He kisses me back passionately, then closes his fingers over mine and squeezes.

"Harder," he whispers, and grunts his approval when I comply.

I don't know what I thought it would be like to touch Holt intimately, but I didn't realize it would be so . . . satisfying. Seeing his reaction to my touch and hearing the noises I'm causing, it's truly the most erotic thing I've ever experienced. And when he whispers urgently that he's going to come, I feel like I've just split the atom or invented the wheel. So powerful and clever.

When he climaxes, I'm in awe.

His whole body tenses, and I mentally claim ownership over his spectacular orgasm. I caused that. Me. Inexperienced virgin that I am, I made Ethan Holt come, and quite explosively I might add, all over his stomach.

I am a sexual goddess.

Holt moans long and loud as he finishes, and I kiss his face as he lies there struggling to get back his breath. Then I go and get a warm washcloth to help clean him up.

When we're finished, he pulls his shirt on and buttons his jeans, and I get a rush of emotion so powerful I don't know what to do with it. He must see something on my face, because he pulls me into his chest.

"Cassie? Hey . . ." He cups my face, concern coloring his voice. "Do you regret doing it? I was joking about pressuring you. I'd never make you do something you didn't want to. I'm not that much of an asshole."

I laugh and shake my head. "No, I really enjoyed it, I just . . ." I blow out a breath and look at him. "I'm just so happy that I managed to make my nonboyfriend come. Is it wrong that I'm proud of myself?"

He laughs and strokes my cheek. "No. Your nonboyfriend is also proud of you. And that was your first time? Damn, woman. I hate to think what you're going to be like after a bit of practice."

"I'm going to ruin you for all other women," I say seriously.

He nods. "Too late."

He gives a deep sigh before grabbing his book and opening it to where we left off. "I hate to say it, but we really should get back to studying. Unless of course you want me to . . . uh . . . you know, return the favor."

I smile and shake my head. "No, I'm good. Although I do have one request before we get all serious with the book learnin' again."

"A request?" he asks with a smirk. "Okay. What is it?"

"Kiss me."

# FIFTEEN

## GREEN-EYED MONSTER

*Two Weeks Later*
*Westchester, New York*
*The Grove*

I look at my hands, too nervous to face him but knowing from the heat at my back that he's there.

"You shouldn't be here," he says. "If you believe the stories about me, I'm a killer. An animal not worthy of love or human kindness."

"I know. I've heard people talk. They'd sooner string you up and dance at your funeral than for one second open up their mind and let in a little reason. They're not happy unless they're miserable, and seeing other people's flaws helps them overlook what they hate about themselves."

"But that's not you?"

"No." I take a deep breath to calm my runaway pulse and look him square in the eyes. "I may not be the cleverest girl in this town, or the prettiest, or the richest, but I know people as well as anyone can. And though folks speak of your evil, I've never seen it. All I've seen is a man who's looking for a second chance but is too proud to demand he gets one."

He swallows as he brushes the backs of his fingers over my cheek. "You can't be saying things like that to me, girl. It makes it impossible to not kiss you."

"That's what I was going for."

Then he's kissing me, slowly, warm lips and soft hands. For a moment I'm confused, because his lips feel different, and his taste is all wrong, but I know those are Cassie's thoughts, not Ellie's.

When we pull apart, there's a huge round of applause as the scene ends. I blink and take Connor's hand as we face the audience.

Tonight our class is performing script excerpts that have been chosen and directed by the third-year students, and even though it was weird to be paired with Connor instead of Ethan, I did my best to make it work. Our director, Sophie, is in the front row clapping and jumping up and down, so I figure she's happy with what we've achieved.

Connor and I bow and exit the stage, and he gives me a brief hug while the next pair is introduced.

"So, I don't want to brag or anything," he says. "But we just kicked ass out there."

I nod and smile. "That screaming applause was the sound of our awesomeness."

He laughs as we walk toward the backstage crossover. "I just need to get my shirt, then we'll head out to watch, okay?"

"Sure."

"See you back here in a few minutes."

I'm grateful, because there's someone I really need to see. As my eyes adjust to the darkness, I can make out Holt near the lighting cage, pacing and mumbling.

Tonight he's performing an excerpt from *Glengarry Glen Ross* with Troy and Lucas, and because we've been rehearsing in separate groups all week, I've barely seen him.

I walk over and smile. He barely looks at me.

"Hey." I'm playing nonchalant really well, considering all I want to do is drag him into the shadowy lighting cage and kiss him all over. "How's it going?"

"Hey." He keeps pacing, taking deep breaths as he goes.

"You okay?"

"Yep. Great. You?"

He's being short with me. Avoiding eye contact. I kind of expected a warmer reception, considering our time apart. I think I know what's wrong, but if I'm right, then he's being ridiculous.

"Holt—"

"Look, Taylor, I have to warm up, so if you don't mind . . ."

He turns away and rolls his neck. It cracks loudly.

I decide not to push. He'll be going on stage soon, and he needs to focus.

"Do you want to"—I lean in so no one can hear—"you know, snuggle? Or I could give you a foot massage if you have time."

He sighs but doesn't turn around. "Nope. I'm fine. I'll see you later, okay?"

I look around. Apart from Aiyah, who's watching Miranda and Jack onstage, there's no one else who can see us, so I wrap my arms around him and hug his back. Then I lay my cheek against his shoulder and inhale.

He smells so damn good, I almost moan.

His body tenses as he whispers, "Cut it out. People can see."

I squeeze him tighter. "I don't care. I've hugged everyone else tonight. Why shouldn't I hug the one person I really want to? I've missed you."

For a second he doesn't say anything, but then his shoulders slump and he places his hand over mine and intertwines our fingers. "Dammit, Taylor . . . I've . . ." He sighs. "Me too."

He steps away, but the way he's looking at me gives away that he's missed me every bit as much as I've missed him.

Maybe more.

I hear footsteps, and Connor appears next to me. Holt's posture is immediately tense.

"Hey, Ethan. Cassie, ready to go out?"

"Yeah, sure," I say, even though I'd really like to stay with Holt a little longer. "So, Ethan, uh . . . you . . . do good, okay?"

I eye-roll my epic lameness.

Holt gives me a halfhearted smile, and I hate that he looks so sick. I'm hoping it's nerves and not me and Connor, but I'm betting it's a little of both.

"Have a good one, man," Connor says and pats Holt's shoulder. "See you after the show."

As we walk away, I'm sure I hear Holt mutter, "Not if I see you first, asshole."

A few minutes later, his group is introduced, and as soon as he walks onstage, I'm mesmerized. Lucas and Troy infuse the scene with the sort of machismo-fueled rivalry that it needs, but it's quite clear from his energy that Holt is the alpha male. He also looks completely edible in his suit and tie.

Their scene ends to huge amounts of applause, and after several more group performances, the show's over. Erika comes onto the stage and makes a speech congratulating us all on a great collaborative effort before wishing us a good weekend.

As Connor and I head backstage to get changed, he puts his arm around me, as usual. It shouldn't make me feel weird, because he's always been physically affectionate, but with things being the way they are with Holt me, I feel guilty. It's bad enough I've spent all week kissing Connor for our scene.

It's not like I have feelings for Connor beyond friendship, but part of me wonders what it would be like to go out with a boy who isn't afraid to show affection in public. Hell, I wonder what it would be like to go *out* with a boy. What Holt and I are doing could hardly be defined as "dating." Mostly we hang out at my place. On the rare occasion we do go out, it's to parties with the rest of our class where we spend the whole night avoiding each other. Then when he drives me home, we paw at each other frantically until someone orgasms.

He hasn't once asked me out on a proper date. He hasn't even invited me over to his apartment.

"See you at the party?" Connor says as we go our separate ways. I nod and wave. I'd like to think that Holt plans to take me, but the only consistent thing about him is his unpredictability.

When I finish getting changed, I grab my backpack and head to his dressing room. I step inside to find him sitting on the couch unlacing his shoes. He's still wearing his suit pants, but his shirt, tie, and jacket are slung over the chair, and all he's wearing on his upper half is a white tank.

*Oh. God.*

I stand there in a state of debilitating lust, watching his arms flex as he tugs at his laces. He looks up and catches me.

He frowns as he pulls off his shoes and socks. "You okay?"

"No." Pretty sure I'm slack-jawed and drooling.

He stops what he's doing. "What's wrong?"

"What's wrong?" I gesture to his shoulders and arms. "*That's* what wrong, mister. *All* of that! I don't see you for five days, then you show up wearing that?!"

He rests his elbows on his knees as he looks down at himself. "Taylor, you've seen my arms before."

"Not recently. And it's not just your arms. It's your shoulders. And your neck. And that little bit of hair on your chest. And all of it together, wrapped up in that . . . that ridiculous piece of clothing you're wearing."

"My tank?"

"Yes! It's like wrapping up the very definition of the word 'sexy' in a layer of irresistible lust." I grunt in frustration and whisper, "It does strange things to me, Ethan. It makes me want to do strange things to you, too."

He stares at me for a second before trailing his gaze down my body, then up again. "What sort of things?"

"You don't want to know."

"I think it's safe to say that I really, *really* do. Show me."

"It's too embarrassing. You'll judge me."

"Taylor, you haven't touched me in five days. Do you really want to keep discussing this, or do you want to do something about it?"

He has a point. "Uch. Fine."

I walk over and kneel between his legs. He watches me with wary eyes as I put my hands on his thighs.

"Flex your bicep," I order quietly. He looks confused. "Just do it."

He shakes his head before clenching his fist and curling his arm, causing the muscles to contract and bunch in ways that makes me bite my tongue to keep from making an embarrassingly wanton sound.

I lean forward and press my lips against the bunched muscle. Holt seems confused.

When I trail my teeth over the soft skin and press into the hardness underneath, he frowns. I close my eyes and suck on the thick muscle. He makes a strangled noise, and when I look at him, I notice he's panting and his pupils are huge.

I give his bicep one final suck before my mortification wins out, and I pull back.

"*That's* the sort of thing it makes me want to do," I say as I sit back on my heels. "Now, aren't you embarrassed you like someone who's so obviously disturbed?"

He lowers his arm and blinks. "You have no idea, do you? You literally have no clue."

"About what?"

"About how insanely fucking sexy you are."

He wraps one arm around me and pulls me forward as he splays his fingers across my cheek and kisses me, sudden and passionate. His mouth is warm and insistent. I react by making more noise than is probably wise considering I can hear my classmates moving around outside the dressing room door.

"Sshhh," he whispers as he pulls me against him.

I'm dizzy, and I clutch at his shoulders as he kisses down my jaw and onto my neck.

"Wow," I say, breathless. "If this is how you react when I suck on your bicep, imagine the fun we're going to have when I get to other parts of your anatomy."

He immediately freezes.

And there it is. The reaction he always has when I imply I'd like to take him in my mouth.

"You know," I say, trying to loosen his arms so I can pull back and look at him, "most men have a completely different reaction when a girl offers to pleasure them orally. Are you afraid I won't do it right, because I have no experience? I can assure you, I've watched enough porn to know my way around a penis. I mean, I don't know if I'll be able to take it all the way in like some of those girls, but I'm sure, with enough practice that I could—"

"Fuck me, Taylor . . ." He lets me go and slumps back against the couch. "You just . . . you can't go around saying that kind of stuff."

"Why not?"

"Because . . ." He rubs his eyes, then looks at me, pained and turned on. "I'm trying not to let things get out of control with you, and if you keep saying that stuff, it's going to be fucking impossible."

"Fine. I won't talk."

I push up his tank and kiss his stomach before moving down to the waistband of his pants. A long, tortured groan pours out of him.

"We can't," he says, his voice cracking. "Someone could walk in any second."

"So?" I unlatch his belt buckle. "I'm sure it's not the first time drama students have been caught pleasuring each other backstage. We're a very horny bunch, or haven't you noticed?"

I stroke him through his pants, and even though his accompanying moan sounds like a protest, he doesn't stop me.

"You're killing me, Taylor. You know that, right? Every time you touch me, you kill me a little more."

There's a rush of running feet outside, and Holt springs off the couch and refastens his pants right before the door bursts open, and a naked Jack Avery streaks into the room.

"Pre-party nudie dash!" He does a quick lap of the room and exits.

"Jesus. I did *not* need to see that." Holt strides toward the open door. "Why don't these goddamn doors have locks? Hide your shame, Avery!"

He slams the door and slumps back onto the couch.

"Actually," I say, "nude Jack has nothing to be ashamed of. Who knew the geek was packing that larger-than-average lightsaber in his *Star Wars* underoos?"

Holt rolls his eyes, and I laugh as I sit beside him and stroke the back of his neck.

"You were really good tonight," I say, running my fingers over his ear.

He raises his eyebrows. "Yeah?"

"Yeah. I love watching you onstage. You're so . . . sexy. And talented. In fact, I think you're sexy *because* you're talented. I mean, you're also ridiculously handsome, but so are soap actors, and they do absolutely nothing for me because they're terrible actors. So yeah, I find your talent a turn-on. Is that weird? Should I stop talking now?"

He smiles and leans forward. "Yes."

He takes my face in his hands and kisses me gently. I grip his arms to steady myself as my heart kicks into overdrive.

He pulls back and sighs. "You're talented, too. Way too talented in too many ways."

"So," I say as I take his hand and stroke his fingers. "Did you see my scene with Connor?"

He tenses. "Uh . . . yeah. I saw it from backstage."

A hint of agitation creeps onto his face, and I can almost hear his brain whispering things that aren't true.

"And what did you think?"

"You were good."

"Uh huh. And Connor?"

He shrugs and stands. "He was all right. He made some obvious choices, but I guess they worked."

He strips off his pants, giving me a very nice view of his butt in dark gray boxer-briefs before he pulls on his jeans.

"So . . . you don't want to talk about anything else to do with the scene?"

He grabs a V-neck sweater and yanks it over his head. "Nope." He pushes up the sleeves and runs his hand through his hair.

"You don't care that I kissed him?"

He sits on a chair opposite me and pulls out his boots and socks from under the bench. "I care. I just don't want to talk about it."

"Why not?"

"Because," he says as he pulls on a sock, "talking about it . . . even thinking about it, makes me irrationally fucking angry."

Wow. He's admitting something. This is epic.

"Holt, you know you have nothing to be jealous of, right?"

He pushes his foot into his boot and tugs roughly at the laces. "Don't I? You looked pretty into that kiss. And it's been obvious from day one that Connor wants to get into your pants."

I walk over and stand in front of him as he laces up his other boot. "I don't think he does anymore. Ever since that first party when I stopped him kissing me, I think he's known that . . . well . . ."

He finishes with his laces and looks up at me. "He's known what?"

I focus on the tiny frown line between his brows. "Even back then, he'd figured out that I . . . you know . . . liked you."

He leans back in the chair and sighs. "Yeah, well, that doesn't mean *he* stopped liking *you*. He just started hiding it better."

"He's hiding it pretty well. During our entire week of rehearsals, he didn't make a single pass at me."

"Apart from all that time he spent sucking your face, of course."

I blink. "Uh . . . yeah. Apart from that."

He stands up and takes a step toward me. "Did he use tongue?"

"A little."

"How little?"

I cup the back of his head and pull his head down. "Kind of like this."

I kiss him slowly, then take his top lip between mine and suck on it gently before repeating the move on his bottom lip.

He makes a noise and pulls back to glare down at me. "Jesus, Cassie, he kissed you like that?!"

"Uh . . . sort of."

"Sort of?!"

"Well, yeah, but . . . it was different because it was our characters, and . . . it wasn't you. And that made it all wrong."

He drops his head. I'm not explaining myself well, but I don't know what to say to him.

"He and I didn't have any of the chemistry you and I do."

"From where I stood, it looked like you had plenty of chemistry."

"It was just acting. Did you see the love scene between Miranda and Jack? It was hot as hell, but it's not like Miranda has traded in her lesbian card and wants to jump Jack. It just looked that way."

He walks around me and grabs a hanger from the rack before hanging up his suit and zipping it into a garment bag.

"Ethan, come on."

"I believe you," he says as he shoves it onto the rack. "Logically, I know you did what was needed in order to make the scene work. But . . ."

"But what?"

He puts his hands in his pockets and blows out a breath. "It made me feel sick, seeing you kissing him." He looks at me, and even now he doesn't seem entirely well. "It made me crazy, Taylor, and I'm not just saying that as hyperbole. I truly felt unhinged. Like I could have beaten the shit out of him for touching you."

"Like you did to Matt when you found out about him and Vanessa?" I ask.

He laughs bitterly and shakes his head. "Jesus, is there anything my goddamn sister hasn't told you?"

I walk over and put my hands on his chest, then stroke him through his sweater.

"Ethan, I wouldn't cheat on you with Connor."

He looks down, seeming more vulnerable than I've seen him for a long time. "I know that."

"I'd never cheat on you, with anyone."

"Yeah, well, technically, you can't cheat on me, because I'm not your boyfriend."

His words at first hit me like a sucker punch, but I have to remember who I'm talking to.

"The funny thing is, you sound a lot like my boyfriend." I run my hands up his neck. "My extremely hot, jealous boyfriend."

I pull his hands out of his pockets and wrap them around my waist. His trademark flicker of fear sparks in his eyes, before he shakes his head and strokes my lower back.

"Taylor, you have sucky taste. There are guys who would be far better boyfriends than I would be. I'd bet Connor would be a fucking spectacular boyfriend. He'd be one of those sickening idiots who'd bring you flowers in the middle of the cafeteria or hire a barbershop quartet for your birthday."

"So are you telling me I should date Connor instead of you?"

"He'd be better for you than I would."

"Oh, in that case, I'd better go find him." I turn to leave, but I only take three steps before he spins me around, presses me into the door, and kisses me, all open mouth and soft tongue.

For the life of me, I can't remember what we were talking about thirty seconds ago.

When he pulls back, we're both breathless.

"So, I'm not sure if you got my subtle subtext there," he says, "but I'd really like it if you stayed the fuck away from Connor, okay?"

My heart is pounding overtime. "If Connor knew you were my boyfriend, he'd know I'm not available. I don't understand why we can't just go public."

He leans his head against mine. "Cassie, I've had high-profile relationships. When things go wrong, it just makes it that much harder to deal with."

"I understand that, but you're working on the assumption that something will go wrong with us. Maybe it won't. Maybe we'll be perfectly happy and never fight."

He laughs. "You have met us, right? We fight all the time." He tightens his arms around me and pulls me more firmly against him. "I just want to keep it between us for a little longer. Okay?"

I nod. "I guess I just . . . I don't want to feel like you're ashamed to have people know you like me, or whatever."

"I'm not ashamed." He cups my face. "Well, actually, I'm a little ashamed of my constant erection, but that's beside the point. I just don't want people judging and talking behind our backs. I'd prefer we keep it private."

I sigh and run my fingers across the stubble on his jaw. "Okay. We can keep it on the down-low for a while longer, but what do I say if someone straight out asks me about us?"

There's a babble of voices in the hallway, and he immediately steps away and shoves his hands in his pockets. "Lie."

"And if Connor asks?"

His eye twitches. "Tell that fucker we're engaged."

### Present Day
### New York City

The foyer of the Majestic Theater is packed with performers, producers, sponsors, and avid theatergoers, all coming together for one of the largest fund-raisers on the Broadway calendar. Each audience member has paid several hundred dollars to see excerpts from some of the best shows currently playing in the theater district, with all proceeds going toward the Variety Performers of America Benevolent Fund.

Holt and I performed a short excerpt from our show as a preview prior to opening, and judging by the audience reaction, our show's going to be a bona fide hit. Even now, as we move through the foyer, people keep stopping us to tell us how much they're looking forward to seeing it. I spy Marco across the room, beaming. It feels good to know that the buzz is positive. It makes my growing anxiety about opening night a little more bearable.

With his hand at the small of my back, Holt steers me to an alcove at the side of the foyer. It houses a particularly bad fake-marble statue of a man with an abnormally small penis, but as least it's free from the noise and crush of the rest of the room.

"Sorry for rubbing up against you," he says. "It was unavoidable in that crowd."

"Yeah, that's what I thought the first three times you did it. Then it was just gratuitous."

He looks shocked. "Taylor, are you implying that I rubbed up against you on purpose?" He moves forward so my back is against the pillar. "That's just insulting. I would never stoop to something so low. If I was going to sexually harass you, I'd be all subtle about it, like this."

He gives me a ridiculously sexy face and presses me into the wall, and although I want to laugh at his antics, the truth is, having his body pressed against me ruins my ability to do anything but breathe.

A loud laugh nearby jolts me back to reality, and a prickle of nervousness runs up my spine as I realize we can still be seen.

"Okay, Sir Humpsalot, cut it out." I push against his chest until he steps back. "There are reporters here. We don't want them getting the wrong impression."

"What, that I enjoy rubbing myself on you? Because that's not the wrong impression. That's an indisputable fact. How do you not know this by now?"

"What I mean is, they might think that we're . . . well . . . you know . . ."

His smile fades a little. "No. Why don't you tell me?"

I sigh and stare at him. "They might think that we're . . . together. And we're not."

A flicker of disappointment registers on his face, but he hides it quickly. He puts his hand on the pillar behind my head and leans down.

"You know, it would be really good publicity for our show if we *were* together. I mean, just think of it, 'Real-life Couple Plays Lovers Onstage.' The press would eat it up."

"Ethan . . ."

"Of course, we'd have to do lots of publicity. I'd have to take you out to high-profile restaurants and make sure the paparazzi were watching when I kissed you . . . and sucked on your neck . . . and put my hand between your legs under the table."

The juncture of my thighs lights up at the thought.

I lean more heavily against the pillar.

"If you really want our show to be a hit," he says as his gaze flickers between my eyes and mouth, "then you'd agree to let me kiss you. Right now. In front of all of these people."

He stares at me, and all I can do is gaze at his lips while my lust wages war with my fear.

"Just say yes, Cassie. Don't overthink it."

His mouth is close. Almost too close for me to deny him anything.

"Ethan . . ."

"No, not 'Ethan.' 'Yes'. Or better yet, 'Yes, please, God, kiss me before we both go insane.' Either works for me. 'Fuck, yes!' with an accompanying fist pump is also acceptable."

I have to smile.

*God, I love him.*

I gasp.

*Whoa.*

*So not ready to face that reality yet.*

He reads the panicked expression my face and drops his head in defeat. "Okay, fine, no kissing, but let me tell you, it's a wasted opportunity. Alcohol?"

"Yes, please."

"Oh, so you can say 'yes, please' to booze but not to me? Nice. Taylor, if our show tanks, just know it's because you didn't get on board with my make-out-with-Ethan-as-often-as-possible publicity plan. I hope you can live with that decision."

I laugh and slap his arm. "Vodka cocktail, please."

"Yeah, whatever." He fake-sulks as he makes his way through the crowd toward the bar, and as soon as he leaves my side, I miss him.

I step out of the alcove and take a deep breath.

As beautiful, and patient, and hilarious as he's being, there's still a shard of something inside me that twists and burns without reason or warning, and it terrifies me, because sometimes it makes me feel like the specter of our past will always be hanging over us, making me push him away even when I want him closer.

I feel a hand slide around my waist, and I flinch in surprise as I turn to see a familiar face.

"Connor!"

Oh, God, *Connor*.

"Hey, Cassie," he says and leans in to kiss my cheek. "How have you been?"

"Really well. You?"

*What's he doing here? Leave. Please, leave now.*

"I'm great. Just about to open in the new production of *Arcadia* down at the Ethel Barrymore Theater."

"I heard! That's fantastic. I can't wait to come and see it."

"Well, let me know when you want to come, and I'll get you house seats."

"That'd be great."

I'll never come and see it. He knows that. I've ruined our friendship.

I'm a fucking terrible person.

We lapse into silence and just look at each other for a few seconds as awkwardness settles between us.

"You look beautiful," he says, and I glance down because I really can't look him in the eyes anymore. "As usual."

"Connor . . ."

"How's the play going?" he asks, changing the subject. "Must be weird working with Ethan again, huh?"

I look over and see Holt at the bar, waiting to be served.

"Yep." I tuck my hair behind my ear and push down my rising panic. "Weird is one word for it. Does he know you're here?"

He shakes his head. "No. I wanted to see you first. Say hi. I . . . I wasn't sure how much you've told him about us. I didn't want things to be awkward."

I sigh. Awkward seems to be where I live these days. Right there on the corner of Freak-Out Avenue.

"I haven't told him anything," I say, wishing Connor would leave before Ethan comes back, "and I'd really appreciate it if you didn't mention it. We open in a week, and I don't want to cause drama."

"Don't tell me you're back together?" he asks, his face turning dark.

"No. We're not. We're just . . . we're trying to be friends."

When I look over, Holt's walking toward us, and I feel like I'm going to have a stroke, my heart's beating so fast.

Connor follows my gaze as a wry smile settles on his face. "Well, I guess some things never change. I can't believe that after what he did to you, you're still completely in love with him."

I look at him sharply. "That's not true."

"Oh, please, Cassie. Even when you claimed to hate him, you were so fixated, you couldn't see other options that were right in front of you."

"Connor—"

"I would have *never* hurt you like he did. But I guess it's all just history now, huh?"

He shrugs it off, but I know how much damage I did, and that knowledge makes me feel like garbage.

"I just hope you know what the hell you're doing, because if he hurts you again . . ." He shakes his head. "You deserve to be happy, Cassie. That's all I'm saying."

I nod. Things might have been so different if I could have made things work with Connor. But I couldn't. I tried. We both know I really tried.

"Hey, Connor!" Ethan hands me my drink and then shakes Connor's hand. To his credit, he looks genuinely pleased to see him. I, on the other hand, am on the verge of two worlds colliding and am about to pass out. "I heard you were doing *Arcadia*, man. Congratulations. The cast looks awesome."

282      LEISA RAYVEN

Connor plasters on a smile. "Hey, Ethan. Yeah, it's great. Bookings are going well, so we're hoping for a nice, long run."

Holt smiles and gestures toward the bar. "Can I get you a drink? They have some decent imported beer. Or if you want to live dangerously, I could get you one of these pink monstrosities Taylor's drinking, although I'm pretty sure it's made from just vodka and sugar."

Connor looks at me and smiles, but there's sadness in his eyes. "Yeah, well . . . she always did have questionable taste."

Something shifts in the air, and when I look back at Ethan he's staring at Connor, his smile fading. Suddenly I think it's really important that Connor leaves.

As if he senses the building tension, Connor says, "Well, it's been great seeing you guys but I've got to get back to the rest of my cast. Hope you can come down one night and see the show." He looks at both of us as he says it, but I know he's only talking to me.

"See you, Ethan," he says, his voice less than friendly. Then he kisses my cheek and whispers, "Take care of yourself, Cassie. Please."

He leaves, and even though the room is full of people chattering and laughing, all I can focus on is the absolute silence surrounding Ethan. He takes several mouthfuls of beer and pretends to look at something across the room, but I can see that his eyes are glazed and unfocused. He's not looking at something as much as he's trying not to look at me. I squirm because I know, without a shadow of a doubt, what he's about to say.

"You slept with him, didn't you?" he asks quietly. He doesn't sound angry, or even hurt. Just . . . resigned.

When I don't answer, he looks at me, and I can see that he's struggling to hold in everything he's feeling. His lips are pressed together and hard, and my heart is pounding so loudly I can hear it in my ears.

"Ethan . . ."

"Just tell me, Cassie. I'm not going to make a scene. I just need to know."

"You already know."

He huffs in frustration. "I need to hear you say it."

I take a deep breath and push down a wave of nausea. "Yes. We slept together."

He blinks but doesn't stop staring at me. "When?"

"You know when."

"After graduation."

"Yes."

"Straight after I left."

"Yes."

"For how long?"

"Three months."

"Three months?!" He laughs, but it's a bitter sound. "Three fucking . . ." He nods and takes another swig of beer, his expression intense. "So you two were . . . what? In a relationship? Dating?"

"No. I mean . . . kind of. He wanted to, but I just . . . I couldn't. I didn't feel that way about him. It was just sex."

He laughs again, and he's looking everywhere else but at me.

"Ethan . . . I was angry and hurting. He was there. You weren't."

He swallows more beer, his jaw clenching and releasing.

"You can't be upset with me for something that happened after you left. That's not fair."

"I know," he says, his voice low. "I know I shouldn't want to smash in Connor's fucking face, but . . . Jesus, Cassie, three months?!"

He takes a deep breath and lets it out slowly before looking at me.

"I know you were with other men after I left," he says. "I overheard you and Tristan talking about it the night I came to your apartment. And as much as it fucking killed me to hear that, I coped by telling myself they were just nameless, faceless guys. One-night stands that fulfilled some urge for you. That didn't mean anything—"

"They *didn't* mean anything. Nothing has meant anything for longer than I can remember."

"Connor meant something."

"No."

"Cassie, you can't tell me you had sex with him for three months without it meaning something. It's one thing to fuck someone you pick up in a bar and never see again. It's another thing to have sex with someone you care about. At the very least, he was your friend, so you had to have *some* feelings for him."

"Obviously whatever I felt for him wasn't enough. Nothing was ever enough for me after you."

When he looks at me, I can tell he's angry. But beneath the anger is hurt, so deep and raw that I can't look him in the eyes, because his pain echoes inside of me.

"Do you think I don't know this is my fault?" he asks as he leans forward. "I know that, all right? And it fucking kills me. And what's worse is that I could have lost you to someone like Connor. Someone who would *never* treat you the way I did."

I glance over to where Connor is across the room. He's looking at Holt and me with concern. He can tell that we're fighting.

Ethan is shifting from one foot to the other, struggling to stay in control.

I don't know what to say to him. His jealousy is pointless. It always was. As if he's ever had anything to be truly jealous of.

"Why couldn't you make it work with him?" he asks and places his beer bottle on a table next to us before looking at his feet. "You said he wanted more. Why didn't you?"

"I've asked myself that question so many times, I've lost count."

"And what's the answer?"

I take a breath. "I don't know. Connor thinks he never had a chance with me because I was still in love with you."

He searches my face, then licks his lips before asking, "And what do you think?"

I fight to keep my voice steady. "I think he's probably right."

He looks at me for a long time, the wheels of his brain processing my words, noting I'd said "was" in love. Not admitting to how I'm feeling now.

I pray he doesn't ask me, because I know I can't say it. Not yet. That would be like cutting open my chest and handing over my heart all over again, and I'm not anywhere near ready to do that.

"So where does that leave us?" he asks, his brow furrowed. "Judging by the way Connor was looking at you, if you said one word to him, he'd walk out of here with you right now."

"And would you let him?"

He stares at me for long seconds before answering. "If that's what you wanted. If you thought he could make you happier than I could."

I take in an unsteady breath and put my hand on his chest, the first voluntary contact I've made for days. He blinks in surprise.

"So, if I said I didn't want you, and didn't love you, and needed Connor in my life instead of you, you'd stop fighting for me? You'd just . . . let me go?"

He tightens his jaw and places his hand over mine before pressing it into his chest. "No."

"Why not?"

"Because you'd be lying."

I let out a shaky breath. "Yes, I would."

Suddenly his hands are on my face, and before I can even get out one word to protest that we're in a room full of people, he's kissing me. My breath catches as his lips move gently against mine, and I'm so devastated by the sensation that I cease to care that Connor, and

Marco, and members of the Broadway press club are standing around us.

My stomach coils and flips as he tilts my head and kisses me deeper, his breath loud and shallow as he half groans, half sighs into my mouth. His hands are on my face and my neck, pulling me closer and stroking me in a way that makes me lose track of time and place and just melt into him, as if we're two highly combustible chemical compounds that ignite when they come in contact.

Part of why I could never get over him is because only *he* can make me react like this. Every other man was like a match, igniting vague passion, but brief and unremarkable. Ethan is like a volcano. A never-ending series of ecstatic, bone-deep eruptions.

He presses me against the pillar, hands cupping my face, and that's when it becomes too much. He's too important, and the feelings I'm having are too big for my stitched-up heart. I push him away and grip his shirt, dizzy and unsteady.

"I'm sorry," he says, breathless. "But . . . well . . . Jesus, Cassie, you can't just say that you want me and expect me to not completely lose my mind. I know you can't give me all of yourself right now, but I just needed to have one small part of you. A piece that wasn't Connor's, or the other guys' you've been with. Just mine. And I hope Connor and every other man in the room saw that fucking spectacular kiss, because anyone who witnessed that could *not* deny that we're meant to be together, especially not you."

I step back and lean against the pillar, panting and trying to calm myself.

He's right. That kiss pretty much destroyed any doubts I had about wanting him in my life again, but that doesn't mean I'm ready to make out with him in front of a roomful of my peers.

I'm so caught up in the moment, I don't even notice how many people have their camera phones trained on us.

# SIXTEEN

## DENIAL

*Six Years Earlier*
*Westchester, New York*
*The Grove*

"Taylor, just stick it in your mouth."

"Don't rush me. I've never done this before."

"Yeah, well, the best way to learn it just to do it."

"I don't know what the heck I'm doing!"

"Stop talking yourself out of it. Just wrap your lips around it and suck. It's not rocket science."

"Oh, my *God*, Cassie," Zoe says as she rolls her eyes. "Either do it or hand it around. Other people want a turn, you know."

She scowls at me as I regard the glowing joint in my hand. I'm tempted to just hand it over, but I don't want to seem like the naive girl I actually am, so I put it between my lips and suck hard. I wind up inhaling a scorching lungful of pungent smoke.

Everyone laughs as I launch into a massive coughing fit.

Holt claps me gently on my back.

"Leave your lips parted a bit when you inhale," he says while trying not to laugh. "That way you'll take in some air with the smoke, and it'll burn less."

"You couldn't have told me that before I did it?" I wheeze as he hands me his bottle of water.

He shrugs and smiles. "Where'd the fun be in that?"

I slap his arm as I take the water and drink.

"Try again," Lucas says and waves his hand at me. "Do as Ethan says and take in more air, then hold it inside your lungs for as long as you can. That's the best way to get a decent buzz."

I do as he says. The smoke still burns, but I manage to hold it inside for a good ten seconds before exhaling.

"Nice," Lucas says, and everyone gives me a light round of applause.

Jack takes the joint. "We'll have you getting high like a pro in no time."

"Awesome," I say weakly as I grab Holt's water again and take a long drink.

"I still can't believe this is your first time," Zoe says with disdain. "What self-respecting American teenager gets to the ripe old age of nineteen without getting high at least once?"

I shrug. "The daughter of the World's Strictest Dad?"

Zoe screws up her face. "Cassie, that's no excuse. Didn't you see *Footloose*? The preacher's daughter did everything but whore herself out after church. Having an overprotective daddy should have made you *more* wild, not less. Sheesh."

For some reason, Jack and Lucas find her statement hilarious and crack up. It makes me smile. Zoe notices, and her face does a really strange dance between being pissed and happy. Happy eventually wins, and she grins at me as Jack passes her the joint.

*Wow. Marijuana has a magical way of making mortal enemies like each other? Why isn't this stuff legal, again?*

Holt takes the joint from Zoe and squints as he inhales. His long fingers splay, and he sucks with pursed lips.

Beside me, Zoe moans. "Fuck me, Ethan, you have the best lips."

He gives her a closed-mouth smile as he holds in the smoke, and I nearly choke trying not to laugh at the expression of lust on her face.

She has it so bad for him.

I know how she feels.

"Jeez, Holt," Jack whines. "Do you have to hog all the girls? How about leaving some for the rest of us?"

Holt hands him the joint and shrugs. Then he turns and leans in as he grabs my head. At first, I'm shocked because I think he's going to kiss me, which is weird because for the past few weeks we've been extremely careful to not show any affection in front of our classmates. But at the last second, he hovers his mouth over mine and exhales, and I realize he wants me to breathe in the smoke.

I inhale, my whole body tingling as he smiles while grazing his thumb super-slowly across my cheek.

*Whoa. Fireworks under my skin. Tingly hot.*

I can definitely feel the marijuana affecting me now. Everything seems to slow down and gain sharper focus, and for the longest time, all I can see is Holt's face in front of me. He blinks slowly, and I can hear his lashes hitting his eyelids. Then he licks his lips, all slow motion and pink tongue. The thudding bass of a Barry White song starts up in my brain.

"Kiss her!" Jack yells before making obnoxious smacking noises.

Holt blinks, but by the time he looks away, my face is blazing hot, and other parts of me, farther south, are even hotter.

"So what exactly is the deal with you two, anyway?" Jack asks, his voice tight as he inhales. "Are you actually fucking?"

Holt shoots him a withering glare before snatching the joint and handing it to me.

"You're so goddamn classless, Avery. No, we're not fucking."

"Then what are you doing? Give us the horny details."

"We're not doing anything," Holt says. "Change the damn subject."

"I'd like to know, too," Zoe says. "After *Romeo and Juliet*, we all thought you were screwing, but you hardly ever touch each other now that the show's over, so we're not sure. Clear up the rumors. Tell us what's going on."

Holt sighs and shakes his head. "There's nothing going on. Taylor and I are friends. Nothing more."

Even though I know he's lying, it still makes me uncomfortable.

"Bullshit, you're just friends," Jack says as he takes the joint from me. "I have a vague recollection of you two making out on my bed on opening night. At least, I think it was you."

Holt laughs before leaning back against a large tree and crossing his arms over his chest. "Avery, you were drunk and stoned out of your mind that night. For about an hour, you spoke to people only in Smurf language. It was smurfing annoying. You were imagining things."

"You're full of shit, Holt," Jack says. "Cassie? Care to confirm or deny that you're smurfing the hell out of Holt?"

My blush intensifies. "Jack, I can say with the utmost honesty, that I'm definitely *not* smurfing Holt. Wait, smurfing means having sex, right?"

How the hell do the Smurfs know what they're talking about most of the time? Is it a noun? Is it a verb? I'm so confused.

"Yes, Taylor, we're talking about sex."

"Well, then no. Definitely not doing that."

*Unfortunately. Smurf it all to hell.*

I exhale as I glance at Holt. One of his hands is in his pocket while he strokes the bark of the tree with his other. I'm mesmerized by his fingertips grazing over the rough texture. I've never been so jealous of a tree in my whole life.

"But you'd like to, right?" Jack asks with a knowing grin. "You'd like to smurf him up real good, huh? Smurf him long and slow? Or maybe fast and hard?"

Holt glares at Jack, who promptly shuts up.

"I know I would," Zoe mumbles. "I'd smurf him 'til his fucking head exploded." She looks up, apparently shocked she'd spoken out loud. "Oh, shit. You guys totally heard that, didn't you?"

"I didn't," Holt says, feigning ignorance.

"Oh, well, I said I wanted to fuck you," Zoe says before covering her face. "Oh, shit. There's no chance you didn't hear *that*, is there?"

Holt smiles and shakes his head. "Afraid not."

"Zoe, you can ride me," Jack says and gestures to his lap. "Climb on up. One decent-sized cock, no waiting."

Zoe raises her eyebrows. "How decent-sized?"

"Seven and a half," Jack says proudly.

Zoe nods. "Acceptable size. Tell you what, Jack, next time I get blind drunk, come see me. I might be able to cope with fucking you if I can't remember it the next day."

"Oh, ha ha," Jack says. "It's your loss. I could give you the best two and a half minutes of your life, lady."

We all crack up.

Our laughter is loud in the quiet woods, and I glance at Holt. He's smiling but staring at me in a way that makes a flood of heat rush through me. My laughter dies as I jiggle my knees to try and help ease the ache between my legs.

If I'd realized pot would make me even hornier than usual, I'd have passed.

"Man, I'm fucking hungry," Jack says beside me.

"Me too," I say to Holt's crotch.

"If we leave now, we can swing past the cafeteria on the way to class," Lucas says.

We all stand and head out of the trees on the west side of the school, heading back toward the Hub. The three boys walk in front of me and Zoe. When I notice her checking out Holt's ass, I'm not even jealous. His ass is incredibly fine. It should be ogled.

"So, you've really never fucked him?" she whispers, as she continues to stare at his butt.

"Nope."

I want to bite his butt. Not hard. Just little nibbles, all over those firm cheeks. Really unsure if this is the pot talking or I just have a weird body-biting fetish. Maybe it's a little of both.

"I bet he's amazing in bed," Zoe whispers. "Just imagine it, all that intensity and passion he has in his acting finally letting loose. He'd be like a sexual stallion."

*Jebus, Zoe, would you shut up? As if I'm not having enough trouble not humping him. Stop making me want him more.*

I drag my eyes away from his butt and watch my feet instead.

*Whoa. Look at the grass. So many blades. So pretty. So green. I wonder what green would taste like.*

"So," Zoe says and nudges me with her elbow, "who's the best lay you've ever had?"

*Well, so far? Holt's thigh. And fingers.* "Um . . ."

"Was there someone back in Washington?"

*Not unless you count my old bicycle, which used to rub against me in strange and not-entirely-unpleasant ways.* "Well . . ."

" 'Cause I've heard some of those small-town boys can be total perverts."

*A boy from my high school videotaped himself having sex with a watermelon. And a cucumber. Simultaneously.* "Well, yeah . . ."

"So who was it?"

I look back at Holt's ass as I try to figure out what to say, because I'm betting that if I stare at it hard enough, the secrets of the universe will be revealed to me.

Do I tell her and risk ridicule? I mean, she's being nice to me now, but what happens when the high wears off?

"Come on, Cassie," she says, urging me on. "If you tell me yours, I'll tell you mine."

"Well, uh . . ." *No, no one must know. Just make up a name. Any name.* "His name was . . ."

*Bob, Sam, Cletus, Zach, Jake, Joanne! Any name will do! Wait, no . . . not Joanne. Or Cletus.*

Zoe grabs my arm and stops short. "Oh my God . . ."

"Zoe—"

"Don't tell me you're a—"

"No, don't say it . . ."

She leans in and whispers, "You've never had sex, have you?" She says it with the same amount of hushed sympathy as if she'd just discovered I was dying of cancer.

I blush and pull my arm away from her so I can keep walking.

"Aw, Cassie, don't be mad," she calls after me. "I'm not going to tell anyone you're a virgin!"

The boys in front of me stop and turn, and Jack and Lucas look at me in disbelief. Holt glances at me nervously before shoving his hands in his pockets and staring at the ground.

"Crap," Zoe mumbles behind me. "Sorry. My bad."

"Taylor," Jack says, a broad smile spreading over his face, "tell me it isn't so. No one has planted their flag in your virgin territory yet? That's just wrong."

Lucas looks at me in genuine shock. "That's impossible. How did this happen? Have you been dating blind men?"

I put my hands on my hips. "Would you stop treating me like I have a rare and incurable disease? I'm not a leper, for God's sake."

"No, of course not," Jack says sympathetically as he walks over to rub my shoulders. "But, Taylor, really . . . what the hell are you waiting for? Are you one of those chicks who's saving it for marriage? Because let me tell you, my mom did that and it was a bad move. Apparently, my dad is a lousy lay. That's why I'm an only child. I'm pretty sure they've only ever done it that one time."

I blush. "I'm not saving it, okay?"

"Then why are you still a virgin?" Zoe asks.

"Because . . ." I don't want to look at Holt, but I can't stop myself. "I just haven't found a guy yet who wants to sleep with me, I guess."

At that statement, he loses all interest in his shoes and looks straight at me, frowning and intense.

"Okay, now I'm going to have to call bullshit," Jack says with a laugh. "Because I know for a *fact* that there are at least half a dozen guys at The Grove who would give their right ball to bang you, me included."

Lightning fast, Holt punches him in the arm.

"Ow, dude!" Jack rubs his arm and scowls at Holt. "What the fuck was that for?"

"Just have some fucking respect, would you?"

"Settle the fuck down. I have respect. It was a compliment. Plus, I want her to know she has options."

Holt looks like his head's about to explode. "Banging you is not an option, you fucking Neanderthal. It'd be cruel and unusual punishment."

Jack throws up his hands. "Why the hell does everyone keep dissing my sexual prowess? I happen to be a very sensitive and thorough lover." He looks back at me and whispers, "Am I selling this at all? 'Cause if you wanted to ditch media class this afternoon so I could relieve you of your virginal burden, I'd be more than willing. I'm just saying . . ."

Everyone laughs except Holt, who hisses something under his breath and looks like he's going to punch Jack again.

I subtly move between him and Jack. "Thanks for the offer, but I'll pass."

Jack shrugs. "Well, okay then, but I'm always here if you need me. Twenty-four hour deflowering services available on request. Condoms provided free of charge."

I sneak a glance at Holt, and judging by the look on his face, he's imagining all the ways he could murder Jack and hide the evidence.

"Actually," I say. "I'm kind of seeing someone, and I'm hoping he might be the one to do it."

*Whoa. Didn't really mean to say that.*

*Or did I?*

*Okay, what I'm doing here will either be completely brilliant or unfathomably stupid. Please, God, let it be brilliant.*

Holt's watching me with a wary expression.

"Wait, what?" Zoe says. "You're seeing someone? Who? For how long? What's he look like? Holt, did you know about this?"

Holt's eyes fill with panic for a second before they set into a steely glare. "Yeah, she may have mentioned something about a guy. He sounds like a dick to me, but apparently she likes him. I'm surprised she's telling you all about him, though. I thought she was going to keep him a secret."

"Well," I say, "I don't really see why I shouldn't talk about him. I mean, I like him. And I don't think he's a dick. He's just . . . complicated."

Holt blinks several times, and his expression softens. "I guess he's lucky you see it like that."

"Well, come on then," Lucas says. "Tell us, who's the lucky guy?"

Zoe takes a step forward, her eyes bright and glassy. "Yeah, do we know him?"

*Okay, brain, I know you're high, but help me out here. Come up with something plausible.*

"I met him while we were doing *Romeo and Juliet*."

*Okay, good. Not exactly a lie but vague enough to throw them off. Good job, stoned brain.*

Everyone exchanges a look, and Zoe says, "Ah, a fan, huh? He saw you onstage and just had to have you?"

I nod. "Uh . . . yeah . . . something like that."

"So, tell us more," Holt says, and crosses his arms over his chest. "You told me the other day that you think he's hot. How hot? Be specific."

A fierce blush lights up my face, because he knows exactly how hot I think he is.

"Jeez, Taylor, check out your face!" Jack laughs. "This mystery guy must know how to press all of your buttons. You're as red as a baboon's ass. And yet, he won't have sex with you?"

I take a breath and shake my head.

Jack scoffs. "What a fucking idiot."

"Maybe he has his reasons," Holt says quietly.

"Are you kidding me?" Jack says in disbelief. "You've kissed Taylor, dude. You know how hot she is. What sort of moron turns that down?" He turns to me and whispers, "Oh, wait. Is he . . . you know . . . challenged? Or one of those creepy religious guys? Ooh, or does he have erectile dysfunction issues? Can't get it up?"

"He doesn't have any fucking erection issues," Holt says emphatically. "And he isn't challenged, for God's sake."

Everyone looks at him.

He shrugs. "I'm guessing that Taylor wouldn't go out with someone who was defective, right?"

"Well, I don't know," I say. "There's must be something wrong with him. Like Jack said, what sort of moron turns this down?"

I shimmy and do my sexy face, and everyone laughs except Holt. He just stares at me, unblinking, and I can't figure out whether he's angry or aroused.

It's kind of disturbing how similar those expressions are on him.

"I once went out with a guy who wouldn't fuck me," Zoe says as we start walking again. "He said he didn't want me to think that sex was all he wanted from me, and that he thought I was special. That we really could have something."

I smile at her. "He sounds sweet. What happened?"

She shrugs. "I dumped his ass. I mean, I have needs, right? If he's not going to give it to me, then I'm going to get it somewhere else."

Holt makes a derogatory noise but doesn't say anything.

"The weird thing is," Zoe says, as we head into the cafeteria, "he's probably the only guy I've ever dated who gave a shit about me, but I didn't realize that until he was long gone. Maybe he was one of those rare guys who didn't want sex without love."

My stomach squirms.

Is that Holt's problem? That he doesn't love me, so he won't sleep with me? It makes sense. Maybe he has no feelings for me beyond pure animal lust.

The thought slithers through my brain, curling and coiling, making my face hot with embarrassment and anger.

"I've given up trying to figure out men," Zoe says as she surveys the stand of candy bars. "They're weird."

*Amen, sister.*

She picks up three chocolate bars and heads to the cashier. Lucas and Jack both have armfuls of chips and chocolate, and I opt for a soft-serve ice cream to help cool my flushed face.

I head outside and sit at a table with the others, and when Holt sits down, I avoid looking at him. Concentrating on my ice cream, I run my tongue around the edge of the cone, catching the drips before they can run too far. I close my eyes as I swallow, and I can almost see the cold as it slides down my throat as spider-veins of sparkling blue tingle in my stomach and out through my skin.

I feel a light brush against my foot and look up to see Holt staring at me, watching my mouth as I eat. He looks into my eyes, and the glittering blue in my body is immediately replaced by sparking orange heat, smoldering and blazing in all the places I want him to touch me. But as I squirm and become uncomfortably warm, it occurs to me that maybe this is all we have—sexual napalm that has no need for friendship or intimacy.

He brushes my foot again, the toe of his shoe grazing up against my ankle and calf, and it's ridiculous that I can feel that touch in every cell of my body.

Oh, I'm going to burn all right. He's going to incinerate me from the inside out.

"I have to go," I mutter as I stand and throw the rest of my ice cream in the trash. "I'll see you guys in class."

"Taylor?"

I sling my bag over my shoulder and don't look back as I cross the quad to the drama block.

Ten minutes later, when I exit the first-floor bathroom, Holt's there leaning against the wall and frowning.

"Hey." He looks around before stepping forward and touching my face. "Are you okay? Sometimes if it's your first time smoking, it can make you want to hurl."

He looks concerned as he pushes my hair back over my shoulders, but as soon as he hears someone coming down the stairs, he steps back and slumps onto one leg, the perfect image of indifference.

I look at him as he shifts uncomfortably, waiting for the student to pass, and I wonder if I imagined the look of concern. Maybe this whole non-relationship of ours has just been me pushing him into something he really doesn't want. Or rather, something he wants but not enough.

"Taylor?" He steps forward again. "You didn't answer me. Are you okay?"

I blink and shake my head. "I'm fine."

We walk toward the lecture hall where our media class is held. There's tension between us, but I resist defusing it. I've always been that girl—the one who sees things that are wrong and tries to fix them.

I don't think I can fix this.

"Jack is having some people over for pizza tonight," Holt says as we climb the stairs. "Want to go?"

*So I can pretend all night that you're just my friend?* "No, thanks."

*God forbid you'd ask me out on a real date, to a place where people could see us touching each other.*

Holt exhales in frustration and grabs my arm. "Okay, that's it. You're being too quiet and way too non-opinionated. What's up?"

I shrug. "I guess I have nothing to say."

"That's impossible."

"We have class."

"So, you're telling me you're okay?"

"Would it matter if I wasn't?"

He frowns as we start walking again, and I know I'm being passive-aggressive, but he's had nearly a month to show me that he wants me in his life as more than just a sexual distraction, yet he's still as emotionally distant as ever. I'm over it.

As we take our seats, I slump down and close my eyes. There's a sharp, hollow ache inside of me, and although I haven't noticed it before, I'm guessing it's been there for a while. It's the part of me that wants someone special. Someone who wants me enough to be brave. Someone who wants to wrap himself around me until it's no longer obvious where he ends and I begin.

Someone who I thought might be Holt, but now I'm not so sure.

The rest of the lecture passes in a blur, and even though I sense Holt looking at me every now and then, I ignore him.

I don't know why the realization that I'm no longer content with having only part of him hit me today. Maybe the marijuana helped clear my mind of the lust that has clouded it since I started having feelings for him. He told me this was how it was going to be, and that I'd want more than he was willing to give, but for some reason I stupidly thought I could change him.

Obviously not.

When the lecture finishes, I mutter that I'll see him tomorrow and head out toward the quad, wanting nothing more than to have a hot bath. The clear weather that we'd had at lunchtime has given way to heavy rain, and I stick to the cover of the buildings for as long as possible before stepping out into the downpour.

"Hey, Taylor, wait up!"

In a few strides, he's beside me, holding his backpack over his head as the rain gets heavier.

"You don't want to hang out tonight?"

"Not really."

"Why not?"

"I just don't. Is it a crime to want to have some time alone?"

A flicker of hurt crosses his face. "No, not a crime, it's just that . . . well, we usually spend time together on Wednesday nights, and judging from the way you were looking at me today, I thought . . ."

"You thought what?"

"Well, it seemed like you wanted to throw me down and mount my face. I figured you'd probably want to fool around or something."

*That's the problem, Ethan. You think we're just fooling around.*

"Nope, I'll pass. Thanks for the offer, though."

I walk faster as my shoes fill up with water. The unpleasant squelching sensation puts me even more on edge.

He keeps pace with me and slings his backpack over his shoulder, giving up avoiding the storm.

"Cassie, what's going on? Are you pissed with me about something?"

I exhale in frustration. "No. I'm pissed with myself. Don't worry about it. Go get out of the rain."

He grabs my arm and pulls me to face him. "I'm not going anywhere until you tell me what the hell is going on."

I don't want to have this conversation now, and I especially don't want to be having it in the bitterly cold rain, but he's not giving me a choice.

"Ethan, I'm just tired of this dance we're doing. It's always one step forward, two steps back with us, and even though you told me it would be this way, for some reason, I chose not to believe you. I'm just sick of pushing you to do things you don't want to do. So . . . yeah . . . that's what's going on. I'll see you tomorrow."

I turn and walk away, trying to outrun the rain, which is pointless, and trying to outpace him, which is impossible.

"Wait! Cassie, talk to me."

He pulls me to face him again, and his hair is plastered to his head as the water drips off his nose.

"There's nothing to talk about. You're you, and I'm me, and you were right when you said we shouldn't start something. We want totally different things, and I guess I'm finally realizing I'm not okay with that."

"What the hell? Is this because of what Zoe and Jack said?"

I grunt in exasperation and resist the urge to shove him in his clueless chest. "No, this isn't about Jack or Zoe, or anyone else! It's about us! It's about me expecting things from you that I shouldn't. It's about me wanting romance, and dates, and intimacy that stems from more than humping and orgasms, and me wanting to tell our friends that the mystery guy I'm seeing who can turn me on with a single look or touch is *you*. And most of all, it's about being angry with myself for falling for a man who told me very plainly not to fall for him! That's what it's about! And now it's too late, and I feel like the stupidest person on the planet, because you're never going to give me what I need, and I should have known better than to expect you to."

He stares at me for a second, blinking as the water streams over his lashes. "I thought you wanted me to try with us. That's what I'm doing. What else do you want?"

I swipe the water off my face, hating the feeling of it running down my cheeks. "God, you're such a clueless idiot sometimes! I want more. Anything. Everything. *Something*, for God's sake! *That's* what I want from you. Can you give me that?"

He stares at me, the muscles in his jaw working overtime. He doesn't answer.

"That's what I figured."

I try to walk away, but he holds my arm. His face turns as stormy as the sky. "So, what? That's it then? It's all or nothing with you? If I don't hand you my balls in a velvet-lined box we can't be together? Where the fuck is all of this coming from? I thought you enjoyed our time together. That you were happy with the way things were."

"Well, I'm not! I hate slinking around like a criminal, acting like what we're doing is wrong. I'm not ashamed of liking you, Ethan, but it seems like you can't say the same. The only reason I've gone along with keeping us a secret is because I thought you just needed time to realize you wanted more, but it looks like I was wrong. You give me as little of yourself as possible, all the while driving me insane with how much I want you."

"You think I don't want you in the same way? Christ, Taylor, are you fucking kidding me with this?"

"I think you want me, but not enough to actually admit it to anyone!"

"Why the fuck does anyone else matter? *You* know I want you! It's not like I can actually hide what you do to me."

"I'm not talking about wanting me sexually, Ethan! I'm talking about you wanting to be with me. I have no idea where I stand with you. I don't know if you have actual feelings for me, or if I'm just a willing body. Convenient but not necessary."

"You think you're convenient?!" He stares at me for long seconds, so angry he can't form words. "You're not fucking convenient! Convenient would have been me not meeting a girl who drives me out of my fucking mind! Convenient would be me being able to concentrate on the course it's taken me *three fucking years* to get into without being constantly distracted by how much I want you! Whatever you are, Taylor, the one thing you're definitely *not* is *convenient!*"

"Then what am I, huh? You tell me! Just open your damn mouth and say something that makes me understand how you feel! I think I've been pretty honest about what I want, but all I get in return is what you *don't* want."

"You want to know what I want?" he says as he throws his bag to the ground. "Fine. I want this."

He grabs my face and pulls it forward. It takes me by surprise as he wraps his arms around me and kisses me like he's drowning and I'm oxygen. There's nothing cautious about this kiss, nothing remotely vague or dishonest. It's passionate and staggering, and his desperation is blazing hot, making me burn despite the cold and the rain. For long minutes he kisses me so hard that the world tilts on its axis, and when it realigns, everything is back to revolving around him.

He kisses down my neck, his voice rough and intense. "This is what I want, Cassie. I can't make it any clearer. Don't even try to deny you don't want it, too. Why are you so intent on complicating things?"

He kisses me again, and everything becomes a blur of hands, and tongues, and lips. It's not fair that this is his explanation, because I can't argue or reason with it. It's too big to describe and too hard to deny, and although it doesn't make things right, it makes me want to forget all the things that are wrong.

But that's what I've been doing all this time. Overlooking and compromising. Being blinded by my want and ignoring my need. I can't continue doing that.

He groans as I pull away, and from the look in his eyes, he knows that what he's offering isn't enough.

I step back, and we stare at each other, both of us breathless and drenched.

"I can't pretend that this is enough for me anymore," I say quietly. "I'm not fooling anyone. Not you, not our friends, and especially not myself. If and when you're ready to be real, let me know."

"Cassie—"

"See you in class, Ethan."

I walk away, every footfall heavy as lead as bile churns in my stomach. As I turn down the path toward my building, I glance back.

He's still standing where I left him, his hands clasped behind his neck and his head bowed. I have the sick urge to run back and tell him to ignore everything I just said. That I'll take whatever part of him he wants to give.

But I can't do that. It would just be another lie.

Instead I shiver as I walk to my apartment and unlock the door with shaky hands. Once inside, I strip naked and head to the bathroom, determined to stand under a hot shower until the compulsion to go back to him goes away.

Sadly, when the hot water runs cold an eternity later, I'm still waiting.

### Present Day
### New York City

I'm standing at the counter of the coffee shop across the road from the theater when I feel a warm hand on my hip. I turn, expecting to see Holt there, but instead it's Marco, smiling at me with a knowing look.

"Miss Taylor."

"Mr. Fiori."

"Have a good time at the benefit last night?"

His tone and raised eyebrow imply he saw Holt and me kissing.

*Dammit.*

"It was fine."

"I'm sure."

"Please don't make a big deal out of it."

"What? My two leads making out in the corner like a couple of teenagers? Wouldn't dream of it."

"It was nothing."

"My dear, I've seen nothing, and let me assure you that what you and Mr. Holt were doing last night was most definitely not it. I thought the way you kissed each other in rehearsals was scorching. Apparently it pales in comparison to the real thing."

"Marco . . ."

"It's all right. I'm not upset. If anything, I'm thrilled. Can you imagine the press we'll get out of this?"

I groan as the barista hands me my coffee. "Really? Do you think they saw?"

"I'm certain of it. Our publicist wants to see us prior to rehearsal. I believe every Broadway website and gossip rag has picked up on it. You two are the talk of the town."

"Oh, God."

He laughs and pats my shoulder reassuringly as he guides me out of the cafe and across the street. When we get into the rehearsal studio, I dump my gear and head to the ladies' room, trying to push down a wave of nausea.

After Holt and I left the benefit, he'd escorted me home.

When we reached my apartment, he'd given me a good-night kiss.

Well, to be honest, it was a little more than a kiss. It was more like a full-body vertical dry-hump against my apartment door. In fact, if Mr. Lipman who lives across the hall hadn't sneezed while he was perving on us through his peephole, we probably would have graduated to an act that's entirely illegal in a public hallway.

When I'd finally peeled myself away, I was more confused than a straight guy at a transgender beauty pageant. I'd promised myself I was going to take it slow with Ethan. I'd *meant* to take it slow, yet in one night, I'd somehow managed to kiss him twice, reach a heavily loaded second base, and get an enthusiastic grip on his baseball bat through the front of his pants.

In anyone's playbook, that's not even in the same universe as slow.

When I walk back into the rehearsal room, Ethan's there. His face lights up when he sees me.

As I stop in front of him, he wraps his arms around me and pulls me into a hug. He doesn't intend it to be intimate, but it is.

His breath is warm on my ear as he whispers, "Good morning. I've missed you." His voice is full of our time together last night—all lusty and a little bit smug.

"Hey." Mine is purposefully flat. Not encouraging.

He pulls back. His smile drops, and the light goes out of his eyes. "Cassie?"

The room is filling up with people. Our publicist, Mary, enters the room like a tiny big-haired tornado, her arms full of papers and iPads.

"Well, you two had an interesting night. I had a whole marketing campaign organized to get the town buzzing about this show, but you managed to take us viral with one well-publicized make-out session. Well done."

She lays all of her materials out on the table. There are several pictures of Ethan and me well and truly lip-locked. Each iPad is cued up with a different film clip of the kiss.

Goddammit, how many people were filming us?

"Wait for it," Mary says as she taps a lacquered nail against one of the screens. "This one has a very artistic zoom that allows us to see actual glimpses of tongue. There!"

Everyone laughs. I want to throw up.

"So," Mary says, "I've already had a dozen requests for interviews this morning, so we need to come up with a strategy. Obviously, I'm all for pushing the whole 'ex-lovers reunited in hot new play' angle, because it will sell tickets. People love it when onstage passion is the real deal. If we're all in agreement, I'll get some draft press releases drawn up and get them out by this afternoon."

She looks between Marco, Ethan, and me.

Predictably, Marco and Ethan are waiting for my reaction.

Just as predictably, my answer is, "No freaking way."

Mary begins to bluster. I don't hang around for it.

"I need to smoke. I'll be back in a minute."

I grab my cigarettes and lighter. When Ethan brushes his fingers over my arm as I pass, I keep going.

Once I'm in the alley, I attempt to light my cigarette, but my trusty Zippo picks that moment to stop being trusty. I flick the roller again and again, but the flint refuses to fire.

"Fuck it!"

I slump back against the wall and close my eyes. When I hear the door open, I know it's him without having to look.

"Cassie?"

I keep my eyes closed. Not seeing him is easier.

"Please look at me."

I can't. I want to be strong, and looking at him makes me the weakest woman on the planet.

"Look at me, or I'm going to kiss you."

That works.

I open my eyes to see him frowning, his arms crossed over his chest. "Would you like to tell me what the hell is going on?"

I throw up my hands. "It's everywhere. Pictures. Videos. Blog posts."

He stares at me, confused. "And?"

"And . . . people are gossiping about us being together."

"Good. As Mary said, it's great publicity." His calm is annoying.

I tense and try to move away, but he grabs my shoulders and holds me still. "Cassie, stop. Why is this freaking you out? No offense, but you didn't seem too concerned last night when we nearly defiled your hallway."

"For a start, what we did in my hallway was between you and me . . ."

"And Mr. Lipman."

". . . not splashed all over every tabloid in the city!"

I push on his chest, and he steps back to give me the space I need to breathe. His face is still aggravatingly serene, and I hate that he's not joining me in my outrage.

"Since when do you care what people think?" he says. "There's no hiding our onstage chemistry. Who gives a shit if they think we're doing it offstage, too? For all they know, I'm actually fucking you during the sex scene."

He doesn't get it, and it's because I'm not explaining myself clearly. Explaining it will hurt him. And yet part of me is totally okay with that.

"Ethan, for everyone who knows us . . . who knows our history . . . I'm going to seem like the biggest idiot in the world for letting you in again, and the kicker is, they're probably right. They know how devastated I was when you left, and now I'm making out with you like nothing happened? How stupid must I be?"

That stops him short. The muscles in his jaw work overtime. "Cassie, I've worked really hard to be in a position to even think about trying to fix things with you. If I thought, even for a second, that I could possibly hurt you again, I wouldn't be here. Can't you just trust me on that?"

I shake my head. "No. And that's the problem here. I don't trust you, and I don't know that I ever will again. Somewhere in the back of my mind, I'm always going to be waiting for the other shoe to drop. For you to get that dead, faraway look in your eyes and run. How can we possibly get back together knowing that?"

His gaze turns steely. "Knowing how we feel about each other . . . how we've *always* felt about each other . . . how can we not? Don't even try to tell me you'll ever love someone as much as you love me, because as arrogant as it is to say, that's bullshit. And I feel the same way about you. Everyone else is just going to be second best for us. Don't you get that?"

I take a deep breath, heart hammering.

We're charging ahead in a rocket car, and I have no idea if we'll end up in paradise or smashed into a tree.

History would suggest the tree.

"Maybe we should just . . . step back," I say. "Get through opening night, then . . . I don't know. Reassess."

He laughs, short and scoffing. "Reassess. Right." He runs his hand through his hair.

"Ethan, reporters can insinuate whatever the hell they like, but when they ask if we're a couple, I'm going to tell them no, and it's going to be the truth."

I see a flicker of pain in his eyes, but he's still not angry. I want to scream in frustration, because that statement should have sent him storming away in a fit of rage. Instead, he's staring at me with an intensity that curls my toes. He moves toward me and puts his hand on the wall next to my head before leaning down until our noses are almost touching.

"Cassie, us agreeing to take a step back is totally different than you pushing me away, which is what's going on here. Let me save you a lot of effort by telling you that you can't get rid of me that easily. I can't live without you, and more importantly, I don't want to. So you go ahead and freak out all you want. I'll still be here when you're done. Understand?"

He stares at me until I nod to acknowledge what he's said. Then he looks at me for another few knee-buckling seconds before saying, "Good."

With that, he walks away and disappears back inside the theater.

Later that day, we do a series of press interviews in which we both deny being romantically involved. Based on the reactions of the interviewers, it's clear no one believes us.

# SEVENTEEN

## SICK & TIRED

*Six Years Earlier*
*Westchester New York*
*The Grove*

I sigh and turn over in bed. Again.

And again.

And again.

I look at the clock: 1:52 a.m.

*Dammit.*

I grab my phone off the nightstand and check it.

Fully charged. No missed calls. No messages.

I don't know why I'm so surprised. Did I really think my little speech in the rain was going to wash away all of his insecurities? Even I'm not that naive.

And yet, here I am at two o'clock in the morning, hurt that he hasn't called or texted.

I dump my phone back on the nightstand, then turn over and shut my eyes.

*Just stop thinking about him. If he comes around, he comes around. If he doesn't . . .*

*Well, if he doesn't . . .*

I pull my legs up to my chest to try to suppress the ache that's growing there.

*If he doesn't . . . life will go on. I'll be okay.*

*I'll be okay.*

I lie in the darkness repeating that same phrase over and over again, and even when sleep eventually claims me hours later, I still don't believe it.

"Wow, you look like crap," Ruby says as I shuffle into the kitchen.

"Thank you."

"He didn't call, huh?"

"Nope."

"Idiot."

"Yep."

I plunk myself down at the kitchen table as Ruby places a plate of grayish scrambled eggs in front of me.

I look at them dubiously.

"Don't start with me," she says. "Even I can cook eggs."

"Really?"

"Dunno. Never done it before. Still, I'm sure they're delicious."

I scoop some into my mouth as she opens the fridge. I almost gag. I'm not sure how someone can screw up eggs so badly, but Ruby has managed it.

"Good?" she asks over her shoulder.

"Awesome," I say with a full mouth. "You should have some." Why should I be the only one subjected to this torture?

"You going to call him?" she asks as she pours me some juice.

"Nope."

"Good girl. You've done all you can. Let him come to you."

I swallow thickly around the eggs and my paranoia. "And if he doesn't? Come to me, I mean."

"He will."

"But what if he doesn't?"

"He totally will."

"Ruby, dammit, what if he doesn't?"

She stops what she's doing and stares at me. "Cassie, that boy is so hung up on you, you might as well be a coatrack. It might take him a little while to realize he can't live without you, but he will. Trust me."

I sigh and push my eggs around the plate. "So, what do I do when I see him today?"

"Act cool."

"I don't know how to do that."

She puts her plate on the table and sits next to me. "Just . . . act polite. Be friendly but not familiar. If he brings up your relationship, then talk about it. If not, stick to neutral topics: the weather, politics, sports teams, how much you want to ride his throbbing hard cock. Hang on, wait." She frowns and holds up a finger. "Scratch that last one. He knows about that already."

I laugh and try not to wince in disgust as I eat the rest of my terrible eggs.

"He'll cave, Cassie," Ruby says and picks up her fork. "Trust me. He probably cried himself to sleep last night and can't wait to see you today so he can declare his undying love. There may even be a proposal."

I roll my eyes as she scoops some egg into her mouth and immediately gags. "Oh, fuck me! That's disgusting! Why didn't you warn me?"

I wear my most innocent expression as I sip my juice.


I have to admit, I take a little extra care when I get ready for class. I apply more makeup than normal, take time to straighten my hair. Wear a boob-hugging top and an ass-hugging skirt.

I didn't think I'd ever be one of those girls who'd use her looks to make a man realize he's missing out on total hotness, but apparently

I am. And yet, one of the reasons we fought is because I need him to want more than just my body.

Hypocrisy, thy name is Cassie.

By the time I take my seat in History of Theater, I'm a mess of nerves.

It turns out my anxiety is unwarranted. Holt doesn't show. At first I think he's just running late, but by lunchtime I have to accept he's ditched for the day.

I can't believe it.

I thought that he'd have mulled over our situation by now and would have wanted to talk, but yet again, he chooses to simply avoid the issue.

Mentally labeling him a bastard doesn't lessen my disappointment, but I do it anyway.

He doesn't call all Thursday afternoon or night, and he doesn't come to class again on Friday. By the time Saturday rolls around, Ruby is sick of me compulsively checking my phone and muttering obscenities under my breath when I see that it is, in fact, working.

"Cass, will you please chill the fuck out? Give the boy some time. He has more issues than *People* magazine. You can't expect him to magically become well-adjusted just because you want him to be."

"I know that, Ruby. I'm being unrealistic and unreasonable, but why won't he call?!" I slump against the couch and put my head in my hands. "I mean, seriously, I'm going insane not speaking to him. How can he just drop all contact? I don't understand."

"Boys are bizarre."

"It's like I don't mean anything to him."

"I'll go out on a limb and say that's not true."

I sit up straight. "I'm going to call him."

Ruby snatches my phone. "No, you're not. You're coming to the spa with me, so you can stop obsessing over him for a few hours. I can't trust you not to call him if I leave you alone."

"I miss him."

"I know."

"I want to know that he's missing me, too."

She sits and puts her arms around my shoulders. "Cassie, he misses you. I'm sure of it."

I'm getting more and more sure she's wrong.

On Sunday, I feel numb.

Well, most of me feels numb. My hoo-hah is hurting like a son-ofabitch because yesterday Ruby convinced me that getting a Brazilian would take my mind off things with Holt.

She wasn't wrong.

For the half hour it took to rip out my pubic hairs by their roots, I completely forgot about Ethan and focused on how many ways I could hurt Ruby without getting arrested. I eventually came up with twenty-three.

Now she's giving me a pedicure to make up for it, but she's still on my shit list.

My phone rings, and we look at each other as we grab for it at the same time. It flips into the air, and we both bat at it like cats until she catches it and hands it to me. I glance at the caller ID and quickly deflate.

"Hi, Elissa."

"Cassie! Thank God you're there! Is Ethan with you?"

I look at Ruby. "Uh . . . no. Why?"

Ruby frowns and leans closer so she can listen in.

"I can't get a hold of him, and when I spoke to him on Thursday, he sounded terrible. Now he's not answering his phone. I'm afraid he's really sick and can't get to a doctor."

"You haven't been home this weekend?" I ask.

"No. I'm staying with Mom and Dad in New York until Tuesday. So you haven't seen him?"

I run my hand through my hair. "No. We kind of . . . well, we had a fight on Wednesday. I haven't seen or spoken to him since. I thought he was just avoiding me."

Elissa pauses. "It's possible. That's something he'd do. But he usually answers when I call, and he's not. Can I ask you a really huge favor?"

My stomach knots. "You want me go and check on him?"

"Yes, please, Cassie."

Ruby shakes her head vehemently and mouths the words "no fucking way," while waving her hands wildly.

I groan and put my head in my hand. "Elissa, I don't know. The way things were after our fight . . . I just don't think he'd want to see me right now."

"Cassie, I wouldn't ask if there was anyone else that could do it. You're his only friend."

"What about Jack or Lucas?"

"Are you kidding me? It's nine a.m. on a Sunday. They'll still be passed out in a garden bed somewhere, half drunk. Besides, if Ethan is sick, do you really think Jack or Lucas would be capable of helping him?"

She has a point. I screw up my face and take a deep breath. "Okay, fine, I'll go and check on him. But if I die from an overdose of extreme awkward, you're paying for my funeral."

"Oh, thank you! You're amazing. Call me when you get there and tell me how he is."

"Wait, Elissa! I need your address."

"You don't have it?"

I sigh. "No. I've never been to your apartment."

I can practically hear her incredulity. "Are you freaking kidding me? In all the time you two have been hanging out, he never took you there?"

"Nope."

"Let me guess, that's one of the things the fight was about?"

"Pretty much."

"My brother's a dick."

*Yes, but I want him to be* my *dick.*

"Well," Elissa says, "Ruby knows where we live. Do you think she'd drive you?"

Ruby rolls her eyes dramatically and throws her arms up in defeat.

"Yeah, I think I can convince her."

"Okay. Thanks, Cassie. I really owe you for this."

"You really, really do."


Twenty minutes later, Ruby pulls up in front of a well-kept apartment building. The whole trip I've been praying that Holt's at death's door, because that's the only explanation for why he hasn't called that doesn't make my chest hurt.

"Their apartment is number four," Ruby says as she points to the second floor. "I'll wait here just in case he's not sick and you murder him. I can't go to prison as an accessory. I'm too pretty."

I get out and head up to his apartment. The building isn't supermodern, but it's clean and stylish. The polar opposite of mine.

I reach the top of the stairs and find number four, then take a deep breath before knocking firmly three times.

There's silence from inside.

I knock again, louder and more insistent. Again there's nothing, and the little grain of hurt I've carried inside me since our fight blossoms into a full-blown ache.

He's out.

Possibly with another girl.

Possibly having the no-strings-attached orgasms he used to have with me.

I push down my pain.

I'm about to leave, when I hear a noise on the other side of the door. There's muffled shuffling, then a bang, followed by a whispered, "Fuck!" When I turn back, the door opens a crack to reveal a bleary-eyed and disheveled Holt squinting at me in confusion.

"Taylor?" His voice is hoarse, and so deep it sounds like Barry White on steroids. "What are you doing here?"

An enormous wave of relief washes over me.

"Oh God, Holt, you're actually sick! Truly, disgustingly sick!"

He frowns and shivers as he leans against the doorframe. "You came all the way down here to gloat? 'Cause honestly, that's just mean."

"No, sorry," I say, composing myself as I take in his greasy hair and sweaty face. "Elissa asked me to come and check in. You weren't answering your phone, and she was worried."

He coughs loudly, causing a horrible rattle to echo in his chest.

"It's just a cold," he croaks as he leans more heavily against the wall. "I'll be okay."

I place my palm against his forehead. He's burning up, and the dark circles under his eyes make it look like he hasn't slept in days.

"You're not okay. You have a fever. Have you taken anything for it?"

"I ran out of Tylenol," he says, then coughs again. "I think I just need to sleep."

He closes his eyes and stumbles a little, and I rush to support him. He's only wearing a thin T-shirt and cotton boxers, and even though he's clammy and hot to the touch, he's shivering.

"Come on," I say, and guide him inside to sit on the couch. "Sit down for a minute." There's a blanket on the back of the couch, so I grab it and drape it across his shoulders. He pulls it around himself as he lies down and closes his eyes. His teeth chatter.

"Ethan?"

"Hmmm?" He's barely awake.

"I'll be back in a minute, okay? We need supplies."

He mumbles something unintelligible as I run around his apartment to take a quick inventory of his kitchen and bathroom, before racing downstairs to Ruby, who's still waiting in the car. I give her a list of things to pick up at the drugstore and ask her to hurry. When I get back to the apartment, Ethan's where I left him, mumbling and groaning.

His fever is bad. Until Ruby gets back with some Tylenol, I'll have to try to get his temperature down. I once had to care for my dad when he'd gotten pneumonia while Mom was out of town at a yoga retreat. I know the procedures pretty well.

"Ethan, can you sit up for me?"

He coughs before struggling into a sitting position. His chest doesn't sound good.

"I think you have a chest infection. You need to see a doctor."

"No," he says in a raspy voice. "The stuff in my throat is green. Bacterial. Doc will just prescribe antibiotics, and I have some in the bathroom, in the cabinet behind the mirror."

"You have antibiotics just lying around the house?"

"Dad's a pharmacist."

"Oh."

I go to the bathroom and retrieve the pills. I read the label as I head back to Ethan.

"It says here you're supposed to take these with food. Have you eaten anything today?"

He pulls the blanket around himself and shakes his head. "Stomach doesn't feel good."

"Well, Ruby is out getting you some soup, so maybe we'd better wait to take these until she gets back."

He shivers as he nods. When I press my palm against his forehead, he closes his eyes and leans into my hand.

I press the backs of my fingers to his flushed cheek. "Do you feel strong enough to take a shower? It'll help cool you down."

He opens his eyes and looks at me, staring for a moment before whispering, "Cassie, you don't have to do this." His voice sounds so husky it makes my eyes water.

"I know, but I want to."

I hold my hands out and help pull him to his feet. He sways for a few seconds before wrapping his arm around my shoulders. He shivers against me as we slowly walk into his bathroom. I sit him down on the closed toilet before turning on the shower and adjusting the temperature.

When I turn back to him, my heart aches at how miserable he looks. He's hunched over his knees, breathing heavily and gripping the blanket around his shoulders.

"Come on. This will help you feel better."

I peel the blanket off and drop it on the floor before tugging his T-shirt over his head. His chest and shoulders are flushed, and when I press my hand against him, he's burning hot. He wraps his arms around himself. His skin prickles with goose bumps as I coax him into standing.

"Do you need me to help with your boxers?" I ask and rub his upper arms to keep him warm.

He shakes his head, and it kind of creeps me out that even when he's as sick as a dog, the sight of him shirtless still does crazy things to me.

"Okay, well, I'll leave you to it, then. I'll be right outside. If you get dizzy, just sit down and call to me. I'll be in here in a second, okay?"

He nods, and I give him a small smile before closing the door behind me.

A few minutes later, there's a knock on the front door. When I pull it open, Ruby's there with two bags of supplies. She heads straight into the kitchen and begins unpacking them.

"I got him several types of soup, as well as some bread, because when the fever breaks he's going to be hella hungry. There's some pineapple juice to help clear the mucus, and I also got Gatorade for rehydration."

"Good thinking."

She finishes unpacking the groceries and moves on to the bag from the drugstore. "There's Tylenol and Advil, plus a decongestant that will totally knock him out and help him sleep."

A huge coughing fit echoes down the hallway, and Ruby screws up her face in disgust. "Okay, don't take this the wrong way, but I have to leave now. Mucus of any kind makes me ralph. You'd better get back to your disgusting patient before he coughs up a lung."

I laugh and walk her to the door.

"You staying here tonight?" she asks as she steps out into the hallway.

"Yeah, unless he has a miraculous recovery in the next eight hours. That okay?"

"Sure, as long as you don't molest him in his sleep."

"Ruby, you act as if I have zero self-control around him." She stares at me and purses her lips. I glare. "Shut up."

"I didn't say anything."

"You judged me with your eyes. I'm telling them to shut up."

"Are you going to be able to cope with being alone with him overnight?" she asks. "Or do I have to make you a chastity belt out of aluminum foil?"

"Ruby, there are two reasons nothing is going to happen between us. One, he's really sick and, yes, disgusting." I neglect to mention that I would still totally do him. "And two, I've drawn a line in the sand as far as our relationship goes, and until he's willing to own up to his feelings toward me, I don't intend to cross it. I do have some pride, you know."

"Yeah, but not much."

"Again, shut up."

She hugs me, and I can feel her smiling against my shoulder.

"Could you call Elissa?" I ask. "Let her know what's going on?"

"Sure. Talk to you tomorrow."

After she leaves, I head back into Holt's bedroom. I knock on the bathroom door before opening it a crack.

"Hey, you okay in there?"

There's a pause and a wet cough. "Yeah. What I'm coughing up looks like something out of a horror movie, but the steam is loosening up my chest a bit." He's losing his voice, but I guess it's to be expected after the amount of coughing he's just done.

"Want to get out?"

"Soon. Give me a minute."

I don't mean to, but I glance through the door and inhale sharply when I see his naked back. His shoulders are straining as he leans his forearms on the wall.

Oh, God.

Naked Holt.

Naked and wet.

I look down to his very fine ass.

God help me.

*Oh, yeah, Ruby, I'll be fine with him overnight. I can control myself. Sure.*

I can't drag myself away from the water sluicing over his muscles. "Idiot."

He turns his head. "Did you say something?"

"Nope. Just talking to myself." While ogling your incredible ass.

I quickly look away and train my focus on his bed. The sheets are twisted and crumpled, and look kind of damp.

I close the door and set about stripping them. While I remake the bed, I try really hard to not think about the glory of his back, legs, and ass, and how they might look sprawled out on the fresh sheets.

As I work, I look around his room. It's messy but not in a gross way. There are haphazard piles of books and DVDs on his desk, as well as a mess of paper and his laptop, and there's a sprawl of video games on the floor near the latest Xbox. Other than that, it's pretty clean and dust free. Not the worst boy's room I've ever seen.

I grab a fresh T-shirt from his dresser and am in the middle of spending way too long in his underwear drawer when the shower turns off. With more than a little guilt, I grab the nearest pair of boxers and shut the drawer.

When I hear the bathroom door swing open, I turn to find Holt wearing only a towel, a halo of steam emerging from behind him.

I'm internally horrified as a Beyoncé song starts playing in my head and everything goes into slow motion. Water droplets glisten on his muscles, and I feel my mouth drop open as I watch one travel from his clavicle all the way down to his belly button.

*Goddamn. Gorgeous.*

"Hey," he says, his voice almost completely gone.

"Hey!" I snap out of my daydream and wave the fresh clothes at him a little too enthusiastically. "These are for you. How was your shower? You're still wet. You should dry yourself. Not with the towel around your waist of course, because then you'd be naked and . . . well, you can use that towel if you like. I mean, it's your bedroom, and if you want to be naked you can. I could watch—I mean, leave. If you want to be alone and naked, I could wait in the living room. Or go for a walk. Whatever you like."

He laughs, or at least I think he does, because he's so wheezy he sounds like a cartoon character. "Taylor, stop talking."

"Sure."

"Give me my clothes."

I hand them over, and he goes back into the bathroom and shuts the door.

Flopping down onto the bed, I put my head in my hands and sigh.

My overwhelming attraction to him, even when he's a virtual cornu-copia of mucus-producing bacteria, is beyond appalling.

The bathroom door opens, and he walks over to me, his hair much drier and his body less naked.

I stand and touch his forehead. "You feel a bit cooler."

"Yeah? Good."

He stares at me for a second, and I'm reminded that if I want to stay away from him, he really shouldn't be allowed to look at me like that.

"Get into bed," I say, my voice breathier than I intend.

He frowns. "Taylor, I'm flattered, but I'm sick. Maybe later?"

"You're hilarious. But seriously, get under the covers. You're shivering."

"That's because it's cold."

"It's really not."

"Whatever." He crawls into bed and pulls the covers up to his chin. "I'm just going to close my eyes for a minute. All that standing up in the shower kind of took it out of me."

"Of course it did. You're an actor. You're not used to working that hard." He glares. "Aaaand that's my cue to go get you food and drugs."

A little while later, I return with a tray laden with instant chicken soup, a glass of pineapple juice, the bottle of cough medicine, the anti-biotics, and Tylenol.

Holt is fast asleep.

"Hey, wake up."

He groans and turns over.

I put the tray down on his nightstand and gently shake his shoulder.

"Come on, Holt. Your drug pusher has arrived. You have to wake up."

His head lolls to the side, but he doesn't stir.

"Oh, no," I say in a breathy voice. "I spilled soup all over myself in the kitchen and had to remove my shirt and bra. I need you to cover my naked breasts with your giant hands."

He jolts awake and looks at my fully clothed form in confusion for a few seconds before flopping back onto the pillows and sighing.

"That was mean and unnecessary. You don't promise a dying man boobs and then renege."

"You're not dying."

"If I was, could I see your boobs?"

"No. That right is reserved for my boyfriend, and since that's not you—"

*Shit, Cassie. Don't blackmail him with your boobs. Low blow.*

"Sorry, that was . . ."

"It's fine," he says before clearing his throat and rubbing his eyes. "You're right."

He looks down at his hands, and I'm aware we need to talk about stuff, but now isn't the time.

"You need to sit up," I say as I grab two Tylenol and the juice. "Take these. Then eat your soup."

He does as he's told.

Fifteen minutes later, he's finished most of his soup, taken his antibiotics and cough medicine, and drunk all of his pineapple juice.

I take the tray into the kitchen, and when I return, his eyelids are drooping.

I pull the covers up to cover him. "How are you feeling now?"

"Sloshy," he says before yawning. "And kind of stoned. What the hell is in that cough medicine?"

"Magical sleep voodoo."

"Oh. I thought it might have just been a sedative of some sort."

"Yeah. That, too."

"It's strong."

"Good. You need sleep."

He yawns again and looks up at me, and it's just wrong how handsome he still is.

Before I can leave, he grabs my hand with his too-warm fingers.

"Stay," he says as he brushes his thumb across the back of my hand. "You need to rest."

"I will. Just stay with me. Please."

In his current state, I know I can't deny him anything. I remove my shoes and go around to the other side of the bed. He turns toward me as I climb on top of the covers.

"After our fight on Wednesday," he says, "the last place I thought you'd be this weekend was in my bed."

I nod. "I have to admit, when I've thought about finally seeing your bedroom, I imagined it would be under far more sexy and far less mucus-y conditions."

"What, my pleurisy cough and laryngitis aren't turning you on? What's wrong with you, woman?"

*Oh, Holt, if you only knew how much you still turn me on, you'd be embarrassed for me.*

He puts his arm under his head and looks up at me. "Is it wrong that seeing you in my bed makes me want to do things to you, even when I'm this sick?" His words are slurred, and I wonder if he'd have said such a thing without the drugs in his system.

"Ethan, we agreed—"

"No, we didn't," he says and touches my thigh. "You told me we had to stop touching each other if we weren't boyfriend and girlfriend. I didn't agree to it. You walked off before I could tell you it was a fucking horrible idea."

"It wouldn't change things if you had."

He looks down. "I know. I stood outside your apartment in the rain for nearly an hour, trying to figure out how fix it. When I realized I didn't have the guts to knock on your door and tell you I was an idiot, I was so fucking angry with myself I came home and got drunk. Then I passed out on the couch, still soaking wet. Woke up in the middle of the night freezing my ass off."

"God, Ethan . . ."

He runs his hand up to the waistband of my jeans and blinks long and slow before pushing a finger beneath the hem of my shirt.

"Your skin is so soft," he whispers as he splays his hand over my stomach. He moves his fingers up until he's touching the underside of my bra. It makes me want to forget all about his germs and shove his hand either higher or lower.

Instead, I take in a steadying breath and put my hand over his, stopping him.

He's sick and full of drugs. He's allowed to have a lapse in judgment. I have no excuse. I'm just horny.

"Ethan, we can't."

"I know." He sounds tired, and his words slur together. "ButIwanto. Somuch. Because . . . not touching youis . . ." He pauses, eyes closing. "It's . . . I hate it."

His head slumps, and his hand falls away, and I thank God he's asleep before he can hear my groan of sexual frustration.


Holt sleeps fitfully, tossing and turning as the fever and drugs work their way through his system. He alternates between shoving me away as he spread-eagles on the bed, and clinging to me with desperate intensity.

After an hour, he starts mumbling and groaning.

"Cassie . . ."

His eyes are closed, but he's reaching for me.

"I'm here," I say as I touch his face. His forehead is hot and slick with sweat. "I'm just going to get a washcloth for your head, okay?"

His eyes snap open, heavy and full of panic. "You're leaving?"

"I'll be right back."

"No . . . please." He pulls my hand to his chest and presses his forehead against my arm. "Don't leave. Please, not you."

He looks so desperate as he grips me like his life depends on it, that I'm not entirely sure he's awake.

He keeps mumbling "Please, Cassie," over and over again, and it's only when I pull him in to my chest and run my fingers through his hair that he relaxes.

"It's okay," I say. "I won't leave. I'll stay with you."

He sighs, and the air is still thick and wheezy in his lungs. "Thank you."

He pushes his head into my neck, and I'm a little shocked when I feel his lips on my throat.

"Ethan?"

He moans and kisses me again as his arms tighten.

"I love you," he murmurs as he rests his head on my shoulder. "I love you so much. Don't leave me."

He slumps back into sleep, and I'm left reeling.

It's not until I feel the burn in my lungs that I realize I've forgotten to breathe.

# EIGHTEEN

## SURE BET

After Holt's unexpected and semi-delirious admission of love, he continues to groan and mumble for hours.

Predictably, he doesn't repeat it.

The balloon of wild hope in my chest slowly deflates.

When I snuggle into his side and try to sleep, he wraps around me like a possessive boa constrictor. It makes me smile.

It's still dark when I become aware of fingers grazing over my skin. They push under the hem of my shirt and trail across my stomach.

"Ethan?"

He clears his throat. "You expecting some other guy in bed next to you? 'Cause I'm not too sick to kick his ass."

He still sounds terrible, but there's something about the rumbling timbre in his voice that gives me goose bumps.

"What are you doing?"

"Nothing. Just wanted to feel your skin."

There's a hint of groan in his voice that worries me, but when I touch his forehead, it's cool. The fever's finally broken.

"How are you feeling?"

"Horny." He moves his hand higher, then warm fingertips stroke my side. "Want you."

He presses against me, hot and hard on my thigh, rocking his hips in a way that leaves no doubt as to exactly how much he wants me.

"Oh, God . . ." My body reacts without engaging my brain, and I tighten my arms around him.

"Cassie . . ."

He slides his hand up to my breast and gently kneads it through my bra. The sensation spirals down all my limbs.

Warning bells go off in my head, because I know if I don't stop him now, what he's doing will rob me of all the reasons I shouldn't let him touch me like this, and I'll be back where I was four days ago.

"Ethan . . . we have to stop."

He pulls back and looks at me. "You think I can't tell how much you want me? You're practically tearing off my shirt."

"That's not the point."

"No, the point is you want me to keep going, but only on your terms. As your boyfriend."

"Is it so wrong that I need to know where I stand with you?"

"Dammit, Taylor, do you honestly not know how I feel by now? I know I'm a good actor, but as far my feelings go, I've been stupidly transparent."

"I need to hear you say it." My voice is barely a whisper.

"I told you earlier."

"I didn't think you were awake."

"I'm awake now."

"Then say it again."

He leans down and kisses my temple, then my cheek, then as close as he can get to my mouth without actually touching my lips.

"I love you, Cassie. I don't want to, but I do. Now, please . . ." He kisses my neck again, lips soft and open as he trails his hand down to the button of my jeans. "Shut up and let me touch you. It's been too long. I'm losing my freaking mind."

I close my eyes as he pops the button and lowers the zipper. Then all I can do is press my head back into the pillow, because he's pushing his fingers into my panties, and any sense of reality completely disintegrates. His fingers are sure and strong, making me arch and pant as he puppet-masters all the strings of my pleasure, inciting noises that are way too loud in his dark, silent room.

He circles his fingers, his breath hot on my throat, my mind spinning as everything inside me curls and tightens.

I groan, because what he's doing isn't enough. I need more. All of him.

"Please," I whisper as I reach between us and find him through his boxers, hard and long.

*"Jesus, Taylor . . ."*

I grip him and move slowly up and down, trying to draw him closer. "Ethan, please . . ."

He makes a low sound and wraps his fingers around mine. *"Cassie, stop. You don't know what you're doing."*

"I do. Want you. Love you, too."

*"You . . . what?!"*

"Ethan . . . inside me . . . Love you."

*"Cassie!"*

Then, I'm being shaken, and when I open my eyes, Holt's looking down at me, frowning and breathing heavily as sunlight spills into the room.

I gasp as my pre-orgasmic tension melts away, and I take stock of where I am.

One of my hands is pressing firmly between my thighs, and the other . . .

*Oh, God.*

The other is on the front of Holt's boxers, wrapped firmly around his very hard erection.

*"Oh, God."*

I let him go, and he sits up as he pulls the blankets over himself. "You were dreaming."

"I'm sorry."

"Talking and . . . grabbing at me . . ."

"Oh, God." My face burns with embarrassment. "How long was I . . . ?"

"A few minutes."

"I'm so sorry."

He sighs and says, "It's okay."

"No, it's not. I . . . I molested you. I'm a sexual deviant."

I put my hands over my face and groan, too mortified to even look at him.

"Dammit, Taylor, stop blushing. It's not all your fault. At first I thought you were awake, and had . . . you know . . . changed your mind about us doing stuff. But then you started talking, and I knew you were dreaming. I could have stopped you, but I'm a man, and therefore genetically programmed to resist removing a woman's hand from my dick."

I pull my knees up to my chest and glance at him. "You said I was talking. What did I say?"

He frowns and picks at the blanket as he clears his throat. "It was a dream. It doesn't matter."

"I'd like to know."

He coughs and takes a sip of water from the bottle on the nightstand, all the while not looking at me. "You were mumbling. Saying you wanted me or something. I couldn't really understand you."

My throat closes up. He's lying.

I drop my head down onto my arms and groan.

Having him hear me say the "L" word is bad enough, but what's worse is knowing I actually meant it. I've never felt this way about someone before. One day, he was just a guy who annoyed the heck out of me, and now, without any warning or permission, he's something else. Someone different.

Necessary and irreplaceable.

If that's love, then it's dumb.

"You know, you talk in your sleep, too," I say, determined not to be the only one in purgatory.

He looks at me sharply. "What did I say?"

I narrow my eyes. "Don't you remember?"

He looks at me for long seconds, and the amount of panic I see in his eyes isn't even worth it. Either he remembers and regrets it or doesn't and is terrified about having said it. Either way, I don't get what I want.

"Don't worry about it," I say. "You were so out of it I could barely understand you. Let's just both agree that dream mumbling should be ignored, okay?"

He's silent for a few seconds before he's hit by a vicious coughing fit. He doubles over and grabs some tissues as he nearly gags on what he's expelling from his lungs. I rub his back until the attack passes.

"You should take a shower," I say as I stroke between his shoulder blades.

"Yeah, I guess." He sounds tired.

He gets out of bed and heads over to his dresser to grab a fresh pair of boxers. He glances at me before looking back into the drawer. "Did you . . . refold my underwear?"

I shrug. "Some of it." Only the ones I felt up like a complete creeper.

"You're strange."

"You're preaching to the choir, sweetheart."

When the bathroom door closes, I flop back onto the bed and exhale. I hadn't envisioned that taking care of my sick ex-non-boyfriend would be such a mortifying experience.

I'm just about to head into the kitchen to prepare breakfast when Holt's phone rings.

The caller ID says "Home," and thinking it might be Elissa, I answer it. "Ethan's phone, Cassie speaking."

There's a pause, then, "Cassie? This is Maggie Holt."

My stomach jumps up into my throat, and my voice cracks as I say, "Oh, hi, Mrs. Holt."

*A girl is answering her son's phone first thing in the morning. This looks bad.*

"So, Cassie, how are you?"

"He's in the shower."

"Oh. Okay."

"That's why I'm answering his phone. Showering."

"I see. So you're—"

"Just hanging out. I know how this must seem, but I just want you to know that there's nothing going on with me and Ethan. We're not sleeping together. Well, actually, we did last night, but that was actual sleep, if you know what I mean. He was pretty doped up. On cough medicine. He's sick. Very sick."

I pinch the bridge of my nose in an effort to stop the ramble.

"I mean, he doesn't need a lung transplant or anything, but he's sick enough to need someone to take care of him. That's what I'm doing here. And answering his phone. Obviously. Wow, your son takes really long showers, huh?"

*Kill me now.*

There's a soft laugh, and I take it as a cue to just breathe. My face is hotter than the surface of the sun.

"Cassie, it's fine. Elissa let us know at dinner last night that he was sick and that she'd asked to you to play nurse. Thank you for agreeing. I know my son isn't the most pleasant patient. When he was a kid, I'd have to bribe him with *Teenage Mutant Ninja Turtle* toys in order to get him to take his medicine."

The image of Holt as a bratty child was almost too adorable to bear. "Really?"

"I'm afraid so."

A huge coughing fit comes from the bathroom, and I hear Mrs. Holt cluck her tongue. "I don't suppose he's been to the doctor?"

"No, but he's actually sounding much better today."

"That's better?"

"Uh huh."

"Poor baby." She pauses, then says, "Actually, Cassie, I'm glad we're speaking. Are you heading home for Thanksgiving?"

"Uh . . . no. I can only afford one return trip this year, and Mom and Dad want me to come home for Christmas."

"So you're free for the holidays?"

"I guess."

"Great. I'd like you to come and stay with us in New York."

"Oh . . . Mrs. Holt—"

"Please, call me Maggie."

"Maggie, I don't know. Ethan—"

"This doesn't have anything to do with him. You're Elissa's friend too, and she'd love you to stay. Besides, we can't have you spending Thanksgiving alone. That would be a tragedy."

"Still, I don't think that—"

"Nonsense. I won't take no for an answer. You're coming, and that's final."

Before I have a chance to argue, Holt emerges from the bathroom, bare chested, with just his boxers on.

He rubs a towel across his hair and coughs before mouthing, "Who is it?"

I hold my hand over the receiver. "Your mom."

He coughs again before gesturing for the phone.

"Maggie? Ethan's out of the shower now. And fully clothed, I might add. Well, not fully. He's not wearing a shirt, but all the important parts are covered." *Oh, for the love of God.* "It was nice talking to you."

"You, too, Cassie. See you next week."

"Uh, yeah. Okay."

Holt takes the phone and sits on the edge of the bed.

"Hey, Mom." His voice is barely there. "I sound worse than I feel. I don't need to see a doctor. Yep, already taking antibiotics."

He pauses then glances over at me. "Yeah, Cassie's been taking good care of me. I'm much better today."

He listens for a few seconds then frowns. "You what?"

He flushes with anger and strides past me into the living room. Even though he drops his voice to a harsh whisper, I can still make out what he's saying.

"Mom, what the hell? You could have at least asked me."

I stare at a pile of books in the corner and clench my jaw. I shouldn't be hearing this.

"Yes, I like her, but . . . Jesus . . . it's more complicated than that."

It doesn't have to be, but it is.

"No, she's not my girlfriend. Having her there would be awkward as hell."

I sit on the edge of the bed and shake my head. Would he honestly rather have me spend Thanksgiving alone?

I really have overestimated his feelings for me.

Holt talks with his mom for a few more minutes, but I can no longer make out what he's saying.

Just as well.

When he comes back into the bedroom, he throws the phone onto the bed and stalks over to his dresser. After he grabs a T-shirt, he yanks it over his head and slams the drawer shut.

"You okay?"

"Yep."

"You're angry."

"It's fine."

"Me coming to Thanksgiving would be awkward as hell, huh?"

He sighs. "Cassie—"

"Why would it be awkward?"

He rakes his fingers through his hair. "You've seen how Dad and I together. There's no way I'd subject you to that again."

I take in a shaky breath. "Okay. If that's what you want."

He takes one look at my face and sighs before sitting beside me. "Cassie, it's not that I don't want you there, but—"

Before he can say anything else, he's struck by another coughing fit.

When it's over, he flops back onto the bed, exhausted.

I guess we're done talking about Thanksgiving.

I lean over and rub his arm. "Is there anything I can do?"

He shakes his head. "I'm just tired. And my chest hurts." His voice is a husky mess.

I go and grab him some painkillers and cough medicine. After he takes both, he crawls under the covers.

I sit beside him and stroke his hair. "You know, my mother used to have this book. It was written by this self-proclaimed swami who believed that if we go against what our souls need, the disharmony in our bodies makes us sick. Like, if we don't say what we're feeling, we'll get a sore throat, or if we do something we know is wrong, we'll get a headache."

His eyes are bleary as he looks up at me. "And if we have a sore throat, a headache, and a chest infection we're . . . what? Emotionally dysfunctional? Heartsick?"

I shrug. "You tell me."

He coughs. "Sounds pretty right. I think my mother invited you to Thanksgiving because she thinks you can fix me."

I run my fingers across his forehead. "I didn't realize you were broken."

He gives me a short laugh. "Maybe not broken, but definitely defective."

"I don't believe that."

"After how I've treated you, you should." He sighs and turns away from me. "I don't work right, Taylor. Don't you know that by now?"

I stroke his back. "If I'd been betrayed by my girlfriend and my best friend, I wouldn't work right, either."

He's silent for a few seconds, then he says, "As much as I'd like to blame all my issues on Vanessa and Matt, I was wrong way before then."

"How long before?"

"Always." He doesn't look at me as he talks. Maybe it's easier for him like this. "As a kid, it was hard for me to make friends. I had trouble showing affection. I always felt kind of . . . off."

He's silent for a long time. Just when I figure he's asleep, he whispers, "One day, my parents sat me down and told me I'd spent the first couple of years of my life in foster care. I don't remember it, but just hearing the words made me have a panic attack. I was nearly three by the time they adopted me."

*Three? Oh, God.*

I used to think his insecurities were somehow augmented by his dramatic prowess, but it turns out he has real, justified abandonment issues.

I stroke his arm, trying to be supportive.

He takes a few shallow breaths. "I've never told anyone this before. But with you . . ." He turns onto his back and looks up at me with tired eyes. "I don't know if my birth parents gave up on me because I was defective, or whether I became defective when they gave up on me, but the end result is the same. After I found out, every time Dad missed a track meet or canceled our weekend plans, I put it down to me not being his real son. That's when we started fighting. I was just some loser's castoff kid he and Mom took pity on."

"Ethan, no . . ."

"Suddenly my wrongness made sense. Like I was an imposter in my own life. And that made me really fucking angry, because I figured,

'Why bother,' you know? Why keep pretending? I'm not a real son or a real brother. I'm no one's real anything. Maybe that's why I'm a good actor. Every character I play is more real than I am."

I take my hand out of his hair and stroke his face. He closes his eyes, and the muscles in his jaw tense and release.

"Ethan, come on. I've seen enough of your family to know that you're absolutely real to all of them. They adore you, even your dad. And as for me, I've never met anyone as real as you in my whole life. Every day you inspire me to stop being what others want and just be myself. So don't you dare sit there and tell me you're not real to anybody. You're surrounded by people who love you, despite your determination to push them away. If that's not real, I don't know what is."

I expect him to argue, but to my surprise, he doesn't. Instead, he searches my face, intense and frowning. "I'm surrounded by people who love me, huh?"

"Why does that surprise you?" I ask as I stroke his forehead. "You're kind of amazing."

His expression changes, and it looks like a smile is trying to escape from a maze of confusion. If it wasn't so damn attractive, I'd find it funny.

"I just— I don't . . ." He squeezes his eyes shut and pulls me over to him. I put my arms around him as he takes in a shaky breath.

We don't say anything else, but it doesn't feel as though we have to. He's told me his darkest secret, and even though it explains so much about why he is like he is, I've decided it doesn't matter. If and when he finally gets up the courage to be with me, I'm all in.

Hell, I'm all in already.


The next day, Holt practically throws me out of his apartment. Not in a nasty way. Just in a one-of-us-should-be-going-to-class way. When I call him that night, he sounds much better. His voice is coming back, and he tells me the coughing fits have become less frequent.

The following day is crazy busy, and it's not until I'm dozing in bed that my phone buzzes.

I look at the screen and smile when I see the caller ID.

"Hey, sicko."

"Hey."

It's crazy that one tiny word from him can make me almost dizzy with happiness. And it's not even a special word. Just a boring old one-syllable greeting, yet I can feel a stupid grin plastered all over my face like cheap wallpaper.

I thought things might have gotten weird between us, since he told me he was adopted, but it hasn't. If anything, it's like telling me has removed a burden.

He still hasn't said anything about getting our relationship back on an intimate footing, but I'm grateful we're not staying away from each other.

"Why aren't you sleeping?" I ask.

"I have been, all day. Now I'm wide awake."

"Take some cough medicine. That'll knock you out."

"I have, but it hasn't kicked in yet. It's probably not a good idea to be talking to you right now. I tend to say stupid things under the influence of that stuff."

"Not stupid. Just stuff you wouldn't tell me normally. I love that cough medicine. I've learned more about you in the past two days than I have all year."

"And yet, you're still talking to me."

"It's a burden, but someone has to do it."

He laughs. Such a beautiful sound.

He's quiet for a second, then he says, "Listen, Cassie, I've been thinking—"

"Uh huh." I can feel his nervousness through the phone line.

"I . . . I know that I was a dick about it the other day when Mom called, but . . . I want you to come to Thanksgiving." His voice gets softer. "I don't think I can go all those days without seeing you. I called Mom and asked her to get the spare room ready."

I'm stunned. And unbelievably touched.

"Ethan . . ."

"You haven't made other plans, have you?"

"Well, sort of. I did buy a frozen turkey dinner for one. I don't know if I can possibly give that up on such short notice. It has 'cranberry-flavored' sauce."

"Oh. Well, yeah. I mean, that's some delicious frozen food. Do you need some time to think about it? Not to sway you or anything, but you know that Maggie runs a gourmet catering company, right? No pressure."

I laugh. "Well, when you put it like that, I'd love to come."

It's not lost on me that this is sounding suspiciously like a date. I resist jumping out of bed and doing a happy dance.

"Good. I'll pick you up tomorrow night. Where will you be?"

"You're not coming to class tomorrow?" My stomach drops knowing that I'm not going to see him in the morning.

"No. I just need one more day to kick the last of this cough. Also, I'm going to need all my strength to survive the weekend with my father. So where can I pick you up?"

"Well, tomorrow afternoon we were all getting together at Jack's place for preholiday drinks."

"Okay, I'll come there. We'll drive to New York for dinner with Mom and Dad, and come back Sunday night."

The thought of spending four days in New York City is dizzying enough, but knowing I'll be living with Holt for that time? The word "ecstatic" is the only adjective that even comes close to how I'm feeling.

"Holt, should I be concerned that you're being all . . . nice . . . all of a sudden?"

He laughs. "Maybe. It's certainly scaring the hell out of me. Be careful what you wish for, Taylor. That's all I can say."

"Pfft. Pinocchio wished to be a real boy, and that turned out okay."

"True. But he was then forever devoid of permanent wood. Think about it."

I laugh, and a few seconds later when he yawns, I join him.

"Go to sleep," he says. "I'll see you tomorrow night."

"Okay, sure."

As we hang up, I feel like one of those paleontologists who works with a tiny brush and spends years slowly clearing away grains of dirt to reveal a precious relic or treasure. I don't think Holt would approve of me calling him a relic, but I'm smiling nonetheless.

By the time six o'clock rolls around the next night, most of my classmates are well on their way to being extremely hammered. Some have gone home to visit family, but for the most part, everyone is waiting until Christmas, like me. Thanksgiving is really just an excuse to be drunk for four days.

Ruby sits beside me on the sofa, sipping an industrial-strength margarita and bobbing her head to the music. I sit next to her, and my leg bounces nervously as I wait for Holt to show up. Ruby orders Jack to get me another drink to help chill me out, but I couldn't chill right now if I were dressed as a polar bear and dipped in liquid nitrogen.

I'm watching Mariska and Troy burn up the dance floor with some impressive swing-dance moves, when they pull apart to reveal Holt in the doorway.

*Oh. He's here.*

There's a huge roar as people see him and crowd around like he's a long-lost mythical creature. People ask how he is and tell him they've missed him. Zoe hugs him. Jack claps him on the back. And even though he smiles and responds, throughout it all his focus is on me.

I can hardly breathe.

"Whoa," Ruby whispers beside me. "Did Holt have some weird

version of bronchitis that increases his sex appeal? Because . . . damn. Boy is looking fine."

He's dressed in black jeans and a dark blue V-neck sweater. His hair's chaotic, and his jaw is freshly shaved. I can't turn away. He looks a little tired, but far less pale than when I last saw him. I have the strangest urge to walk over to him, wrap myself around his torso, and cling to him like a limpet.

Of course if I did that in the miniskirt I'm currently wearing, I'd look like an extremely slutty limpet. The kind the other limpets would shun and talk about behind her back.

I stand up and move toward him. I need to be near him.

When I stop in front of him, Jack's in the middle of a story about how Lucas simulated masturbation in acting class today, and how Erika had surprised everyone by praising him for being brave.

"I swear, man," Jack says as everyone laughs, "Beneath that hard-faced-bitch exterior, Erika's a complete sex freak."

Holt smiles at me and shoves his hands in his pockets as I mouth "hi" to him.

"Hey."

Jack slaps his shoulder. "Can I get you a drink? Beer? Shot of bourbon?"

"No, thanks. We're not staying long."

"We? Who's 'we'?"

"Me and Taylor."

Jack looks around at the crowd and raises his eyebrows. "You and Taylor? Well, well, well. What's going on here?"

For a moment, there's panic in Holt's eyes, but he takes a deep breath and says, "She's spending the holidays with me in New York."

*Oh.*

*Wow.*

Jack stares at us, stunned. By this time, Lucas and Zoe have joined him.

I can feel that my mouth is open, but I'm too shocked right now to shut it.

"Seriously?" Jack asks. Holt nods, and Jack turns to me. "Taylor, won't your mystery man have something to say about you spending time with tall-and-intense here? I mean, he saw you two in *Romeo and Juliet*, right? This could be an epically stupid move."

I try to think of something to say to deflect Avery's attention, but it turns out I don't have to. Holt has it covered.

"Actually, Jack," he says before swallowing nervously. "I'm her mystery man. And I'm completely okay with her spending time with me."

The room goes deathly quiet. The music has stopped, and if I listen real carefully, I can probably hear the wind blowing through the tumbleweeds outside.

I stop breathing, terrified that if I move, I'll wake from this awesome dream.

Jack stares between Holt and me in disbelief. "I'm sorry, but what? *You're* the guy she told us about? The fucking moron who won't sleep with her?"

Holt glowers and gives him a tight smile. "Yep. That's me. Fucking moron, in the flesh."

*Oh my God. Please don't let me wake up. Let it be real.*

There's a pregnant pause before Jack punches his fist into the air and yells, "Yeaaaaaaah!"

The room explodes with chatter, and Jack turns and high-fives the people behind him. "All right, everyone who had Taylor dating someone other than Holt, pay up. Markers are due, people! The eagle has landed! Repeat, the eagle has landed. Someone remind me to pay Erika."

The living room looks like the floor of the New York Stock Exchange, with cash and tickets being waved in the air while people chatter and laugh.

"Wait a minute!" Holt yells and glares at Jack. "You . . . you ran a fucking book on whether or not Taylor and I were together?"

Jack's face drops. "Well, yeah. But it was all in fun, man. You two have been making goo-goo eyes at each other for freaking months. We had to have fun with it somehow."

"Dude!" Holt says stiffly. "I do not make goo-goo eyes."

Lucas pats him lightly on the shoulder. "Sorry to break it to you, bro, but you totally do. Lucky you two got good crits for *Romeo and Juliet*, because in real life? You totally suck at acting."

Holt looks at me in shock, and I step in and put my hand on his chest.

"Um, so . . . wow. "

He blinks and shakes his head. "What the hell just happened?"

"Good question."

He stands there for a few seconds like a goldfish, watching the action around him with a look of confusion. It's only when I trace along the skin at the neck of his sweater that he snaps out of it and looks at me.

"Hi. I'm Cassie Taylor. I don't believe we've met."

I know it's quippy, but it's the truth. Who is this open and declarative man in front of me?

His ears turn pink. "Uh . . . yeah. Hi."

"So, that was . . . unexpected."

"Yeah. But good unexpected, right?"

How can he possibly think otherwise when I'm smiling up at him like I'm high?

"Very good unexpected. Did you mean to out us when you came here tonight?"

"No. Well, yes. I mean, I didn't know for sure, but when I saw you, I . . . I guess over the last few days I've realized that what I want with you outweighs how much you scare me. And I'm tired of depriving myself. It's too fucking draining. I want to be with you."

I put my arms around his neck. To his credit, he only looks around once to see who's watching before focusing on me.

"Stop freaking out."

His breathing gets faster as he stares at me. "Make me."

I pull his head down. When he kisses me, it's soft and chaste, but the way he inhales and tightens his arms around me tells me his reaction is anything but mild. There are various whoops of approval around us, but we ignore them. It's kind of easy when all my focus is directed at resisting the urge to become a slutty limpet.

He kisses me more firmly, and through my lusty haze, I'm impressed that he's being so bold in front of everyone. I know this is kind of a big deal for him.

I'm proud.

He pulls back as the entire room applauds, and he gives them all a good-natured bird flip as he drags me down the hallway into the deserted study.

When I close the door behind us, he sighs in relief and runs his fingers through his hair.

"See?" I say. "After all these weeks of secrecy and denial, was that so hard?"

He pulls me against him, not being shy about running his hands over my butt as he stares down at me. "Taylor, I can say with absolute honesty, that yes. It was, and is, extremely hard."

He kisses me again, less restrained now, and walks me back toward the wall. He's groaning in a way that makes me want to crawl inside his throat and rub myself on his larynx. The sounds I'm making are embarrassingly loud. For so long, I've been waiting for him to just let go and give in to this thing between us, and now that he is, it's so much better than the fantasy.

There's no hesitation. No self-consciousness. He's kissing me like he's afraid to stop. Like he's trying to make up for all those long days of separation.

Part of me is still convinced this isn't reality, but when he lifts me up so he can grind against me, I decide I don't care. Whatever it is, I'll take it.

"We should really stop," he says as he kisses down to my clavicle.

I grip his hair. "Of course we should. Best possible solution to all this burning lust between us. Good plan."

He cups my breasts, and caresses them through my sweater. "Don't mock me."

"Then don't stay stupid things like 'We should really stop.'"

"You have a point. I didn't declare us as a couple in front of everyone so that you could continue not touching my dick, that's for sure."

"On it." My breathing is loud as I palm him through his jeans.

He puts his hand on the wall behind me and hangs his head. "Sweet Jesus."

I squeeze him through the fabric, and he drops his head lower until his forehead is resting on mine.

"At the risk of being mocked again," he says breathlessly as he pulls back, "you really need to stop doing that. We kind of have to get on the road if we're going to make it to Mom and Dad's for dinner."

With reluctance, I remove my hand. He steps back and sighs. "Just give me a minute. Jack probably has a bet going that I'll be walking out of here with a hard-on."

"Maybe I should go put some money down. I could win big."

"Especially if you continue to stand there in that nonexistent skirt."

"You like this?"

"If I said no, would you take it off?"

"Only one way to find out."

He explores under my skirt, long fingers grazing my thigh.

"Ethan," I say breathlessly. "If you go there, we're absolutely not getting out of here any time soon. You know that, right?"

"I know. I just have a very hot girlfriend, and when my hands are on her, I get carried away."

All the breath leaves my lungs. "You're admitting I'm your girlfriend? Finally?"

When he answers, his voice is soft. "Yes, Cassie. You're my girlfriend."

My stomach flips.

I don't think I'm going to get tired of him saying that word any time in the near future.

Although he's smiling, I also see a little panic in his eyes.

"Just saying it is freaking you out, isn't it?"

"A little."

"Do you think you can get used to it?"

He strokes my neck and thinks for a second. "I hope so. I want to."

My cheap-wallpaper grin is back. "Me, too."

He smiles, and I wrap my arms around him. "Was this what you were afraid of? Because even though I really don't have much experience with this sort of thing . . . I think it's going well so far."

His smile fades. "Taylor, I have to warn you once again that I suck at relationships. I've made that clear, right?"

I stand on my toes to kiss him. "We'll be fine. Stop thinking so much."

He nods and sighs, and for a moment, he's completely open.

Like that, he's the most beautiful thing I've ever seen.

# NINETEEN

## NEW YORK, NEW YORK

*New York City*
*The Holt Residence*

From where we're standing on the pavement, the Holt brownstone looks huge and imposing. I shudder.

*Okay, Cassie, be cool. You'll be fine.*

When I look at Holt, I notice he seems nervous, too.

I take a deep breath. "So, what's the plan?"

He frowns. "The plan?"

"How do we behave in front of your parents? Are we hiding that we're together?"

"Do you want to?"

"No."

"Then we won't."

He says it with conviction, but I don't miss the flash of panic.

"So, what? We're going to tell them we're boyfriend and girlfriend?"

He hesitates for just a second. "Uh . . . yes."

I'm still not convinced. "So, you're my boyfriend, Ethan, bringing home his girlfriend, Cassie, to meet his parents?"

"Yes." Less hesitation that time, but it's still there.

"Just a normal *boyfriend* and *girlfriend*, spending time with your folks and doing normal boyfriend and girlfriend things. All boyfriendy and girlfriendy—"

"Okay, stop saying 'boyfriend and girlfriend.' It's annoying."

"I'll stop if *you* say it."

"Why?"

"So I know you can."

"I said it at Jack's."

"That was ages ago. Say it again."

He rolls his eyes. "You're my girlfriend, okay? My very hot, very *irritating* girlfriend."

"Aw, *boyfriend*, that's the sweetest thing you've ever said to me, your *girlfriend*."

He shakes his head and tries not to laugh. "Will you stop now?"

"Of course." I wait a second before asking, "Can I call you 'sweetie'?"

"No."

"Cupcake?"

"No."

"Angel-cheeks?"

"Fuck, no."

"Okay, fine. Just so we're both on the same page."

He laughs, and I join him, but I'm so faking it. At least laughing helps me pretend I'm not terrified.

"But listen," he says and takes my hand. "Let me tell mom and dad when the time is right, okay? A few days ago, I swore up and down to my mother that you weren't my girlfriend, and I said the same thing when I told her you were coming to stay. I don't want to just walk in here and blurt it out, or I'll look like a jackass. Just give me some time, okay?"

I want to argue that he's hiding how he feels about me again, but after what he did at the party, I know that's not what this is about.

I look up at the door again, and my nervousness expands. I've never

met a boyfriend's parents before. Heck, I've never had a boyfrien
before, let alone parents to meet. I mean, yes, I'd met them before
but I wasn't his girlfriend then.

Holt must notice my tension, because he leans down and kisses me
tender and lingering. When he pulls back, I feel a little better.

"Cassie, you're going to be fine. Stop freaking out."

"What if they hate me?"

"Don't be ridiculous. They've already met you, and I can confidentl
say my dad prefers you to me. I'm the one who should be nervou
here. If Mom gets drunk, she's likely to pull out the family photo al
bum and show you naked pictures of her boy."

I stifle a laugh. "Would they be recent pictures? Because . . . hmmm
I'd like to see those."

He shakes his head, goes to the trunk, and removes our bags. "Yes
my mother has a full set of pictures of her grown son, naked. That'
totally normal."

"Hey, a girl can dream."

He locks the car, and when I go to grab my bag, he shoos me awa
before he picks it up and gestures for me to head up the stairs.

"Such a gentleman with the bag carrying," I say.

He gives me a wry smile. "If you still think I'm a gallant gentle
man after I've been your boyfriend for a while, it'll be a first. Bette
start lowering your expectations."

"Never. Like my hemlines, my expectations will remain high."

He gives my legs a sultry appraisal, before he opens the door an
leads me into the entranceway of his home. "Mom! Elissa! We're here!

I hear a high-pitched yapping, followed by scrambling claws on th
wooden floor. Then a furry ball with legs explodes into view at th
end of the hallway. It bounds toward us in a blur of long, tan fur an
pink tongue. When it reaches Holt, it jumps up at his knees and beg
to be picked up.

He drops the bags and scoops the puppy into his arms, then holds it away from him, as it tries to lick his face.

"Jesus, Tribble, cool it. We have company." The tiny dog squirms and yaps, and although Holt's scowling, I can tell he's smitten. "Tribble, this is Cassie. She's going to stay with us for a few days, so behave yourself."

I go to pet her, but Holt stops me.

"Careful. She's weird with strangers. Especially women."

Tribble watches me suspiciously with black eyes as she sniffs my hand. Then her lips pull back, and she emits a tiny growl. If it were any other dog, it might be frightening, but coming from her, it's adorable.

Holt pulls her away and glares. "Tribble, no. Stop being a bitch."

When he puts her on the floor, she eyes me with disdain before turning on her heel and trotting away.

"Sorry about her," Ethan's mother says as she comes down the hallway. "She hates everyone except for Ethan. She tolerates Charles and me because we feed her, but it's a tenuous relationship at best. Welcome, Cassie. So nice to see you."

She gives me a hug before she kisses Ethan on the cheek. There's something about the way he smiles at his mom that makes me melt.

"Dad's not home?"

Maggie shakes her head. "No. Working late."

It doesn't escape my attention that news of his father's absence makes Ethan's whole posture relax.

"So," Mrs. Holt says, "dinner's almost ready. Why don't you show Cassie to her room, so she can freshen up? Elissa will be home in about fifteen minutes, and then we'll eat."

Holt leads me up the stairs into a comfortable bedroom and sets my bag down on the bed. I can feel him eyeing me for approval, as I look around.

"So, this is it," he says with a wave of his hand.

"Nice."

The décor is modern but comfortable, and the bed is huge. Considering I'm used to a lumpy single, this is luxury. I flop back to test the bed's bounce-ability. It's only when I turn to Ethan that I realize he's staring. Straight at my boobs.

"Bathroom's down the hall," he says, his expression intense. Never before have bathroom directions been so arousing.

"Where's your room?" I notice how tall and broad he is as he stands above me.

"Next door down."

"So, close then?"

"Very."

"Can I see it?" Pretty sure I'm still talking about his bedroom.

I don't know why the thought of seeing his childhood bedroom turns me on, but it totally does.

He tries to play it cool, but the way he taps his fingers on his thigh tells me his anxiety is rising. "Sure."

This is a big step for him, showing me parts of himself he'd probably like to keep hidden.

He leads me down the hall to the next room and gestures for me to enter first, then drops his bag inside the door.

The room is much neater than the one in Westchester, and over the bed are framed posters of old movies like *Taxi Driver*, *On the Waterfront*, *Raging Bull*, and *Butch Cassidy and the Sundance Kid*. If I were a betting woman, I'd wager his favorite actors come from their cast lists.

On the wall opposite the door are shelves, filled not only with books but also trophies and photos. I wander over to get a closer look, mindful that Holt is still hovering in the doorway like an anxious vulture.

There are so many trophies and ribbons, it's hard to take them all in. I pick one up and read the inscription. *All-State Track Champion— Ethan Holt*.

I turn to the frowning man in the doorway. "So you were a pretty fast runner, huh?"

He shrugs. "I was okay."

"Sure. They always give dozens of trophies to people who are just *okay*."

I lean over to get a closer look at the photos. One shows Holt leaping over a hurdle, front leg extended, back one bent. His hair is longer than it is now, and there's a look of fierce determination on his face. Another picture shows him crossing the finish line, head thrown back, arms wide, a victorious smile on his face. He almost looks like a different person; Ethan's less intense younger brother.

Further down, there's a group photo of boys in varsity letter jackets with girls wrapped around them. My breath catches when I see he has his arm around a girl. He's looking at her with obvious affection. Then I realize that she's not gazing back at him but at the blond boy on her other side.

Oh, God.

*Vanessa and Matt?*

He reaches around me to turn the picture face down. "Don't know why I keep that out. I should've gotten rid of it years ago. I mean, I was an idiot for not seeing it, right? It was obvious they were screwing while we were together."

When I turn to him, he looks down and shoves his hands in his pockets.

"Hey, don't be too hard on yourself. I mean, clearly the poor girl was delusional. And maybe blind. Choosing that chump over you? What the hell was she thinking?"

He relaxes a little, but I know the part of him that was damaged by the situation doesn't believe me.

"Yeah, well . . . whatever. Matt was a decent guy. At least I thought he was, right up until I found him screwing my girlfriend."

"Ethan?" I put my hand on his chest, and after a few seconds, he meets my gaze. "I've never met Matt, and I'm sure he has his good points, but somewhere there's a plaque declaring that Vanessa choosing him over you is the Stupidest Girl Fail Ever. Trust me on that."

He leans down and kisses me, and although it's slow and intense, our inhales are loud and simultaneous.

Damn this boy and his mouth.

It's crazy how quickly he has me frustrated, and before I know it, I'm pushing him down onto his bed so I can straddle him.

"So," I say, as he sucks gently on my throat, "apart from Vanessa, am I the only girl who's been in this bedroom?"

His voice vibrates against my skin when he answers. "Yes."

"Good."

I push him down and kiss him with a fierce sense of possession. He makes a noise that I think indicates he enjoys it, and it gets louder when I roll onto my side and pull his thigh between mine.

*Oh, hell yes. I love his thigh. Awesome thigh.*

"We should stop." His breathing is ragged, and he glances nervously at the door.

I kiss down his throat. "Stopping is bad. Except maybe if you lose control on an icy road and are hurtling toward certain death. Then, it's pretty much essential. But in this case? Definitely bad. Terrible. Worst idea ever."

I suck on the racing pulse in his neck, and when he speaks, his voice is strained and low. "Taylor, you know my mother could come up here at any second, right? Do you really want her to catch you riding her son's leg?"

I stop dead in my tracks. That's when I hear footsteps coming down the hallway.

*Oh, God*

Within half a second, I'm on my feet and straightening my clothes and hair, while I try not to look like the horny virgin I am.

Ethan chuckles and sits up, then grabs a pillow to cover his erection

The footsteps get closer before Elissa appears in the doorway. She rolls her eyes as she looks between us. "Oh, please. Don't even pretend you two weren't just making out. When I was at the bottom of the stairs, I could hear Ethan's disgusting groaning. He sounded like a bear with heartburn. Plus, Ruby called and told me all about the spectacle you made of yourselves at Avery's party. Thank God. I was beginning to think I was going to lose that stupid bet."

Holt glares at his sister. "You bet on us, too?"

"Pfft. Of course. As far as I was concerned, it was easy money. Especially after Cassie agreed to check on you while you were sick."

"Elissa!" I say. "You asked me to go over there because you wanted to win a bet?"

She sighs. "No. I asked you to go over there because I was worried about Ethan. And because you were both being stupid about being together." The next sentence is much quieter. "Me winning a hundred bucks and buying a new purse is just a bonus, so yay for me."

"Fuck me," Holt says with a scowl. "Why does everyone in this family think I'm incapable of making my own decisions about my love life?"

"Because you haven't had a love life in four years, big brother," Elissa says. "You're like a little kid who won't go back in the pool because he swallowed some water once upon a time. Thank God you finally manned up with Cassie. If you hadn't, I was considering buying you a few dozen cats and being done with it."

"Elissa, get the fuck out of my room."

"No. Cassie's my friend, too. You need to learn to share."

"I'm not sharing her. Now, get out."

"Make me."

"Happily." He strides over to her, picks her up in a bear-hug, and deposits her outside the door before he slams it in her face.

Her voice is muffled by the wood when she yells, *"You're such a tool!"*

Holt snatches the door open and whispers, "Oh, and by the way,

I haven't told Mom and Dad that Cassie and I are together, so if you could keep your giant trap shut, that'd be sweet. Thanks."

She puts her foot in the door before he can slam it again. "In that case, you'd best be nice, or I'm going to broadcast it to the whole neighborhood."

He frowns. "I hate being nice."

"And I hate being discreet. Deal with it, and let me in."

Ethan pushes the door open and goes to sit on the bed as Elissa walks over to give me a quick hug. "Cassie, I can't even tell you how glad I am you're here. At last I'll have someone to talk to other than butt-munch over there."

"Bite me," Holt mutters while absently flicking through a *Rolling Stone* magazine.

Elissa sighs. "You said you'd be nice."

He leans back on the bed. "Sorry. Bite me, *please.*"

She nods. "Better."

I laugh, because even though they're being snarky and immature, underneath it all there's affection, and it makes me realize how much I've missed out by not having a brother or sister.

We chat for a while, and discuss plans for the next day and which parts of New York they'd each like to show me. Holt wasn't joking when he said he didn't want to share me. Every time Elissa suggests taking me somewhere, he tenses up. Part of me finds his jealousy incredibly hot.

At one point, Elissa catches me staring at him as he unpacks his bag, and she smiles. I feel my face heat up.

When Ethan leaves to take his toiletries to the bathroom, Elissa shakes her head. "Man, you have it so bad for my brother, don't you?"

My face flames again. "Shut up."

She laughs. "I'm not making fun of you. I think it's awesome, but he's not exactly low maintenance. I was beginning to wonder if he'd find a girl to take on all his baggage."

"He's not that bad."

"That's because you have a knack for handling him."

"You think so? Sometimes I have no idea."

She glances at the door before she whispers, "If you want to understand him more, ask him to show you what's in the bottom drawer." She nods in the direction of the tall chest of drawers on the far wall.

"Why? Is he keeping human body parts in there?"

She laughs and stands as Ethan comes back. "In a way. I figure he's seen yours, so you should get to see his."

Holt eyes his sister suspiciously. "What the fuck are you talking about?"

"Nothing." She kisses him on the cheek, then disappears down the hallway.

He gives me a dark look. "What did my sister just say to you?"

"She told me I should ask to see what's in your bottom drawer." I lean forward and lower my voice. "Is it porn? Because that's something I'd really enjoy looking at with you."

Rather than laughing it off as I expect, his face turns red and stormy. "Fucking Elissa."

"What? What's in there?" I didn't really believe it was human body parts, but now I'm not so sure.

"What's in there is no one's business but mine," he says, as he grabs the remaining clothes out of his bag and slams them into drawers.

"Ethan . . ."

"Just drop it, okay?"

"You're really not going to tell me?"

"No."

"Why not?"

"Because it's private, all right? Just because we're going out doesn't mean you get to know everything about me."

"Uh, actually, I kind of thought that was the point." I walk over and lay my hands on his chest. "Aren't we supposed to show each other all our ugly parts and see if we like each other anyway?" He tenses when I push under his shirt to touch his warm skin.

"Taylor . . ." His eyes get heavy when I explore his muscles.

"I mean, apart from you murdering someone and burying them in your backyard, there's nothing you could tell me that would make me not like you. You're aware of that, right?"

He breathes heavily. I move my hands around to his sides, then run my palms over his ribs and up to his shoulder blades. He closes his eyes and drops his head. "What are you doing?"

"Convincing you." I run my fingernails down his back, and it makes him groan. "Ethan, please tell me what's in the drawer."

He exhales, and I can tell he's wavering.

"If you tell me, I'll kiss you. A lot."

"Low blow."

"I'll do that, too."

He squeezes his eyes shut. "If I tell you, you have to promise not to give me shit."

"When do I ever—?" I stop myself and sigh. *Yeah, can't even pretend to deny it.* "Okay. I promise."

"And you have to make good on your promise to kiss me. A lot."

"Definitely. And the low blow?"

The look he gives me makes me shiver. "Don't tempt me. My mother is downstairs."

"Okay, fine. It's a deal."

He sighs then walks over to the chest of drawers. "Remember, no mocking."

I draw a cross on my chest.

He pulls his key ring out of his pocket and uses a small brass key to unlock the bottom drawer.

"I don't fucking believe I'm doing this," he mutters as he pulls the drawer open.

I step forward and peer inside. It's full of plain, fabric-covered books

"Um . . . okay."

He's waiting for a reaction. The only one I can give him is confusion. "I'm sorry, Holt, I don't understand."

He sighs. "Remember when I read your diary? I was a total asshole and yelled at you for writing all that shit down where people could find it? Well, this is why. I was scared someone might find these. That *you* might find these one day, and . . ."

What he's saying becomes clear. "Oh my God."

He bends down and picks up one of the books.

"These are all . . . ?"

"Yeah."

He flips open the front cover and holds it up for me to see:

*The Journal of Ethan Holt. Keep the fuck out.*

"You keep diaries!"

He drops the book back into the drawer and shoves it closed with his foot. "Journals, Taylor, not diaries. There's a difference."

"Oh, please. How is a journal different from a diary?"

"It just is, okay? Men don't keep diaries."

"Well, obviously they do."

"Goddammit, you said you wouldn't mock."

I hold up my hands. "You're right. I'm sorry." We're silent for a moment, then I ask, "So what do you write in there?"

"The same sort of stuff you write in yours, I suppose."

"Really? So you're also a sexually frustrated virgin who's obsessed with a handsome actor's penis?"

He sighs and drops his head.

"I'm sorry," I say, laughing. "But you gave me such a hard time after you read my diary. Aren't I allowed to have a little fun?"

"A little," he says grudgingly.

"So, do I feature in your diary?"

His ears pink, and he shoves his hands in his pockets. "Maybe. Not these, but the one back at my apartment."

"Are you ever going to let me read something? Quid pro quo, and all that."

"Not in this lifetime. Or the next, for that matter." He looks at the floor, and I feel bad for poking fun. Revealing this to me is a huge step for him, and I shouldn't make light of it.

I walk over and touch his face, then rise on my toes to kiss him lightly. "Thank you. For showing me. It means a lot."

He looks away. "Yeah. Sure."

I kiss him again, longer this time, and after a moment's hesitation, he responds. Strong arms wind around me as he kisses me more passionately, and just as I register his giant hands are cupping my butt, I hear a throat clear behind us.

We both turn to see Maggie in the doorway, trying not to smile. "Sorry to interrupt, but dinner's ready."

Without another word, she disappears.

Holt exhales and drops his head to my shoulder. I notice his hands remain on my ass.

"Well, I guess now we don't have to tell Mom we're dating."

"Nope. Guess not."

When we get downstairs, Elissa and Maggie are already seated. Tribble guards a chair I guess to be Ethan's. I swear she sneers at me.

"Sit, please," Maggie says and gestures to the remaining place settings. "I don't know about anyone else, but I'm starving."

Tribble growls as I sit next to Holt, and he chastises her under his breath.

When his mom passes him a plate of pasta, he clears his throat and says, "Mom, I . . . uh . . . I wanted to tell you earlier about Cassie and me, but . . . well . . ."

"It's fine, sweetheart," Maggie says and offers me a bowl of salad. "I already knew."

Holt shoots an accusing glare at his sister.

"Hey, don't look at me," she says and holds up her hands defensively. "I haven't said a thing."

"Then how did she know?"

"Sweetheart," Maggie says, "when you're a mother, it's easy to read the emotions of your children. It's been obvious to me you have feelings for Cassie, and I'm glad you finally acted upon them. I'm very happy for you."

Holt looks dubious as she hands him the salad.

"Oh, all right," she says. "Jack Avery called earlier to say that my bet last week had paid off."

Holt's face drops, along with his fork. "What?!"

Maggie wrings her hands in embarrassment. "Well, darling, Elissa told me the odds Jack was offering, and after I saw you two in *Romeo and Juliet*, I figured it was a sure thing."

"Mom! Jesus!"

"Darling, don't be mad. Momma needed a new pair of shoes."

He rubs his eyes and groans.

My nervous energy manifests as too-shrill laughter, and as I snort indelicately, three surprised faces turn to me. Four, if you count the dog.

"I'm sorry," I say as I try unsuccessfully to stop. "But that's kind of awesome."

Maggie laughs along with me, and Elissa joins in.

Ethan shakes his head. "Why are all the women in my life determined to torture me?"

I lean over and kiss him on the cheek. I'm rewarded with a hint of a smile.

The rest of the meal passes quickly, and I'm blown away by the amazing feast Maggie has whipped up. By the time I'm finished, I can barely move. My poor, distended stomach is in both heaven and hell, and I curse the years of eating my mom's sad excuse for cuisine, in which the chickpea was held sacred and anything that tasted good, like butter or salt, was treated like a deadly poison to be avoided at all costs.

As she serves dessert, Maggie questions me about myself and my family, and even though I'm usually nervous about being scrutinized so openly, it doesn't seem like she's being nosy. She just wants to get to know her son's girlfriend.

A couple of times I catch her watching when Holt and I talk to each other, and she has that same optimistic look in her eye my mother used to get whenever she tried to convert me to veganism. I'm hoping Holt and I work out better than my short-lived relationship with Tofurkey and rice milk.

As for Holt, I like to watch him interact with his mother and sister. He and Elissa fight incessantly, but it's good natured, despite his efforts to seem like a badass. And the way he is with his mom? It makes me all kinds of swoony.

They say you can tell a lot about how a man will treat you by the way he treats his mother. If that's true, I expect to be treated like a queen.

# TWENTY

## DESPERATION

Four days later, Thanksgiving is over and we're back in Westchester. Holt's barely gotten my apartment door open before I'm on him, kissing him with everything I have.

He drops my bag in surprise, and we almost trip over it.

"Cassie, slow down . . ."

"Don't tell me to slow down," I say, and push him the short distance to the couch. "Four days, Ethan. Four days of interminable fondling, interrupted orgasms, and family drama. The time for being slow has passed. Now, please, shut up and kiss me."

Whatever he's going to say next is smothered by my mouth, and I straddle him as I bury my fingers in his hair.

He feels amazing. Tastes amazing. How one man can taste so good is completely beyond me.

I know I'm out of control, but he's made me this way. Our weekend with his family ended up being pretty enjoyable, despite some tension when his dad was around. But being in close quarters with him for twenty-four hours a day was sexual torture. Between sightseeing with his sister and family meals, we rarely got time alone. And when we were, he'd always stop before we got to the good stuff. The whole weekend turned out to be one giant round of excruciating foreplay, and if he doesn't stop stalling and give me some relief pretty damn pronto, there's going to be a girl-parts rebellion the likes of which he's never seen. I'm wound tighter than Jane Fonda's latest facelift, goddammit.

"Take off your shirt." I kiss all over his face, then move down his neck while I add in some nibbling, because I know it makes him crazy.

"Wait . . . just— Oh, fuck . . ."

I bite down at the point where his neck meets his shoulder and suck hard. He pushes his pelvis up so suddenly, he nearly bucks me off his lap.

"Jesus, Cassie!"

"Shirt! Off!"

I tug and yank it over his head. His hair looks like I've electrocuted him. With the way my neurons are firing right now, I probably could.

When I throw his shirt away, it smacks into the lamp beside us and knocks it to the floor in an explosion of porcelain.

He drags his mouth away from me long enough to assess the damage. "You murdered the lamp."

I circle my hips. "Stop talking. Lamp's not important. Getting naked is."

I fumble as I unbutton my shirt. He says something in protest, but I tear it off anyway. It lands on the floor next to the lamp corpse and leaves me just in my bra. I press my chest to his and exhale in relief. I want to lick him all over. I start on his neck and revel in the salty and sweet of his skin, as I move my hips to rub against him.

Ohhh, he's hard and perfect. All of his other parts taste good, and I wonder if that would, too.

Just thinking about it makes me even more desperate, and something's seriously gotta give before I burst into flames.

"Pants," I say, and it's barely even a word. More like a hoarse bark.

"What?" He's doing something amazing to my boobs.

I can barely form words, but I try. "Holt, for the love of all that's holy, take off your damn pants!"

My yelling shocks him into stillness, so I take matters into my own hands. He makes vague protests as I fumble with his belt, but at this point, all of his arguments are invalid.

His belt is the stupid type that just has a solid metal plate held together with pins or something. I tug at it, frustrated.

"Crap . . ."

"Cassie—"

"How the frack does this thing work?!" I grab it with both hands and pull and push in an attempt to make it come apart with brute force, but it won't budge. "Dammit, Ethan, help me!"

I feel like I'm in a disaster movie, and that belt is the iceberg that's going to sink the good ship Orgasm. It must be destroyed.

At last, the buckle gives way, and I make a small victory noise before I frantically unbutton his jeans.

"I want you," I say as I push my hand into his boxers.

*Oh, God, yes. That, right there. That's what I want.*

"Ohhhhh . . . Jesus." His eyes glaze over when I close my hand around him.

"Please, Ethan." I'm so whiny, I'm almost ashamed. "Ruby isn't going to be home until tomorrow. We have the whole place to ourselves. Please."

The look on his face tells me he's about to say something I don't want to hear, so I kiss him to shut him up and stroke him slowly. He moans and grips my thighs. Neither of those things makes me any less frantic.

I stand and unbutton my jeans then tug them down to my knees in record time. I try standing on them to get them off, but they're skinny jeans, and the stupid things won't go over my giant feet.

"Dammit!"

I yank my right foot up and try to pull it free, but I end up over-balancing and face-plant into Ethan's crotch. My chin hits something soft, and he doubles over and cups himself.

"Fuuuuuuck, woman . . ."

"Sorry! Oh my God, I'm so sorry!"

He collapses sideways on the couch. I try to stand, desperate to help in some way, but my feet are still encased in my jeans, so I just end up falling over again.

"Fracking frack!"

Holt groans, his face half turned into the couch cushion. "Taylor, if you're going to be a badass who destroys her boyfriend's balls, you're going to have to start using real swear words."

I sit on the ground and tug at my jeans until my feet are free, then I kneel in front of him. "I'm so sorry. Are you okay?"

His voice is strained when he says, "Well, I don't have the problem of coming in record time anymore, that's for damn sure."

I lean down and stroke his hair. "I'm sorry."

"You keep saying that. It doesn't help."

"I don't know what else to do."

He eyes my jeans, which are like a denim pretzel beside me. "You're the only person I know who can turn getting undressed into an extreme sport. What the hell is the rush?"

"I just . . . I want you."

"I want you, too, but that doesn't mean we have to have sex this very second. We haven't even been to third base yet."

"Yes, we have."

He scoffs. "No, we haven't. I'd remember you going down on me. Or me going down on you, for that matter."

All of the blood that isn't currently pulsing down south now rushes to my face. "You haven't— I mean . . . *That's* third base?" I have a flash of self-consciousness about him being all face-friendly down there. "I . . . uh . . . I thought that was fourth base."

He sits up and frowns. "Cassie, fourth base is sex. How many bases do you think there are?"

I don't know, but I want him to teach me about all of them.

I lean in to kiss him, but he pulls away. "Just . . . stop, for a second okay? What's going on with you?"

"I'm sorry, I just—" I slump back onto my heels, feeling frustrated and foolish. "You make me crazy, and I want to do stuff to you and have you do stuff to me, but you keep stopping and I . . ." My eyes prickle. I can't pretend his continued rejections don't hurt.

"Come here." He pulls me up onto the couch, and we lie side by side.

I sigh when he grazes the backs of his fingers across my cheek. "I just get the feeling I want this more than you do, and that sucks, you know?"

He looks at me like I've accused him of liking Adam Sandler movies. "You think—" He shakes his head. "You think I don't *want* you? Are you fucking serious?"

He runs his hand down my side and reaches the bare skin of my thigh. "How can you possibly think for even one second I don't—" He looks down. "Fuck me, what are you wearing?"

My panties and bra don't match, but he doesn't seem to care. He runs one fingertip around the edge of my lacy boy shorts. It's the closest he's ever come to delving beneath the fabric, and my heart rate immediately goes into overdrive.

"You like these?"

He closes his hand over my hip. "I like *you*. Your panties are just a bonus. If you understood . . . if you had any idea how much I—" He looks at me, eyes heavy and dark. "Cassie, I want you, *all the time*. Too much."

He leans forward to cover my mouth with his, and the light suction almost distracts me from the way he runs his hand down my leg to grip the spot just under my knee.

"I have to be careful with you," he says between soft, slow kisses. "Because if I screw this up . . ." He kisses my neck, almost talking to himself. "I really don't want to screw this up."

"You won't." I take his face in both hands to make him look at me. "Besides, what's the worst that could happen, right?"

He grazes fingers across my stomach, then slowly moves up to my breasts. He teases me there as he kisses my neck, then my chest, then the swells at the top of my bra. Just when I think he can't inflame me any more, he moves his hands lower. And lower. Then he's *right there*, over my panties, touching gently at first, then pressing harder, making my breathing shallow. He takes control of my pleasure like he has an instruction manual, watching my face the whole time to gauge my reaction.

How is it possible? How can he know what to do to my body when I'm still fumbling and clueless?

Within sixty seconds, he has me closer to orgasm than I can get in ten minutes on my own. I subconsciously rock against his hand, to try and find the magical fulcrum of sensation that will tip me over the edge.

"That look," he says, as I press my head back into the cushions. "That belongs to me. The way your mouth drops open. Your eyelids flutter. That look is all mine."

Then I gasp, because he pushes *into* my panties and brushes aside the lace. He's never done that before, and ohhhhh, dear God, his fingers . . .

His perfect, virtuosic fingers.

I squeeze my eyes shut as he touches parts he's never touched before.

He groans, too, and presses his forehead against mine. "Jesus . . . so soft. And bare. What the fuck are you trying to do to me?"

"Ruby." I'm panting and barely coherent.

"No, I'm Ethan. But if there's some awesome lesbian tale you'd like to tell me about you and your roommate, I'm all ears." He presses harder.

"No," I say, barely able to get the words out. "Ruby forces me to get Brazilians. That's why I'm bare. It hurts like hell."

He moves his hand faster, and I can't keep my eyes open.

"Right now, Ruby is my hero. I've never felt anything like this."

"Oh, God . . . Me neither."

Then it feels like he's kissing and touching everywhere at once, and everything is hard breaths and low noises. He tightens and coils me, until I think I might pass out from the intensity.

"I love making you come," he whispers, right before it happens. My back arches, and all the tightrope strands of me snap and unfurl.

*Oh God, oh God, oh God, oh God . . .*

He murmurs his approval as he watches me spiral through layers of pleasure, and whispers encouragement until I'm panting and boneless beside him.

Wow.

Just . . . *wow.*

The last few shudders fade, and I melt into his arms, beyond relaxed. Endless days of frustration and sexual tension disappear, and I'm so heavily satisfied, I can't move. Thank God at least one of us knows how to get me off.

He pulls my panties back into place. I take deep breaths, but it seems to take forever for my pounding heart to slow down.

When I open my eyes, I see him looking at me with an expression that makes my pulse race again. But as soon as our eyes meet, something shifts, and his emotional shutters slide down.

I stroke his face in an effort to keep him with me. "That was . . . amazing."

"Yeah?"

"Lord, yes. So, you're telling me that was . . . what? Second base?"

"Uh huh."

"Wow. Second base rocks."

"Do you feel less . . . frantic now?"

"Yes. I feel like a sloth on Valium." I trail my hand down the front of his jeans and feel how hard he still is. "So, can I help you relax now?"

He tenses. "I'm relaxed."

"First of all, you're hardly ever relaxed. Second, *this* part of you is definitely uptight. I'm guessing he'd like a little trip to third base. Or maybe even a home run."

"Cassie . . ." He moves away and sits at the other end of the couch. "We're not going to have sex tonight."

"Why not?"

He turns to me. "How can you be so blasé about having sex for the first time?"

"I'm not blasé, I just don't think it's that big a deal."

"That's the definition of blasé."

I sigh. "Okay, fine, but I think I'm ready. And I can tell you are, too, so I don't understand why you keep saying no. I mean, aren't you uncomfortable? Don't you want some relief?"

He gives me a wry smile. "Do you think all of those trips to the bathroom during our stay with Mom and Dad were to pee? You must think I have the smallest bladder in the world."

"You mean, when you went to the bathroom you were . . ."

"Yep." He says it with very little shame.

Just the thought of him pleasuring himself makes my face flame. "In your parents' house?!"

"I grew up in that house. I've been masturbating there since I hit puberty. Besides, it was either that or walk around for the whole weekend with a hard-on, and believe me, that would have been worse."

"But if I turn you on so much, why aren't we naked in my bed right now?"

He adjusts himself and runs his hand through his hair. "Cassie, I'm hyperaware that you're a virgin, and apart from the pain you're going to feel the first time, it's also going to be a milestone in your life. You'll never get to have a first time ever again, and I . . . I just don't want to screw that up for you."

"How on earth could you screw it up? It's not like you don't know what you're doing. I mean, judging by what you can achieve with just your fingers, having your whole body is going to rock my world."

"I'm not talking about the actual sex."

"Then what are you talking about? Because I'm kind of confused here."

He looks down at his hands. "What if we do it, and you figure out I can't be the boyfriend you need and end up hating me? The memory of your first time would always be tainted."

"Why would you even think that?"

He takes a deep breath. "Because it happened to me." He clasps his hands in front of him and squeezes his knuckles until they crack.

It takes me a few moments before the penny drops. "Oh! Vanessa? She was your—"

"Yes."

We sit in silence for a few seconds, and I feel bad for doubting he wanted me. It never occurred to me he was trying to make sure I didn't jump headfirst into a sexual relationship I'd end up regretting.

"I just don't want you to make the mistakes I did," he says.

I nod. "Okay. I can see where you're coming from."

His eyes are guarded but tinged with the lust I saw earlier. "You can?"

"Yeah. I kind of think . . . well, it's actually pretty sweet of you."

He frowns. "Don't call me sweet. Call me hot. Or awesome. Or well-endowed. Kittens are sweet, not me."

I try not to laugh. "Okay, fine. You're a hot, awesome, well-endowed bad-ass."

He nods. "Better."

I poke him with my foot, and he grabs it. He gives it a gentle squeeze before he brings it up to his mouth so he can kiss my ankle.

*Oh, sweet Holy Mother . . .*

"So," he says as he kisses my calf, "my point is, I might have a lot of issues, but not wanting you isn't one of them. Controlling myself around you, on the other hand . . ." He looks pointedly at my panties and bare legs. "That's a definite problem. You have me so turned on all of the time, I'm embarrassed to think how short my fuse will be when we finally seal the deal."

I move over to straddle his hips and wind my fingers in his hair. "But we are going to seal the deal?"

He puts his hands on my thighs and strokes slowly. "Maybe. If we try this boyfriend-girlfriend thing for a while, and you don't want to murder me."

"Yeah, I'll go out on a limb and say that even if I wanted to murder you, I'd still want to have sex with you. Are you sure you don't want to do it tonight? Ruby has, like, a thousand condoms in her nightstand. She wouldn't miss one. Or four."

He drops his head back and half groans, half laughs as I kiss his neck. I know how much he likes it when I nibble and suck. Am I trying to make him forget all the noble reasons we should wait? Maybe. All I know is that the longer I spend kissing him, the hungrier I get. He thinks I could end up regretting sleeping with him. I doubt it. But I do know that if he leaves here tonight without making love to me, I'd definitely regret that.

I kiss him all over, trying to break down his resistance.

His chest is warm, and I use soft lips and gentle fingers. When I look up, I find him watching me. As I move farther down and explore the ridges of his abs, he tilts his head back and exhales.

I whisper things into his skin. I tell him how beautiful he is, how special, how much I need him. He replies with a frown. I don't think he believes me, but I'm determined to make him.

When I go back to his mouth, he lets me see more of his need and kisses me so deeply, he makes me dizzy.

When I reach for the fly of his pants, he pulls back, breathless. "I thought we agreed to not have sex tonight?"

"No. You said we should wait. I didn't agree."

"But you said you understood. You thought it was sweet."

"I do understand, and your concern is sweet. I just think it's completely unnecessary." I graze my fingers across his chest and watch as goose bumps form. "If you really don't want to take this any further tonight, no problem. Just tell me to stop." I kiss his neck. Taste his skin. Salty and warm despite the chill outside. "I'll do whatever you want."

He grips my hips as I grind against him, but he doesn't say anything.

"Do you want me to stop, Ethan?" I kiss his clavicle, his pec, just above his nipple. He squeezes his eyes shut. "Or do you want me to keep touching you?"

When his eyes open, there's fire there. Deep and hungry.

He wraps his fist in my hair. "You don't think I can stop, do you?"

"I know you can. I just really hope you won't."

He stares at me for a few seconds before pulling me in for a searing kiss.

Lips. Tongue. *Oh, God. His tongue.*

He tastes like lust. Smells like it, too. Even though I can feel him trying to resist, I know his erogenous zones just as well as he knows mine, and I use them against him.

After a few more minutes of coaxing, his hands are everywhere, pushing under elastic and tugging at straps. When I sense him becoming greedy, I pull back. His gaze heats my skin as he watches me remove my bra. Then just like that, he doesn't seem so cautious any more. He makes a sound, and I swear it's the last of his willpower snapping. He stands, taking me with him, and it's like he's all around me. Hands, and mouth, and dark, needy noises.

Then, everything seems to happen in a blur. My back is pressed against walls and doors as he moves us toward the bedroom. I tug on his hair. Sink teeth into his shoulder. He carries me with one arm and uses the other to tug at his clothes.

We're both needy. Urgent hands push and probe, not satisfied with anything but unencumbered skin. For me, every layer that hits the floor feels like a victory. Every low noise he makes becomes my new anthem.

Each time he crushes against me, I can feel more of him, and the more I feel, the more I need.

When we're finally both naked on the bed, the sheer volume of his skin against mine makes me stop dead in my tracks and gasp for air.

When I stare up at him, my awe is reflected in his eyes.

"Cassie . . ."

I stop him with a kiss. "Say you want me."

"You know I do, but . . ."

"Then make love to me."

He drops his head and exhales. "You deserve—"

"You. I deserve *you*. Stop second-guessing this and make love to me. You said you want my first time to be special. Well, *make it* special. I want it to be you. Don't you understand? This is the most special thing you can give me. Please."

He squeezes his eyes shut. His body is bound up with tension from so many different sources, I don't think he can figure out how to unwind himself. I push him onto his back and straddle his hips before leaning over so my hair brushes his chest. I stroke his arms to try to loosen his emotional knots.

"Stop thinking," I whisper, and kiss down his neck. He sighs when

I move down to his chest and lifts my hair so he can watch. "For one night, just be with me. No fear. No guilt. Just us."

I move down and kiss his stomach. Warm skin. Sparse hair. Muscles tremble under my lips as he tightens his hand in my hair.

"It's not easy to just switch off my brain," he says, his voice quiet.

"Then let me help you."

I move down to where he's hard and graze with fingers first, then lips and tongue. He makes a long, strained noise that vibrates through all of his muscles.

Lord, how he sounds. How he feels. How every stroke makes him let go just a little bit more.

I look up and see he's watching me, enraptured. For once, he's totally here. Not lost in his head somewhere. His expression is breathtakingly vulnerable as I bring him pleasure.

"God . . . Cassie . . ."

He strokes my face gently, the expression on his face reverent. I move my mouth over him, making every touch say something.

When he swears under his breath, I know he's close. Before he can finish, he lifts me up and away and pushes me onto my back. He kisses me then moves down to the rest of my body to explore all of the parts he hasn't seen before.

The look of astonishment on his face almost makes me laugh. I have no illusions that I have a perfect body or that I'm the most beautiful girl in the world. But the way he looks at me makes me feel like I am.

He trails fingertips over my nipples and makes me shiver. His mouth follows.

*Yes.*

Every dip and groove of my body is explored. Touched and kissed. Sucked and nibbled. He worships my skin, and makes soft noises that peak louder than most of the words he's ever said.

Like this, he's mine. Completely. It's so clear in the way he watches me. As if he's looking for every new milestone of pleasure while he convinces all of my nerve endings to dance for him.

I'm desperate to ask him if this is normal. If the other women he's been with have come so thoroughly undone by him. But I decide to believe this is extraordinary for both of us. That this bizarre chemical eruption we bring out in each other is unique.

I go into a haze as he pushes his hand between my thighs. Gentle fingers. Tight circles. I clutch and grip at him; whisper his name to urge him on. Needing, needing, needing.

Long minutes stretch and ebb. He strings me along, gentle but determined, and when he finally lets me come, I cry out as all of my muscles tremble and spasm.

I grip his shoulders throughout my climax, and he kisses my forehead. He seems to be breathing almost as heavily as I am. When I come back to my senses and open my eyes, he looks confused. Almost like he can't believe what he just witnessed.

"I'll never get tired of seeing that," he says and shakes his head. "It's freaking ridiculous how someone else's orgasm can give me so much pleasure."

He collapses onto his back, and I kiss down his neck, to his chest, then press my lips over his heart to feel how fast it's pounding. I notice how it speeds up when I reach between us and take him in my hand.

"Ohhhhh, God . . ."

The feel of him makes me want him even more. Like I'm holding the exact shape of my need. I wonder if I'll ever see anything more magnificent than Ethan in the throes of pleasure. I highly doubt it.

"You are so beautiful," I whisper.

He opens his eyes, and for just a moment, I think he lets himself believe it.

I kiss him. His response is hungry and desperate, and I've never needed anything more than I need him inside me. He either need it, too, or he finally understands my relentless determination, because he grabs his jeans off the floor, tugs his wallet free, and pulls out a condom.

I've never seen a man put on a condom before, and although it seems like it wouldn't be an inherently sensual act, watching Ethan do it is incredibly arousing. He moves quickly, hands sure and confident, and a shiver runs up my spine.

*We're going to have sex.*

*I'm going to lose my virginity.*

For the first time in my life, I'm going to have another person . . . a man . . . *Ethan* . . . inside my body.

I'm overcome by a wave of nerves. For so long, I've sworn black and blue that my virginity was nothing more than a burden, but as Ethan kisses me and rolls between my legs, the reality of what's about to happen dawns on me.

I tense up. He's so close to where I've wanted him for months.

He stops and frowns. "What's wrong?"

I shake my head. "Nothing. I just—"

"We can stop. We probably should . . ."

"No! God, no, please." I touch his face. "I'm just . . . this is kind of a big moment, you know? I didn't think it would be, but it is. After this . . . everything will be different."

His expression darkens. "I'm going to hurt you."

"I know. But it has to happen, right?"

He doesn't answer. Regretful already.

"When it comes to that part, just do it, okay? Quickly. I'd rather it be fast and over with than all drawn out."

He pauses as his fear builds. "Cassie . . ."

I wrap my arms around him and pull him down. He kisses me deeply, but the sound he makes almost feels like a protest. As if he wants to stop but can't.

"I'll be all right," I whisper and stroke his face. "Don't worry." He's pressed against me, and I can feel how hard and ready he is. I kiss him once more. "Ethan?"

"Yeah?"

"I'm really glad it's you."

He swallows and nods, and when he kisses me again, I feel him reach between us. I hold my breath. There's pressure, much more than with his fingers, and it increases as he pushes forward. He doesn't get far. We grunt against each other's lips before stilling, forehead to forehead.

"You okay?"

I nod. "Don't stop."

He moves again, and the pressure starts to burn. When I close my eyes against the pain, he stops.

"No. Keep going. Please."

"Look at me."

I open my eyes and see strain and worry on his face. "Just keep looking at me, okay? Don't think about the pain. Be with me." He moves forward again until he can't go any farther. I grunt in frustration. He pulls back before he thrusts with more force, and this time, it really hurts. I groan, and he tries to distract me with his mouth.

"You feel amazing," he whispers against my lips. "I knew you would but . . . Jesus." He thrusts again, and I cry out when a sharp pain shoots through me. I dig my nails into his shoulders.

He stops for a second, but I urge him on.

When he pushes forward, it hurts. Muscles and tissues stretch and ache. A flash of panic hits as I think he's not going to fit.

*God, no. What if he doesn't fit?*

He rocks back and forth and manages to go a little deeper each time. His brows furrow in concentration, and he alternates between asking if I'm okay and kissing me.

"I'm sorry it hurts," he whispers. I grit my teeth when he moves deeper. "I never wanted to hurt you. Ever."

Another thrust. Then another. I push out a long breath, and so does he. Then his hips rest against my inner thighs, and I realize . . . he's inside me.

Fully.

His body joined with mine.

*Finally.*

I look up at him in surprise. The pain has been replaced by a throbbing burn, but it doesn't stop my mind from being blown. Everything he's feeling is reflected in his eyes. Joy, shock, lust, love, regret, elation. Like this, he's an open book. Nothing hidden or buried.

Just us. Joined in so many more ways than just the physical.

It's the most incredible thing I've ever felt.

Full to overflowing with him, I can barely breathe. This is what I've waited for. What I've craved for months. I understand why he's been hiding from these feeling all this time. They're too powerful and too scary. If you never see paradise, you don't know what you're missing.

But we see now. Both of us. He's been blinded from seeing, and as much as he wants to look away, he can't.

Neither can I.

"Cassie . . ."

"I'm okay."

He moves a little then freezes. All of his muscles tense. "God . . . I can't. You feel . . . unbelievable."

He drops his head into my neck and just breathes. I hold him and savor the moment. Stroke his back. Take in the all-over rightness of him.

I'd thought I didn't want special, but here it is. His face is pressed into my throat, and I can tell he's trying to control himself. Being with him like this is more than special. It's essential. I can't imagine giving this part of myself to anyone else. I try to take a mental snap-shot, because I know in the album of my life, this moment is irre-placeable.

He pushes up onto his elbows, and when he moves, he does it slowly. He watches me with a look of concerned concentration. I think he's trying to hide how much he's enjoying himself. Like it's wrong he's feeling pleasure while I'm in pain.

He needn't worry. With each thrust, the burn diminishes, and af-ter a couple of minutes, I'm breathless and arching from the deep slide of him.

His thrusts become more confident.

"You're inside me," I say.

He kisses my shoulder and presses his forehead against it. His voice is strained when he says, "Only fair. You've been inside me for months. Are you okay?"

"Hmmm. You feel amazing."

He pushes in deeply and groans. "I feel amazing? Are you kidding me? You feel . . ." He closes his eyes and shakes his head. "Cassie, there aren't enough words to describe how incredible you feel."

He keeps rocking, and although neither of us can talk anymore, the noises in the room speak volumes. Groaning breaths. Raspy sighs. All manner of murmurs as we kiss and grip each other.

He pushes onto his hands, and I can't tell whether he's trying to hold on or let go. His face is beautiful. Every nuance of what he's feel-ing is playing out in intricate detail. He's showing me all the parts of him I knew were buried inside. Sure, the fear is still there, but so is the strength, the courage, the raw vulnerability and profound emo-tion. I want to tell him how breathtaking he is, but I don't have the words. I'm too mesmerized to even attempt to find them. Too hesi-tant to look away in case he disappears.

Soon, I can't keep my eyes open, so I close them and just feel. Fingers grip. Hips connect. Muscles tremble and skin heats. Tension coils inside me, and I open my eyes to find him looking down at me, open-mouthed and heavy-lidded.

"Cassie . . ."

He whispers my name in the moments when his mouth isn't on me. It sounds likes he's begging. For what, I don't know. Whatever he wants, it's his for the taking. Having him like this has ruined me. How could I ever want anyone else after experiencing him?

He's so deep in me, he's tattooed himself on every nerve ending. Pleasure and pain and gasping perfection.

"Cassie, I can't. I'm going to . . . Oh, God. Oh, God."

His face crumbles. His thrusts become erratic, and all of his exhales sound more like moans. He wraps around me and holds me so close it feels like we share the same thundering heartbeat. The pleasure burn inside me has blossomed into a full-blown fire. It's all I can do to keep my eyes open and watch him.

A guttural sound vibrates in his chest, before the thrusting stops. He falls forward and mumbles incoherent whispers into my chest.

I sigh under the weight of him, feeling heavy and sated. I can't move and don't want to. We breathe against each other, and I can still feel him inside. For some reason, tears spill onto my cheeks.

I think part of me believed we'd never get to this point. That he'd never agree to be a part of this most intimate act. And yet, here we are, naked and breathless, having given each other a part of ourselves no one else has.

I try to swallow down my emotions, but I can't, so I just let the tears fall.

Is this what being in love feels like? Overwhelming gratitude that the other person is with you as you share something astonishing? Knowing that the most astonishing thing they can share is themselves?

"Thank you," I say, trying to keep my voice steady.

He squeezes me, and I'm surprised to feel moisture on my shoulder. I try to see his face, but he keeps it buried in my neck.

"Ethan?"

He stays silent and holds me. His breathing is shallow. I can feel his heart pounding through his ribcage, and I stroke his back to give him a moment.

Eventually, he exhales. It's deep and shaky. He lifts his hips to withdraw slowly, and when he's completely out, a strange emptiness expands inside me. Without meaning to, I tighten my arms around him. He kisses me before he pushes back onto his heels and removes the condom.

"Come on," he says. He gets out of bed and holds his hand out to me. "Let's get you cleaned up."

In the bathroom, he fills the tub and makes me soak for a while. I close my eyes as he washes my back. I ache but not more so than when I exercise muscles that aren't used to being worked.

Ethan's quiet, but he keeps one hand on me at all times. Makes sure I'm okay.

When we climb back into bed, I snuggle into his chest. His heartbeat sounds weird. Kind of like there's an extra echo in his ribs. But he strokes my arm and soon, it's just a rumble beneath my ear.

When I drift off, I dream about him.

Dream Ethan stands in front of me and gets dressed. He pulls on layer after layer, and covers all the parts that just made love to me. The brave parts. The loving parts.

I try to stop him, but he's determined. Eventually, everything is hidden again. Covered and protected.

*No. We're beyond this now.*

He mouths something. I study his lips as they meet then pull apart.

What is he saying?

For a moment, I think he's telling me he loves me. Saying it so softly I can barely hear. But then I hear . . .

"I'm sorry."

He says it time and again. Quiet and regretful.

When I wake up, a crawling sickness overcomes me as I realize it wasn't a dream.

# TWENTY-ONE

## EPIPHANY

**Present Day**
**New York City**
**The Diary of Cassandra Taylor**

Dear Diary,

Good news! Ethan wants us to get back together, so I'm now magically healed and we're off to live happily ever after!

In case you missed it, I typed that sarcastically.

The truth is, as much as I believe Ethan's changed, it's not enough.

If only I could go back in time and beg myself not to fall for him so hard. Not that young me would have listened. I knew he was damaged, but I figured what we had was strong enough to smooth over all the cracks and fissures.

For a while, it was, but it was just an illusion, like when snow covers over giant holes, making it look like the ground is perfect and solid.

Holt and I have never been solid. Just varying degrees of screwed up. Always teetering on the edge of our vast insecurities.

And now, he's asking me to walk that slippery slope again, and he's taking such care with me, I'm tempted to believe it's safe.

The problem is, no matter how careful he is, I'll always remember the

*other falls, and no matter how much he tells me he's different, I'll al-
ways know it was at my expense.*

*It took breaking my heart twice to grant him an epiphany strong enough
to make him change. Fucking good for him.*

*What's going to grant me mine?*

I stand at the bar and sip my vodka cocktail. It's my third, and I'm
finally starting to feel less. Or maybe I'm feeling more. It's hard to
tell.

I can hear my castmates in the far corner of the restaurant, laughing and talking. They're celebrating our move into the theater next
week. Tech rehearsals. Previews. Getting the play as perfect as it can
be before the world judges us on opening night.

I should be with them, but I'm not in the mood.

Marco raises his glass to me and smiles. So happy with what he's
created. Onstage, Ethan and I are flawless. It's made him confident
in my abilities.

I give him a smile before looking into my drink.

He doesn't realize he's trusting someone whose emotions are slowly
choking them.

Deep laughter rumbles across the room, and I turn to see Ethan
chuckling as Marco gestures wildly. He looks so happy.

I finish my drink and order another. Maybe four is my lucky number.

A man sits on the barstool next to me. He gives me a smile as he
orders a Scotch. He looks a bit like Ethan. Dark hair and blue eyes.
Attractive. Expensive suit. Tie loose, shirt unbuttoned.

I must be staring because he glances at me as the bartender deliv-
ers his drink. "I'd offer to buy you one, but it looks like that one's
still fresh."

I blink and look away. "Uh . . . yeah. I'm good."

"Are you here alone?"

That's not what he's asking, but I answer anyway.

"I'm here with friends," I say and gesture to the loud table in the corner. Holt's doing an impersonation of someone. Possibly Jack Nicholson.

The stranger nods. "Ah. Taking a break from the fun?"

"Something like that."

Heat prickles up my spine, and I turn to see Ethan, his gaze sharp and blazing from across the room. He's stopped mid-impersonation. I've felt subtle glances from him all night, but this is different. I'm no longer alone.

I get a flashback of him before his personality makeover. Always so jealous.

I turn back to the bar and try to ignore him.

The stranger leans over, and the Scotch on his breath makes him smell like Ethan.

"You're far too beautiful to be alone," he says. "Is there anything I can do to help?"

I've heard variations of that line countless times over the years, and on many occasions I let those men help me. And when I fucked them, I did so desperately. Using them and hating them afterward for not being Ethan. Hating myself more for still wanting him so much.

Hating *him* most of all.

The stranger is still waiting for an answer, hopeful my delicate emotional state will result in him getting laid. In the past, it probably would have.

"I'm just going to drink for a while," I tell him and smile, aware that Holt is watching my every move. "But thanks for the offer."

I touch his arm. Start at the tricep and run down to the elbow. My words say "no" but that touch says "maybe." I don't mean "maybe," but Ethan doesn't know that, and perhaps I want him to squirm. Perhaps I'm petty enough to test his newfound serenity and see if he's really changed as much as he says.

I chat with the stranger. Give him a coy smile.

Ethan's glare burns me every second I continue. I take sick comfort in it.

I wonder how far I'd have to push him before he breaks.

Another cocktail. More conversation. I can feel Ethan's frustration like a ripple in the air, vibrating against me, telling me that what I'm doing is wrong.

It's hurtful.

Vengeful.

After five cocktails, I've lost the ability to care. The stranger has his arm around me as he whispers in my ear. Tells me how beautiful I am. How much he wants me.

I laugh, because I don't feel beautiful. I feel like trash.

The man plants a soft kiss on my neck. I don't tell him to stop. When he does it again, Holt appears beside me, muscles bunched and expression brooding.

"Okay, Cassie. Time to go."

"Wait a minute, pal," the stranger says and tightens his arm around my waist. "The lady and I were having a conversation."

Ethan practically growls at him. "Your conversation is over, *pal*. Take your fucking hands off her."

*Ah, the caveman cometh.*

It's kind of a relief that he's not so perfect after all. Makes my imperfections seem less vast.

The stranger frowns and puts down his drink. "Who the hell are you to tell me what to do?"

Ethan leans over into his face. "I'm the guy who's going to put your fucking head through the bar if you touch her for one more second. Anything else you want to know?"

With a flash of fear, the stranger lets me go, and Holt helps me up. I feel guilty for leading the stranger on, but not as guilty as I do for screwing with Ethan. I can't even look at him as he walks me outside.

When we're on the pavement, he stands me on my feet. I stumble over the gutter and brace myself against a parked car as I try to hail a cab. Everything is tilted and wrong, and I know that only he can make it right again, and that makes me fucking angry.

"Cassie, what the hell is going on with you tonight?"

Another cab passes as I wave sloppily, and I almost fall before strong arms wrap around me and pull me up.

"Jesus Christ, would you stop? You're going to get yourself run over."

I grip his shirt as my legs sag, and all I feel is warmth, and arms, and lips on my forehead as I breathe in the so-right smell of him.

"Come back inside."

"I have to go."

"Then I'm coming with you."

"No. I can't do this."

"What?"

"This!" His face is too close. Mouth too enticing. "This!" I push on his chest, hand over his heart. "You!"

I'm agitated. Bitter about things I can't change and too frightened to think about the things I can.

He glares at me with barely repressed anger. "Would it make it easier if I was some douche in a suit who just wants to fuck you? Could you deal with me then?"

My legs give out again. He pulls me tight against him. Now I'm off my feet, and we're chest to chest, face to face. He's killing me with closeness.

"That's it. I'm taking you home."

I shake my head, wishing he could understand that if I stay with him any longer, he'll unstitch me, and I really can't fall apart now. Bitterness is the only thing holding me together. Without it, I'm shapeless.

Lost.

My breath hitches, and he loosens his embrace. Puts his hand on my cheek.

"Fuck." He hugs me to him. Whispers in my ear. "Don't cry. Please. I'm sorry. Whatever's going on tonight, you're going to be okay."

I don't believe him.

He holds me with one arm as he hails a passing cab. It stops, and he puts me in the backseat and passes the driver money with instructions to help me to my door if necessary. Then his face is in front of mine, concerned and unhappy.

"Call me when you get home, okay?"

I study the back of the seat.

"Cassie, I'm serious. Look at me."

My head is so heavy. It's all too hard.

He cups my chin to help me lift it.

Somber eyes look into mine. "Promise you'll call me when you get home, otherwise I'm coming with you."

He stares until I nod.

A knot tightens in my throat as he kisses my forehead.

Why does he insist on making everything seem easy, when it's clearly impossible?

He disappears, and the door slams. When we drive off and I know he's not watching anymore, I crumble.

When I stumble into my apartment, Tristan's there. He's seen me like this before and knows what to do. He helps me into the bathroom and orders me to shower. Makes the water cold. Then he helps me into bed, brushes my hair away from my face, and whispers that everything's going to be all right.

I must doze off at some point, because when I open my eyes again, he's gone, but sitting on the nightstand are two Tylenol and some water. I take them and gulp the water down.

I feel dry inside.

Emotionally desolate.

I grab my laptop and open Holt's e-mails, needing some part him. Feeling too full and inconsolably empty all at once.

I pour over every word. They're filled with vague ramblings of regret, but there's one thing he never said. One thing I needed to hear so much back then to reassure me that what I'd felt for him wasn't completely one-sided.

I'm nearly asleep when my phone rings, and without looking at the screen, I know it's him.

"Hey." My throat is dry.

"You said you'd call." His voice is hard. Worried.

"I'm sorry."

"Dammit, Cassie, for all I knew that cab driver could have raped you, murdered you, dumped you in Central Park. What the fuck is going on?"

"I don't know. I'm sorry." And I am, for so many things.

He sighs. "You just— You can't do that to me. You have no idea how much I— I mean, I want to . . ."

He's quiet for a second. "I'm sorry for snapping." He sounds as tired as I feel. "I'm just worried about you. I've tried to give you space for the past few weeks. Distance so you can get a better perspective, or whatever. But you let that guy paw you tonight and I . . . Dammit, you had to know how I'd react."

"I know."

"I haven't felt like that in a long time. I wanted to annihilate him."

"But you didn't."

"I wanted to break his fucking fingers. Was that reaction you were after? To drive me insane? To hurt me?"

"I guess."

"Yeah, well, mission accomplished."

The admission doesn't give me comfort. In fact, it makes me feel like crap.

I'm so tired of feeling this way, but I don't know how else to be.

A long time ago, I thought that two people who cared for each other could work out any issue as long as they talked about it, but now I see it's not that easy. Talking actually requires a person to have the courage to express what they're feeling, and I'm all out of courage.

"Would you have gone home with him if I hadn't been there to-night?" he asks.

"No."

"Why not?"

"Because . . ." I struggle to find the words. "If I'd taken him home I'd . . ." I sigh, prickly and defensive. "I would have just pretended he was you, anyway, so what's the freaking point?"

There's a long pause. My heart is pounding erratically as I wait for him to respond.

"Have you done that before?"

"Yes."

"How often?"

"All the time. Every time."

He inhales. "What does that mean?"

He's pushing, but despite my discomfort, some part of me wants to be pushed. I'm not going to be able to do this without him.

"Cassie?"

"After you left . . ." I swallow. "I missed you so much, I wanted them to be you, so I closed my eyes and tried to make them you. All of them. Even Connor. *Especially* Connor. It didn't work. None of them even came close."

My breathing seems obscenely loud in my quiet bedroom, and the tick from my clock fills the long seconds.

"Jesus . . . Cassie . . ."

So now he knows. For better or worse, he knows.

"I thought . . ." He stops, regroups. "When I found out about the men you'd been with after I left, I figured you did it to forget about me. Or punish me."

"That was part of it. But not the main part."

"And tonight?"

"I wanted to push you. See if you'd revert back to your old self. And, like you said, hurt you."

Saying it makes me realize what a low blow it was. How far I've fallen. How poisonous I've become.

"I get that. I know you think I deserve some pain, considering what I did, but you don't understand." He takes a breath. "I know you suffered when I left, but I suffered, too. That European tour was the most miserable time of my life."

My resentment flares. "Oh, yeah, I'm sure parading around all those exotic places with beautiful girls adoring you was really hard. Deciding which one to take home each night. It must have been like a freaking smorgasbord."

"Is that honestly what you think happened? That I could do that? Jesus, Cassie, when we were together, I never so much as even looked at another girl. Do you think I could forget about you so easily?"

"After you gave up on us, I thought you were capable of anything."

He laughs. "Yeah, well, the reality was a little different."

"How different?"

I wish I could see his face. But all I have is his voice, low and resonant.

"In Europe, even though I was always surrounded by people, the time I spent apart from you was the loneliest I've ever been. At first I couldn't handle it. I was drinking a lot, sometimes during the shows. I'd go to bars. Get into fights. Then, I'd go home and think about you. Google you. Dream about you. I missed you so much, it made me physically ill. Sometimes I considered taking someone home with me, so I could wake up beside another body. No sex. Just . . . company."

I feel his pain. So similar to my own.

At least I'd found Tristan.

"So, yeah," he says. "Other stuff happened that made me reassess everything about myself and what I needed to do to get you back, but that's a story for another time. The point is, I wasn't having a party while I was over there. I was completely miserable. And alone."

"But surely you had other . . . relationships . . . while we were apart?"

"No."

His answer confuses me. "But you had . . . *sex*. I mean, I'm not sure why I'm asking because the thought of you and other women is . . ." I shudder. "But you did, right?"

I close my eyes and wait for his answer, tensing in anticipation.

*Say "hundreds." Give me fuel for my fire. Let me be hard.*

*Please.*

He's quiet, but every word is filled with heavy sincerity. "Cassie, you have no idea how many times I wanted to have meaningless sex, just so I could get you out of my mind, but I couldn't do it. Every time I tried, I felt like I was cheating. Eventually, I stopped looking at other women. It was fucking pointless. None of them could ever come close to replacing you, even if I'd wanted them to, which I didn't."

I can't believe what I'm hearing. "Are you telling me that . . . the last time you had sex was . . ."

"With you." It's hushed, like he's confessing.

*No.*

*Not possible.*

"But that was . . ." *That* night. *The* night. "The night before you left?"

"Yes."

It takes a moment for my brain to respond. "But . . . that's . . . that's . . . goddamn, Ethan, three years?!"

He laughs. "Believe me, I know. I don't say this to make you feel bad, but between my self-imposed dry spell and doing this show with you, my balls are bluer than the entire cast of *Avatar*."

I still can't comprehend it. "Unbelievable."

"You're making me feel like a freak."

"I'm sorry, I just can't understand—"

"Look, it's simple. I didn't have you, and I didn't want anyone else. End of story."

"So, if we don't get back together, you're just going to continue being celibate?"

There's dead silence for a second, then he says, "First of all, us not getting back together isn't even a possibility in my mind. And secondly, I was never celibate."

"But, you said—"

"I said I hadn't had sex with anyone, but being celibate means abstaining from all sexual pleasure. I've had plenty of sexual pleasure, usually while having erotic thoughts about you."

The thought of Ethan masturbating to images of me instantly turns me on.

"In fact," he says, "I'm having some very erotic thoughts about you right now."

He lets out a quiet moan, and I have to draw my knees up to my chest to cope with how much I burn for him.

"Can we please talk about something else?"

"Definitely," he says, quiet and lustful. "Talk about something that will distract me from how much I need to make love to you. Please."

"Ethan—"

"Fuck, yes, say my name."

"I'm only going to keep talking to you if I know both of your hands are in plain sight."

"I can see my hand perfectly well. It's wrapped around my aching—"

"Ethan!"

I hear fabric rustling, followed by a resigned sigh. "Fine. Hands re above the covers. Killjoy."

His tone is so petulant, it makes me laugh.

"So," he says before yawning. "You in bed, too?"

"Yeah."

"Doing anything interesting?"

His innuendo isn't lost on me, but I don't bite. "Actually, I was read-ng some of your old e-mails."

There's a pause before he says, "Why?"

"I don't know. I guess I'm trying to figure out how I feel."

"About me?"

"Yes."

Another pauses. "Did they help?"

"Not really. I keep looking for something that isn't there."

He's quiet for few seconds before saying, "Did you know that I have whole folder of draft e-mails? Stuff I wasn't brave enough to send?"

"What sort of stuff?"

I hear shuffling and the tapping of fingers on a keyboard. "Hang n. I'll send you some of the less embarrassing ones."

Almost immediately my inbox lights up with two new messages.

*From: EthanHolt <ERHolt@gmail.com>*
*To: CassieTaylor <CTaylor18@gmail.com>*
*Subject: Too much of a pussy to send this to you.*
*Date: Thu, February 9, at 1:08a.m.*

*Cassie,*
*We're in France. I've stopped drinking and have been getting help for over six months now. I'm learning to take responsibility for my mistakes.*

*I take responsibility for hurting you. If you'd never met me, you wouldn't be in pain right now. I hate that I did that.*

*Of all the people in my life that I fucked up, you are the one I regret the most.*

*I think about you a lot. Dream about you.*

*I wish I had the guts to send this to you, but I probably won't. Still, writing it soothes me. I'm working on being open and honest with you, but I guess I'm not there yet. When I am, rest assured, you'll be the first to know.*

*France is beautiful. I stood at the bottom of the Eiffel Tower today and looked up at it. There are very few times in my life I've felt so small. The day I left you was one of them.*

*I miss you.*

*Ethan.*

I opened the second e-mail.

*From: EthanHolt <ERHolt@gmail.com>*
*To: CassieTaylor <CTaylor18@gmail.com>*
*Subject: I need you.*
*Date: Mon, June 9, at 12:38a.m.*

*Cassie,*

*It's my birthday. I don't expect to hear from you, but fuck, I really need to.*

*I want you here, in my apartment. In my bed. Kissing me and making love to me and telling me you forgive me.*

*I need it like air. I'm drowning without you. Please.*

*Please.*

*Earlier, I was sitting on a bench on the banks of the Tiber, and there were all these people there holding hands and kissing. Happy and in love.*

*They made it seem so easy. Like giving their heart to someone else isn't the scariest thing in the world.*

*I still don't understand that.*

*Don't they know the power they're giving to that other person? The absolute future-forming dominion?*

*Don't they understand how much it's going to hurt when it all goes wrong? And let's face it, ninety percent of those couples won't still be together a year from now. Even six months from now.*

*And yet, there they are, hugging and lip-locking, completely oblivious to the pain that's coming for them.*

*Unconcerned and trusting.*

*That was always something I struggled to be.*

*It was almost impossible to turn off the internal countdown clock that screamed at me daily about all the ways you could hurt me. After all, history proved that eventually, everyone leaves me. Why would you be any different?*

*Now I know that you were.*

*Are.*

*The thing is, underneath all the bullshit that made me push you away, there were parts of me that clung to you when I left, and now, without you, I struggle to function.*

*The thought that keeps me up at night is that I had my chance to be whole and right, and I blew it.*

*Please tell me I'll get another chance. Don't tell me this is how I have to live now.*

*I can't. Being without you is too hard.*

*I miss you so much it hurts.*

*Ethan.*

feel like I've been punched in the chest.

This is exactly what I'd needed to hear, so many times.

I realize I'm gripping my phone to the point of pain. "They . . .

od, Ethan . . . They're beautiful. Why didn't you send them?"

He sighs. "I don't know. I thought you hated me."

"I did, but . . . if I'd read those e-mails, maybe I would have hated you less."

"I wish I'd had the guts to lay it all out for you back then, but just wasn't ready."

"And now you are?"

"Ask me anything you like, and I'll give you a straight answer."

"Anything?"

"Absolutely."

I take a breath and ask him the question that's haunted me for years. "In all your e-mails, why didn't you ever say you loved me?"

I can almost hear his shock. "What?"

"You never said it. In any of them."

"Cassie, I did say it. All the time."

"I've just read through them all for the hundredth time, and you didn't say it once. You said you missed me, that you wanted to be friends, but there's nothing about love."

"There's no fucking way that's true. I . . . I—" He takes in a shaky breath. "I thought it all the time. It seemed to be in every word I wrote to you but . . . I— Shit, Cassie."

He growls in frustration.

"Ethan, it's fine."

"It's really fucking not. Of all the things I should have told you, that's at the top of the goddamn list. But whether I said it in the e-mail or not, you have to know that I— I really do—"

"Ethan, stop."

"Cassie—"

"No. I don't want you to say it just because I brought it up."

"That's not the reason."

"Still, just don't, okay? Not tonight."

He exhales, and thankfully, he doesn't push it.

We make small talk about the show for a few minutes, but when I stifle a yawn, he tells me to go to sleep. I don't argue.

In the morning, I feel like crap. My hangover isn't too bad, but I had terrible dreams in which Holt left me, over and over again, and each time, I took him back, all the while getting angrier with myself each time I did it.

I've barely shuffled out of the shower, when my phone beeps with a text from him.

*<You have mail.>*

Intrigued, I open my laptop and find a single e-mail.

When I open it, my screen explodes.

I LOVE YOU, I LOVE YOU, I LOVE YOU, I LOVE YOU, I LOVE YOU, I LOVE YOU, I LOVE YOU, I LOVE YOU, I LOVE YOU, I LOVE YOU, I LOVE YOU, I LOVE YOU, I LOVE YOU, I LOVE YOU, I LOVE YOU, I LOVE YOU, I LOVE YOU, I LOVE YOU, I LOVE YOU, I LOVE YOU, I LOVE YOU, I LOVE YOU, I LOVE YOU, I LOVE YOU, I LOVE YOU, I LOVE YOU, I LOVE YOU, I LOVE YOU, I LOVE YOU, I LOVE YOU, I LOVE YOU, I LOVE YOU, I LOVE YOU, I LOVE YOU, I LOVE YOU, I LOVE YOU, I LOVE YOU, I LOVE YOU, I LOVE YOU, I LOVE YOU, I LOVE YOU, I LOVE YOU, I LOVE YOU, I LOVE YOU, I LOVE YOU, I LOVE YOU, I LOVE YOU, I LOVE YOU, I LOVE YOU, I LOVE YOU, I LOVE YOU, I LOVE YOU, I LOVE YOU, I LOVE YOU, I LOVE YOU, I LOVE YOU, I LOVE YOU, I LOVE YOU, I LOVE YOU, I LOVE YOU, I LOVE YOU, I LOVE YOU, I LOVE YOU, I LOVE YOU, I LOVE YOU, I LOVE YOU, I LOVE YOU, I LOVE YOU, I LOVE YOU, I LOVE YOU, I LOVE YOU, I LOVE YOU, I LOVE YOU, I LOVE YOU, I LOVE YOU, I LOVE YOU, I LOVE YOU, I LOVE YOU, I LOVE YOU, I LOVE YOU, I LOVE YOU, I LOVE YOU, I LOVE YOU, I LOVE YOU, I LOVE YOU, I LOVE YOU, I LOVE YOU, I LOVE YOU, I LOVE YOU, I LOVE YOU, I LOVE YOU, I LOVE YOU, I LOVE YOU, I LOVE YOU, I LOVE YOU, I LOVE YOU, I LOVE YOU, I LOVE YOU, I LOVE YOU, I LOVE YOU, I LOVE YOU, I LOVE YOU, I LOVE YOU, I LOVE YOU, I LOVE YOU, I LOVE YOU, I

LOVE YOU, I LOVE YOU, I LOVE YOU, I LOVE YOU, I
LOVE YOU, I LOVE YOU, I LOVE YOU, I LOVE YOU, I
LOVE YOU, I LOVE YOU, I LOVE YOU, I LOVE YOU, I
LOVE YOU, I LOVE YOU, I LOVE YOU, I LOVE YOU, I
LOVE YOU, I LOVE YOU, I LOVE YOU, I LOVE YOU, I
LOVE YOU, I LOVE YOU, I LOVE YOU, I LOVE YOU, I
LOVE YOU, I LOVE YOU, I LOVE YOU, I LOVE YOU, I
LOVE YOU, I LOVE YOU, I LOVE YOU, I LOVE YOU, I
LOVE YOU, I LOVE YOU, I LOVE YOU, I LOVE YOU, I
LOVE YOU, I LOVE YOU, I LOVE YOU, I LOVE YOU,
LOVE YOU, I LOVE YOU, I LOVE YOU, I LOVE YOU,
LOVE YOU, I LOVE YOU, I LOVE YOU, I LOVE YOU,
LOVE YOU, I LOVE YOU, I LOVE YOU, I LOVE YOU,
LOVE YOU, I LOVE YOU, I LOVE YOU, I LOVE YOU,
LOVE YOU, I LOVE YOU, I LOVE YOU, I LOVE YOU,
LOVE YOU, I LOVE YOU, I LOVE YOU, I LOVE YOU,
LOVE YOU, I LOVE YOU, I LOVE YOU, I LOVE YOU,
LOVE YOU, I LOVE YOU, I LOVE YOU, I LOVE YOU,
LOVE YOU, I LOVE YOU, I LOVE YOU, I LOVE YOU,
LOVE YOU, I LOVE YOU, I LOVE YOU, I LOVE YOU,
LOVE YOU, I LOVE YOU, I LOVE YOU, I LOVE YOU,
LOVE YOU, I LOVE YOU, I LOVE YOU, I LOVE YOU,
LOVE YOU, I LOVE YOU, I LOVE YOU, I LOVE YOU,
LOVE YOU, I LOVE YOU, I LOVE YOU, I LOVE YOU,
LOVE YOU, I LOVE YOU, I LOVE YOU, I LOVE YOU,
LOVE YOU, I LOVE YOU, I LOVE YOU, I LOVE YOU,
LOVE YOU, I LOVE YOU, I LOVE YOU, I LOVE YOU,
LOVE YOU, I LOVE YOU, I LOVE YOU, I LOVE YOU,
LOVE YOU, I LOVE YOU, I LOVE YOU, I LOVE YOU,
LOVE YOU, I LOVE YOU, I LOVE YOU, I LOVE YOU,
LOVE YOU, I LOVE YOU, I LOVE YOU, I LOVE YOU,
LOVE YOU, I LOVE YOU, I LOVE YOU, I LOVE YOU,
LOVE YOU, I LOVE YOU, I LOVE YOU, I LOVE YOU,

LOVE YOU, I LOVE YOU, I LOVE YOU, I LOVE YOU, I
LOVE YOU, I LOVE YOU, I LOVE YOU, I LOVE YOU, I
LOVE YOU, I LOVE YOU, I LOVE YOU, I LOVE YOU, I
LOVE YOU, I LOVE YOU, I LOVE YOU, I LOVE YOU, I
LOVE YOU, I LOVE YOU, I LOVE YOU, I LOVE YOU, I
LOVE YOU, I LOVE YOU, I LOVE YOU, I LOVE YOU, I
LOVE YOU, I LOVE YOU, I LOVE YOU, I LOVE YOU, I
LOVE YOU, I LOVE YOU, I LOVE YOU, I LOVE YOU, I
LOVE YOU, I LOVE YOU, I LOVE YOU, I LOVE YOU, I
LOVE YOU, I LOVE YOU, I LOVE YOU, I LOVE YOU, I
LOVE YOU, I LOVE YOU, I LOVE YOU, I LOVE YOU, I
LOVE YOU, I LOVE YOU, I LOVE YOU, I LOVE YOU, I
LOVE YOU, I LOVE YOU, I LOVE YOU, I LOVE YOU, I
LOVE YOU, I LOVE YOU, I LOVE YOU, I LOVE

I scroll down pages and pages, stunned, until finally, I reach the
bottom.

*Just in case you didn't get what I was doing, I've written "I LOVE
YOU" 1,162 times—one for every day I was away. And please don't
think this was some quickie copy and paste declaration. I typed each
and every one individually as penance for being too much of a
dumbass to make it crystal clear how I felt about you.*

*I know you think I left because I didn't love you, but you're wrong.
I've always loved you, from the moment I first laid eyes on you. I
ranted and railed about love at first sight, because the concept is fucking ridiculous to me. But the very first day I saw you at the auditions
for The Grove, it happened, and you ruined me without even saying
a word. I saw you there, trying desperately to be something you weren't
just so they'd like you, and I wanted to pull you into my arms and tell
you it was going to be okay.*

*From that moment, I knew you were meant for me. But I was pigheaded enough to refuse to accept it.*

*I have no idea how or why you were able to love me. I was an asshole, so busy trying to run from my feelings, I didn't figure out you were my gift; the precious reward I'd somehow earned with all my pain. I'd spent so long believing I got what I deserved when people left me, that I didn't stop to think I got what I deserved when I met you. I couldn't comprehend that if I stopped being an enormous insecure jackass for five minutes, that maybe . . . just maybe . . . I could keep you.*

*I want to keep you, Cassie.*

*That's why I came back. Because as much as I used to think you were better off without me, you're not. You need me as much as I need you. We're both hollow without the other, and it's taken me a long time to realize that.*

*Don't be as stubborn as I was and let the insecurities win. Let us win. Because I know you think loving me again is a crapshoot and that your odds are grim, but let me tell you something, I'm a sure thing. I couldn't stop loving you if I tried.*

*Am I still terrified of you hurting me? Of course. Probably the same way you're terrified I'll hurt you.*

*But I'm brave enough to know it's absolutely worth the risk.*

*Let me help you be brave.*

*I love you with everything I am, and I swear to God, I'm not going to hurt you again.*

*Let yourself love me back.*

*Please.*

*Ethan.*

I sit there and look at the screen for a long time, alternating between laughing and crying.

Somewhere in there, the fire in my bitterness sputters and dies. Th sensation is strange, because it's what kept me going when nothing else would, and without it I feel naked in the worst way. Soft and vulnerable and more fragile than glass.

Yesterday I'd wondered what it would take to grant me my epiphany to change. I guess Ethan baring his soul in an e-mail did the trick.

One of Tristan's favorite sayings is, "Be the change you want to see." I guess that's what Holt's done. He's made himself strong enough for both of us.

My hands tremble as I send him a text.

*<I need to see you.>*

I've barely pressed send when there's a knock at the door.

Ethan and Cassie have a second chance at love,
but can her shattered heart be repaired?
Or is their epic romance better left in the past?
Their story continues in

# BROKEN JULIET

Coming soon

# ACKNOWLEDGMENTS

So many people were instrumental in making this dream of publishing a reality, it will be impossible to mention them all, but I'm going to give it a red-hot go.

My unending thanks go out to the following people:

First, bestselling author Alice Clayton, who not only encouraged me from the start but who blessed me with incredible generosity and support. You are astonishing, Alice. None of this would have happened without you. Truly.

To my agent, Christina, who took a chance on an unknown Aussie and made her dreams come true in the most epic of ways. You and the whole team at Jane Rotrosen Agency have been astonishing in your guidance and kickassery. You're all rock stars in my eyes.

To my editor at St. Martin's Press, Rose, who has infected everyone around her with boundless enthusiasm and belief in this book—lady, you're a marvel. I can't thank you and your team enough. (Well, I could, but it would get embarrassing after a while.)

To my Sprinkle Queen, Victoria Lawrence, who contributed so much in helping shape these words, and to my lovely pre-reader, Heather Maven, who held my hand when I was freaking the hell out about this whole process. Without you lovelies, I'd still be climbing a wall somewhere, devoid of words and sanity. (PS. You're both pretty.)

To my beautiful Filets—the most amazing group of supportive, helpful, and hilarious women a girl could ask for. I don't know what I would have done without you—especially you, Nina. (Hint: It probably would have involved lots of alcohol and ugly crying.)

To my darling Catty-Wan, Caryn Stevens—you were there from the beginning. You were the very first person to say, "You know what? You have talent," and ever since then you've been my partner in crime, my loudest cheerleader, and my shoulder to cry on. I love you.

To my wonderful friends, especially my tireless and spectacular bestie, Andrea—that you still bounce with excitement over these characters after all of this time still makes me smile every damn day. You complete me.

To my parents, Bernard and Val, who have always supported everything I do, no matter how harebrained—I love you stupid amounts. And to my brothers, Chris and John, who put up with a little sister with an overactive imagination—guess all that playacting as a kid finally paid off, huh?

To my wonderful husband (the best person I'll ever know)—thank you for pushing me to do something with my writing. You're so amazing, it's actually kind of annoying. And to my sons, who endured Mummy spending countless hours locked away exploring the worlds inside her head—darling Dr. X and Special K—no matter how proud I am of these books (and let's be honest, I'm *bloody* proud), you guys are, without a doubt, my most spectacular creations. Forever and always.

And last, but absolutely not least, to all the readers who loved this story from the start and encouraged me to get it published—you gave me so much inspiration, support, and love that I'll always be eternally grateful. This book is for you.

Thank you all.